Wildwood Whispers

WildWood Whispers

WILLA REECE

REDHOOK

Redhook Books/Orbit
Hachette Book Group
1290 Avenue of the Americas
New York, NY 10104
hachettebookgroup.com

First Edition: August 2021

Redhook is an imprint of Orbit, a division of Hachette Book Group.
The Redhook name and logo are trademarks of Hachette Book Group, Inc.

The publisher is not responsible for websites (or their content) that are not owned by the publisher.

The Hachette Speakers Bureau provides a wide range of authors for speaking events. To find out more, go to www.hachettespeakersbureau.com or call (866) 376-6591.

Library of Congress Cataloging-in-Publication Data
Names: Reece, Willa, author.
Title: Wildwood whispers / Willa Reece.
Description: First edition. | New York : Redhook, 2021.
Identifiers: LCCN 2020047787 | ISBN 9780316591768 (hardcover) | ISBN 9780316591782 (ebook)
Subjects: LCSH: Paranormal fiction. | GSAFD: Fantasy fiction.
Classification: LCC PS3608.A69775 W55 2021 | DDC 813/.6—dc23
LC record available at https://lccn.loc.gov/2020047787

ISBNs: 978-0-316-59176-8 (hardcover), 978-0-316-59178-2 (ebook)

Printed in the United States of America

LSC-C

Printing 1, 2021

For Todd

WildWood Whispers

Prologue

April 2009

I was prepared.

I was always prepared.

Before recess, I opened my locker and felt the bottom of the Wonder Woman book bag hanging on the hook. The lumps created by several tightly rolled T-shirts, shorts and pairs of underwear made me feel better. In another locker, one hall away from mine, Sarah's book bag was also carefully packed.

I wished I could check it too, even though I already had before we left our foster home that morning.

Recess was never okay. And it was even worse now that I had a "sister" to protect. Bullies seemed to know when you didn't have adult backup. No loving mom or dad who would swoop down and save you if things went south.

I had been saving myself for a long time. Unlike Sarah, I'd been in the system for as long as I could remember. I pulled my hand back from the book bag and slammed the locker door harder than I should have.

The bang sounded loud even in a hallway full of students rushing toward the one free half hour out of the day. I didn't look up. I cringed inside and forced my fists to relax. I laid my palms flat on the cool, dented metal of the closed locker as if I could shush it now. Too late. I'd called attention to myself. It felt like a hundred sets of eyes were on my bowed back.

So, I did what I had to do.

I turned, straightened my spine, and squared my shoulders.

I was already over five feet five inches tall. Bigger than most of the kids in my grade. And on my head was a wild cap of muddy brown curls that added a couple more inches to that. Tall or not, the whole world still considered me just a kid. *I'm ancient only on the inside.* I met the first set of staring eyes I came to and locked on with my best "What are you looking at?" face. The boy looked away. I did that several more times until the whole crowd moved on.

Recess was a daily challenge I faced with the grim determination of a soldier marching onto the battlefield. Before Sarah, I could always find a quiet corner, and my size made me less likely to become a target. Sure, there were rumors about me. Bored people can make up some crazy shit. But teachers talk too and sometimes their voices carry between districts.

I hadn't always known to lay low.

The system didn't like fighters. It had taken me eleven years to learn that. I kept our book bags packed because flight was best. Bugging out instead of hitting back was always the plan. Caseworkers liked that. Runners got extra counseling. Different placements. Sympathy from overwhelmed men and women "just trying to do their jobs." Sarah didn't understand all the tricky stuff yet. She was a year older than me, but inexperienced in spite of what she'd been through.

If you didn't contribute to the blood and bruises, you were much better off.

Sarah Ross had come into the foster care system in Richmond from far away. She spoke like every word was a song and she didn't know anything about bullies or living in the city. She was small and so vulnerable my fists clenched again thinking about it.

She was the first best friend I'd ever had. Only I knew her real last name. To everyone else she was a "Smith" like me.

Three months ago I'd been *Jane* Smith. No name. No family. No hope that anyone would adopt a girl with a record of anger management issues. But Sarah didn't care that I had been born a fighter into an unfair world that made me use my fists and punished me for using them at the same time. Maybe she even liked it a little. My hot anger was the opposite of Sarah's icy grief. Our friendship had been instant. We'd pinky sworn our sisterhood at midnight by the glow of a superhero night-light.

Sarah had given me the name Mel the very next day. And I had run with it, feeling more like a Mel than I ever had a Jane.

"Sarah's trapped at the top of the monkey bars and Jason is posting upskirt shots online," a girl shouted at me as I exited the building and started to look around. Wendy Solomon sounded more pleased than upset. As if recess was much more fun with a little torture and sexual harassment going on.

Most of the students had abandoned whatever they'd been doing to gather in a ring around the monkey bars, where the biggest kid in school, even bigger than me, had cornered Sarah.

Sarah was quiet and peaceful and way too old for playground equipment, but she could never lay low when the sun was high and the playground was open. Something about the outdoors drew her as if every scrubby blade of grass was a miracle. Sarah never seemed to notice the noise of traffic or the pollution haze across the sky. Or the bullies that stalked her because they liked her rounded shoulders and hollow eyes.

I didn't pause. I didn't even consider walking to the other side of the playground where an empty bench might help me to stay out of it. I wouldn't leave Sarah to the small huddle of teachers near the basketball court where a weed-clogged fence gave them cover to smoke. Not even when butting in would further wreck my file.

But I didn't run. I walked, as carefully as I could, across the playground. No one paid me much attention. Rumors were one thing. Personal experience another. I'd never scrapped at recess here. I'd avoided bullies and pretended to be chill.

Only Sarah knew better. And right now, only Sarah watched me head in her direction.

I could imagine how it had all gone down. The spring day was warm and clear. Butterflies flitted over the dandelions that poorly paid landscapers hadn't even bothered to poison and kill. Sarah had eagerly run outside while I was dragging my feet. She'd scrambled up to the top of the monkey bars to get even closer to the white cottony clouds she loved to watch.

And Jason Mews had been right behind her.

I should have rushed outside. I should have been there to guard the ladder and protect my friend from pervs.

I was close enough now to see Sarah's red eyes and flushed cheeks. I could see her white-knuckled grip on the rusty metal bars and the sheen of tears on her face. And the hot, hard knot of anger that always wrapped around my insides, squeezing my lungs and holding me back, broke loose and set me free.

I ran.

I ran at Jason and slammed into him with the force and fury of ten thousand times when I'd wanted to but hadn't. He was knocked off his feet and his cell phone flew from his fingers. It fell in the mulch beneath Sarah, and my foot came down on the screen, hard, once, then twice, while Jason caught his breath.

"Mel," Sarah said. Her voice trembled, but it sounded hopeful and relieved.

I needed to warn her that this wasn't going to end well. The system didn't favor heroes. Victims were better, quieter, more easily managed. But, before I could put the complicated lesson into words, Jason swung out a long leg and kicked me off my feet. I went down with a thud into the mulch that was so thinly spread hard-packed earth showed in a bunch of places.

My chin found one of the bare spots and pain exploded in bright flashes behind my eyes. I tasted blood and gasped its sickly metallic flavor down my throat. I hated that taste. I always hated it. The taste of blood was usually followed by worse things.

"What? You the only one that can peek at the hillbilly's pink lace, Ankle Bracelet?" Jason asked.

I'd never had to wear a juvenile court monitor, but rumors had inspired the nickname and I hadn't bothered to deny it. Maybe, in the back of my mind, I'd figured it would be true, sooner or later. Laying low was hard.

I gagged and spit blood into the dirt. Kids were yelling now. Some encouraged Jason to kick me again. Their shouts somehow hurt me more than the fall had. Others warned the teachers were coming. I ignored them. I also ignored the pain. I grabbed two fistfuls of mulch and pushed myself up on my knees.

"Stay down, Ankle Bracelet," Jason warned, then he turned away from me to clown with his friends as if he was already sure I would listen.

Sarah and I were only foster kids. And no one was going to save us.

Staying down would have been the right thing to do. Oops. I fell. Just an accident. No reason for a teacher to get involved. So far, I'd only shoved a much bigger kid. Stomped his phone. Big deal. There was no blood *on him*. No bruises. Me being the bloody one might actually work in my favor. The problem was he deserved so much more. Especially when I glanced back at him and saw him still looking up Sarah's dress.

I ignored his warning. My jaw ached, but I struggled back to my feet. Handfuls of mulch made my fists bigger.

The problem with lying low was that bullies like Jason deserved to bleed.

"They're pink, guys. And the elastic is torn and hanging out on one leg," Jason said, then he laughed. Because poor kids were funny. Because if he didn't mock and laugh and hurt someone else bad stuff might happen to him too. He was cruel because if he was kind he might feel our pain. Some of his friends in the crowd laughed and shouted nasty suggestions, but others got really quiet because they had seen me stand.

The first teacher was pushing her way through the students who had ringed the scene when Jason turned back toward me, warned something was up by stares and gestures. I didn't hesitate. This chance couldn't be lost. He was bigger, but I was madder. I put all my weight behind the swing. Blood flew from Jason's busted lip as my knuckles connected with his smirking face. His body spun halfway around before he fell, hard, knocked off his feet. Mulch scattered in a satisfying spray as he came to a rest. Stunned. The whole playground was stunned. Except for Sarah, who had seen the blow coming from a hundred yards away.

The momentum of my swing carried me forward and into the teacher's arms as she burst through the crowd to join us under the monkey bars. The look on Ms. Tatum's face pretty much confirmed my philosophy about lying low, but I focused on Sarah instead. My best friend. My sister. Family. She looked down at me from her perch with the first huge grin I'd ever seen on her face. The smile made her seem less pale. Like okay could be possible if we held on to each other. Jason howled curses from the ground at my feet. Ms. Tatum's hands closed cruelly around my upper arms. But our bug-out back-packs waited in our lockers and Sarah was smiling.

I'd always been a fighter.

But I hadn't always known family was worth fighting for.

April 2019

Mel didn't wear perfume. She didn't have to. Even though her chest-nut curls were always kept back with strong clips and a perky visor with the coffee chain's logo on it, the scent of coffee permeated her hair and skin and clothes. No wonder. She worked, constantly, picking up extra shifts and volunteering for overtime and inventory because nursing school wasn't cheap. Sarah had always wanted to be a nurse.

Nearly always.

She could remember a time when she'd dreamed a different sort of dream. Growing up in the western Virginia mountains with her herb-alist mother, she'd always assumed she would be a healer. She shied away from thinking about why that goal had morphed into another, with Mel's help.

Sarah breathed deeply of Mel's comforting coffee scent.

She could never go home again. At least not while she was living. It wasn't safe. One day, she would be buried there. With her mother. Until then, she would learn to heal in more modern ways.

The fragrance of Mel's job filled the apartment that morning as she drank the cup of herbal tea Sarah had made her. Beside her cup, nothing but crumbs were left of the toast Sarah had also made, but she knew better than to try to make her eat more. Mel's budget consciousness begrudged every piece of her own toast consumption while usually urging Sarah to eat more than her share.

Never had an actual sister worried over a sibling the way Mel worried over Sarah. At first, it had been a relief to accept Mel's caretaking. When the loss of her mother had been sharp and fresh. When the new sights and sounds and expectations in the city were so different from the hushed world of the whispering woods where she'd grown up.

Mel had pushed back, literally, against the bullies who would mock Sarah's accent or her backwoods ways. Against the people who would have preyed on her because she didn't know anything about surviving as an orphan and she'd been so slammed by loss she'd been too slow to learn. She'd come to the Richmond Children's Home completely wrecked by the ruin of the only life she'd ever known.

And Mel had caught her as she was falling, before she could hit the ground.

Never mind that Mel, as an unplaceable foster kid, had her own problems. She had taken Sarah under her wing and taken care of everything from that moment on. And Sarah had let her. Until now. After six months of nursing school, Sarah realized that Mel wasn't going to sign up for classes too, like she'd promised. She wasn't going to stop making do with less food, less clothing, less of everything, so that Sarah could have more.

Not unless Sarah forced her to.

A daunting thought. No one forced Mel to do anything she didn't want to do. She was ever and always immovable. Like the sun...or maybe more like the moon. Definitely more night than day. Sarah brought the warmth to the tiny family they'd made. With tea and crotchet. With houseplants and silly texts to try to make Mel smile. Mel brought the predictable power of the tides. She propelled their lives, but always for Sarah, never for herself. Only Sarah knew that there was more to Mel, beneath the work and worry.

"You need more time away from the coffee shop," Sarah said. Mel's eyelids drooped with exhaustion, but her mouth still managed to smirk at the very idea of rest.

"I'll sleep all afternoon. I promise," Mel said. She'd tossed the hated visor on the table beside her plate and now she pulled the clips from her hair. They often caused her to have headaches. She pushed her hands into her hair to massage her scalp, probably dealing silently with one now rather than complain about it.

But Sarah often knew things others didn't know.

For instance, she knew that Mel wasn't meant to brew coffee for the rest of her days. She just didn't know how to make her shift her focus from caretaker to taking care of herself.

"They'll call you in early. And you'll go because I won't be here to stop you," Sarah said. Mel shrugged and sipped some more tea, not bothering to deny it.

She wanted to tell Mel that trouble was brewing. Beyond Mel's workaholic ways, there was something else nibbling at the edges of Sarah's senses. A warning. She heard it in the call of the doves on the ledges outside their apartment windows. She heard it in the wind whistling through the trees on the street. There was still some nature in her life and Sarah couldn't ignore what it was trying to say. But she wasn't sure how to convey this knowing to Mel without adding to the already heavy burdens she was determined to carry on her strong shoulders.

Her sister in every way but blood stood up and drained the rest of the tea from her cup. She placed it back on the table with a decisive clunk. But she did pause beside Sarah's chair and lean to kiss the top of her head.

"Get to class. I've got this," Mel said, bumping her hip against Sarah's side. It didn't negate the affectionate kiss. But it did punctuate the end of their conversation.

Sarah watched Mel retreat from serious conversation to her room. Where, in spite of the valerian tea, she would probably toss and turn over how to pay for Sarah's residency scrubs and how long she could ignore the fact that she needed new shoes. When Mel's bedroom door closed, Sarah reluctantly reached for the "For Fox Sake" cup she'd saved pennies to buy for Mel last Christmas. She needed to see the dregs of the ground valerian root in the bottom of the cup, although she dreaded what they would say.

Her heart pounded and her eyes went wide. The lumps and swirls in the bottom of Mel's cup negated the fox's cartoon smile. Sarah dropped the cup to the table. It clattered over onto its side. She glanced toward Mel's bedroom door and halfway rose to go to her—for comfort? To warn her? It was no use to try either. Her glance moved to the apartment door down the hall and froze there. The three extra dead bolts Mel had installed weren't going to protect them forever. The danger that had driven Sarah from the mountain still stalked her, and even Mel wouldn't be able to catch her when she fell this time.

And who would catch Mel?

Sarah gathered up the breakfast dishes quietly and washed the dregs down the sink, hoping she was wrong. While she cleaned, she strained her ears for answers, but the cooing doves outside the window had nothing more to say.

One

Twelve-year-old Sarah Ross reached *quickly for the fragrant charm beneath her pillow the same way she would have reached for a parachute ripcord if she'd been rudely pushed from a plane cruising at ten thousand feet. It was only an imaginary fall, one that had propelled her awake, as bad dreams do, but her trembling fingers clutched at the familiar shape of the tiny crocheted mouse like a lifeline. The charm her mother had filled with sage and lemon balm was supposed to help Sarah sleep, and it did, usually, but the dream fall had cannoned her awake with stomach-swooping dread, as if the entire world had disappeared beneath her sleeping body.*

This time her knuckles didn't stop hurting even after the bed solidified under her. She wasn't falling. She was awake. Her soft bedding still smelled like sunshine from its time on the clothesline.

Her hands hurt.

It was only a ghost pain that had haunted her first waking moments since she was a little girl. There was nothing wrong with her fingers, her knuckles, or the palms of her hands. The mouse usually banished the pain by grounding her in the real world.

Not this time.

Sarah didn't take the charm with her when she sat up. She left it where it lay, hidden, because she was twelve years old and shouldn't need to clutch a faded pink mouse for comfort. Her heart still pounded. Her stomach doubted the assurance of solid floorboards beneath her bare feet. Sarah walked over to close the window anyway.

Maybe the chilled morning air had woken her.

But sometimes a Ross woman felt things and knew things that couldn't be explained away by ordinary circumstances.

Predawn light barely lit the sky outside. Sarah strained her ears. There was no whip-poor-will calling in the distance. There were no coyotes laughing their way to their dens for the day or runaway roosters calling triumphantly from hidden bowers far from their barnyard homes.

The wildwood was quieter than it should be.

Unease suddenly woke her completely and diminished the ache in her knuckles. The cabin felt wrong around her, and the wrongness stretched out from where she stood, silent and still, to the Appalachian wilderness that ran for hundreds of miles around her home.

Sarah almost went for her mouse charm again, but then she remembered today was her birthday. There would be apple stack cake and presents and maybe, just maybe, her mother would finally let one of her friends ice Sarah's earlobes and pop a needle quickly into each one. She could wear the new earrings that were sure to be in one of the brightly colored packages in her mother's bedroom.

Happy thoughts.

And, still, Sarah's heart wouldn't stop beating more quickly than it should. The quiet forest and the dream fall didn't explain it. The phantom pain in her knuckles was too common to rush her heartbeat. Something was wrong. It was the wrongness that had woken her. Not the cool breeze from the window. Not a bad dream. Not the occasional pain in her fingers on waking that her mother said would probably be explained one day.

Last night when she'd gone to bed she'd opened the window to release a frightened luna moth caught between the screen and the wavy glass panes. The thumping of her heart against her rib cage reminded her of the frantic beat of the luna moth's wings. Helplessly trying to fly free. She'd released the moth, but there was nothing she could do for the racing heart trapped in her chest.

The floor was cool against her feet, but she didn't pause to find socks or shoes. She hurried out of her loft bedroom and over the small landing that led to the half-log stairs. They were covered with rag rug treads so her slapping feet fell silently as she slipped down to the cabin's great room.

All the lights were off, even the one in the bathroom off the hall that led to her mother's bedroom. Her mother always left that light on in case she had to get up in the night to answer the door. She was a healer, and on the mountain a healer was often woken up in the middle of the night even now, when a modern clinic was only forty-five minutes away.

The unexpected darkness was temporary. The sun would come up soon. There was a hint of pink around the shadowed edges of things.

Sarah went to the kitchen instead of running to wake her mother. She wasn't a baby, in spite of the fluttering moth in her chest.

She was twelve. She was going to get her ears pierced, and pretty soon she would be helping her mother when it came to helping others. She'd already learned a lot by her mother's side—the growing, the grinding, the tinctures and tisanes. She was getting too old to be nervous over dreams and premonitions.

The pain in her knuckles was gone. And its meaning could wait.

The refrigerator hummed a reassuring sound as she opened its door. She reached for the orange juice her mother always kept in a carafe on the top shelf. The familiar sweet tang soothed her. At least, that was what she told herself until she put the juice back and closed the door. It had been the light that soothed her. When the door snapped shut and the refrigerator light went out, she was left in the strange darkness once more, and no thoughts of sun-rise or cake stopped her from finally hurrying to her mother's room.

The dark didn't matter. She knew every familiar step down the hall. She'd lived her whole life in the cozy cabin her great-grandmother had built. Just as her mother and her grandmother had.

Sarah stood in the bedroom doorway for a long time when she saw her mother wasn't in bed. The fall was there again in her stomach and, oddly, in the back of her throat like a choked-off scream. She reached for the doorframe and held it with white-knuckled fingers that were whole and strong and uninjured. Nightmares weren't real. Melody Ross must have risen early to sweep the front porch or grind herbs in the stump that held the stone mortar bowl generations of Ross women had used.

But even hearing in her mind the sound of the oaken pestle, smoothed from the friction and the oil from so many hands, grinding against the mortar didn't convince her.

Because she was a Ross, and Ross women knew that premonitions were as real as the scatter of paper on her mother's bedroom floor.

Sarah let go of the doorframe and rushed forward. She fell to her knees in the pile of paper, but even the rustles as she gathered them up to her chest hardly allowed her to accept the reality of their desecration. Something her mother never would have allowed if she were okay.

Darkness outside had given way to a washed-out gray.

The pages had been ripped from the Ross family remedy book that normally sat on her mother's bedside table. They were worn and stained from years of use. The familiar scripts and scrawls of all the Ross women who had come before her had been carefully protected and preserved.

Until now.

The wrongness swallowed Sarah. The feeling of falling blossomed out from her stomach to take her whole body down into black despair. And still, she gathered up the pages before she struggled, wobbly, to her feet. Every last one.

With the growing light, she could see what she'd missed before.

More pages led down the hall and into the sitting area. And still more led out the open front door. The moth of her heart had risen up into her throat to lodge there so solidly she could hardly draw breath. She ran forward, gathering up the pages because she knew it was what her mother would want her to do.

The book had been a part of her life since she was a baby. She was a Ross. And by the book she would heal and help, bind and brew, nurture and sow the seeds of tomorrow. Hot tears ran down her chilled cheeks. Mountain mornings were cold. Her thin nightgown didn't provide enough warmth. But she didn't go back for a robe. She shivered, cried, and gathered up page after page as her feet became wet and icy in the dew.

She didn't leave any of the pages in the damp grass, even the ones that were sticky with blood. She gathered those too as gasps of despair made it past the moth in her throat and her stiff, cold lips.

The pages led her down a path into the forest. She didn't hesitate even though the woods were still and dark around her. She knew these wildwood shadows. She'd been taught every plant, every root, every tree and every vine since before she could walk and talk. But the wrongness had preceded her here. The morning breeze in the leaves wasn't a welcome sound, because another joined it—a rhythmic creaking that made her clutch the rescued pages to her chest.

Cree-cree, cree-cree. An unnatural sound in a place that should be wholly natural.

Sarah came to the end of the path that led from the backyard to the garden, and unlike every time she'd come to the clearing before, she paused in dread. The creaking was louder. It roared in her ears, drowning out the sound of her pounding heart and the trickle of the mountain stream that usually gurgled a welcome to her at this point.

The cree-cree was ominous. Her mind tried to identify it and shy away from it at the same time.

But what if some pages had fallen into the water?

Panic pushed her forward.

She had to save the pages that had been ripped from the book. It was the only logic she could grab in a morning that defied normalcy.

The sudden revelation of her mother's body hanging in a black locust tree stopped her again. All logic fled. All reason escaped her. The rope around her mother's neck strained and rubbed on the crooked branch that held the other end—cree, cree, cree. Sarah's arms went limp and all the pages she'd gathered fell like crimson-speckled leaves to the ground. Some did fall into the stream then. They were the lucky ones, washed away on rivulets and ripples while Sarah stood frozen, inside and out, staring at her mother's body.

Finally, she released the moth that had been stuck in her throat on a wavering scream. Her cry broke the silence that had gripped the mountain. The stillness also broke, as sleepy crows were startled up from the roosts they had claimed around the gruesome scene. Sarah ran to her mother's blue-tinged pendulum feet. To help her. To protect her. Although it was obviously too late.

There was blood on her mother's nightgown, black splashes of dried blood, stark against the pale pink cotton. Her mother was always clean and neat, strong and prepared, full of energy and delight. Someone had hurt her. Someone had dragged her from the house, leaving a trail of blood-stained pages in their wake.

Sarah wasn't ready. Twelve years of apprenticeship wasn't enough. She needed more than charms and remedies. She needed more than the wildwood garden. The moth was gone. Only groans remained. Sharp and ugly, they parted her lips with jagged wings that cut like glass. Her mother was gone too. There was nothing left but a pitiful shell of the wisewoman Melody Ross had been. Her eyes were glassy and empty. Her mouth would never smile again. Her dark curls were tousled and damp and lifeless where once they had gleamed in the sun.

It had taken Sarah too long to make it to the garden. She must have heard a noise. She must have sensed the terror. It had woken her, but she'd hesitated over her mouse and the dark house. She'd tried so hard to make everything okay with juice and birthday wishes. She was a Ross, and nothing was ever as simple as cake and earrings.

A howl of anger and fear met the sun as it broke over the horizon. Nothing as sweet as a crochet charm would ever soothe her again. Sarah fell to her knees at the base of her mother's locust tree, shocked at the sound she'd made. It would be a long, long time before she was capable of making another.

The ashes sat exactly as I'd left them. The stainless steel urn hadn't tipped over as I slept to spill Sarah and her horrible memories onto the floor. Grim dust hadn't risen up to haunt my usual faceless dreams with nightmare precision, sharp and detailed. The hit-and-run accident that killed my best friend had left me with nothing but a mild concussion...and Sarah's ashes.

It had been a month since I'd picked up her remains.

No one else had claimed her.

The hollow chill of that responsibility made me into a shell of a woman through the days and far too receptive to the gnaw of terrible thoughts at night.

I was the one Sarah Ross had turned to after her mother was murdered and I hadn't lived up to the task. I hadn't kept her safe. I hadn't kept her at all. Just as I hadn't kept anything in all of my twenty-three years...except Sarah's memories.

I had held her hand when we'd first met, and through a succession of midnight confessions I listened as she'd whispered about the morning she'd found her mother.

She'd been so small.

I'd been awkward, a giant beside her petite frame. She'd been placed in the same foster home as me and they'd had only one bedroom for us to share. Her size had fooled me for only a few seconds. She was the older one. By a whole year. But her age hadn't stopped me from knowing instantly she needed a protector. Something about the bruises under her eyes and the sickly pallor beneath her fading tan skin. Her lips had been dried and cracked. After hours of tears, the salt from her sadness had leached the moisture from her mouth.

I brought her a glass of water and sat on the floor beside her bed. She'd taken a few sips, enough to moisten a parched throat, and then she started talking. I'd taken her hand and held on for dear life.

Until she died, I hadn't known I'd memorized every word she'd said.

The nightmare inspired by her raspy whispers came every night after the accident. It always jolted me awake at the same moment and sent me wandering for reassurance. Every night I found the urn. Confirmation there would be no comfort.

The harsh light from the ceiling fixture caused a glint on its surface almost like glass. In it, my reflection was distorted. The strange, softened face of a woman I didn't recognize caused me to back away and close the door.

The second bedroom of the Richmond apartment I soon wouldn't be able to afford on my own had become a tomb.

On the way to the bathroom for some pain medication, I checked my phone. No notifications. There was nothing left of Sarah there. No messages. No texts. I'd deleted them all and there would never be more. Why hadn't I saved them? Because the evidence that we'd enjoyed a normal life for a while was more than I could bear.

Besides, my heart was as empty as the screen.

I laid the phone on the hall table and focused on the throbbing at my temples and in various other battered and bruised parts of my body. It was time for another dose. The tiny white pills were probably as responsible for my lucid dreams as anything else, but I couldn't sleep without them and the night was only half over.

Sarah would have brewed some valerian tea. Over the years, I'd learned to like the slightly minty, slightly bitter concoction she remembered from a family recipe.

Sarah had never fully recovered from her mom's murder. She'd stayed pale, surrounded by an aura of fragility only I was allowed to penetrate. I was tall, strong and walled off from the world. Only Sarah managed to penetrate that. But we'd managed to find "okay" together. For a while.

Now, there was a hole in that wall where Sarah used to be and the nightmares slipped through it to freeze my soul. I'd made a promise to Sarah. To take her back home when she died.

It was one I intended to keep. Eventually. I wouldn't let the last thing between us become a lie. My body didn't try to fight the effects of the pill when I lay back down. It was too tired and too sore. Truth was, even my mind was quick to welcome the embrace of hazy unconsciousness. Nightmares were the only place I was sure to see Sarah again. Fear wouldn't stop me from going to her. It never had.

Two

It wasn't far from Richmond to Morgan's Gap, Virginia. But distance between communities isn't really measured in miles. There was no Global Positioning System that could have prepared me for the world I discovered at the top of Sugarloaf Mountain. One of those maps a reader finds in fantasy novels would have been more fitting than the slightly robotic voice that directed me to a land of morning mists and deep forest shadows so far removed from crazy commutes and cappuccinos. It was late spring and I drove from dull cement and asphalt into myriad shades of green that dazzled my eyes.

When I finally arrived in Sarah's hometown and pulled into a parking space on the street, the sunrise was so deeply pink on the horizon it seemed the perfect surreal light for an alien landscape. The GPS informed me the nearest familiar coffee chain was forty-five minutes away—back the way I'd come. I was lucky the navigation system worked at all. My cell phone had only a few bars of signal. I sat in the rental car in a sort of stunned, uncaffeinated silence while the pink sunrise turned into an orange-tinted morning. I was a barista.

I'd grown too accustomed to easy access. Some part of my brain was awake enough to translate the nearest restaurant's name into visions of heavy white porcelain cups filled with plain black liquid. The idea came from a movie scene, not from any real experience I'd had, but my need for stimulant urged me out of the car. It was more than the lack of caffeine or missing the familiar morning ritual of obtaining it that had me on edge.

The ashes were in the backseat. I'd put the urn in one of Sarah's storage boxes. The kind with the old-fashioned botanical prints she'd always favored. This one was covered in roses. Big cabbage roses the size of saucers. Would the pretty box entice a thief to break in and steal what would turn out to be a horrible surprise? My empty stomach plummeted at the thought and I quickly shrugged out of my jean jacket and laid it carefully over the box.

Truth: Nothing in life prepares you to handle cremated remains. Everything you do feels disrespectful. For the first time, I thought maybe I understood some of the traditions surrounding death. I didn't have traditions. I was adrift. Grief doesn't pair well with inexperience and awkwardness.

Or fear.

I was dressed in my usual camouflage—black skinny jeans, black high-top sneakers, a logo T-shirt from a defunct bar and the faded jacket I'd discarded. Only here my city camouflage achieved the opposite effect. I felt exposed on the sidewalk. Too dark, inside and out. I was doing what I'd promised to do, but it felt like I'd brought Sarah to foreign soil. The strange sunrise didn't help to negate the horror in my dreams.

Somewhere not too far from this sunny street, there was a black locust tree where a body had been found, so maybe I wasn't too dark for this place after all.

I placed my hand on the top of my jacket to make another promise to Sarah. This one was wordless and more about steadying my nerve. *I'm here. I'll see this through.* Then I hurriedly backed up to slam the car door shut.

Sarah was gone. I'd promised to bring her home. Those were two absolutes I couldn't change. Besides, hiding in my apartment had never been an option.

I hadn't hidden since I was five. There'd been a closet and an abusive foster mother. There'd also been a toy clown that hadn't saved me any more than hiding had. I'd huddled for all I was worth with the pitiful little clown. For hours, I'd ignored my bladder as it became painfully full and the cramps in my legs as they'd stayed curled up under me too long in the tiny space. When she finally found me, she'd ripped the clown from my arms. She'd torn the stuffing from it. The white fluff had fallen onto my upturned, tearstained face like snow. It had clung to my lashes and stuck to my lips and I'd never forgotten the stale cotton taste. Once the clown was destroyed, she'd wrenched me to my feet onto stiff, numb legs that would barely hold me.

They didn't stay numb for long when the beating began.

I'd never hidden again. I'd faced and dealt with whatever punches came my way. And once Sarah came into my life I'd faced a few for her too.

I walked into the diner looking for a fight. I wanted to hit back at the universe the same way I'd hit Jason Mews in middle school. All I found was the heavy aroma of bacon and a waitress frenzied by a "crowd" of three occupied booths and one guy on a stool at the counter. I walked past him and settled at the last booth with my back to the wall and my face toward the door. I played with the sugar dispenser while I waited for the lone server to see me. The click, click, click of the sliding metal lid was soothing, until I noticed the dispenser reflected my face back at me in the same distorted way the urn had done the night before.

Who was I now that Sarah was gone? I'd been eleven when we'd met and, by necessity, wholly focused on making it through each day. My intense self-preservation had expanded immediately to encompass the tiny girl who would become my world.

"We have fresh rhubarb pie this morning if you're interested," the waitress said. She rushed up to my booth carrying the scent of coffee and bacon with her. I had to admit it was an appealing perfume. The bacon made up for the lack of imported bean scent that normally permeated my hair and skin. My stomach growled even though I had no idea what "rhubarb" could be. The rest of the menu was above the counter on a chalkboard that had seen better days. Someone had tried to offset its dilapidation with jaunty smiley face emojis. They hurt me the same way the stuff I'd deleted from my phone had hurt me. Too happy, too ordinary in a life turned empty and cold. Again. Loss was such a simple way to describe the hollow I'd become.

"Coffee and toast," I said. "Please." The last was added as an afterthought when my first words had come out curt and clipped and totally out of place compared to the chalk emojis. I was definitely not going to take my edginess out on a server just doing her job. Nerves, lack of sleep, grief and fear were no excuse. None of those things should be allowed to negate the empathy I'd developed on the other side of the counter.

"Okay. But I'm going to bring you some of my blackberry preserves because you look like you need something sweet," the waitress said. She didn't have a name tag. She was wearing faded black jeans and a T-shirt with the diner's logo on the front. The mascot on her chest was a pig in a chef's hat. The pig had a huge smile on its face I couldn't quite reconcile with the scent of bacon in the air. She wasn't being snarky. A quick glance from the pig's grin up to her face found a more relaxed and natural smile there.

She was being kind. My body responded by flooding my eyes with hot moisture.

The waitress didn't wait for agreement. She hurried away and I breathed a sigh of relief because every interaction I'd had since the accident felt like walking on shattered glass. Her rush allowed me to widen my eyes so the tears would dry before they could fall.

There were harder things I would have to face in Morgan's Gap than a server's kindness. I had to say goodbye to Sarah. I had to endure the scene of my nightmares to do it. And I had to decide where to go from here.

I was on the second cup of coffee so acidic a third might dissolve my esophagus, downing each gulp like a bitter medicine I had to endure, when the door opened. A woman entered to greetings from the rest of the customers. Calls of "Granny" met her from everyone in the place and for a crazy second I wondered if they were all related.

The lone guy at the counter disrupted that chain of thought. He stood to face the older woman and nodded at her as he also said "Granny" with a curtness that suggested she was not his grandmother. And yet, he didn't get out his wallet to pay. He hadn't risen to leave. He moved the stools beside him closer to the counter to get them out of her way. Then he stood as if at attention while Granny passed by. It seemed a gesture of respect, but one strangely tinged with wariness. His back was straight. His shoulders stiff. His jaw tight. He didn't speak again, but he watched until she had walked all the way to my booth.

As the woman walked, my attention met the lone guy's gaze over the top of her head. Only for a second. I looked away quickly and he sat back down, but not before I had seen that the intensity of his dark green eyes didn't match the casual ruggedness of the rest of his appearance. His fall catalog clothing suggested simple outdoor pursuits. His boots were worn. His hair thick and tousled. But the weight of his stare seemed complicated. Why did he seem wary of a little old woman? And why, in spite of his wariness, did I find his old-fashioned deference to her charming? I was too jaded for chivalry to make an impact. But, as with the waitress, genuine consideration was another thing altogether.

I've made coffee for all kinds of early morning patrons—from politicians to construction workers. The guy at the counter had more on his mind than hiking. I was sure of it. His caution and the respect he'd shown her in spite of it made me look closer and harder at the woman than I initially had.

Granny—whoever's grandmother she might be—arrived at my booth as if it had been her intended destination when she got out of bed that morning. She hadn't even paused when the man stood. And, unlike me, she hadn't seemed to be affected by his eyes, his courtesy or the certainty he had more on his mind than the fried eggs on his plate.

In a Richmond coffee shop you're more likely to hear a grandmother referred to as Louise or Beverly. Maybe NeeNee or Nan. But the instant I met this woman's eyes I couldn't imagine her being called anything else

"Coffee. Should have known. Damnable stuff. Always interferes. Never drink it unless you need to counteract…Oh well, Sarah wouldn't have remembered everything, would she? Bless her and you," the old woman said. "I was a friend to her mother and her grandmother before that. Even knew Great-Granny Ross. Not that she was exactly friendly with anyone. Did my best for you girls. Wasn't good enough. But here you are and that's what's meant to be."

She sat in a flounce of colorful fabrics with so many layers I didn't know where one sweater ended and a shirt began. I'd thought at first she was soft and round, but it was her clothing that padded her with extra inches, not body fat. In spite of the layers, she wasn't messy. All was clean and bright about her, including her sharp blue eyes. As I took in her bohemian appearance, she reached into a pocket and pulled out a tiny net pouch tied with a thin yellow string. Suddenly, I was certain her layers hid numerous pockets, each prepared to fulfill whatever requirements she might encounter as she went about the business of her day. And nothing about her suggested her business would be the ordinary type you'd expect an elderly woman to undertake, including the fact that she obviously thought she knew me even though I'd never heard of her.

The waitress came rushing back to our table with a steaming cup. She placed the cup in front of Granny and the old woman plopped the net bag into what appeared to be water. It was all done in the fluid motions of habit. As if it was commonplace for this particular customer to brew her own tea.

"I promised Sarah I'd bring her home," I said. My jostled brain wasn't at its best and my lack of sleep might be beginning to mess with my perceptions. I was compelled to confide in her as if I'd been waiting for her to join me.

"At least she knew to tell you to bring her home. Even if she didn't remember to avoid coffee. She didn't forget the garden," Granny said. She sipped from her cup and the scent of peppermint rose into the air as the liquid was disturbed. From the wild mop of graying curls on her head to the voluminous patchwork skirt that fell to her knees to the polished black hiking boots on her little feet, I'd never seen anyone like her. The phrase "jolly old elf" kept running through my brain, but some niggling instinct honed from years of living out of a backpack told me her jollies might be of a darker variety than I expected.

"She found her mother in the locust tree," I said. It wasn't a secret and yet I whispered the words as if I was oversharing. The whole town must have known about the murder, including the longtime denizen across from me. The diner still existed around us. The waitress still rushed. The man at the counter finished his eggs. Several other customers came and went. But I saw what Sarah had seen on the worst morning of her life superimposed over it all.

"You helped her. You shouldered the weight of her burden. Seeing you now I'm not surprised. Your strength is palpable," Granny said as she sipped her tea. "Exactly what's needed. You actually worked with coffee? You brewed the stuff and drank far more of it than you should have."

My eyes were hot again. For so long, I'd been strong for Sarah. Now that she was gone I felt insubstantial. Not strong at all. As if one stiff breeze would blow me off my feet. It was oddly comforting this woman seemed to know about me when normally I would prefer not to be known. Like I needed the reminder of who I was or who I was going to be.

And that increased the edginess the caffeine hadn't soothed.

"Bah. Coffee. Not good for you at all. Bring another cup, June!" Granny ordered. She pushed my coffee cup away from my elbow and reached into the folds of her clothing to pull forth another net bag. This one was tied with a green string and the second it hit the water in the cup the waitress had rushed to our table, a familiar scent rose on the steam to tease my nose.

"Valerian tea," I said. No tears actually spilled. Although the world glistened around the edges. "Sarah used to make it for me."

"She left us young, but she'd already learned a lot from her mother," Granny said.

Wary or not, there was nothing in me that could resist the tea that reminded me of my sister. I picked up the cup and carefully sipped while the bag of herbs continued to steep. The flavor brought it all back—the friendship, the loss, the confidence of togetherness, the certainty that, now, I'd be alone for the rest of my life.

"It's too soon. I wanted you both to grow older and wiser before you came back. But here you are. You're too young," Granny said. "And I'm too old. But seeds scatter where and how they may." She was even older than I'd initially thought. Her movements were quick and certain. Her eyes sparkled. But a close look at her face revealed a tiny network of lines around those eyes and more lines around her lips. She drained the last of her tea and placed the cup in front of her on the table, then untied the yellow string to allow the damp herbal mix contained in the net bag to dump out. She looked down into the bottom of her cup and chewed her lower lip as if she was contemplating the secrets of the universe.

"I'm supposed to take her ashes to the garden near her mother's cabin," I said. Her tea and sympathy had caused me to relax my guard. I needed to share this solemn, horrible duty with someone and I had no one else.

"She wants you to do more than that," Granny said.

She reached for my cup, but I held fast to the handle. For some reason I suddenly didn't want her to tug on the green string and release the valerian mixture. And by "didn't want her to" I mean my heart was pounding as if I was hiding in the closet with a plush clown while my abusive foster mother turned the doorknob with a determined rattle that was going to break the flimsy lock.

I didn't know this woman.

Not her intentions or her motivations.

Granny's hand was surprisingly strong on my cup, but she accepted my resistance. She slowly released the mug and lowered her hand with nothing more than an arched brow that said she didn't need to see the herbs in the bottom of my cup to know what she knew.

Hadn't Sarah always known things? She was that girl who always stopped to stare at lost pet notices. After a while, I didn't even try to pull her away. She'd found so many of them. Knowing things was something you accepted about Sarah Ross. The sun would rise tomorrow. Sarah would feel out the exact location of that missing bichon frise. Finding someone like Granny in Morgan's Gap didn't exactly shock me. Sarah had told me to bring her ashes home without any doubt I'd find the way.

Still. Accepting Sarah's otherworldly qualities had happened gradually over time as we'd grown up together. Granny was too sudden. Sarah had been a spark of special in a world too often dingy and dull, but my self-preservation instincts were overwhelmed by the unexpected discovery of more sparking, here, of all places, where coal dust might still smudge attic keepsakes.

"There have been Ross women in Morgan's Gap since this area was settled by Irish immigrants after the Whiskey Rebellion. Some say they were here waiting when the first folks arrived. They were wisewomen, you understand," Granny said.

"They knew things," I said, but my tone was reserved. Accepting something about your best friend didn't mean you comfortably accepted it about anyone else. Or the world. The hair on the back of my neck had risen to attention and my stomach had gone light as if it was suddenly filled with helium instead of herbal tea. This woman had been expecting me in town this morning even though I had decided to come myself only in the wee hours after I'd "lived" through Sarah's mother's hanging multiple times.

"That's one way of putting it," Granny said. "Another way is to say they knew how to influence this world. To prick. To nudge. To help.

To heal. But whatever you call it in these parts if you know something you shouldn't—if rain's going to fall or some couple is going to marry—they say you must have Ross blood. Some deny it. Some claim it. Some fear it. But no one has disturbed the Ross cabin or the garden. You can take Sarah to join her mother and grandmother and great-grandmother there." The old woman stood up and slid out of the booth. She retrieved several tiny envelopes from yet another pocket and laid them beside her cup. "Ginseng powder for June's mother," she said, nodding toward the packets. "She's undergoing cancer treatments and her energy is low. Come see me when you've finished at the garden. We'll have more to talk about then."

The man at the counter was looking at us again. Unaccountably more tense than before. This time, Granny turned toward him and shushed him as if he'd spoken.

"Don't you worry, Jacob Walker. I'm no poacher. This ginseng was legally harvested from private land," she said. To me, she continued, "As if I'd endanger a single leaf in the whole of the wildwood. He's a biologist. Works for the state. He should know he and I both worship this mountain, just in different ways."

The biologist didn't turn away. Our glances caught and held again long enough for superstitious tingling to give way to a different sort of tingling and I sat stunned. I was too guarded not to notice when I wasn't guarded enough. Why was I so disarmed by his moving a couple of barstools a few inches to make way for an elderly lady to walk by? Or had it been the standing? The respect he'd shown her? He was just a guy eating breakfast. A stranger who happened to be polite. I was terrible at guy meets girl. I always had been. So, I usually dealt with that kind of tingle by ignoring it.

But today was proving to be even tougher than I'd imagined it would be. I didn't want anyone to see my pain and I was afraid the man saw my unshed tears and more before he finally turned around to focus on his breakfast.

Granny didn't seem to notice my reaction to Walker. She reached into another pocket as if I wasn't furiously blinking my eyes to dispel the moisture. I'd seen a slight softening around his lips when he'd noticed my emotion. Vulnerability wasn't acceptable. If he looked this way again, he'd see dry eyes and a hardened jaw. But he didn't look and this time Granny pulled out a rolled piece of paper. It was faded and smudged in her brown fingers. By now I understood her work with herbs—harvesting and preparing—must stain her fingers. Her dark curls were shiny and shot through with silvery glints of gray. Her cheeks were pink and her clothing fresh. The stains weren't dirt. They were more like the earth left its mark on her in order to recommend her services to the community.

"This was set down for your eyes a long time ago," she said. She offered the paper to me on her outstretched palm and I took it because her gravitas wouldn't allow me to reject it.

The paper was difficult to unroll because it had been curled for so long, but I was finally able to read the bold script. The ink had faded, but I made out what appeared to be directions. Several lines were followed by a larger signature. The initials *M* and *R* were even bolder and hardly faded at all. They had been the most protected by the roll with several layers of paper between them and the sun, air and moisture that came with the passage of time.

How could I trust a note written by a stranger and given to me by a woman I'd just met?

"Those directions will take you to the Ross cabin. The garden is a ways behind it. Follow the trail. You'll see where Sarah's ashes belong," Granny said. She stepped away and I started at her sudden movement. I dropped the paper and it curled back up. I'm not sure why, but I reached for one of Granny's stained hands to prevent her from leaving. I hadn't touched anyone since Sarah had died. It wasn't in my nature to reach out. Lash out, occasionally, yes, but not reach. Granny was surprisingly cool beneath my fingers as if her circulation had gone poor with age. She lifted her other hand to pat my wrist, a warm gesture in spite of her cold skin. I couldn't guess her exact age, but she'd surely laid friends to rest before. I hadn't wanted her to see too much in the herbal detritus left in my cup. This was similar. Too soon. Too close. Too much.

I could offer empathy by being polite to a waitress I didn't know. Accepting it from someone else over tender feelings of grief made me edgier than before.

And yet, I had reached for her and I didn't let her go.

"Best to get it done. Then we'll talk again," she advised. "Come and find me when you're finished." She moved her free hand from my wrist to the back of the hand that lightly gripped her. She urged me to release her other hand. Then she curled my fingers in on my palm until she helped them to form a loose fist. "You're a fighter. Sarah needed that. She still needs that. Don't give up. This isn't the end. It's a beginning."

I didn't uncurl my fist when she released me to leave.

This time, the biologist stayed seated when she walked out of the diner. He didn't note her passing at all. Again, I found his behavior oddly charming. She had places to go and things to do and he was merely staying out of her way. I don't know if he looked my way again when I finally opened my fingers and asked for my bill. I was too determined not to look his. I was aware of Walker on a sensory level that made me nervous.

I was several feet away from the biologist's back as I passed his stool to leave. My body mapped every inch of those feet as if it needed to know how quickly it could get to him should I give it permission. What's more, the strange awareness I felt might have gone both ways. I could have sworn his shoulders tightened when I walked by. I kept walking. By the time I made it to the door, my jaw hurt from clenching my teeth and my eyes burned with determined dryness.

He probably didn't notice or care. I proved nothing to anyone but myself. I was okay with that. In this odd little town that seemed less sleepy than it should before 9:00 a.m., I needed to rely on myself to stay steady and strong. I'd created calm out of chaos a long time ago. And I'd survived Sarah's death. Hadn't I? Mostly? I wasn't going to lose it now over a pair of intense green eyes and a fay grandmother with pockets full of herbal tea.

Three

I wasn't used to following written directions, but the Ross cabin had no address and my GPS would have been spotty this far out of town. My phone might still be capable of sending and receiving calls, but the one lone bar in the top right corner of its screen seemed almost apocalyptic.

So, I tried to find the landmarks the directions referenced with an anxiety-filled process of hit or miss that left me hoping I'd filled the car with enough gas.

I finally found what I thought was the cabin's driveway past a rock formation M. R. had called "Standing Stones." The three large boulders piled side by side looked more like "Rocks Too Large for Highway Construction to Blast." I signaled and cut the wheel even though the delineation of grass to road wasn't clear.

The rental car bounced on the overgrown road. A tall grassy streak in between two dirt tracks was enough to impede the car's progress. The flow of flattened grass swished beneath the chassis. It sounded like driving through water. I navigated with care, passing through forest and fields, steadily climbing higher. Before the slope where the Ross cabin rested against the mountain, the road split a field of wildflowers in half. To my left was a faded red shed with a rusty tin roof and a bright splash of turquoise paint where an old pickup had been left for nature to reclaim. Vines mostly obscured its windows and frame, trailing over and under, around and through, as if to trace the automobile and remake it as a green and growing thing.

A "No Pipeline" sign had been stuck into the ground by the side of the road. Time and weather had caused it to fade and tilt to one side. I'd seen similar signs on the way into town. I knew enough from statewide news stories that natural gas companies wanted to build conduits from their fracking sites in northern Virginia to the rest of the state. Apparently, a lot of people on Sugarloaf Mountain didn't want the hassle.

The condition of the road and the faded sign calmed my fears about encountering other people. Someone visited occasionally. Possibly Granny. Otherwise it would be completely overgrown, but all was quiet and still when I stopped the car in front of the cabin. I didn't pause, because if I did I might head back down the road. I climbed out and slammed the door. I opened the back door and pushed my jacket aside. All quick and sure as if I carried my heart to be scattered in the mountains every day.

The urn was cool in my hands. I clutched it close to my stomach and closed the door with my foot.

Maybe letting go of Sarah's ashes would end the nightmares. I needed peaceful sleep, but dreaded it at the same time. Right now, I was with her again, in a way, every night. But a promise is a promise. I couldn't break my word to my best friend even if fulfilling her last request broke me.

The cabin had been built a long time ago. Its logs were weathered and gray. The chinking between them stood out in faded stripes. But it seemed sturdy. Straight and square with an unblemished metal roof. The hollow in my gut I'd lived with since the accident echoed with Sarah's tears when I saw bright red rubber boots beside the front door. Unlike the shed and the cabin, they didn't seem faded at all. I'd lost Sarah. She'd lost her mother. No wonder the hollowness in the nightmare stayed with me even when I was awake. The cabin had a porch across its front. On one end an empty swing swayed in the breeze, at once inviting and heartbreaking.

Peace. Tranquility. And all of it was a lie.

The middle of nowhere wasn't immune to pain or danger. Those red boots had probably belonged to Sarah's mother. A woman who had been murdered near this spot ten years ago. Their cheerful color reminded me of the much less cheerful red I'd seen in my nightmares.

I didn't go up on the porch. I couldn't bear the sag of the steps beneath my feet where Sarah must have played. Lingering here would only put off the inevitable anyway. I'd come to bring Sarah's ashes to the garden. I'd have to see the tree that haunted my dreams. I'd have to walk on the moss in the clearing by the creek where the remedies had washed away.

When I came around the corner where a riotous wild rose had been urged to grow up a trellis made of faded white lattice, the view behind the house stopped me in my tracks. The rose hadn't been pruned in a while, but the backyard was pristine. And it was the yard I walked across every night in my nightmares. The sun had dried the dew hours ago, but I'd been here, exactly here, as Sarah, so many times.

My body quaked.

Exactly.

The tingling of superstition I'd experienced in the diner morphed into a finger of cold dread down my spine. Had Sarah described this place so perfectly that I'd managed to envision it as it had been? The back door to the cabin was closed, but it was the same batten and ledge door made from weathered wood. I'd walked over its familiar threshold dozens of times.

I walked to the door, but I hugged Sarah's ashes rather than reach for the handle. What if the inside of the cabin was familiar? I turned away from the house and faced the forest. An opening in the trees revealed where the trail began. It was well traveled by someone. For a second, I imagined Sarah's footsteps going to the black locust tree every night, taking me reluctantly with her. The dark whimsy didn't ease my dread.

The dirt was smooth and packed firmly beneath my feet. As it had been beneath Sarah's, every night, in every dream. But a real person must keep it worn. I couldn't allow myself to get carried away by coincidence.

Suddenly, I was more nervous about encountering another person than superstition had made me moments before. I needed to take Sarah's ashes to the garden. Afraid of an audience and uncertain of whom that audience might be, I kept walking.

I wouldn't find a woman hanging in the tree. There was nothing to be afraid of beyond the possibility of sharing my grief and loss with a stranger.

I plucked a stalk of lavender as I passed the fence on the way to the opening in the trees. I brought it to my nose and breathed deeply of its soothing scent. The fragrance unlocked an image of pale purple dust created from petals crushed in the palm of Sarah's mother's hand. The path was smooth, but the forest surrounding the trail needed to give way when I entered it. I gently pushed past tendrils of hanging vines and the tickling fingers of branch tips, unsure if I was an intruder or a welcome stranger. I walked into the wildwood for the first time as I imagined Sarah's mother opening her calloused fingers and allowing the lavender dust to fall into the steaming bathwater she prepared for her daughter.

The pain had been sharp in Sarah's fingers that morning, so this evening her mother prepared a special lavender bath before bed. Sarah was only five, but she knew the pain might be back in the morning, brought on by dreams that could sometimes bring ponies or cotton candy instead.

Her favorite nightgown was already laid out on her bed and her mother had aired her favorite quilt on the clothesline as she often did in summer. The quilt was a masterpiece of handwork made by her mother's friends where colorful scraps of bright cloth had been sewn into intricate kaleidoscope patterns Sarah had traced with her fingers for years.

Her whole bedroom smelled of sunshine and warm grass. And while her mother filled the large claw-foot tub with steaming water, she sang. The song was from the Ross remedy book. It wasn't one most people would have heard. The tune was strange and lilting and filled with words Sarah couldn't pronounce herself.

Not yet.

One day she would sing them. That's how being a Ross worked.

Her mother had shown her how to make a daisy chain a long time ago. Stem to head and head to stem. You always ended the chain by connecting the end to the beginning to form a circle. Sometimes they made a giant chain together, working all day long to form a huge circle that wound around the cabin. Then they held hands and skipped seven times around singing the names of all the Ross women who had come before them so they'd never forget.

Fair-Margaret-Ann-Elizabet-Berta-Katherine-Mary-Beatrice-Melody-Sarah.

The powerful women who had come before her were known by the Ross name on the mountain. If they married at all, it was under the moon and stars with trees as witness and forest creatures as deacon and clergy and wedding guests. Sarah didn't know her father, but even at five years old she knew Ross blood flowed throughout the community in many different homes and families. Some was just more diluted than others, like a strong, bitter tea that had been weakened with cream and sugar. The drink became something else altogether, easier to stomach for some. Gentler. Sweeter.

The bath was full and her mother's song had become a wordless hum. Sarah shrugged out of her shirt and pants while her mother tilted a mason jar full of dried blossoms with one hand to tap some of its contents into the palm of her other hand. She closed her fist on the petals and worked her fingers until the dried lavender became a fragrant dust that she released over the length of the bath. It sighed as it hit the hot water and steam carried its fragrance to scent the room with spring.

"There, now. That should do the trick. You'll sleep soundly and wake without dreaming for sure," her mother said. But Sarah knew Melody Ross wasn't sure her daughter wouldn't dream. Sometimes a Ross was restless. Sometimes a Ross knew things that woke them in the wee hours of the morning. The knowing was never certain. It sighed and dissolved in their minds the same way the dried lavender dissolved in the bath, leaving nothing but a hint of it behind.

Sarah took her mother's dusty hand, and her mother helped her into the tub. She sank down into the water even though it was hot enough to make her skin rosy beneath the lapping waves.

Once she was settled, her mother handed her a bar of homemade soap. The vanilla of the soap didn't fight with the lavender. They went together and worked together. They were c-o-m-p-l-e-m-e-n-t-a-r-y. Sarah had known how to read and write before she started school because of the remedy book. As she foamed the soap in her hands, she carefully hummed the tune her mother had hummed without trying to sing the words. She was learning. She was always learning. But becoming a wisewoman would be a lifelong task. For now, she was content to be a girl. She let the bar of soap go and watched it float on top of the soothing lavender water. And as she toed the bar this way and that she imagined it was a boat gone to pick her up a pony to ride away from the pain in her dreams.

I dropped the lavender from my fingers. Unlike my nightmare, my connection to this "memory" was hazy and vague. The whole thing could have been a fancy, brought on by the fairy-tale woods around me. It was midmorning. The heat of the day was already beginning to rise. But the shadows of the trees made the trail cool and comfortable. Suddenly, the reality of a damp, dewy morning replaced thoughts of hot lavender baths in my mind. But my steps didn't falter. I was here now. There were no torn pages to pick up off the ground. No blood. I carried Sarah's ashes clutched to me instead of the pages I'd clutched as Sarah in the dreams.

Birds sang in the trees and insects whirred by on incomprehensible errands. Water rippled over rocks in the distance and the soft tread of my tennis shoes scuffed on the ground. I heard no other footsteps. Especially not those of my best friend's cold bare feet.

My toes were chilled as I drew closer and closer to the sound of running water. Pressure built in my chest. Blood rushed in my veins and roared in my ears. The air I forced into my suddenly constricted lungs was rich and loamy, thick with rotten leaves and fresh with green growth.

As I rounded the bend, I heard the sound of the rope against the tree limb. The squeak of its coils protesting against the friction and the dead weight. Dead. My mother. No. Not mine. Sarah's. I wasn't trapped in a nightmare. I was only bound by my promise.

I didn't expect how full of life the garden would actually be when it came into view. My pent-up breath released in a whoosh of surprise.

Lush and vibrant, filled with sprouting, budding, flourishing things, the well-tended garden could have graced the cover of a magazine. Instantly, I could see every bush, every plant, every vine had its place in carefully maintained rows and raised beds, but the explosion of green leaves and colorful blossoms was pure exotica to me. I recognized nothing. I knew pavement, cement and brutally trimmed city trees. Here, there were lush blossoms of pink, gold, royal purple and dusty blue. There was every shade of yellow from butter to nearly orange. The living rainbow fluttered en masse as the breeze brushed over the unusual clusters and silky groupings of petals I'd never seen. I knew the trees that framed the four corners of the garden only because Sarah had named them and because the deep ridges of their bark were so distinctive. They were black locust trees of different sizes. The differentiation told their age, one for each Ross woman who had been scattered to rest beneath their unusually gnarled branches.

The condition of the road and this cultivated ground didn't match. The garden echoed what the well-worn path had said. I might not be alone for long. I clutched the urn even tighter to my chest.

"It's illegal to plant on public lands. This is a national forest, but I'm not sure the first Ross gardener knew or cared, a pretty common mentality in the Appalachian region."

I turned quickly to find the biologist from the diner. *Jacob* Walker. His name came to me on a whisper in my mind very much like the rustle of the breeze through the golden petals on the tallest stalks in the garden.

He stepped into the clearing from the trail moments after I had, but he spoke conversationally, as if he'd been my companion for a while. Had he followed me from town? Then followed me all the way up the path without speaking? Granny had seemed to know him well. His sudden appearance startled me, but I didn't think he was here to harm me. He was still wearing the same clothes—ripstop gray cargo pants and a long-sleeve shirt with a well-known outdoors brand above its right chest pocket. His boots were expensive, but a sturdy choice and worn enough to be real, not an affectation. A biologist probably spent a lot of time outdoors. His hair was still tousled. Within its chestnut mass, lighter curly strands were picked up and blown by the same morning breeze that seemed to whisper inside of me, a soft echo of the wind in the trees. He stepped closer, jumping effortlessly over a fallen log I had skirted around.

In his left hand he held the broken piece of lavender I'd dropped. He had picked the flower up rather than crush it beneath his boot. I wasn't happy about his intrusion, but I couldn't help wondering why the flower held carefully in his fingers caught my attention. It reminded me of the deference he'd shown Granny. The breeze settled as I focused on the flower and everything in me and outside of me became still.

"The garden has been here much longer than you or I," I said. "I don't think it cares about public or private. Seems to be thriving."

A small pack rested on his back and a collapsible hiking stick was hooked to a lanyard on one of its straps. His eyes were active and bright, cataloging everything his gaze brushed. But I'd noticed that before. In the diner. Hadn't I? He stopped and looked me over from head to toe in a quick assessing manner. I was no different than I'd been in the diner either, but both of us stared as if it had been longer than an hour since we'd met.

Or as if our eyes had found that meeting too brief and wanted to make up for it now.

"There are plants in that garden that have been officially extinct for fifty years," he said. "I still haven't decided if I should report it or gather all the seeds I can this autumn."

A sudden flurry of butterflies rose from the patch of tall stalks topped by yellow thistlelike blooms, and I watched them fly out of the garden to rest lightly on Mr. Walker's shoulders and head. Their delicate decision to favor the biologist with the tickling prance of their feet and brush of their wings drew my eyes back to his. He didn't look at the fluttering insects. He looked at me. Our gazes locked again and my jaw was too soft, my eyes too dewy. I'd been better prepared in the diner. I wasn't prepared now.

As if he was a priest and the forest was his cathedral, I found myself confessing.

"My friend Sarah's mother died here. Ten years ago. In that black locust with the hooked branch," I said. "I've brought Sarah's ashes. I'm not sure who planted the sapling, but Granny told me I'd know where to sprinkle her remains."

He glanced at the locust trees. I should have been relieved, but I wasn't. For some reason I hadn't wanted him to look away.

"I'd heard about the murder," Walker said. "But I hadn't heard about your recent loss. I'm sorry." He lifted his hand and twirled the lavender in his fingers. I noticed his digits were colored with earth like Granny's, although I was pretty certain his stains would still wash away.

"Do you take care of the garden?" I asked.

"No. I only wondered who had dropped this so soon after picking it," the man said. "I use the Ross cabin as an access point for field research sometimes." He shrugged out of his pack and it rattled as he placed it on the ground. He pulled a small field journal from the side pocket and pressed the lavender in its pages before putting the book away. He unhooked the hiking stick and telescoped it to its full length before he shrugged his free arm back into one strap of the pack.

All of this was completed with an efficiency of movement that startled me. He was above average in height and build, but there was a grace to his physicality that made him appear as if he belonged among the flowers and trees. Sarah's wildwood didn't make way for him. It enveloped and accepted him. This was a scientist? I'd never met one, but my preconceptions of tweed and stuffy laboratories were suddenly, glaringly wrong.

"I only use this trail occasionally. I spend a lot of time on the mountain, but I've never disturbed the garden. Not that I haven't taken a closer look at some of the rare plants." Walker's eyes flicked toward the garden as he mentioned the rare plants. He pushed the end of his hiking stick into the ground, gripping it with both hands until I could see the white of his knuckles stand out in relief against the dirt stains. "Granny is a well-known herbalist in this area. There's a community of people around here who comb the woods for ingredients. Dyes. Medicines. Most of them don't bother to think about what they might be doing to the environment. Ginseng is a threatened species now. It's worth big bucks on the black market. And its illegal harvest and sale is driving other dangerous activities like money laundering."

So, maybe his intensity had a logical explanation?

He wasn't only a scientist or a casual hiker. He was a man on a mission. Still, hunting plant poachers didn't seem to fit the serious preparedness I sensed in him either. I wasn't only a barista. I was a survivor. I'd been on my own for a long time before Sarah came into my life. Overworked caseworkers and jaded foster families didn't count. Walker had me on edge worse than Granny had and I wasn't sure if it was attraction or an early warning system. My body and my brain couldn't seem to agree. The intent in his eyes didn't match the rest of him, mission or not.

"You haven't reported the garden because you think it should stay hidden. That maybe it'll be pillaged if word gets out," I guessed. "I suspect the Ross women and people like Granny would rather die than hurt the forest."

"It would have been sacrilege. The way your friend's mother was killed. The murderer didn't only take her life. He or she tainted the locust tree..." Walker began.

"And polluted the wildwood," I finished.

Saying the words aloud suddenly felt like the reason I'd come. The manner of her death and the way the killer had disposed of her body hadn't only been cruel and violent and evil. It had been an abomination of all she held dear. Including Sarah. Whom I'd also held dear. Dearer than myself. I wasn't tied to anyone or anything now that Sarah was gone, but I felt ghost tendrils from this garden and the Ross way of life reaching out to me. Sarah's beliefs had brought me here with her ashes. She would soon become a part of this place again as if she'd never left it. Walker and the garden became distorted as my eyes swam with unshed tears.

"I'm sorry I disturbed you. I should have walked around," the biologist suddenly said.

My jaw clenched. I refused to cry. But even without tears, my hold on the urn gave my emotions away. Of course he noticed. My white knuckles. My wet eyes. His were filled with understanding. I was immediately on guard. He might be observant, but I didn't want him understanding me better than I understood myself. My grief was a vulnerability I didn't want to share with a stranger.

Suddenly, I was saved. One second, he was Mr. Walker, calm lavender-scented biologist, and in the next he stood straight and alert with his shoulders back and his hiking stick gripped like a weapon. He wasn't muscle bound. He had the kind of understated strength that hid until it was needed. I gasped and took a step back from the

changed man, but then I whirled because he had obviously been react-
ing to a threat behind me.

"Tom," Walker said. I could tell he had instantly relaxed. His voice
was deep and assured. But it came from inches behind me. When I'd
whirled to face the forest, he must have stepped forward. Much closer
than I'd expected him to be. The move seemed protective, but it didn't
calm me. His proximity was bothersome in part because I wasn't as
bothered as I should be by this changeling of a man. "You planted a
sapling for Sarah Ross," Walker continued.

The new man barely looked our way, but he nodded constantly as
he carried a large bucket of water to the locust sapling Walker had
referred to. I noticed an angry red scar that ran from the corner of one
eye down in a diagonal slash across both of his lips to the other side of
his face. He was a big man but was obviously no threat, silently tending the Ross garden as if we weren't there.

"It's okay. He tends the garden. I've seen him here several times
before," Walker said. He hadn't moved away. So I did. Several steps to
the side didn't lessen my body's reaction to his confidential tones muttered so close to the back of my neck. He hadn't touched me or over-
stepped any sort of bounds. The reawakened tingles along my spine
were my fault not his. From the corner of my eye, I saw he'd lowered
his hiking stick back to the ground. He'd returned to his casual, outdoorsy science-guy act. But that didn't stop me from cataloging his
sudden protective reaction as not very academic-like at all.

"Granny said I'd know where to put Sarah's ashes," I said.

Tom had finished his watering task and now he moved around the
garden pinching off dead leaves and examining vines and flowers. He
paid no mind to me when I approached the locust sapling and opened
the urn.

It took far too long for me to tilt the container. I stood. I waited.

In the end, it was only a tremendous force of will to honor my promise that allowed me to sprinkle Sarah's remains on the damp ground. Strangely, it seemed as if every individual particle of ash flicked off the lip of the urn to pause, infinitely defined against the air, before it fell. The birds sang. The insects whirred. And I laid Sarah to rest—the person who had known me better than anyone had ever known me—in the company of two men I barely knew.

I couldn't handle a spoken eulogy. No words could convey the sentiment for Sarah that beat in my heart. The urn was too light afterward. I replaced its lid and stood, not quite knowing what to do. Walker hovered. He seemed torn between leaving and offering support. Truthfully, I was so unused to the offering I didn't know how to respond. My usual was frightening people away before they reached out. It's easy in Richmond. The crowds. The rush. Nobody questions a "leave me alone" vibe.

"My name is Mel," I said to the biologist. He watched my every move and I was aware of his every breath. It seemed stupid not to introduce myself to the man if I was going to be that attuned to his respiration. He was a part of this understated memorial where everything about and around Sarah's black locust tree seemed suddenly portentous.

The dark, twisted trees were a memorial, but also vaguely unsettling. Their tortured limbs didn't seem at peace as they scratched at the sky.

"Nice to meet you, Mel," he replied. He looked from me to the forest around us and nodded as if we'd been more formally introduced by the leaves in the trees.

The ashes had settled onto the dirt and they darkened as they soaked up the moisture Tom had sprinkled on the ground. There was no sense of relief. No sudden sense of closure claimed me. Granny had warned me. It felt like a beginning instead of an end. My first noon on Sarah's mountain. I tingled with the knowledge that it wouldn't be my last. "You and Granny don't get along," I said. I wanted to pin him down. To define him. In the course of one morning he'd been too changeable for the keen perceptions I usually could count on.

"I noticed she gave you some tea. Be careful. That old woman is always brewing something," Walker said.

"You think she doesn't know what she's doing," I surmised. I crouched to place the urn on the ground and only when I rose with empty hands did my heart spasm in acknowledgment of what I'd done. Sarah's life was over and every contraction of muscle that continued to give me life caused me pain.

"Oh, she knows exactly what she's doing. I'm just not sure you know what you're getting into," Walker said. My chest burned inside the way ice burns against skin, but even though I was painfully numbed from the heart out, I turned because his voice had come from farther away. He was finally moving toward the place where the trail resumed on the other side of the garden's clearing. "It would be safe to assume that every bag of herbs she hands out has strings attached. And I'm not talking about the ones that tie them."

"You're a scientist. You can't believe…" I began. My screaming heart thumped harder in my frozen chest than it should. I'd been drinking a Ross herbal brew for years and I was fine. Perfectly fine. Not hexed or bespelled in any way. *But hadn't Granny said the coffee interfered?* I didn't believe in hocus-pocus. I'd believed only in Sarah and Sarah was dead. *Even a fighter could get tired.*

"What I believe is that I won't be drinking one of Granny's concoctions anytime soon," Walker said. "And neither should you. You should head back to Richmond. Say goodbye to your friend and go back to the city while you still can."

"While I still can?" I asked. The tone of his voice was lighthearted, but there was no mistaking the warning in his words.

"Once the wildwood has you, it never lets you go," Walker said. He had paused at the opening to the trail. Behind him, cool green shadows waited. I noticed his eyes were the same moss-in-shadows green. In fact, the colors around him didn't only echo the color of his eyes. The multiple browns and golds in the waves of his hair and his lightly tanned skin blended with his surroundings so it was hard to tell where the woods began and he ended.

"Does it have you?" I asked softly. My heart went warm and quiet without my permission. Ice thawed. Thudding eased. He suddenly looked nothing like a scientist and everything like a being who belonged among the trees. He was a creature of hush and masculine grace that somehow looked more at home in the wilderness than he would look among men.

How could I be comfortable with this chameleon man? Even for a second? Loss had obviously made my radar spotty and my defenses faulty.

"Always has. Always will," he said.

He turned and walked into the forest with a light, steady stride that would eat miles before the end of the day. In seconds, he was gone. Only then did I realize I was all alone in the garden. What's more, the urn was gone. Tom must have silently cleared it away when he left. It hadn't belonged here, a stark, terrible object wholly unnatural in a garden. My usual defenses were faulty here for a reason. Frigid veins didn't belong. In the city, I could stay as detached as I pleased, anonymous in the crowd. The wildwood demanded warmth. Inspired it. I could grieve, but I also had to live on. Here, there was a natural cycle of birth, growth, death and rebirth that had to be maintained.

The black locust with the crooked limb caught and held my

attention for several macabre moments. I could almost hear the sound of the rope from my nightmare. Murder wasn't natural.

Cree-cree, cree-cree.

A woman had died here. I'd seen her corpse as clearly as if I'd been the one standing at her bloodstained feet.

Clouds suddenly covered the sun and I shivered in the shadows. Even in the clearing, the forest had taken over the garden as soon as the sun was hidden. I looked up and was comforted by the slide of fluffy white over the bright orb, confident its beams would be back in a little while.

I didn't wait.

Granny would be waiting for me. She'd told me to come and find her. I brushed my fingers along the leaves of Sarah's sapling. Not to say goodbye. I would be back. In spite of the nerves that skittered along my spine when I walked past the crooked locust, I didn't consider accepting Walker's advice on leaving.

The ghost tendrils had taken hold. My heart squeezed in their grasp. Sarah had wanted to come back because this was her home. Granny had said this was a beginning and I could feel the start of something in me. Curiosity fought to clear the fog of grief. I wanted the nightmares to end, but I also wanted to understand what was happening. I couldn't do that by running away.

Four

*H*e *hadn't been here* for a long time. Dirt against paws. Damp earth. Bitter bark. Spit after nibble. Not good to eat. He sneezed several times. Explosive shudders were pleasant. Cleared the house dust from his nose. He kept to the edges of the strip of bare ground he followed. The cover of undergrowth gave cool, blanketing shadows. Tickles in his ears and in his gut whispered, "Safe. Safe in the shadows." But there was a burning too. Like hunger but not. Like seeking a mate but not. The burn forced him from his soft hidey-hole indoors.

Nose and ears. Constant twitching. Run. Smell. Listen. Taste. He'd been quiet, hidden for an age.

But he'd been waiting.

Crafted from a love ferocious, he'd risen when his innards rustled in response to a newcomer. But he'd been too slow. Frayed threads and moth-chewed herbs became flesh and blood. Pain. Then the burning began. Go. Go. More than a charm. Go. The newcomer had gone, but his gut still burned. Down the stairs. And through to outside. Moving answered the burn. Joy after years of hibernation.

No whispered songs revitalized him. No new garden growth freshened his insides. No needle and thread repaired his wear or fade. All different now. He hadn't felt the touch of a powerful hand in so long. His once lavender heart pounded in his chest. He breathed. In and out. Too fast. Frightened.

Different. But he remembered enough.

He followed the scent of the newcomer's footsteps to the wild place. Many times, long ago, he'd been carried to the wild place in a pocket. This time, he had to dodge around death. A long, slithering deathly thing. Slick. Quick. Swallower of him. But not. The burn made him quicker, slicker. He escaped, and then froze in a clump of tall grass. More tickles to teach him. He hid. The shadow of a hawk flew over. Chilled him to his newly formed bones.

But nothing stopped him.

And the longer he continued the stronger and clearer he became.

He was old and frayed, but he'd been created with a loving intent that gave him life. There were bad dreams to be battled, still, and fear to be soothed. This was the burn in his belly. His purpose. Not for the girl who'd had to leave him when she'd been taken away. She'd been very brave to place him, one last time, wet from tears, beneath her pillow before she left. But even he knew with his lavender brain that he couldn't stray far from the plants and wild place of his making. Else he'd be nothing but string and dried stuff.

The girl had left him so he wouldn't "die." Maybe she had known he should watch and wait for another.

Finally, he made it to the wild place. He sniffed every tendril and vine. The tickle and the burn led him to the ones he needed.

This was his freshening. And the reason he'd been given the gift of movement. He nibbled here and there. He filled his belly until the burn was soothed. Then, sniffed his way—smell, listen, look—to a tiny sapling where the girl's ashes had been spilt.

He sat there for a while, remembering her pockets and the dreams he'd calmed for her, before he turned to make his way back to the cabin. He couldn't follow the newcomer. He could barely sense her now. She'd gone too far away for even a ferociously woven mouse. He would have to wait some more.

His movements were more coordinated after several hours of practice, but he was still slow to notice the blacksnake he'd avoided earlier had coiled in the same clump of grass where he'd hidden from the hawk. He was new to the world of scents and sensations. Only the shine on the snake's scales saved him as the sun suddenly broke from behind the clouds to illuminate deadly intent.

The blacksnake struck and he leapt without ever having leapt before. But the wild place, the wildwood garden, had fueled his minuscule muscles well. His tiny gray body flew up into the air and he curled and rolled to where he could clamp down on the back of the blacksnake's head with his teeth when he came down.

What followed was more in keeping with the ferocity of his maker than his current incarnation as a living, breathing mouse. He'd been made as a protective charm. He had to protect himself to fulfill his purpose. Blood flowed. The snake writhed in death throes that should have dislodged its killer. He was more than a charm now. And more than a mouse. Although he wasn't yet what he had been crafted to be...

Between She who will come and She who came before,

Fair-Margaret-Ann-Elizabet-Berta-Katherine-Mary-Beatrice-Melody-Sarah.

Between the wildwood vine and beating heart,

connect, guide, protect.

He didn't open his jaws until the snake stopped moving. Pain was new. Wildwood emissary or not, a wisewoman's familiar or not, his little mouse body hurt from heroic effort. But his once lavender brain had quickened along with the rest of him. As he left the dead snake on the path behind him, he thought about being more than he had been before.

He would be here, freshened, when the newcomer needed him.

Melody Ross had ensured it.

Granny's house had gingerbread trim like well-turned teeth all around its edges. The first person I'd asked had known exactly where to find it. The woman had been exiting a corner hair salon and she'd lowered her voice and whispered the directions with furtive glances up and down the sidewalk as if she didn't want to be seen or heard giving me the information I'd asked for. Strange considering how everyone had greeted Granny in the diner.

Of course, she'd also looked me up and down as if my black skinny jeans and high-top sneakers were breaking some kind of dress code I didn't understand.

I approached the Queen Anne Victorian cautiously through a spiky wrought iron gate, reminding myself I'd been invited. However, the toothy trim and curtain-covered windows didn't seem to welcome me. The house was the largest and oldest on the block at the very end of a cul-de-sac turned mostly to black gravel from the crumbling asphalt. The other houses were sided with painted boards or cheap vinyl that probably covered deteriorated wood, but the yards were mowed and the weeds whacked back, and here and there was evidence that families with children resided in some of the homes—a swing set, a sandbox, a bike with training wheels leaned on a fence.

Granny's house was faded brick, but still solidly handsome, fronted by a dominant cylindrical turret. On top of the turret, a large black crow in the form of a weather vane squeaked rather than cawed as it twisted to and fro. I thought maybe the woman from the hair salon considered Granny and her house eccentric. The woman's hair had been smoothed, sprayed and teased into a very conventional soccer-mom style. I'd known Granny only a short while, but with all her layers, pockets and patches, not to mention her wild curly hair, she was definitely outside of the norm, even for Richmond. In this small town she was probably seen as more wild than wise.

One of the "No Pipeline" signs was displayed proudly by her front walk.

It took me a flustered few minutes to figure out the doorbell after I'd climbed the stoop to reach the entrance. There was no button, only a knob you pulled instead of pressing, and the result of the pull wasn't a buzz. The knob tugged a cord in the wall that mechanically jangled a bell inside.

Footsteps responded to the bell, walking in a stride I remembered from the diner.

Granny opened the door.

Her cheeks were flushed pink and her curls were more frazzled, the silvery strands sticking out all over like exclamation points. She wore a voluminous apron over the clothes she'd worn that morning, another layer added to her already impressive regalia. More pockets, seen and unseen. So many I couldn't count them. When she moved, the con-tents of her pockets rustled or clicked or rattled, adding a mysterious layer of noises to her persona.

"I've baked you some cookies," she shouted above the cry of a giant fat tabby—he'd had more than his share of cookies—twining around her ankles.

The air released from the house carried the warm scent of sugar and vanilla, but it was combined with a mixture of other scents not as pleasant. Devil's breath? Furniture polish? Burnt toast? Pixie dust? I could only imagine. When I stepped inside and she closed the door behind me, my reaction was a little too panicky, considering the door supposedly opened from both sides.

"There, now. That's finished. The hard part is over. The rest will be a breeze," Granny said. She enveloped me in a bear hug, an impressive undertaking since she was much shorter than an actual bear and I towered over her by more than a foot. Still, I suddenly felt supported and completely understood. It wasn't merely a big hug from a small woman. It was a Sarah hug, and for a few seconds I had come back to see Granny for this, nothing else. No purpose or mission or goal beyond this embrace. The problem with building a wall as a defense against the world is when you're finished you're there with yourself with nowhere to hide.

I disengaged after those few seconds of weakness and I couldn't tell if Granny had given me something or taken something away.

"The dreams have put you through the ringer. You need a rest. Some reprieve. And I've baked just the thing," Granny said.

She prodded me forward down a long hall that led to the back of the house. It was a tight squeeze through clutter that must have accumulated over many years. I tried to take in all the individual details of bric-a-brac and furniture, but a nude bronze, a tufted ottoman, umbrellas and photographs, crystal decanters and a grinning plastic piggy bank I recognized as the diner's logo rushed past.

We burst through the swinging door of the kitchen with a slap of Granny's stained palm against its surface. And, there, a different sort of clutter began. Copper pots hung from the ceiling. Baskets and barrels lined the floor. Bins and tins filled every shelf, and bottles with meticulous labels of tiny script marched along the counters in orderly rows.

Granny left my side to rush to the largest oven I'd ever seen. A white enamel monstrosity with rounded edges and chrome accents, the appliance must have been as old as Granny herself. Or older. But when she opened its door and used the corner of her apron as a pot holder to retrieve a cookie sheet, I could see that the cookies were golden brown and cooked to perfection.

There was still a hint of something unusual—I couldn't decide if it was burnt toast or devil's breath—but vanilla and sugar predominated now. So much so my stomach gurgled and my mouth flooded with saliva. I'd nibbled jam and toast that morning, and I'd skipped lunch altogether. The distance of the drive between town and the Ross cabin had taken up much of the day. Suddenly, thoughts of devil's breath led me to thoughts of Persephone and Hades's pomegranate seeds. Was I really going to sit down and eat as if I hadn't been warned away from this eccentric woman's mixes and mischief?

Granny grabbed a spatula from a pottery crock on the counter and moved cookies from the hot tray to a cooling rack she must have previously prepared.

"We have a lot to discuss while these cool. Pull up a chair and see there what I have for you . . . besides a good night's sleep," Granny said. She nodded toward a table beside a picture window that looked out into a backyard that was more riotous than the neighbors' yards I'd seen. The other houses had seemed to have towny, trimmed landscaping. Unlike the ordered lushness of the wildwood garden, Granny's yard was basically a kitchen garden gone crazy.

But she hadn't nodded toward the riot of herbs growing outside.

The Ross Remedy Book sat on the kitchen table.

I'd never seen it whole before, though I'd seen it destroyed a thousand times in my dreams. Sweat beaded on my brow and above my upper lip. My mouth went dry. This was my nightmare come to life. This was also, somehow, Sarah. Her past. Her heritage. Her mother. Gone, but not forgotten. Never forgotten.

I once dragged Sarah from a foster home in the middle of the night because our new "dad" had hugged us both a little too long before bedtime on a night our new "mom" had been traveling out of town on business. I'd found us a safe place to crash with nothing but the few belongings we kept stowed in our backpacks for times like those.

I'd done it with dry eyes, even knowing our caseworker wouldn't believe we were in danger and there was no assurance that the next placement would be any better.

But for the millionth time today my eyes weren't dry. The hold I'd had on myself for years was loosening and I didn't know how to reset my grip.

I walked to the table and sat down. I reached for the remedy book and touched the pages, in real life, for the first time. No. I wasn't going to run away. Caution with Granny might be a good idea, but retreat wasn't an option.

"I repaired it. I dried the pages and sewed a new leather binding to the old leather covers. I saved it for Sarah," Granny said. She came over and sat across from me, leaving the cookies to cool.

The binding was obviously new leather. It stood out, a pale caramel, compared to the nearly black walnut front and back covers that had been polished by thousands of hands over time. I'd never noticed the faded imprint of a tree that had been stamped into the leather of the front cover. I lightly traced its branches wondering if Sarah had done the same, and many of her ancestors before her. I flipped through the book, certain some of the splotched pages were ones Sarah had saved from the dew the morning her mother had been killed. I could feel the sturdiness of the binding Granny had created, but repaired or not, I was also certain some of the stains on the covers and the pages weren't from the stream. The pale bloodstains, if that's what they were, didn't seem gory; rather they seemed a testament, a recording of lives and events as carefully kept as the words on each page.

"Sarah would want you to have it," Granny said.

Many of the recipes and concoctions were signed with the same bold cursive initials I'd seen on the scrolled paper Granny had shared with me in the diner. I traced the *M* and the *R*, knowing Sarah had given me her mother's name back when I didn't have one of my own. It had been a tribute and an honor. It had been her way of adopting me when we were both unwanted and alone.

"Mel" had suited my temperament better than "Melody." The nickname had stuck. But I'd never tried to claim "Ross." I'd gone from Jane Smith to Mel Smith without looking back. I'd had it legally changed as soon as I was old enough to make it happen.

"Jacob Walker told me to leave while I still can. He told me not to drink your tea or stay too long in the wildwood," I said.

"Did he warn you away from my cookies too?" Granny asked. "Because the recipe is in that book. Great-Granny Ross put it down in her chicken-scratch scrawl." She reached across the table and flipped the pages until the book opened on a recipe illustrated with thistles like the yellow ones I'd seen in the Ross garden. There were notes in the margins that had obviously been added more recently than the recipe itself. Chicken scratch was a good description for the original handwriting on the page.

"Hers are always the hardest to read. Her daughter and granddaughter clarified a lot of them in the margins. She was self-taught. No schooling at all. Save for what she learned by her mother's knee," Granny explained.

I scanned the ingredients. No devil's breath or toadstool juice. "Ground sunwort" was the only thing I didn't recognize.

"It's a mild soporific. These will help you sleep. And that's the only hoped-for result stirred into them," Granny said. She wasn't as jolly as she'd been that morning, but she was still elfin. Her eyes glinted with knowledge in the waning light from the setting sun. The sun's reddish glow warmed the kitchen around us, reflecting off the copper pots and pans.

While I hesitated between the lure of a deep sleep and Walker's warnings, the tabby pushed his way into the kitchen. I followed his surprisingly graceful movements until he leapt up on the counter directly across from the table. He sat with regal privilege where most cats wouldn't, without nosing around the cooling rack of fresh cookies, and met my attention head-on without blinking. His eyes were as green as the biologist's and as intent, but there was something unusual about his expression that seemed to come from neither man nor beast. The tabby's irises seemed to swirl with non-catty thoughts I couldn't ascertain.

"This is where you belong, but you have to make that decision. And stay or go isn't something you have to decide right away. For now, rest or run. It's your choice. Walker is wiser than he lets on, I'll give him that. But there are some things he can't understand...about Ross women and what they've been through. Sarah's mother was murdered. Now, Sarah is dead. I can only go by the tea, the roots, the flowers and the trees, but the mountain whispers to me and I don't like what it says," Granny said.

"It was a hit and run," I blurted. Maybe it was the scent of cookies. Or maybe it was the hug. Suddenly, there was no stopping the rest. "They never found the unmarked van that clipped us in the rain. Sarah was driving. She never trusted me behind the wheel. I was too aggressive in traffic. Too prone to road rage. She was always so careful. Slow and steady wins the race. But not that time. The rain was heavy. It was just before dusk and the storm made it dark as night. The van came out of nowhere. They were speeding," I said. Hot tears finally overwhelmed my control. They streaked down my face. I'd held them back all day. For weeks, even. My heart had felt ice-burned in the garden. Now, my tears burned embarrassing acid trails on my cold cheeks. I'd had no one to talk to about the accident. I gulped back on the torrent that had burst from my aching chest. I knew better than to overshare. Even to an apparently sympathetic ear.

Granny stood and walked to the counter. The tabby didn't move. Even his tail was still. She slowly placed cooled cookies onto a porcelain plate.

"It was just a horrible accident," I said. There were no tears left. My cheeks had dried, tight and sticky. Granny came to the table and placed the plate of cookies between us. Then, she fetched glasses and a carafe of milk from the old-fashioned refrigerator that matched her oven. She poured us each a glass of milk and then poured some for the tabby in a bowl on the floor I hadn't noticed before. Thankfully, the cat acted exactly as I thought a cat should. He broke eye contact with me to jump down and lap up the fresh milk. Granny picked up a cookie and bit into it as the cat drank. She chewed and swallowed thoughtfully before she replied.

"I sent Sarah away. I hid her as long as I could. I think I failed. I think she was found," Granny said. "But all hope isn't lost yet because Sarah found you."

"I'm nobody. Only a student. Not even really that. We couldn't afford classes for both of us. I wanted Sarah to get her nursing degree first. So, me? I'm only a barista," I said, drawing my attention away from the now normal tabby. I pressed my fisted hands on the table on either side of the pretty cookie plate. My knuckles were still red from the wounds I'd caused when I'd tried to free Sarah. If the window hadn't been cracked and damaged by the accident, I might have broken my fingers trying to break shatterproof glass. They would probably carry scars to remind me of those frantic moments forever. The pain in them had been nothing compared to the pain of seeing Sarah dead and trapped in the car. But I would always wonder if the phantom pain Sarah had experienced before she met me had been a premonition of what I would do to my hands after the crash.

She'd told me the ghost pain had never bothered her again after I'd held her hand that first night we'd been together.

"So. You're a barista. Brewing is more important than you know. Than anyone knows. Much more. It's a lost craft. The Ross women knew it. They practiced it," Granny said. "I'm getting old, but I'll help you learn it. A student is exactly what I need. If you don't run away, I'll help you brew through this book. Sarah's book. And the wildwood will show us what to do."

"I don't believe in your craft. It seems like the same kind of magic they always asked us to believe as kids—happy families, the good guys win, love conquers all," I said. "That there would be a home for us one day."

"You believed in Sarah. You believed in the sisterhood you shared. That's all that matters," Granny said.

I did believe in Sarah and our sisterhood. She was right. That belief hadn't disappeared. I could feel it in my gut, a hint of warmth like smoldering coals. Maybe I could stir them back to life if I honored her memory this way. There was nothing for me in Richmond but a cold, empty apartment. At least here I could explore Sarah's childhood world. What she had believed. The people she'd known. Just for a little while I wouldn't have to completely let her go. I uncurled my fists and reached for a cookie. I dunked it in the milk in my glass.

Granny did the same and then she lifted her dripping cookie toward mine. Exactly as Sarah would have. Had she eaten Granny's cookies as a child? We clicked them together as Sarah and I would have before we each took our bites. A sweet explosion with a hint of bitterness on the back end filled my mouth as I chewed.

"Sometimes the mountain whispers more pleasant things to me," Granny said. The twinkle was back in her eyes, but she closed them as she drank from her glass so I couldn't read her mood. When she lowered the glass, the twinkle was gone, but I thought I heard it in her next words. "Walker might have warned you away, but he won't be sorry to find you're still here."

Mischievous twinkle or not? I was suddenly too sleepy to know for sure. I only knew that I wouldn't dream about Sarah's mother hanging in the black locust tonight. But not because of bittersweet cookies. Granny had filled my mind with thoughts of shadowed eyes and tousled hair, and it would be the mysterious biologist who followed me into my dreams.

Ignoring the tingle definitely wasn't the same as not feeling it. And maybe a little loosening in the privacy of my own thoughts wasn't a bad thing after all.

Tomorrow would be soon enough to accept I'd come to Sarah's wildwood not to lay her to rest but to find her again in this place of lavender and secrets.

Five

*S*ummer was the best *time. Sarah's feet were toughened by mid-June and she rarely had use for the recess-worn sneakers she'd had to endure during the school year. They sat, faded and forgotten, by the back door, while the tops of her feet turned golden brown in the sun.*

She didn't care about the mosquito buffet of her briar-scratched legs or the wild tangle of her curly hair, kept as far as she could keep it from brush or comb. From dawn till dusk, and often well after the lightning bugs began to flicker and flash, she was free to play in the wildwood as long as some of her play involved lending a helping hand or bringing a ladleful of cold spring water to her mother in the garden.

Her mom was always busy, but she was busiest in the summer when the garden became a jungle of fragrant ingredients that had to be tended, to just this side of tame, in order to be ready for harvest. Sarah learned what she could touch and what she shouldn't right around the time she learned to walk. And yearly practice made her an expert at playing in the garden's moss-carpeted clearing by the time she was ten.

Enough of an expert to invite her best friend to play along with her, which was perfect because her best friend's mother was best friends with Sarah's mother. While the adults plucked suckers from fledgling tomatoes and dead-headed marigolds, the young girls set up a dollhouse made of sticks and stones by the creek. They used poplar leaves for rugs and pine knots for chairs. They twined honeysuckle vine into beds and bathtubs and used a large flat rock for a dining room table. Up from Sarah's bedroom, they carried fashion dolls that had been improved with berry-tinted hair and dresses made from color-ful silk scarves Tallulah Rey had found in her grandmother's closet.

And, of course, Lu sang.

She was a singer. Had gotten in trouble at school for singing just as Sarah had gotten in trouble for knowing things when she shouldn't—like which teachers were courting or when Mr. Thompson snuck away for an after-lunch cigar at recess. They were often in trouble together, standing in time out against the wall of the school, humming nice and low. Sarah could catch Lu's tunes as soon as she thought them up. They were both "unique," but not stupid. Way back then, they'd learned there was a time for singing and a time for pretending to care about coloring inside the lines and cutting care-fully around the edges of things.

Lu's song was like Sarah's feelings. It bubbled up constantly until Sarah could see it in her eyes even when she made no outward sound at all. At best, Lu could try to tend it, just this side of tame, like the garden—but it was always barely controlled, she said, still wild in her chest.

So, they were different together.

Lu could sing as often as she liked in summer, and every now and then the adults in the garden would pick up what she sang and go along with her. But only Sarah was able to sing the new songs that came from Lu's own head. She knew the words and the tune almost as soon as Lu knew them herself. Sarah had learned never to sing those songs with Lu at school, but the wildwood garden loved Lu's songs, so here, in the summertime, they usu-ally sang while they played, as carefree as could be.

Today, the adults had started whispering about something sad and serious and the girls had gotten distracted from their play by the sweet nectar of honeysuckle blossoms. It was a game they liked even better than dolls. So, they became fairies and abandoned their dolls to their sap-stained chairs. They flitted from vine to vine in order to pluck and suck the perfumy sweetness from the bottom of each bloom. For a while, the sweet nectar held their mothers' whispers away. Fairies didn't care about such things. They only wanted to flit and fly and race the bees from bloom to bloom. But girls who were only pretending to be fairies needed more than honeysuckle to offset scary talk of a disease that the garden couldn't cure.

"I'm lucky to have May to help. She's crazy about Lu. Did you know she decided to make her a dulcimer? Tom brought her some walnut from a tree at the old homeplace up the road. The one the lightning felled last August," Lu's mother said.

"Tom always knows what you need before you know it yourself," Melody replied. "My great-gran would have said he hears the wildwood's whispers." Sarah's mother stood and stretched her back before dusting the dirt from her hands. She draped an arm around her sick friend's shoulders. "I wish there was more I could do."

The honeysuckle girls looked at each other above the blossoms. Sad, sad talk. Sorrowful times. It was summer, and that made it worse. Cancer was even more terrible with the buzzing of the bees and the tickle of moss between your toes.

But there it was.

The garden grew, and even as it did, parts of it died. Leaves turned brown and withered on the vine. Petals curled and wilted and fell to the ground. Tallulah's mother wasn't going to be well. Not ever again. Lu's song was only a temporary softness before the hard goodbye.

Sarah no longer felt like drinking nectar. Instead, she moved closer to her best friend. This nearness was a different kind of support than singing along by the schoolyard wall. Less rebellious and more a simple offer of comfort.

A sudden rush of steps came from the undergrowth on the north side of the clearing. A young woman ran out of the trees and stopped to blink at them in surprise, as if the garden hadn't been in these woods for a hundred years or more. Her dress was torn and her kerchief was loose, but Sarah could tell from the faded homespun fabric of her clothing she was from the Sect community on the other side of the forest.

"Are you okay?" Melody Ross asked. Sarah stepped toward the Sect woman at the same time as her mother.

But before they could reach the panting woman's side, Tom came from the trees behind her. He always managed to walk through the wildwood without making a sound. He knew the hidden trails and pathways better than anyone else. This time his sudden appearance made them all jump because they'd already been spooked by the frightened Sect woman.

"They're looking for you, Mary. You can't lead 'em here. Come with me," Tom said. He took the young woman's arm—it was always hard to tell how old the Sect people were because of their scrubbed faces and covered hair— and no one protested when he led her away. Not even Sarah's mother.

"Girls. Head to the house. We'll be right behind you," she said. "Don't drag your feet. Don't look back. Just go," Melody ordered.

Summer was the best time, but something had gone wrong. Even more wrong than the disease that was hurting Lu's mother. There had been acceptance in the adults' conversation earlier. Resignation. Grief. But now Melody Ross stood facing the wildwood in the direction the young woman had appeared. Her chin was up and her dirt-smudged hands were fisted at her sides. Mrs. Rey went to stand with Melody even though her steps were slow and unsteady.

"But . . . Mom," Sarah said. Lu's hand closed over hers. Suddenly too human again, they stood together surrounded by sweet-scented drifts of

honeysuckle blossoms. The honeysuckle would be no protection against whomever the woman had been running from.

"If he follows her here…" Lu's mother began.

"Shhhh, Ruby. Let the girls go," Melody warned. "Go," she repeated to Sarah without turning her head. Summer was wild and free, but her mother was the law and even during summer Sarah obeyed.

Melody Ross was Mom. But she was also the closest thing to a real fairy queen Sarah could imagine. Wisewoman. Caretaker. Wildwood tender. Whichever "he" might come from the trees would find Melody Ross and her garden in this clearing and he'd better back away. Sarah's chest loosened. Her heart still pounded, but her fear became a feeling closer to ferocity.

Lu followed when Sarah tugged her back toward the cabin. They heard nothing else. No shouts. No confrontation. If her mother was capable of rousing a honeysuckle blossom army, it fought silently while she and Lu huddled in Sarah's room, no longer able to fly away.

I stepped through damp morning mist and onto the sidewalk that hugged the slightly curved hook of Main Street.

Nothing was straight and simple in Morgan's Gap.

The hollow where the town had been built opened up enough to allow streets to sidle this way and that, but here and there buildings backed up against the craggy hills. "Gap" was a misnomer. The rocky, rolling and often narrow landscape made the layout of the town haphazard. A walk through it seemed like a fun house stroll.

The whole place and the people in it might as well have sprung up between boulder and brick like unexpected dandelions reaching for the sun.

It had rained the night before and the moisture was rising as the sun began to heat the air. Granny kept a strict schedule. Early morning was for deliveries. Midday was for kitchen work—grinding, mixing, steeping and stewing. Late afternoon, when the sun had done its work to dry the plants from earlier dew and damp, was for the garden.

The scent of tended soil and fresh growth—the acidity of lemon balm; the bitterness of aloe; the sharp, stinging aroma of mint leaves—was a welcome respite from feeling lost. Granny must have been a teacher many times in her long life. Her process was firmly in place. I'd slipped into the vacant slot of apprentice with an ease I didn't usually feel. Maybe it was because my connection to Sarah made every task seem vaguely familiar, even though my own hands had never completed them before.

Yesterday, I'd applied careful script to new labels for jars of dried herbs that had hung in Granny's pantry since last fall. My label script was neater than my usual handwriting, but still a sort of proclamation. I'd never really been the type of person to leave my mark:

Mel was here.

"Good for arthritic knees" or "soothing for headaches" Granny had directed me to write on labels. I'd stared at the completed project for a long time after, wondering why the coals in my belly were kindled by such a simple task.

I spent every evening before bed examining the pages of the Ross Remedy Book, trying to better understand my nightmares and the strange connection that still existed between me and the friend I'd lost.

Granny had seemed to suggest that the hit and run hadn't been an accident. That Sarah had been in danger even after she'd been sent away. In my whole life, I'd never felt truly safe, but the idea that a killer had been stalking Sarah for years seemed crazy. I was used to more mundane threats—bill collectors and customers more interested in getting your phone number than a cup of latte.

I wasn't a Ross or a wisewoman. The strange scribbles and sketches in the book meant nothing to me. I was simply the delivery girl for Granny's stomach cures and wrinkle cream for customers who preferred to receive their products in the early a.m. before the town woke up. I allowed the simple routine to soothe me. The rental car service I'd used had an agreement with a local garage for pickup. Last week, a pimply faced teen had driven off with my best means of running away.

So, instead of running, I walked everywhere I went.

My last stop this morning was at a handcrafted dulcimer workshop that sat proudly in a prime spot on Main Street between a barbershop and an antique gallery housed in a former drugstore that still had the remnants of a soda fountain on display. Tallulah Rey was a well-known singer and songwriter in addition to being an artisan who custom crafted the instrument she also played. Her mountain dulcimers were treasured all the way to Nashville and beyond, as was her singing voice and her way with words. She probably could have left Morgan's Gap years ago, but she hadn't.

The mountain was where the walnut wood grew in the thickets of her family's homeplace not far from the Ross cabin. And her blind grandmother had known the mountain well before her eyes had failed. She'd be lost anywhere else. In Morgan's Gap, she could still "see" as well as anyone else.

I already knew the dulcimer craftsman. She was Lu in my dreams. Sarah's best friend before she was forced to leave Morgan's Gap. The shop didn't open until ten o'clock, but Granny had told me all about Lu and her grandmother. They lived above the workshop where Lu made the dulcimers with lathe and chisel and her two gifted hands.

In the shop's window, a "No Pipeline" sign was taped beside an advertisement for sheet music.

"Granny always knows when May runs out. Never have to ask," the young woman said when I came through the shop's door. It wasn't locked. On the second floor, window boxes full of trumpet vines seemed to be the only sentinels to guard against theft... or worse.

"She hears the wildwood's whispers," I softly replied, remembering what Sarah's mother had said about Tom. Lu didn't know we'd already been introduced by my dreams and Sarah's memories. The sun couldn't warm away the chilling memory of the Sect woman being chased through the woods. I stopped in the middle of the polished cherry floor and held on tight to the basket in my hands. Maybe it was my background that made me see the shadows around things. Maybe it was my nightmares. But suddenly I wanted to warn the African American woman who greeted me like an old friend that her smiles were too open and welcoming in a town that might still harbor a killer.

"Everyone is already talking about Granny's houseguest. She takes an apprentice from time to time," the blind woman, May, said from her plush seat on a cushioned rocking chair in the corner.

"I'm Mel," I replied. As always, the darkness I carried wherever I went made me feel awkward. My friendship with Sarah had caused it to recede somewhat over the last ten years, but her death and the lucidity of my dreams had brought it rushing back. The trumpet vines should have heralded a warning when I arrived. Maybe I brought the shadows instead of simply seeing the ones already there.

"Granny never had an apprentice in my lifetime," Lu mumbled with a smile and a roll of her eyes her grandmother couldn't see.

"And you're only twenty-three. I guess you know something," May corrected with a tsk-tsk of her tongue against her teeth. Her eyes had failed, but her hearing was fine. The strands of gray in the thick braids she wore wound at the top of her head turned the coils into a silvery crown against her smooth, dark skin. As she spoke, she worked to place strings on the rosewood fretboard of a freshly made instrument in her lap. Her gnarled fingers carefully fitted the steel cord with quick, sure movements.

I stood, still rooted, embarrassed because I knew I didn't deserve special treatment from Granny, a woman these two people seemed to admire. But neither May nor Lu seemed to notice the scars on my hands or the shadows reflected in my eyes. They merely continued their morning routine while including me by offering up a third cup of steaming chicory, its bitterness cut by a dollop of heavy cream.

It wasn't coffee, which Granny had forbidden in no uncertain terms, but it was similar enough that I closed my eyes to savor the richness of the creamy liquid in my cup.

"My mother taught me to like chicory over coffee. She came up from New Orleans. Married in Morgan's Gap and stayed awhile," May said. "Lu's mother, rest her soul, was my daughter-in-law." She'd set aside her work on the dulcimer to rock and sip.

"My mother sang too. Oh, how she sang. Wish you could have heard her sing. You need a song. I can tell," May continued. She hummed what I thought was an old hymn in between sips.

As if May had thrown down a challenge, Lu set her cup down with a clink of china and turned to pick up a dulcimer that was obviously hers. Its box had a smooth, worn patina that only being constantly and lovingly played could have created, and it went to her lap as if it subtly conformed to the slight curves of her thighs. Seemingly without effort, Lu picked up the tune her grandmother had begun. Her deft calloused fingers picked and strummed in a rapid dance that was far too quick for shadows to catch.

And then she sang.

Her music was like the garden. It rose up from the wood, but it also seemed to rise up from her heart and soul, her blood and bones. My blood quickened in response, in a way I couldn't explain. I was an outsider, but warmed by the chicory brew and the sweet contralto of Lu's voice, I was somehow, not.

I belonged.

It had to be because of Sarah. My love for my dead friend forged a connection between me and the people who had loved her too.

When Lu was finished, she set the instrument aside and picked up her cup as if she hadn't casually given a stunning performance that had changed her audience.

"Just like that," May said. "Just like that. My Tallulah has her great-grandmother's music in her. Yes, she does."

Lu had welcomed me, but her music had done something more. The sound had flowed through me to leave vibrations between the two of us that didn't end when the song was over.

"Thank Granny for the arthritis cream, Mel," Lu said with another smile. Unlike her grandmother's braids, Lu's were a riot around her face, accented with colorful beads and a freed inch at each end left to curl this way and that in a hundred lash-like ways. She was beautiful, but I had to admit some of her beauty came from the superimposed ghostlike image of the girl she used to be courtesy of my dreams. She might be older, but something told me she would still sing whenever she needed to, come hell, high water or arithmetic lesson. Sarah told me. I could practically hear the words in her slight mountain accent so like Lu's. "You're welcome. Anytime. Granny says we'll be friends. I've no cause to doubt it."

My smile was odd on my face. Not forced. Not faked for politeness' sake. Lu made me smile. This quick and certain kinship had happened to me only once before. The preciousness of it caught my breath and tightened my throat around words it was too soon to say.

"Lu's got a new song coming on. I can always tell. She gets wistful. Waiting. Listening. I thought you needed a song, but I was wrong. I do believe you brought a song with you this morning," May said.

I had been Sarah's protector. I'd failed. I couldn't be anyone's muse. But, for some reason, after meeting Lu and hearing her song, Granny's confidence in me no longer felt impossible. I was strengthened. Fortified. The music had worked on my hesitancy.

Lu and her dulcimers were good. I had seen and felt enough bad to know its opposite, and without warning my protective instincts flared. What if Granny was right? What if Melody's murder hadn't been the end of danger? Would learning the teas and tisanes and creams and oils in the remedy book be enough? Shouldn't I do more? Now. Right now. To help. To heal. To keep from harm.

Granny, the remedy book, my dreams and now Lu's music... I hadn't truly believed in mountain magic. The wildwood kept its silence with me. Didn't it? Or maybe I'd mistaken my unwillingness to hear for silence. I thought about the bottles I'd labeled all lined up in their neat rows. Life didn't line up like that. It was more jumbled and confusing. Sarah had deserved to live a longer life. She'd been a healer from the day she'd been born. Had someone cut that short? Intentionally depriving the world of what she should have been? People like Granny, Lu and her grandmother deserved to live in peace. But could there be any peace in Morgan's Gap as long as someone had gotten away with murdering a mother and her child?

Six

L u walked me to the door because the shop was her home and also because lingering goodbyes were as Appalachian as the music she played. I'd been here a couple of weeks. Long enough to see people rise and chat from interior door to interior door, through kitchen and hallway and living room, until they could do nothing but pause on their feet in the archway of an open front or back door and chat some more before a brave soul actually followed through with goodbye. The farewell ritual normally made me impatient. I was used to rushing from place to place without making eye contact or slowing down at all. But not as much with Lu. I turned to thank her, but my words died on my lips. Lu's smile had disappeared. In its dazzling place was a hard jaw and storm-cloud eyes. My shoulders tightened. Lu's disapproval wasn't for me, and once again, the urge to defend her stiffened my spine. I turned to face whatever troubled her without hesitation.

"Every Wednesday like clockwork he parades them through. Best to stay out of the way," Lu said. Gone was the warm rhythm of her lyricist's voice. In its place was a stark monotone I barely recognized.

Up the center of the street with no regard for vehicles or empty side-walks more appropriate for pedestrian traffic, a flock of women came. They moved in a nervous flutter of blue homespun fabric and gray kerchiefs that completely covered their hair. I'd seen this outfit in my nightmare. The kerchief had wide straps wound tightly around their plain pale faces and the identical nature of the head coverings and calf-length skirts made them all seem eerily similar. Like a murmuration of starlings or chimney swifts they flocked up the street, their individual nervous movements oddly coalesced into unified purpose.

But, Lu's frown wasn't for the women either.

She stared at the tall black-clad man walking with purpose behind the women. He was dressed in an outdated suit and flat-brimmed hat, funereal in their severity. As they came closer, the man's expression became clearer. It matched his garb, grim and plain.

But his sharp gaze wasn't as plain as the rest of him.

It followed the women's movements. This way and that. Catching and observing. Every finger twitch. Every sigh. Every stumbled step. Every furtive glance toward shops with colorful window displays. His eyes were as active as the movements of his flock, unquiet and unceasing.

"That's Reverend Moon," Lu said. A warning not an introduction.

My throat tightened. The women's starling motions were wrong in a way I hadn't been able to define until I saw Reverend Moon's eyes. The obsidian chips of his pupils allowed them no ease.

The other people on the street made way for the man and his nervous flock. Cars pulled to the side with blinkers flashing. Pedestrians stopped and turned away. One mother pulled a staring child into the barbershop. A man tipped his baseball cap then stared down at his feet.

Moon herded the women up the street and his manner suggested he would keep them in formation. Away from all the shops' windows. From Lu and her grandmother's music. From my basket of herbal tisanes.

Like the young woman in my dream, these women were all impossible to age, but some of their unlined, shiny faces made my gut clench hard on the toast I'd grabbed for breakfast.

If the people around me sensed the wrongness of this parade, they did nothing to stop it. I stepped forward. One stride. Then two. Lu made a guttural noise as if she was taken by surprise. I gripped the basket's handle until my knuckles were white. My reddened scars stood out on my fingers and the backs of my hands. I continued stepping until I was on the street and in the flock's path. Until I disrupted their progress, I didn't know I'd intended to.

I only knew I had to do something.

Not one woman said a word. They simply stopped to mill around me in a flurry of faded sunshine-scented clothes that must have been hung out to dry time and again. Lu called my name from the edge of the sidewalk as if the street was lava and I was breaking the rules of a game we'd played as children.

Reverend Moon came through the milling women. He didn't have to raise his arms and shout a command. The frightened birds moved in unison away from him, naturally avoiding all contact with the man.

They instinctively evaded the dart-eyed shepherd in their midst.

I wanted to flutter away too.

"You won't find anyone here who is interested in your devil's wares, girl. Fly away with your filthy potions," Moon said.

But I wasn't one of his birds, so I stood my ground even though I didn't know why I'd stepped into the street in the first place. The women weren't in chains. Many of them even mumbled Moon's words in soft whispering echoes that were as creepy as their instinct-driven movements. The man's black irises drilled into me and my eyes burned in response, dry and angry.

I refused to blink to moisten them.

He's coming.

The slow throb of my heartbeat connected this darkly watchful man to the threat Sarah's mother had faced in the nightmare of the night before. It was the dresses and handkerchiefs. That was all. He was in the middle of the street in broad daylight. He posed no danger to me. Yet…

Go back to the house, girls. Don't look back.

My spine was made of icicles. My breath came up through a tight throat and out stiff, cold lips. The basket trembled in my hands.

But I didn't step aside.

My feet suddenly had roots that reached down, down to the dirt beneath the asphalt.

Reverend Moon's dark eyes narrowed and his attention left his flock to thoroughly examine my face from brow to chin.

"Are you looking for a taxi? You're going to be out of luck. They say there hasn't been one of those in Morgan's Gap since prohibition. Supposedly a gangster drove up from New York looking for home brew. The Lumstons had a lucrative side business in the stuff until well into the sixties," Jacob Walker said. I didn't jump. Not even when his calloused hand closed over my clenched fingers on the basket's handle. I was not relieved. I refused to be. He casually encouraged me to loosen my hold on the basket as he spoke as if he wasn't interrupting a standoff in the middle of the street. He took it from me with one hand and used his other to direct me toward a running Jeep that had been left with its door open on the side of the street.

I was reminded of his subtle moves to edge the barstools out of her way so Granny could pass in the diner. And of his sudden defensive stance against a possible threat in the wildwood garden. Was I like the discarded lavender? Was he picking me up from Moon's path before I could be crushed underfoot?

Moon watched, but didn't say another word as Walker walked me around to the passenger-side door.

"You can toss your devil's wares in the backseat," Walker continued.

I held the basket on my lap instead as Lu came forward to close my door while Walker circled back around to get behind the wheel. I turned to meet Lu's serious gaze. The biologist was trying to defuse a situation that couldn't be defused.

Sometimes the shadows I sensed around every corner came out to play and sometimes they screamed.

"The women were pregnant, Lu. All of them. Every. Single. One." I didn't have to tell her. She knew. Everyone knew. The whole town couldn't have missed the various stages of rounded bellies beneath the dresses the women wore. Women? Some of them were too young for that designation. I didn't have to expand upon the observation and what it implied. Some of the deferment I'd seen on the street from the townspeople had been respect. But some of it had been fear.

"The devil isn't in your basket," Lu said. "He walks bold as can be by my shop when the Sect comes to town."

I looked down at the few bundles of herbs that were left after my deliveries. The scent of rosemary and mint rose up to tickle my nose. My eyes were still wide and unblinking. They might crack like the ground after a drought. I might never blink again. The flock of pregnant women had already begun to move. Reverend Moon had resumed his place behind them. What kind of cult was the Sect? It was suddenly hard to believe I hadn't stepped back in time. Sarah had always warned me a woman's freedom in our society was illusory. Had she grown up seeing women—and even girls—treated this way?

"What were you going to do?" Lu asked. Moon looked our way, but neither of us had the stomach for more direct eye contact with the man. Or at least that's what I told myself. I remembered Sarah's mother in the clearing facing the trees. She'd sent Lu and Sarah away, but she hadn't backed down. She'd watched and waited for whatever might come through the wildwood. Had one of Reverend Moon's flock tried to run away? Had he been chasing her that day?

"I was going to stand," I replied. "I needed to get in his way." Lu leaned in through the window and touched her forehead to mine, confirming the connection I'd sensed earlier with skin to skin that was comfort not imposition, until Walker revved the Jeep and pulled away.

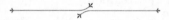

By the time Walker made the five-minute drive to Granny's house, my body was shaking. He pulled the Jeep into a driveway nearly hidden by overgrown Althaea bushes heavy with rose-red buds as I clenched my teeth so they wouldn't chatter, but the rustling of dried-herb packets in my basket gave me away. I'd been flooded with adrenaline during my strange confrontation with Reverend Moon. Now, it was gone and I was both flushed and chilled by its sudden absence.

Had I just met someone who might have had something to do with Melody Ross's murder?

"Damn," Walker said. He struck the steering wheel with his palms and the thud made me jump. "Damn," he repeated, but before I could form the words to question why he was angry he'd flung open the driver's-side door and strode around the front of the vehicle. He wrenched my door open and reached in to grab me by the hand and pull me from the seat. "Walk it off," he said.

He didn't give me the chance to refuse. I left the basket on the seat and rushed to keep up with his quick strides. He was only slightly taller than me, but he pulled me around the Althaea and into the yard with surprising speed.

It was the cure I needed, but not in the way he intended. Suddenly, I had a new challenge to face—one with curly brown hair and intense eyes who had no right to notice my vulnerability or try to tell me how to handle it.

"Stop," I said. I came up short and pulled my hand from his. To his credit, he immediately loosened his hold and let me go. "I'm fine. Believe me. I've faced worse than creepy cult leaders in my life."

"Debatable that anyone is worse than Moon, but your face was so white for a second there I thought you were going to pass out," Walker said. He'd stopped to face me with his hands on his lean hips. Today he wore a yellow plaid shirt with sleeves rolled to show muscular tanned forearms. The goldenrod color brought out the highlights in his hair... and in his eyes. Flecks of sunlight dwelled in his irises, the opposite of the shadows that must have been in mine.

That intimate discovery caused my temper over his arrogant handling to stutter and ease. Our bodies were too close together and it didn't feel like a challenge. It felt like... possibility. We were hidden from the world behind the verdant bushes. Had he pulled me here to give me privacy to recover or because he wanted to be alone with me?

"I wasn't faint. That was fury. Something about that man..." I began.

"The Sect is a religious group that broke away from the Mennonite tradition fifty years ago. Moon is their leader. They live in a community outside of town," Walker said.

"From the other side of the forest," I whispered, recalling Sarah's memory of the Sect woman running away. He gave me the history lesson as a way of changing the subject from his observation of my pale skin. He'd noticed how upset I was. He'd cared. Enough to get personally involved. Now, he was backpedaling. He was the biologist again, not a concerned friend. Good. I'd never handled concern well and I rarely made friends. The Althaea might wall us off from the world, but my walls were even more effective. Usually.

"Let me guess. Model citizen. Respected religious leader," I replied. My stomach still churned when I thought of Moon's darting eyes.

"By some," Walker said.

"But not you," I guessed. I could see his disgust for Reverend Moon. It tightened his lips and hardened his jaw. It also soothed me more than the walk had done. I liked that he agreed with my instincts about the freaky reverend. He edged back from me as if our nearness was suddenly a bad idea. I was glad. I needed to be far away from the sunlight in his eyes even more when we agreed on something.

"His word is law with the Sect people. He's their messianic figure and they take his opinions as holy truths," Walker said.

"And you think I should stay away from him," I gathered.

"Ask Granny what she thinks about Reverend Moon," Walker advised.

"I should trust her opinion, but not her brews?" I asked. I plunged my hands in the back pockets of my jeans to give them something to do now that I wasn't holding Walker's hand. Okay. Yes. I was probably hiding my scars. Had he felt the rough patches and ridges when he'd grabbed me? Not vanity. Vulnerability. And it pissed me off.

"I told you to leave. You became a kitchen witch's apprentice instead. Are you always this rash or does she have you under a spell?" Walker asked.

"I think the preferred term is *wisewoman* and I don't believe in spells," I replied with a tilt of my chin and set to my teeth that Sarah would have recognized as trouble.

Walker either didn't see my temper or he wasn't intimidated by it.

He took a step in my direction and it was all I could do, temper or not, to hold my ground. He might be a scientist, but the glitter of anger in his eyes sparked off the gold flecks in the green like flint on steel.

I wasn't afraid of Jacob Walker. I was drawn to him. And that scared me.

"There are logical reasons not to self-medicate with natural ingredients of unknown potency and origin," he said.

I slowly pulled my hands from my pockets, surprised by his sudden deadly seriousness.

"Granny has lived on this mountain for at least sixty years if not more. She isn't some rando with a pop-up Internet shop. She has traditions. Recipes. And her own garden. We're good here, Mr. Walker. What's really bothering you?" I asked.

Was this about his precious ginseng or something else I couldn't understand? His intensity didn't jibe with our level of acquaintance. It was another mystery added to an already overwhelming puzzle I didn't even know if I wanted to solve.

"Work with Granny if you must. She'll cure whatever ails you, I'm sure. But stay away from Moon and stay out of the forest," Walker said. "There are dangers from plants and insects and animals there it would take years for you to understand. Not to mention the isolation. People who get lost are sometimes found in much worse shape than you'd expect—exposure, falls, black bears and bobcats. You've been through something." He nodded toward my scarred hands. "I can see that…"

I was done. With his warnings and his keen observational skills.

"Never through. Always in the middle of something," I corrected. "Usually in between the threat and someone being threatened. And right now, I've got work to do."

I left him standing in the midmorning light behind the Althaea bushes. I'd been certain after listening to Lu's song I needed to take my studies with Granny more seriously. That hadn't changed because of Walker's concern. In fact, his warnings only made me want to understand the wildwood he acted as if he alone could know and navigate. Yes, it was vast and dangerous. I could easily believe elements of it were deadly. Yet, the garden was part of it and the garden and Sarah were intertwined.

The basket was where I'd left it and I collected it quickly and headed inside. It was a strategic exit not a retreat. But I was glad there was only a fat cat to see me lean with my back against the front door once I was inside.

Seven

In October on the *mountain, fall wrapped around Sarah when she stepped outside, even before the sun was up. She couldn't see the changing leaves, but the slightly musty scent of them dying was in the air. And there was a chill unlike the chill of an August morning. By noon, the sun would chase it away, but it was sharper with a boldness that said it would be back, longer and longer each day. This morning, she snuggled into a pale blue hoodie, but in a few weeks she'd be needing the violet plaid peacoat waiting on a hook upstairs.*

It was apple butter time.

All over Morgan's Gap, folks were rising early and gathering their things—a favorite paring knife, an apron, boxes of mason jars that had been sterilized after they'd been emptied, as well as brand-new packages of lids.

Sarah's mom had already loaded their supplies in the back of the old Chevy truck she called "Sue." They would drive into the town like everyone else to meet at the small cannery by Tinker Creek.

There, the Baptist women would have already set up their yearly contribution, an ancient iron kettle lined with hammered copper large enough to simmer elephant stew, but intended only for the overripe apples that had been delivered the previous week from orchards all around. The Baptists also filled a couple of picnic tables with homemade ham biscuits, piled high and so buttery Sarah's mouth watered just remembering the rich flavor from years past.

The heavy oak paddle used for the constant stirring that would take place for at least twenty-four hours was the proud responsibility of the Presbyterian men. Every year they took turns making sure the heavily spiced apple mixture didn't stick before it became the thick, smooth texture Morgan's Gap was known for. By then, the apple butter would be almost black—a brown so dark it matched a Ross woman's eyes, they said. And everyone knew a Ross had eyes that could flash dark as midnight when they laughed... or cursed.

Sarah clambered up into the truck. As always, when Melody Ross climbed behind the wheel and turned the key she mumbled, "Sue has seen better days." As if it was a prayer or a spell intended to keep the fifty-year-old vehicle running once its chugging engine turned over.

The unpredictability of it probably contributed to how much Sarah loved the rattly vibration of the moth-eaten seat beneath her and the dusty scent of dried lilac her mother had hung from the rearview mirror. Tom was always bringing her mother flowers and, even though they grew plenty of flowers themselves, it was nice. Little bunches of blooms everywhere always made her mom smile.

Melody had said nothing about the Sect women who had started coming to the cabin more and more over the summer. Or about who might have chased that first one through the wildwood. She'd been growing too quiet in the evenings and it wasn't the easy silence of working in the kitchen or the herb pantry either. That kind of industrious quiet was the kind Sarah was free to interrupt anytime with questions or attempts to work alongside.

No. Last night her mother had curled up in her favorite quilt on the overstuffed sofa in their tiny living room. She'd asked for Sarah to bring her charm and she'd placed her lips against his crocheted side so that her words were too muffled for Sarah to hear.

But the air had tingled the way it did when Melody Ross was working a powerful spell.

Afterward, her mother had sipped valerian tea, but even an extra cup brought by Sarah before bed hadn't soothed her mother's brow. That telltale forehead crinkle had caused Sarah to clutch her reclaimed charm all night long, and this morning the crocheted mouse was in the pocket of her hoodie just in case.

It was apple butter time, but something not as pleasant was brewing on the mountain. Something Sarah didn't understand. She could only feel it in her chest as if her lungs were squeezed before every breath. The Ross blood she shared with her mother made her anxious when something was wrong. Even when she couldn't say exactly what wasn't right.

The horizon was pink when Melody parked with a firm jerk of her arm that set the old truck's gearshift firmly in place. Today was always a good day to come to town. There wouldn't be time for staring today, or whispers. Besides, all sorts of people came together to complete the task of peeling and cooking hundreds of bushels of apples. Baptist, Presbyterian, Methodist, Episcopal, and even Sect people, all hurried this way and that.

And there were wisewomen in almost every group.

Sarah and her mother didn't go to church.

"The ceiling of our sanctuary is the sky," Melody Ross said almost every Sunday.

Still, for apple butter, all transgressions were forgiven, so besides the herbalists there were also other sorts of "backsliders" mixed among the gathering townsfolk. Drunken Jack Whitaker, mostly sober at dawn but with bloodshot eyes as usual. Definitely not a Baptist, although his mother was already taking ham biscuits from a Tupperware container. The thought of salty country ham sandwiched between flaky crust made Sarah's stomach rumble. Tiffany Banks in the highest heels and reddest lips Sarah had ever seen. Definitely not a Presbyterian, although her father was one of the stirrers.

Sarah's mother tied an apron around her lean middle and Sarah smiled because a Ross apron had more pockets than most. A giant wooden spoon stuck out of one, but all the others would be filled with net bags and paper packets she'd pass out to other women as the day wore on—for headaches and cramps, for sadness and fatigue, for rashes and sorrow and clear skin and undisturbed sleep.

Sarah's apron was getting too short for her and it had only two pockets, but she would be helping to peel so she had her own small paring knife. The knife had belonged to her great-grandmother Ross and the polished bone handle fit perfectly in Sarah's hand.

Her mother grabbed her and pulled her in tight against her warm body for a quick squeeze. She felt a familiar hand pat the pocket of her hoodie where her charm was hidden as if to impart an extra bit of potency to the crochet mouse hidden there.

"Grab a biscuit before you get to work," her mother said into her hair.

She didn't need to be urged twice. Especially because Lu was Baptist and she'd already seen her friend helping her sick mother to a chair near the biscuits and a large maple that would shade her once the sun rose high.

Sarah headed toward the shuffle of people grabbing breakfast, but Lu had already seen (and probably heard) Sue arrive, so she came running with a biscuit on a paper towel.

"I'll have to stick close to Mama today, so I won't be peeling," Lu said.

"Mom brought molasses cookies for after lunch. I'll bring you some," Sarah said around the mouthful of buttery biscuit she was already chewing.

Lu ran back to her mother's side while Sarah finished her breakfast on the way to the picnic pavilion where the peelers would be.

She'd never heard anyone tell people where to work and what to do, but apple butter day always resulted in apple butter, enough for the churches to sell for fundraising and festivals and enough for each family to take at least a few jars home for their labor.

The long tables under the pavilion were draped in checkered plastic table-cloths and the benches were already getting filled. The apples started off in bushel baskets. From there, they graduated into metal tubs where they bobbed in a spring-water bath until they were grabbed and peeled. Older, stronger teens lifted and shifted the baskets and tubs. Younger people and much older people pared with flashes of knives that had probably been sharpened the night before.

Sarah took the last bite of biscuit and used the paper towel to wipe grease from her fingers before tucking it in her spare pocket with her paring knife. Large metal trash cans were set up for peels not garbage. Later they would be claimed by folks with hogs to feed. With her growling stomach satisfied, she walked down the length of the nearest bench until she found a place wide enough for her to sit. She heard a few giggles, but mostly people were too busy for teasing. And most of the kids she went to school with had given up ever getting a reaction from her.

Wisewomen heard the whispers of the wildwood and no other whispers mattered.

Sarah pulled her paring knife from her apron pocket and reached for an apple from the closest tub on the table. Around and around and around. Drop. Then, reach for another and around and around and around again. When all the apples in the washtubs were replaced by peeled apples, men came to carry the tubs to the corers who used longer knives to complete the harder task. There were several older men operating stainless steel appliances that cored and peeled the apples at one time as they turned long-handled cranks, but their apples were messier than the hand peeled ones, still speckled with bits of bruised fruit and red peel.

Soon the sun was high enough to heat the sticky apple juice that seemed to coat everyone and everything. The sweetness attracted yellow jackets as busy as the peelers. Whirling and sipping, with their sharp rear ends ready, daring anyone to shoo them away. The bees drew Sarah's attention from the task at hand, and for the first time she noticed the homespun fabric of a Sect woman's dress beside her.

A yellow jacket had landed on the back of the woman's busy hand and she simply ignored it, bravely continuing to peel. Sarah looked up from the bee to the woman's face to see if she was afraid. And suddenly she recognized Mary, the woman Tom had led away from the wildwood garden earlier in the summer.

Sarah's knife slipped.

She nicked her finger with its sharp tip and quickly sucked the bead of fruit-flavored blood while she looked at the girl with eyes that felt too wide in her face.

"Be careful," the Sect woman whispered. Sarah knew she wasn't talking about the cut or the paring knife in her suddenly trembling hand. Mary and her two simple words explained the tightness that had been building in Sarah's chest since that day. But she was a Ross. She'd seen her mother handle life and death in the blink of an eye. She'd helped when no older and wiser hands were there. Sarah swallowed her fear and went back to peeling as if a premonition of danger and doom hadn't filled her lungs when the woman spoke.

Only after several ordinary-seeming minutes had passed did she risk a glance up at the world from beneath her lashes. Mary was still calmly peeling. Around and around and around. Drop. She'd been scared before. Out of breath. Panting like a rabbit running from a fox. Now, she was in town as if nothing had happened. Her kerchief was tight and neat. Her freckles and dark brown eyes as ordinary as anything. But she'd chewed her lips pink and tender like Sarah sometimes did when she was nervous. And Mary's face was pink too.

Had the work made Mary's cheeks hot or something else?

Sarah couldn't guess Mary's age. But she was younger than she'd thought. She was peeling after all, and this job was for young and old, not the in-betweens.

"Always," Mary whispered again. "Always be careful." Her lips barely moved as she easily peeled the apple in her hands, still ignoring the threat of the bees all around.

Ignoring.

The.

Threat.

She was so brave about the bees while lots of other girls squealed and shooed them away. Sarah continued to peel, but she looked up and around at the rest of the people who had come to help. Outside the pavilion where the peelers worked there were other tasks being done.

But not everyone had come to help.

There were spectators too.

Lu's mother was reading a book to a circle of children too young to work, but across the path beaten from the parking lot to the cannery entrance, in the shadows of the building's long, low overhang stood a man dressed in a black suit. He wasn't working. He was watching. Sarah forced her hands to continue peeling even though the man's shadowed face made her heart stutter. He wasn't looking at her or the Sect girl. But his attention was hard and fast on something or someone in a way that made her think of rabbits and foxes all over again.

Sarah followed the direction of the man's attention only to see it was trained on her mother and Tom, near one of the big spice pots that bubbled on an open fire. Melody Ross would be one of the women responsible for the perfect mixture of cinnamon and cloves, brown sugar and ginger that would flavor the town's apple butter.

Her throat closed up and she dropped her apple and her knife.

The shadow man was why her chest had been tight all morning.

Sarah reached for the charm in her pocket, forgetting her sticky fingers. Her mother sensed her distress. From yards away, her chin rose from her spices and she met Sarah's frightened gaze. Only then did Sarah realize she was standing.

Tom must have noticed the change in Melody because he looked around to see what had bothered her. Sarah saw Tom look toward the shadow man. Did he recognize him? Could he see better from where he stood? Sarah couldn't be sure. But Tom stepped between the shadow man and Melody Ross. Her mother looked back to her spices, scooping more brown powder from a large cloth sack to add to her pot as if nothing had interrupted her.

Sarah understood.

She sat, her heart beating so hard it hurt.

Her mother's calm meant there was nothing wrong. At least not here and now. Soon. Or later. There would be. But life had to go on even when something scary was felt or seen. Her mother had taught her that a long time ago.

The Sect woman was gone. When Sarah had dropped her apple to stand, Mary must have slipped away. Standing wasn't careful. Noticing the shadow man was bad because it might mean he would notice them. Sarah Ross knew that. Sensed it somehow with a sense that couldn't be named. Did the Sect women know that too?

But Sarah wouldn't run away. That special sense she could never ignore told her the shadow man's identity was important. The sun's light would penetrate the shade of the building where he stood in another hour. So Sarah endured the careful work of peeling under his watchful presence while she waited for his face to be revealed.

Because he watched her now.

Sweat trickled down Sarah's forehead and into her eyes. It stung behind her lashes like tears even though she refused to cry. Her body shook, but she didn't stop the motions of her knife. Not again.

Always be careful. Be careful. Be careful.

Around and around and around and drop.

After each apple, as she allowed each sticky orb to drop with a splash into the water, she flicked her eyes up to check on the shadow man. Each time she saw him still there, her heart stuttered and her breath caught as she reached for another apple. The building's shade continued to shrink. The heat continued to rise. Older teens continued to come and fetch the tubs of peeled apples.

And still the shadow man stared.

Waiting to see his face was the hardest thing Sarah had ever done. She wanted Tom to make him leave. She wanted to go and hug her mother and never let her go. Instead, she peeled. She dropped. She flicked her eyes up for only a second. Three more apples and she'd be able to see. Two more apples and she'd be able to see.

When the yellow jacket landed on her leg, it wasn't nearly as threatening as the man in the shadows. She ignored it as well as Mary had. But the girl next to her didn't understand about the shadow man or a Ross woman's ability to sense more than most saw. Before Sarah could urge her to be careful, the girl beside her swatted at the yellow and black wasp.

The sting was sharp and sudden and then burning hot. The heat spread beneath Sarah's skin and she couldn't bite back the cry that burst from her lips. There had already been a few stings that morning and the last one had resulted in an allergic reaction that had set all the adults on edge.

Sarah didn't have a yellow jacket allergy, but that didn't stop numerous adults from running to check on her when she cried out. In the middle of all the fuss, Sarah risked another glance up to check the sun's progress. The shade was gone. But the shadow man was gone too. Before she'd had a chance to see his face.

The sting was nothing. As her former first grade teacher, Mrs. Bennett, held an ice pack to her leg, it was the shadow man's disappearance that made Sarah's skin go clammy. Autumn's chill had found her again in the middle of a sunny day and, this time, no amount of afternoon sun would make it go away.

Eight

A *familiar tickle interrupted Sadie* Hall's morning basket weaving. She looked down to see a honeybee doing the waggle dance on her bare forearm. In seconds, she understood what the worker bee was telling her. It was time. Bees communicated with each other through a complex series of movements and emission of pheromones. They could indicate to their hive mates where the best food sources could be found with precise instructions. They could signal for danger and satisfaction.

But today the dance on Sadie's arm marked an important event.

Swarm.

A virgin queen would fly and begin a new hive. She would need to be presented with an alternative to a hollow tree in the wild if her hive was to become a part of the apiary Sadie cared for.

Setting the basket she was working on to the side for future completion, Sadie stood and flexed her sore fingers. She looked down at her knobby knuckles and the thick calluses she'd developed over the years from twisting grasses and twigs into useful shapes. Her hands were a wisewoman's hands like her mother's and her grandmother's.

And like the women who came before, she reached for the bee balm to smooth into her palms and over each toughened digit to soften and maintain the flexibility she needed to continue her work.

"Beekeepers, we are. First and foremost. The balm we make from the melted wax will help us to continue weaving, but it also soaks into our skin and makes us smell like home to the bees we keep," Sadie's mother had told her years ago when she was first taught to rub the ointment into her fingers.

Hall women don't get stung and they can take the fire out of a sting if they're of a mind to.

Their honey was prized for miles around—no need for labels or advertisement. Word of mouth was all it took to create demand. Some called it "mountain honey" and it was certainly that. Some called it "apple blossom honey" because the main food source for the apiary was the nearby orchard. But Sadie's family had always called it "wildwood honey." Everything they were and everything they possessed had come from the wildwood, and a wisewoman knew to give credit where credit was due.

The bees themselves had originally come from overseas. Honeybees weren't indigenous to North America. Good hardy stock from the Old Country had been sealed into woven skep hives with protective coats of dried manure. The queens and drones had lain dormant for the crossing. Then, the wildwood had welcomed them when they were released. The bees Sadie kept were descendants of those first bees, fed on mountain fields and flowers long before the orchard was cultivated.

"Home," Sadie said as she rubbed the balm over her forearms once she had finished with her palms.

She and her friends decided where the golden jars filled from each honey extraction would be shared. Needs let themselves be known. And she, Kara and Joyce—her trio—generally listened if Granny suggested a recipient or if the oldest wisewoman asked for a jar. Honey had antimicrobial properties. It could help heal wounds and ease gastric complaints. It was rich in antioxidants and could also help build immunity to pollen allergies.

Wildwood honey had deeper and less-scientifically-measurable benefits than those, of course.

Sadie was already whispering words long forgotten by most folks in Morgan's Gap. The bees that came and went from her arm carried the words with them to the hive. Prayer. Song. Hymn. Spell. All one and the same when invoking a blessing on a new queen.

"Was a time when there wasn't such a distinction between believing this or that. I believe in the bees and the blossoms. I believe in the grass I twist and the twigs I weave," Sadie's mother had said often enough it had become almost a mantra for the young daughter learning to make baskets at her knee. "And I believe in the wildwood that gives us those things."

Sadie was forty-nine. Times had changed a lot in her almost fifty years in Morgan's Gap. Either that, or a person could see clearer as they got older. See the things that had always been there—quiet and creeping—until you were old enough to understand.

Her mother hadn't talked much about the Sect. They just were. Sadie learned over time that they were at odds with the wisewomen. The Sect was austerity. Wisewomen were abundance.

The Sect was like a disease. Hurting its members by disconnecting them from everything beyond what Reverend Moon allowed...and he didn't allow much.

"I believe in the bees and the blossoms," Sadie whispered as she picked up the old wall phone that was still connected to town by miles of wire strung across tarred wooden poles. "I believe in the grass I twist and the twigs I weave."

Granny was the opposite of Moon. It was as simple as working to heal rather than promoting weakness. Granny didn't fear the power of her people. And, suddenly, she was leading the wisewomen into action. They were extracting, brewing and stirring up more than they had in a generation.

Knowing of the existence of evil and doing something about it should go hand in hand. But it was easier to weave and keep than it was to reach out and stir up trouble.

Sadie was nervous and the bees could tell. They danced worrisome warnings against her waxed skin as she pressed in Granny's number on the old butternut-yellow telephone with "Bell" stamped on its face. Melody Ross had been the most powerful wisewoman Sadie had ever known. Melody's powerful connection to the wildwood hadn't saved her. Or her daughter. But Sadie had promised Granny she would help her with her new apprentice anyway. The Halls had a little Ross blood from one marriage a century ago. Joyce and Kara had a bit in their heritage too. And they'd always been proud of it. Sadie couldn't turn her back on that now.

"I believe in the wildwood that gives us those things."

Elsewhere in Morgan's Gap, two of her dearest friends sensed her fear. She could tell when Joyce and Kara dropped whatever they were doing to send her support through the connection they shared. It was like that sometimes in Morgan's Gap. Always three. From birth. As if tendrils of the wildwood itself weaved and wafted through their souls, binding them together. Danger was to be triply feared then. But the battle and the triumph could be triply shared as well.

They had grown up together. Taking their conjoining for granted until they saw other trios fall to sickness or disinterest or outside interference. People grew up and moved away. People died. People became so involved with the modern world they couldn't hear the wildwood anymore. Invisible ties could be tenuous if they weren't purposely nurtured and kept. Over the years, their trio had grown into caring about maintaining their ties, their strength, their purpose.

They were the last surviving trio in town. They might have only a smidge of Ross blood to share between them, but Granny needed them. So all together, it would have to be enough.

"The bees are swarming and Sadie needs help luring the young queens into new hives," Granny said. I'd heard the phone ring and her quiet voice in hushed conversation through the open kitchen window. I had been pinching the small shoots off the joints in the tomato vines to prevent the plants from becoming too sprawling to be productive. When Granny came to the back door to speak, I straightened with my hands at the small of my back. The sun had risen, but dawn shadows still lingered under the trees.

I had been up and working as the birds began to sing.

Granny gave me dozens of daily tasks and errands. I was so busy I often collapsed into bed much earlier in the evening than I would have back in Richmond. I was also recharging. Idleness would have driven me mad. It was better to keep my hands and mind occupied. The daily time in the sun warmed me. My hands and feet in the earth calmed me. I ate and drank what we grew. Constantly sipping and nibbling as I learned about flavors, potency and properties.

Focusing small—on leaves, roots, stems and petals—helped me to acknowledge my own smallness in the scheme of things. And yet, the interconnectedness of all permeated my consciousness in a way it never had before.

I weeded and watered all while being nurtured myself. Working for Granny felt more like a cottagecore vacation than it should at times.

But, whenever I caught a glimpse of a Sect woman shadowing me, I was reminded of the danger lurking around the edges of my new life. It had been two weeks since I'd seen Moon himself. But I hadn't forgotten how the women had eerily echoed his words. In what other ways had they been programmed to obey? Would their interest in me ever go beyond creeping around?

"You aren't allergic to honeybees, are you?" Granny asked. I noticed she didn't look nearly as alert as I felt. The early morning showed in the shadows under her eyes, oddly like the ones under the trees in her yard.

In the last few days, she'd been moving more slowly and occasionally her joints would pop and creak. I'd seen her sigh and massage her elbows or knees when she thought no one was looking.

"No. I've had a few stings in my life. Never much swelling," I replied. I dusted my hands together as if the chlorophyll stain from the tomato vines could be merely wiped off. The tips of my fingers would be green until I scrubbed them with a nailbrush and soap.

"You'll need to take the bike and wagon. Sadie's got some honey for us from a recent extraction. The apiary isn't far outside of town," Granny continued. "Wear good sturdy shoes. No sandals. She'll have the rest of what you'll need."

I'd taken the large three-wheeled contraption Granny referred to as her "bike" a couple of times. Long ago, it had been a bright red and white, but those colors had faded to an almost uniform color that was more rust than paint. It rattled and shook beneath the rider's body. I usually ended up hovering above the cracked vinyl seat to save my bones from jarring. It had no gears and pushing the pedals was a Herculean task even without a loaded wagon. "Not far outside of town" didn't really sound promising. Neither did "luring" bees.

But even as I thought about not relishing the chore, I noticed the dark circles under Granny's eyes again. She had eccentric notions about what my job should entail, but she'd given me a place to stay. I still wasn't sure about how long I was going to accept her hospitality, but I definitely didn't want her to decide to go after the honey herself.

"I've never seen honey outside of a jar," I said. "This should be interesting."

"Sadie has been keeping the bees all by herself since her mother had a stroke. She'll be glad for some extra hands today," Granny replied. "But that's not the only reason I want you to go. You can learn a lot from the bees. Listen. Watch. Do as Sadie tells you to do and don't be afraid."

"I'm not afraid of a sting," I assured Granny as I wiped my feet on the mat and climbed up the back stoop. I would need to wash up and change before I headed out.

Granny smiled until the sparkle in her eyes almost negated the shadows under them.

"Stings happen. But I wasn't talking about that," she said.

"Stings happen" repeated in my brain all the way down the multiple roads that led to the apiary. Granny had given me the directions as if I regularly navigated winding country lanes made up of more dirt than asphalt and gravel. Once I left the town limits, I was struck again by the wilderness around me and the quiet isolation. The only noise was the sound of the bike's protesting squeaks and groans... except for my own groans as "not far" proved to be hell and gone from the fitness level that could have tackled the distance with ease.

And the wagon I towed behind me was empty.

How much did honey weigh?

By the time I reached the apple orchard that marked the place I was supposed to look for Sadie's driveway, I was already dreading the trip back to Granny's house.

The trees were heavy with blossoms. On the mountain, their blooming came later than in the valleys below. A welcome breeze stirred and a flurry of pinkish-white petals were swept from the branches to swirl through the air like blushing snow. A sudden downward slope allowed me to relax and I lifted my face to the falling flowers. In spite of my exhaustion or maybe because of it, I was charmed by the butterfly kisses on my forehead and cheeks. Their scent was mild. Barely a sweet suggestion in the air. But I inhaled deeply anyway. I was winded. I caught my breath and allowed my eyes to drift shut, but for only a few seconds. The sound of an approaching car jerked me to attention.

I gripped the handlebars tightly and maneuvered as far to the side of the road as I could to allow the car to pass. Then, when it didn't, I risked a look behind me. A dark sedan—faded black or covered in dust, I couldn't tell which—followed behind my wagon far closer than it should. It was a huge old car. The kind whose hood stretched in front of it forever so that the person behind the steering wheel was a distant silhouette hidden by glare on smudged glass. All I saw before I had to turn my attention back to the front was a hulking shadow in the driver's seat. Tall grass grew on the sides of the road. The vegetation covered the ditches, making them a mysterious threat—could be inches, could be a bottomless chasm. It wasn't safe for me to pull over much more than I already had.

The car accident hadn't been that long ago. My heart raced with memories of squealing tires and Sarah's scream. It wasn't raining today. The sun illuminated the world with a cheerful midmorning light. But the sedan's engine was loud. Did I feel the heat of its engine on the backs of my legs? Impossible, but I tried to pedal faster.

Apple blossoms still blew around me, but now their kisses fell against numbed cheeks.

I was all alone in the middle of nowhere.

When the car began to go around me, my sudden push for speed had diminished, but the sedan crept even slower than I did. Inch by inch, the hood came into focus beside me, and the bulk of the car was a looming threat of rubber and steal. I turned to look because I had to see who would drive so closely and so slowly beside a cyclist. But I barely saw a flash of white (more grimace than smile) before the car suddenly accelerated. I jerked the handlebars in reflexive defense and ended up bouncing with protesting rattles into the overgrown grass. It was the weeds that saved me from a crash. They tangled in the rusty spokes so my lurch was halted inches before solid ground ran out.

I hadn't worn a helmet, but if the driver had decided to run me down, skull protection wouldn't have been enough to save me.

My thrill of relief was short-lived. As I climbed off the bike onto shaky legs, the sedan skidded to a stop. Its taillights gleamed red in the shade of the trees that hung over the road at the bend. Maybe the driver realized what he'd done? Maybe he was checking to see if I was okay? But somehow, I didn't think so. The pause seemed more sinister. I imagined the driver's malevolent gaze trained on me in their rearview mirror. My hands loosened and I allowed them to fall from the bike. I had been prepared to wrench it back onto the road. Now, every muscle I had quivered and bunched to prepare for flight.

Would the driver get out of the car and come for me on foot? Or would they try to run me down for real this time?

I could abandon the bike and run into the orchard.

That was my plan when the lights went out, signaling that the driver had taken their foot from the break. But the sound of a loud motor on the road behind me made me look before I leapt. A shiny red pickup truck was approaching. Maybe the sedan driver saw the truck too. Maybe they *had* only been checking on my welfare before going on their way. Cold certainty that they'd meant me harm crystalized in my gut like ice. Ridiculous. I'd never know for sure.

The woman driving the red truck beeped a hello. The driver's-side window was open and her hair was a wild, wind-tossed mane of faded brown shot through with silvery highlights that glinted in the sun. After her horn greeting, she cut the large steering wheel hard and swerved onto two well-worn ruts in the gravel road Granny had told me would lead to the beehives.

The sedan was gone.

I reached with shaking hands to drag Granny's bike back onto the road. I was more than ready to see a friendly face. I followed the red truck with relief. If the sedan turned around and came back, they wouldn't find me alone. I would worry about the return trip later.

After several yards it became steep and I was forced to get off the trike and push. Lucky for me, the pushing was much easier than the pedaling had been. My heart slowed. The ice in my gut thawed. I was already beginning to doubt that I'd been in any real danger.

I had time to catch my breath and think about Granny's words again. "Stings happen, but I wasn't talking about that."

Thankfully, I came to the cluster of beehives Granny had told me to watch for fairly quickly. Arranged in a large U shape like open arms reaching toward the apple orchard in the distance were twelve squat off-white boxes made up of layered levels. Even from a distance, I could see the bees swirling around the hives. Although I couldn't see their keeper yet, parked by the side of the road near the hives was the red pickup truck, dusty now, with its tailgate down and what must be beekeeping accouterments laid out, waiting. For me.

As I came closer, the hum of thousands of insect wings filled the air.

The vibrations enveloped me. I didn't just hear the bees. I felt them. In my chest. Along my skin. Deep in my inner ear. The noise was a sentient entity. I wasn't alone.

A movement drew my attention toward a shed that had been hidden behind the bulk of the truck until I got closer. I recognized the woman who had been driving the truck from her silver-shot hair. The woman I assumed to be Sadie was definitely older than me, but much younger than Granny. She moved with a quickness and confidence that came from a lifetime of activity that was nowhere near to slowing down. She noticed I'd arrived and she raised her hand in greeting. I awkwardly waved back as she approached.

"I cannot believe you rode that thing all the way out here," she exclaimed.

It was only then I noted the red truck had come from the direction of town. Why hadn't Granny arranged a ride for me rather than sending me out on the trike?

"Fresh air and exercise," I said with a shrug. If she knew Granny, then she knew the old lady worshiped nature. She refused to drive, walking everywhere she went in town in spite of her advanced years. And she'd expected me to do the same. In my short time in Morgan's Gap, I'd already developed a warm glow to my skin in spite of sunscreen.

"She can go overboard sometimes," Sadie said. "She used to hike or bike all over this mountain. Wherever she was needed. These days she'll accept a ride if she has to go very far, but she's too stubborn to learn to drive. Take care of yourself and don't be afraid to say no, every now and then, if she pushes you too hard. It does her good to face occasional opposition."

"I'll keep that in mind," I said.

"You do that. I'm Sadie, by the way. Sadie Hall. You must be Mel,"

Sadie said. "Welcome to the apiary." She was close enough now for me to see the crinkles around her eyes that matched the silvery streaks in her hair. But I could also see the straight square shoulders and muscular set to her arms and legs. As well as a highly alert glitter in her hazel eyes. She looked me up and down as well. Evaluating my merits, or the opposite. My spine stiffened, but then she pointed at the pile on the tailgate of her truck. "You'll find coveralls there. And some gloves. I think they'll fit. Get suited up and then I'll introduce you to the bees."

The apiary. *The* bees.

Not *my* apiary or *my* bees.

Their noise still stirred the air, a physical manifestation of sound.

"I'll help you with the hood and net when you get to that point. There are zippers and Velcro to prevent any access points. The bees are generally very focused on the queen when they swarm, but you'll need to take care," Sadie said.

I left the bike and met Sadie at the tailgate. Before I shrugged into the coveralls, she used wide tape around the openings of my jeans and sleeves to seal them close to my skin. After, she helped me with the Velcro on the sleeves and neck of the coveralls.

"Sometimes a new person can upset them. They're more aware of their caretakers than most people think. Especially these mountain bees. There's been an apiary here since before my grandmother was born. Quite likely as far back as the settlement of Morgan's Gap. And we've never brought in any bees from elsewhere. We've established new hives with local wild bees or from colony swarming. It's made them particularly hardy and healthy. But less...tame," Sadie said as she brought the oversized hood up and settled the netting around my face.

Suddenly, I felt claustrophobic. I could see through the netting, but it was thick and coarse enough to alter my vision and my breathing. And just beyond the net the hum of the bees was like another layer separating me from the rest of the world.

"It's okay. You'll be fine. And I really do appreciate the help," Sadie said. She patted my shoulder as if she had sensed my unease. "My mother and I used to do this together. She just isn't able to anymore."

"Will the bees be aggressive toward an outsider?" I asked. The sound in the air had altered. Either the hood changed the acoustics of the hum I'd heard when I first arrived or the colony was getting louder and higher-pitched. Even entirely covered in canvas, the hair on my arms rose in response to the... warning?

Sadie looked toward the hive as if she'd noticed the alteration in the bees' hum as well. Her hand settled more firmly on my shoulder and she held me in place for several long seconds. The sound stabilized at the higher pitch without climbing higher.

"Nothing to worry about," Sadie said then. But the netting didn't obstruct the slight furrow of her brow.

She wasn't wearing coveralls. Her safety equipment consisted of tall rubber boots and gloves paired with jeans and a faded canvas barn coat she'd zipped to her throat. After looking toward the hives for a few seconds, she dug a netted hat from a sack in the back of the truck as if she hadn't intended to wear it at first, but had changed her mind.

"I got the smoker going when I arrived. It's over by the shed," Sadie said. Her brow was covered now and I couldn't tell by her voice if she was still concerned. She certainly moved decisively enough back the way she'd come earlier. I followed. The coveralls swished when I walked. Made with plenty of excess material to distance stingers from skin, they were cumbersome and uncomfortable, but now I found them reassuring rather than claustrophobic. Not being afraid of stings was easy when you were dealing with random insects flying around a garden or park. I recognized the tingle of fear now as my body responded with adrenaline to the presence of thousands of bees.

The smoker was a battered old tin tool with a pointed lid that made me think of *The Wizard of Oz*. From its spout, a thin trail of smoke curled upward. Sadie picked it up off the ground and showed me how pumping the handle engaged a small bellows that turned the smoke curl into cloudy puffs.

"This is another precaution. It prevents them from detecting alarm pheromones if any bees become distressed. They should be distracted enough by the new queens that we won't need it. But..." Sadie looked again toward the hives. I could see only the shadow of her face behind her netted hat, but I sensed her hesitation.

Something was wrong.

The hair on the back of my neck joined the hairs on my arms at attention. The vibrations in the air shouldn't have affected me through the layers of protective clothing, but they did. Several bees flew around us as Sadie looked toward the hive for longer than mere seconds this time. I shifted from foot to foot, trying to tamp down the flight instinct that was probably better honed than most people's.

Granny had said beekeepers dealt with swarms every year. It was a natural part of the bees' cycle. But Sadie's sudden tension seemed out of place. And, yet, it wasn't Sadie's tension that had me worried.

It was the bees' tension. Which made no sense at all. I had never worked with bees. I knew next to nothing about them. I certainly wouldn't understand if their buzzing wings had something to say.

Finally, Sadie seemed to shake off whatever was bothering her. She turned back to me with surety once more.

"I keep woven skeps in this building. We'll use them to lure the queen and her followers and then transfer them into the boxed hives I've prepared," Sadie said. I reached down to pick up two of the bell-shaped, basket-like containers she indicated. The scent of fresh straw rose from the skeps combined with the cloying sweetness of honey. "Be careful. I've coated the inside with honey. Some beekeepers use artificial pheromones or a combination of beeswax and resin called propolis. But these mountain bees seem to prefer their own honey."

Sadie held the smoker. I held a skep in each hand. Together, the three things felt very small in comparison to the sound of the bees that seemed to echo inside my head.

"What do I do?" I asked, trying not to shout.

"We'll carefully approach a swarm and offer them the skep. It will be obvious where the queens are because they'll be surrounded by a mass of bees that have split off from the original hive. Come, I'll show you," Sadie said.

I had come to help, so I continued in her footsteps in spite of the hum in my head and the adrenaline response of my body. If some nuance had reassured Sadie, then I should be reassured as well.

Because of my impeded vision, I didn't notice at first that the wind had shifted. Apple blossoms no longer floated through the air. Now, it was a flurry of honeybees that brushed along my hood and net. Once I noticed, I watched hundreds of little insects dancing around Sadie's form in front of me. Rather than act like she didn't notice them, she slowed and moved more carefully as if she was hyperaware of her body in relation to the bees' environment. No sudden movements. No jarring steps or turns. I tried to mimic her, but had much less experience. Several times, I felt the impact of a fuzzy bullet against me. Kamikaze or accidental collision? I couldn't be sure. Maybe the bees dive-bombing me were simply attracted to the honeyed skeps I carried across the yard.

"We're good. They're keyed up, but we're good," Sadie said. I didn't correct her because I thought my inexperience and fear made dive bombs out of regular flight. "And it looks like the saplings I planted have done the trick."

In between the beehives and the split-rail fence that separated the apiary from the orchard, a row of young trees had been planted. I immediately understood why when I saw the pulsing balls of bees that hung from low branches on two of the trees.

"Looks like we'll be starting two new hives this year," Sadie said. "Just as I thought." I could hear pride and satisfaction in her voice. I was happy for her. Really. Until I fully understood what she needed me to do.

I was dizzy as Sadie led the way around the box hives to the first tree. The sound of the bees pulsed in my head until it actually interfered with my equilibrium. She wordlessly directed me with gestures to raise the bell-shaped skep with the open end under the vibrating ball of the bee swarm. Then, Sadie began to scoop handfuls of bees into the skep. They didn't resist. They didn't leave once they were there because more joined them, handful after handful, until finally Sadie uncovered the virgin queen. She was much larger in size, but I doubted I would have been able to identify her as readily as Sadie.

The seasoned beekeeper reached into her pocket and pulled out a piece of plastic that looked almost like a hair clip. The bulk of the bees were in the skep I held now, but there were many stragglers flying around us. That changed when Sadie opened the clip and closed it to form a safe plastic cage around the queen. Once she placed the clip in the skep, most of the straggler bees followed. I hadn't realized how tense Sadie was because of the net covering her face. When the queen was relocated, she patted me on the back and I saw her shoulders relax.

"I've prepared an empty hive, but we'll turn the skep over on the grass in front of it and let them settle in together for a little bit first," Sadie said. "We can lure the other swarm while we give this one a minute to eat and calm down."

Sadie helped me turn the skep over and place it on the freshly trimmed grass in front of the empty hive. I was sure the clumps of bees would fall out, but they were clinging to each other and the woven edges of the skep, busily eating the honey coating Sadie had gifted them.

"Now, I'll hold the skep this time and you'll urge the bees into it," Sadie said.

I reluctantly let go of the second skep. I was getting used to the sound of the bees and I was beginning to trust the suit that protected me from stings, but even with gloves, I wasn't sure I wanted to hold handfuls of bees for the seconds necessary to move them from tree to skep.

I didn't have time to gather my nerve before the loud roar of a car engine interrupted us. We both turned toward the road to see that the old sedan was back. Instead of parking behind the truck and Granny's bike on the road, it had cut over the grass toward the hives as if the driver thought he was driving a sport utility vehicle instead of something resembling a hearse. Even over the car's engine and the humming roar of the bees, I heard Sadie gasp as the sedan came to a stop barely a foot from the farthest hive. She stepped forward as if she would have thrown herself between the chrome grill and the bees.

But she brought herself up short when a Sect man jumped from behind the wheel of the car. He was carrying a jar of honey. And then he was brandishing it in the air. His face was red under his wide-brimmed black hat and he stomped forward without a care for the bees that whirled around him.

"Reverend Moon warned you. He's warned all of you. We don't want your filth anywhere near our women. None of your lotions or drinks. None of your unguents or balms. We will not abide your unnatural meddling," the man shouted.

He raised the jar of honey over his head and threw it. It sailed in an ugly arc straight toward Sadie's head and she dropped the skep she was holding, to either try to catch the jar or shield her face I couldn't be sure. The Sect man pulled my focus. I raised my hands and pointed them toward him. The jar fell sooner than its trajectory said it should. It fell at Sadie's boots and busted open against a rock on the ground.

But I couldn't worry over spilled honey.

I had room in my mind for only the buzz of thousands of bees. They roared between my ears and the roar turned into fury. I didn't even try to fight it. It matched and melded with my own. And with my raised hands and pointed fingers I told it to fly.

The Sect man finally noticed when he was hit by the fourth or fifth tiny projectile. He wasn't wearing protective coveralls or a net. When the bees hit, they were able to sting. Six, seven, eight, nine, ten.

He had attacked us. Now we were defended. The vibration in my mind and all around me seemed to have soaked all the way to my heart. Interloper. Intruder. Invader. For once in my life, I wasn't the outsider.

"Stop," Sadie said. I heard the sob in her voice more than I processed her command. "Every sting is a death. He's not worth their lives."

I couldn't stop. I didn't know how. I didn't control the bees. They controlled me. I was a swarm of rage and I had to protect my queen and my home.

The Sect man was shouting in fear now. Swatting at the stinging bees that pelted him from all directions. He jigged from foot to foot, no longer looking as if he could ever tell a group of women how they should live or what they should do. Like a marionette on strings, he danced as sting after sting spurred him on.

"Mel, lower your arms and close your eyes." It wasn't another command from Sadie. She had gone silent. But I recognized the voice. I looked toward the speaker. "No one's in danger now. He's not going to hurt Sadie or the apiary."

Jacob Walker must have approached from the orchard. He'd climbed over the fence and stepped toward us with his hands out as if he was talking to a person with a loaded gun. But his deep, calm voice interrupted the angry buzz of the bees. I blinked. I shook my head. The roar between my ears faded. And my hands came down.

The biologist stopped several feet away, giving me space to process what had happened, but before I could, the Sect man yelled a garbled prayer for deliverance.

Walker and I looked toward Sadie, but she had disappeared. In her place, a giant swarm of bees had massed over Sadie's form. Her arms were stretched out to her sides. Her legs were planted shoulder width apart. A sheet of bees covered the net over her face and they danced angrily over and around her entire body in a constantly moving suit made of bees.

We both stepped toward her at the same time. Me, with no idea how to help. Could she breathe? Would they sting? We both stopped short when she began to speak.

"You made a mistake coming here. We will protect home. Always," Sadie said. Only it was more than Sadie, amplified and reverberated by the vibrations of thousands of wings. Her voice sounded changed, augmented by an alien colony intelligence I would never truly understand. She also sounded completely unafraid.

The Sect man was already running for the open door of his sedan. He slipped several times and each time he squealed as he struggled to keep his footing. From this distance, I could see that one of his eyes was already swelling shut and his face was covered in welts. I thought his mouth looked misshapen, and there were no more prayers tainted with misogynism from his lips.

The sedan's tires spun on the grass, digging deep rivets in the earth as the Sect man floored the gas pedal. He finally got traction on the road and with a shriek of gravel he sped away. I hurried over to where he'd been standing. At my feet, dead and dying bees covered the ground. Hundreds of them. Tears burned my eyes. I didn't know what had happened or what exactly I had done. But I knew I'd done something wrong. I turned to face whatever judgment the bee-covered Sadie meted out.

But she was no longer covered in bees.

Walker had gone to her and helped her remove the hat and face net. In spite of the bees. But if he was stung, he didn't flinch. Not once. I reluctantly joined them. Abandoning the evidence of the carnage I had caused. The buzz of fury was only a remembered echo in my mind. The ferocious defensiveness against an attack had faded, leaving me shaken as adrenaline drained.

"I'm sorry," I said.

Sadie didn't look at me. Maybe she couldn't bear to see my face. The killer of her bees. Or maybe she was just exhausted because she leaned against the nearest hive as if to prevent her collapse. The bees that had engulfed her body had broken back up into individuals. Many had gone back to their hives, but some still flew around the entrances as if they too were shaken.

"I came to tell Sadie about a wild hive I found. In a tree that was struck by lightning last year," Walker said. Neither of us had asked him about his presence. I didn't know about the older woman, but I was becoming used to him showing up. Especially during trouble.

"This was my fault. I didn't know you would be able to hear them or help them," Sadie said. She finally looked up at me. She didn't look angry only resigned. "They would have attacked him anyway. You simply gave them direction. You helped them to coalesce in purpose.

I was so shocked. I counteracted with direction of my own. I called them home. To me," Sadie said.

My shakes were dissipating. I wasn't at all tired or depleted, while Sadie looked like she might need help to get to her truck. Had I really controlled the bees? Had I directed them to attack? I couldn't deny their buzzing had made me feel funny from the moment I'd arrived at the apiary. The noise had seemed to get inside my head. And even though I'd been swathed in thick coveralls, I had definitely felt the bees urgently bumping into me when I followed Sadie to the hives. Had some of them been coming to me the way they came to Sadie? I hadn't consciously called them. I wouldn't know how to even if I tried.

Walker had moved away from us. He was gathering up the sticky pieces of broken glass, carefully avoiding the bees who were attracted to the spilled honey. How had he known? And how had he known what I needed to do?

"Granny was right about you," Sadie said quietly, for my ears alone. "You need to open yourself up to training. You've been closed off, but that's changing and you'll need to learn how to handle what's happening to you."

"I've been studying the remedy book. And helping Granny," I replied. But my voice wavered. A healthy dose of skepticism had helped me to survive more times than I could count in my life. It was one thing to be inspired by the connection I'd felt to Lu and her magical music. It was another to be possessed by angry bees.

I'd felt the bees' ferocity. It had melded with my own, increasing it, and I hadn't known how to control that connection. Jacob Walker had snapped me out of it. He had interrupted before I'd decimated the apiary.

Sadie was right. I couldn't handle what was happening to me. Not alone. I'd been studying the remedy book, but I'd missed a valuable lesson—wisewomen believed in community. I'd been learning about how everything was connected, but I'd still been keeping a part of myself in reserve. My bug-out bag was always packed. I hadn't been prepared for the sudden, total, consuming *oneness* with the bees.

Sarah's special abilities had always seemed to come so naturally to her. If she had somehow bequeathed even a portion of her affinity for the natural world to me, I was certainly not handling it well.

Sadie patted my shoulder. Could she sense the lingering shakiness beneath her hand? I stepped away just in case and she allowed her arm to drop without protest, but the look on her face was sad. Walker had finished cleaning up the glass, but he didn't come back over to us. He stood, looking toward me with tight lips and a furrowed brow.

The bees had revealed my biggest weakness. One I hadn't really acknowledged to myself. Togetherness was terrifying. And if practicing Granny's wildwood beliefs depended on me completely connecting with anyone or anything, then I was pretty sure I would fail.

Nine

J oyce Mayhew was a Sunday school teacher and a dear old friend of Granny's. She was also famous or infamous—depending on who was doing the talking—for her dandelion wine. It was already warm on an early sunny Saturday morning in June when Granny woke me to help with the dandelion harvest.

"This is Joyce's pet project and it's as good a time as any for you to introduce yourself. She can be a little standoffish with outsiders. Best to jump right in. Show her what you're made of," Granny said from the doorway. "Normally I would help, but hours in a sunny field might be a little much for me today. Sadie will bring me by Joyce's house later. I'll help strip the petals and fill the fermenting crocks."

"Will I be taking the trike?" I asked. I'd used the bike around town since the apiary incident, but I dreaded taking it back on country roads.

"No. No. Joyce has told Alan to stop by and pick you up. You can't ride a bike that far in your Sunday best. But you've got time to get ready. The dandelions have to be fully open and dried out by the sunshine before they're picked. Alan will be by around ten o'clock,"

Granny said. Even though she said there was plenty of time, her wrinkled cheeks looked flushed as if she was flustered. Maybe because she
was still in a voluminous white cotton nightgown. Had she overslept?
If it was such an event, I wondered why she hadn't told me about the
dandelion harvest ahead of time.

"Sunday best?" I murmured. Granny had already disappeared.
Probably to get dressed herself. It wasn't usual for her to still be in
sleepwear at this time of morning. Sarah and I had never been church-
goers. But I assumed Granny wanted me to wear a dress. A tricky turn
of events. I had exactly one dress that Sarah had gifted me several
years ago. It was a summery thing I almost hadn't packed. If it hadn't
been a present from Sarah, I never would have worn it in the first
place. But I fished it out of the back of my suitcase and shook it out.
Thankfully, it was made of a light, crinkly material that didn't need
ironing. Or hanging up. Or caring for in any way beyond laundering.

It even had a built-in white slip beneath the opaque outer dress.
Unlike most of my other clothes, the dress was a cheerful robin's-egg
blue instead of black.

I felt self-conscious the minute I put it on. Like I was a cosplayer.
But Granny seemed satisfied when I came downstairs. She didn't even
frown at my white canvas shoes which probably were not "Sunday
best" by any stretch of the imagination.

"Just in time," she said as the sound of a large vehicle pulling up to
the curb came from outside.

Granny opened the front door and I was startled to see an ancient
school bus waiting for me. Only a little orangish yellow showed through
the many layers of paint the bus had seen in its repurposed lifetime. I
thought maybe the children that waved and shouted at Granny from
the bus windows must have helped with the current rainbow theme
and the scribbled lettering on the side. "Crooked Creek Methodist

Church." I grabbed my bag and a floppy straw hat Granny must have placed beside it. The driver had waved at Granny without getting out.

"Be sure to thank Alan for the ride," Granny said as I hurried out the door.

Maybe Granny hadn't prepared me for the dandelion harvest because nothing would have prepared me for it. The laughter. The singing. Alan's jovial welcome followed by a careening ride through town picking up dozens more children that waited by mailboxes with their parents. Easter had come and gone while I was alone with Sarah's ashes in Richmond. But I imagined this is what children looked like on Easter morning, dressed all in suits and flouncy dresses and carrying baskets as if they were going on an egg hunt.

Even I was swept up by the enthusiasm and holiday atmosphere. I waved. Several times. And Alan caught my eye once in the rearview mirror with a cheeky wink and a grin. He was a giant of a man. In height and girth and smile. A Santa Claus with a snowy white beard somehow transported from the North Pole to Morgan's Gap. And his bigness obviously impacted his personality as well. Some of the children called him Mr. Alan and I thought that was fitting because even with his grins and his seemingly reckless piloting, he seemed very in charge of getting a whole town's worth of children—and me—to Joyce's dandelion field safely.

The children cheered when the bus pulled to the side of the road. Through the windows, the field of dandelions was an explosion of color that was welcoming and intimidating at the same time. In the summer sun and breeze, the fully opened dandelion heads made me dizzy from the expansive floral waves of yellow—from amber to butter and back, again and again. I waited in my seat as a hundred kids that seemed more like a thousand pushed and pulled and tumbled down the aisle and steps. I wasn't prepared for the feelings that hit me when I noticed the trailing ribbons and untied shoes, the mussed hair and smudged clothes. They had all been so pressed and perfect when they'd been picked up. And already they were loosened, as if driving into the country had freed them somehow. From Crooked Creek Methodist Church to the wildwood. Or almost. I could see the forest framing the edge of the field, a distant rustling of green shadows and towering trees.

"Thank you, Mr. Alan," I said when I rose and approached the front of the bus myself.

"You're welcome," he replied. "I'll take you all back to town once the picking is finished."

Joyce Mayhew had been waiting for the bus to arrive. Alan had parked behind her sedan on the side of the road. It was plain and proper compared to the bus. And Joyce was the same. She was younger than Granny but older than Sadie by at least several years. Her graying hair was in a set-and-sprayed style I'd seen only in movies and her skirt suit was polyester and a pink shade never seen in nature. The children had all lined up like fidgety soldiers for review.

My chest tightened as Joyce walked up their ranks as if preparing to do an inspection.

I came off the bus ready to defend kids I didn't even know, but my rush was brought up short by laughter.

"Watch for bees and help your younger friends," Joyce was saying. "And there'll be cookies and lemonade once your baskets are full!"

Her eyes cut to me and the laugh crinkles at the side of them eased as if she wasn't nearly as pleased with me as she was with the children. *Watch for bees.* I set my teeth against the urge to cringe.

"Let's show Granny's new friend who can pick the most dandelions today. Ready. Set. Go!" Joyce shouted above the shrieks of children who were already running into the field, stomping as many flowers as they were plucking.

"They're so happy," I said. I could easily imagine a young Sarah just like some of these girls, laughing so hard that they could barely manage to get any dandelions in their baskets.

"They'll grab leaves and stems too. We'll have our work cut out for us. Cleaning away all the greenery so the wine won't be bitter," Joyce said. Vehicles had started to arrive. Men, women and older teens got out. Many I recognized from bus stops earlier that morning. "They like to get pictures of the children with the dandelions, but don't want the kids to miss Alan's bus ride. He brought many of them to this field when they were small too."

Suddenly, the bright day and the joyous chaos was a lot for me. Sarah should have been one of these parents one day. Now, she never would be. And the continuity, the tradition, the belonging of it all made me even more aware that I was on the outside looking in on an alien world. An ache pulsed deep in my gut. I thought of the dying bees writhing on the ground.

"Well. You're here. Might as well get to picking," Joyce said gruffly. I didn't know if she'd noticed my emotion, but she definitely noticed my idle hands.

There were spare baskets piled by the road. Joyce must have brought them for anyone who had forgotten theirs. I picked one up and waded into the field a little more carefully than the children had. I noticed that most of the kids had run for the middle. I kept to the edges. Picking the dandelions that had been stepped over and forgotten. Step by step, I made my way around the field toward the trees. I didn't purposefully stay to myself and move away from the families taking photographs and enjoying the day together. But by the time I came to the undergrowth that indicated the beginning of the forest and the end of the dandelions, I was far away from the others.

The laughter and exclamations in the distance didn't penetrate the wildwood. From the sunbaked field at my back to the shadowy forest in front of me, there was at least a five degree difference in temperature. The floral green scent of the dandelion breeze suddenly changed to a fragrance that hinted at mossy secrets and moist leafy carpet.

At first, I was refreshed. I stretched my back and lingered in the shade. I had filled my basket. It had been painstaking work. My fingers were pollen-stained and my shoulders were stiff. And still I had managed to get some greenery in with the dandelion heads. I sank down to my knees beneath a tree and began to pick out the stems and leaves while I rested.

I wasn't sure how long I worked before a twig snapped. I only knew I was wholly focused on presenting a clean batch of flowers to Joyce. I wouldn't have noticed anything happening around me. The sudden sound jerked my attention from the task in my lap. The closely packed tree trunks didn't allow me to pinpoint the direction of the snap I'd heard. Now, there was only silence. There were no scurrying squirrels. No birdsong.

The absence of sound made me aware of my isolation.

I rose to my feet, dusting off my dress as if I wasn't strangely unnerved by the quiet forest. What had seemed like a haven from the hot, bright sun and the crowd now seemed more like a chill warning...of what?

I stood in my pretty dress with my basket clutched in front of me, straining to see into the woods. Every squat stump seemed like a crouching animal. Every spindly sapling seemed like a skeletal figure, gone frozen while my eyes tried to focus, but surely ready to skulk toward me whenever I blinked.

Ridiculous to be scared. A whole field of children played only a half an acre away. I remembered the flock echoing Moon's condemnations and Moon's burning eyes. I remembered the Sect man's fury at the apiary and how his sedan had seemed to threaten me on the road.

When the Sect woman revealed herself beside a curtain of vines that trailed down from an old twisted oak several yards away, a rush of adrenaline flooded my sun-warmed skin. The homespun blue of her dress was in sharp contrast to the festive dresses in the field behind me. Her gray kerchief was tied tightly around her hair, cutting into her face. Her cheeks seemed to bulge from the sides.

And her eyes bulged too. As if she was shocked to see and be seen, as if she didn't know what to do now that she'd been discovered. But her fists were clenched. And her mouth was drawn down in a frown. Her gaze dropped to the basket of dandelions in my hands.

"Do not drink the witches' brew," she hissed. Her admonition wasn't for me. The singsong quality of her voice was like the repetitive echoes of Reverend Moon's flock. She was only repeating what she had been told.

"I'll drink it by the gallon if I like," I said loudly. My voice rang out among the silent trees. "And I'll help to brew it too."

She actually took a step forward with her fists raised. I'd faced aggression from my earliest days, but this was different. After the church bus ride. After sundresses and Mr. Alan and the happy chaos of the children and their supportive families. Even after Joyce's less than enthusiastic welcome.

This woman's irrational anger made the wildwood seem fifty degrees colder than the dandelion field and it chilled me to the bone.

The face-off lasted for only a few minutes. When I didn't back down, when I didn't run away, the Sect woman turned and slowly walked deeper into the forest. Her measured, careful steps didn't seem like a retreat. She hadn't meant to be seen, but now that she had been, she seemed to boldly claim her right to stalk me. I watched her back until she was swallowed up by darkness. I stared at the dark until I was certain she'd gone away.

My study of the remedy book that night was halfhearted. Thunder rumbled in the distance and it was a comfort to curl under a faded quilt beneath the shelter of Granny's painted tin roof.

Granny had said the remedy book held all the answers I was looking for. So far I hadn't found any revelations in its pages. Although I had to admit I noticed something new every time I opened it.

As the storm came closer and closer with such flashing that the bedside lamp wasn't the only illumination on the book's brittle pages, I was suddenly startled by an illustration of a honeybee I'd never noticed before. A crash of thunder sounded directly overhead and a jagged bolt of electricity rent the sky beyond the filmy fabric of the curtains. The bee seemed to glow on the page in the lightning's light. Done in ink, then colored with a yellow pigment that had faded to pale buttercup, the bee accompanied step-by-step directions for attracting pollinators to a garden.

It wasn't as simple as that, was it? The storm had been moving steadily, but now it seemed to have slowed, lingering above Granny's house. The erratic patterns of shadow and light on the page should have made it harder to read, but my chest tightened and I had to moisten dry lips caused by sudden rapid breaths because the lightning flashes seemed to highlight several words, one after another, again and again.

Bergamot. Water. Offering.

Only after I imagined a revelation did the storm move on, leaving darkness and a steady rain pattering on the metal roof above my head. Now, lit by only the lamp, the illustration of the bee seemed faded and dull and the instructions were once again an ordinary listing of which plants would draw bees and how to cultivate them.

I flipped back to the previous page and forward to the next. I recognized directions for a freckle poultice I'd laughed at before and a
recipe for citrus jelly to be made from something that resembled a lime
called a maypop. I'd seen that before too. But not the two-page spread
about bees in the middle?

The lingering guilt from the traumatic events at the apiary had
made me notice it. That was all. Regret burned my cheeks and messed
with my perceptions. But when I finally closed the remedy book to go
to sleep, I'd already memorized the instructions. They followed me
into dreams filled with the poor dead bodies of bees.

The next morning Granny was busy in the pantry when I left for
deliveries. Several of her regulars didn't mind the occasional discreet
Sunday visit when most people were in church. The basket had already
been packed and left for me on the counter with a list of recipients.
It was cowardly to shout a goodbye and leave without any morning
conversation, but I still wasn't sure what to say. Granny must have
heard from Sadie by now. The phone had jangled several times since
sunrise.

In the center of Morgan's Gap—if any point nestled in the quirky,
twisting hollow could be called "center"—was a park that was more
rock than respite. There wasn't much to it. A few ancient trees that
seemed prone to blight. An ancient gazebo more gray than white
with previous colors showing through its chipped paint. And several
patches of sparse grass. I'd passed around it on the crooked, rolling
sidewalk many times, hardly noticing it at all. No one gathered there.
There weren't any flowers or picnic tables. There was no playground
equipment. Maybe a town surrounded by plenty of green and growing
spaces didn't feel the need to put much energy into a park, but, today,

I stopped and stared once my basket was empty. I didn't like the idea that the heart of Morgan's Gap was barren and still.

"I would offer a penny for your thoughts, but your eyes are too dark. Something tells me I shouldn't ask," Lu said, instead of saying hello. She didn't wave because her arms were wrapped around a large container that held a bright red flowering plant. She came to stand beside me on the sidewalk. "Haven't given this place much attention, have we? I've mainly focused on the farmers' market. Donated proceeds from my first album. At first it was all about music, but that liveliness drew others in. Give an artist space and freedom to express themselves, however they see fit, and suddenly you've got a community."

So Lu crafted dulcimers and created music, but she also gave back to her roots, creating a place for other artists to come together. You could see the enthusiasm lighting up her face. Community. She made it sound appealing.

Even when she wasn't singing, her voice was melodic. I'd heard the mountain in other people's voices, including Sarah's, but no one's was as vibrato and compelling as Lu's. My Richmond voice was sharply staccato in comparison.

"What's wrong with the trees?" I wondered. Many of the branches were leafless, covered by a pale green lichen that must have been leeching whatever life remained out of them.

"Should probably be removed before they fall, but the mayor lives there." Lu's hands were full so she tilted her head toward an ugly walled house with colonial columns at the edge of the blighted park. It was a sprawling monstrosity compared to the other houses in town, with disjointed, modern additions that made the square of its original structure seem to dully squat in shame. "Most people just leave this park to him. A sort of neglected backyard. It suits, believe me."

The flower in Lu's container kept drawing my attention again and again. I suddenly recognized it and my entire body flashed cold then hot with the strange coincidence. I wouldn't have been surprised if lightning had cut across the sky even though it was a sunny day.

"Is that bergamot?" I asked. I already knew. The illustration of the bee had been accompanied by sketches of the flower Lu held. Petals. Stem. Leaf. Whole blossoms. They hadn't been colored, but the shape was distinct.

"Yes. My mother calls it bee balm. It's for you. Been trying to track you down all morning," Lu said. She held out the container toward me and I couldn't help stepping back. The eerily lit page. The words illuminated one by one. The surety that the storm had moved on once I'd seen what I needed to see. The equal certainty that I'd never seen the bee pages before. As if they'd appeared when I needed them.

"Wh-why?" I asked.

Lu wasn't fazed by my nervousness. She stepped forward as I stepped back and nudged the pot into my arms. My basket was empty and the handle looped over my arm. My hands were free. I had to take the container. Once I did, the scarlet flowers trembled, giving my mood away.

"I'm not one to place much store in mountain superstitions. But I guess I've always followed my heart and intuition. It's where the music comes from. Since you came, I've been writing more. Stuff bubbling up from someplace I'd forgotten. You brought Sarah's ashes home. And maybe that's part of it. But since she's been laid to rest I shouldn't be so restless. Last night, when the storm rolled through, I couldn't sleep. Went out back and dug up this plant like a woman possessed by lightning light. And all I knew was you needed it," Lu said.

"Something bad happened. At the apiary Sadie Hall keeps. Bees died. And it was my fault." The confession I hadn't been able to give to Granny poured out to Lu. The bee balm quivered in my arms. "Last

night, I think I learned what I need to do to make amends. To…
apologize to the bees."

She would tell me I was crazy. She would take back the plant and
walk away. She didn't. Lu reacted the same way Sarah would have
reacted. She waited for me to tell her what I needed to do. Her ready
acceptance made me nervous. This was connection. More intimate
than the bees because Lu was a person. A person I liked. Someone I
was drawn to in the same way I'd been drawn to Sarah. If I accepted
that we shared thoughts and ideas, inspirations and aspirations, then
I'd have to accept the risks as well. Of losing her. Of letting her down.

"It's coincidence. You couldn't have known I was reading about bergamot last night. You couldn't have known about the bees." I stilled
the plant in my hands and dared any breeze to blow.

"One way or another, there's no harm in planting some bee balm.
This is the place, isn't it? That's why you were standing here looking
at that sad, sorry grass," Lu said. There was laughter in her eyes. She
was so calm and easy in the face of the wildwood bringing her a friend
like me. I wanted to warn her away. There and then. Put an end to any
idea of us being linked together. But she waited so expectantly and the
compulsion to apologize to the bees was stronger than my usual flight
response. We were here with a plant that would improve the park.
Plain and simple. I was suddenly certain it was what I wanted to do.
Needed to do. Before rational thought stopped me.

"I don't have a shovel," I said. If we were being compelled by some
kind of remedy book spell I'd inadvertently unleashed, it wasn't a very
practical force. The ground beneath our feet was rocky and hard when
we left the sidewalk to find a place to plant the flower. We wouldn't be
able to turn the soil with our hands.

"He'll have one," Lu said. She paused as a familiar Jeep pulled up
to the sidewalk. "Maybe I'm not the only one who was thinking about

you last night." More laughter and this time it flashed in her eyes like leftover electricity from the storm.

Jacob Walker got out of his Jeep and stood on the curb. If he had pulled a trowel from his back pocket, I wouldn't have been surprised. But he looked as clueless as I had been moments before when I'd felt like I was seeing the barren park for the first time. It was Lu who shouted a hello and asked him if he had a shovel we could use.

He did more than let us use his shovel. He dug the hole. No one walked by. This part of town was quiet at this time of day. I thought I saw a curtain sway in the mayor's house, but if it did it fell back into place without a sound. Once the hole was dug, Lu helped me pull the bergamot plant from its temporary container, but then I stepped away with the plant in my hands. I had killed the bees. I was the one who needed to place the bee balm into the ground. I'd been working with Granny long enough to know how to arrange the roots and cover them loosely with a soft layer of dirt. My fingers were pale against the brown soil. I burrowed them into the earth for several seconds. I emptied my mind of everything except goodwill toward the bees and regret for any part I'd played in their deaths.

And gratitude.

That emotion was a surprise. But I'd been glad we'd driven the Sect man away from Sadie and the apiary. No sense in pretending otherwise. I was grateful for the bees' sacrifice. There was no humming in my ears. I didn't feel anything but the dirt between my fingers. I had no idea if what we were doing mattered at all. But the gratitude felt like as much of a revelation as the illuminated words had felt the night before. Less dramatic, but no less impactful.

"I have some water in the Jeep," Walker said. He left to retrieve it and Lu reached down to help me up. I dusted my hands off on my jeans, trying to ignore the looks Lu was cutting between me and the biologist in the distance.

"Seems to show up often when you're around," she noted. I glanced away because I was not going to watch him coming back to us with the bottle of water even if his easy strides could have been considered watchable.

"It's a small town," I said. "Besides, you showed up too."

"But my arrival didn't make you all hushed and hesitant like a deer in the headlights," Lu noted.

I didn't know how to deal with the instant attraction I'd felt for the biologist or the continuing awareness between us. That Lu noticed my discomfort wasn't a surprise, but it did make me even more determined to hide it.

When Walker reached us and stretched out his hand toward me to offer a large water bottle still three-quarters full, I forced myself to take it from him without hesitation. As I did, I noticed a small tattoo on the underside of his wrist I hadn't seen before. It was a tiny tree. Not so unusual for a biologist, I guess.

"Thanks," I said. And I meant it, discomfort or not. I unscrewed the cap and poured the water around the plant. Water. Bergamot. Offering. "Come and get it."

There were no bees in sight, but it was done. My chest was no longer constricted. I breathed a sigh of release.

"Well. If that's it, I need to get back to the shop," Lu said. She shoved her hands in her pocket, acting like she was no longer certain why she'd come to find me at the park with a plant she'd been compelled to dig up at midnight.

"I was headed out when I saw you. I guess I'll get back to work as well," Walker said.

I thanked them both again, but we were all suddenly awkward and out of place. Like three adults who had found themselves throwing a penny in a wishing well in broad daylight. They left me there, alone, staring at the bee balm as if it held answers for me in the network of fine veins sketched across each green leaf.

Walker hadn't said why he had stopped or why he had decided to help us. Like Lu had said, he showed up too often for coincidence to explain it. She'd been teasing about him thinking about me before, but I wondered if he *had* been gripped by the same compulsions that had hit Lu and I last night. Something was nibbling at my perceptions. I was drawn to Lu. I was drawn to Walker. I'd blamed it on chemistry with the biologist, but now I wasn't so sure that completely explained it.

Connection. Community.

I'd grown up with Sarah. We'd been together for years, but it was hard to imagine her abilities rubbing off on me. Sarah was special. People sensed it the second they met her. Like she was dancing to music no one else could hear.

But, in Morgan's Gap, I found myself straining my ears, listening for the tune Sarah used to know.

Lu and Walker had been gone awhile when an itch between my shoulder blades made me look around. The curtains in the mayor's house were still. There were no cars on the street. No people on the sidewalk. But a strange awareness prickled along my skin. I squinted at the edges of distant buildings and trees, but I saw no movement. The sun glared on the glass of the windows, near and far, so I couldn't tell if anyone was looking at me. I hadn't seen any Sect women following me that morning, but it had taken only a couple instances of their creeping to make me feel like I was being watched all the time.

If I was being watched, what would someone think about us

planting a lone bergamot in the rocky earth of a practically abandoned park? There were some folks in Morgan's Gap who wouldn't find us coming together to complete a bee-apology ritual strange at all. But there were others, like Reverend Moon, who would probably find our actions offensive.

The whole town around me seemed deserted. No matter how I strained to detect any hint of a watcher, I didn't see a scurry of skirts anywhere that would have betrayed a spy's rush to report what she'd seen.

Ten

As the end of June approached, I was able to match many names with faces. My deliveries had been Granny's way of introducing me to the town and the town to me. Most of the time now I was comfortable with our usual customers and I made my way to Becky's beauty salon, Lu's music shop, and even Joyce's perfect picket fence with no problem.

Occasionally, if I took a shortcut between streets or if I visited the flourishing bee balm too late in the evening, the sunny, bustling atmosphere would dissipate. Sleepy secrets rose up in those times. I would stop and peer and all too often a homespun figure would be lurking in the distance, roughening the shadows.

I could never be certain they were following me. They were always too far away to identify as the man in the sedan or the woman in the woods near the dandelion field. But I knew they were Sect and the Sect as a whole didn't smile my way.

The constant watch frayed my nerves, but I refused to let it wear me down.

Today, I had a special delivery of rheumatism ointment for a friend of May's. Next week was the Fourth of July and many people had driven to Rivers Crossing, the larger town down in the valley, for fireworks. Morgan's Gap was nearly deserted as I walked to May's house. I passed the firehouse swathed in patriotic bunting and a couple of families out for evening strolls with young children who were content to wave sparklers in the gloaming. A humane society volunteer I often saw around town waved from across the street as she tried to tug a dog almost as big as she was after her three young sons before they disappeared around the corner. She was always with a different dog, usually named after country music stars. Plus she'd named her children rhyming names which made remembering who was who tricky even if they'd ever stood still. I was relieved they were on the opposite side of the street so I was off the hook.

But once the harried mother and her boys disappeared, the sidewalks were empty. The street was quiet. I couldn't help checking the edges of buildings and trees for Sect kerchiefs and skirts, for wide-brimmed hats and homespun fabric.

I saw no one following me, but that didn't mean they weren't there.

Lu's grandmother lived in a shotgun bungalow that Lu had renovated when it was no longer possible for May to live in the old family farmhouse outside of town. A cousin with two children and one on the way had been happy to move to the farmhouse so it wouldn't be abandoned. May's friend, Charles, had lived with her for twenty years and he'd moved to town with her. They were an iconic couple, beloved by everyone, in spite of May's unconventional decision not to remarry no matter how often Charles proposed.

I loved visiting the bungalow. The craftsman-style porch had two rocking chairs that sat like thrones on either side of the often-open front door and extra ladder-back chairs stacked in the corners for company. Charles had filled the yard with the birdhouses he built, so there was always a chorus of songbirds flitting in and out, raising their broods, squabbling over seeds and otherwise filling the place with a flutter of wings.

"Well, now, I am glad to see you," Charles said from the open door of the garage that sat beside the house. The garage was older than the man who used it for his woodworking supplies. I thought maybe it had been a carriage house at one time. The two broad doors had upper and lower halves as if they could have been opened for a horse's head to poke out before cars became the norm. Charles had a cobbler's bench he sat on to put his birdhouses together. He was on one end of it now. A half-constructed house was on the other. I was always fascinated by the intricate houses he built, each one a replica of a house or a shop in town.

"Don't get up," I scolded as the man with obviously stiff joints tried to rise. "I'll come to you."

"Move it or lose it," Charles replied, standing. But I knew he stood because I was a woman and that's what a gentleman of his age did to be polite. As always, he was dressed in one of what he called his "walking suits": a steamed and pressed blazer and pants paired with a starched white shirt. There was only one dry cleaner in town and Charles was probably their best customer. He was also at the barber shop across from the hardware store every other Friday at ten on the dot when the Black barber from Rivers Crossing came to Morgan's Gap for his clientele. Charles's perfectly clipped hair was all salt, no pepper, showing off the barber's expertise in sharp edges around his face. He smiled at me because he knew what I was thinking. Mischievous man. No wonder May loved him. Everyone in town, including a newcomer like me, was on his side in the Great Marry Me Conspiracy.

I hadn't needed the bike or basket today. I'd carried the bottle of ointment in hand. May had called Granny asking for a stronger batch and I had been the one to stir it up this morning because Granny was feeling tired.

"This has a very medicinal scent, but it should help," I said. Charles took the bottle I offered. "Can May help you reach your shoulder blades?" I asked.

"No. But Jacob can help me with that," Charles said.

As if he'd been conjured by name, Jacob Walker came down the staircase at the back of the garage. He was dressed for hiking with his usual backpack slung across one shoulder. The sun had already disappeared over the horizon. The sky was darkening by the second. How often did he go on night hikes? And were ginseng poachers dangerous? A twinge tightened my jaw, but Walker's safety really wasn't my concern, was it?

"The least I can do because they refuse to charge me for the bed upstairs," Walker said.

Just then, May and Lu came out on the porch and saved me from any awkwardness caused by my concern and Walker's sudden appearance where I least expected him. Never mind that I should be getting used to his sudden appearances by now. And to my reaction to him.

"Jacob helped Charles with Granny's birdhouse too. He wanted to finish it in exchange for the ointment, but his shoulders have been bothering him and slowing him down," Lu said.

"As if Granny wouldn't have been happy to wait another week or two for that house," May said as she sat in a rocking chair. Lu came down the front stairs to join us and I cut my eyes from her to Walker to let it be known that I wasn't happy about not being warned.

"May offered Jacob the room for whenever he's not out in the woods. There's a bed and bath up there. Not much. But better than a cold mountain stream," Lu explained. Her eyes were sparking. I tried to ignore the knowing quirk of her smile.

"And while I like streams, cold or not, I am deeply appreciative of that soft bunk," Walker added.

Bunks, baths and sore muscle massages weren't really topics I was comfortable with around the handsome biologist. But Lu's eyes were twinkling and I refused to blush under her teasing. Not to mention Walker's watchful glances. He seemed as surprised to see me as I was to see him and I realized that no one had informed him of the special order.

"Can you get Granny's birdhouse?" Charles asked Walker. He went to a shelf and brought back a birdhouse in the shape of Granny's Queen Anne Victorian complete with a turret and toothy gingerbread trim.

I couldn't help it. I exclaimed and stepped forward to examine the house closely even though Walker hadn't given it over to Charles. The gentlemanly artist had included every element from the tiny knob of the doorbell to a fat porcelain cat glued to the inside of the kitchen's picture window.

"All that's missing is you," Walker said softly. *Jacob.* They all called him Jacob. Suddenly, I realized I hadn't let myself think of him that way, and yet, the more formal *Walker* had taken on a familiar intimacy in my mind. Our faces were closer together than they should be. I pulled back, but not before I was lost for several seconds trying to understand what was hidden in his eyes.

After Walker left, Lu and I sat alone together in the dark on May's porch. In the distance, an occasional bottle rocket would soar high and pop, lighting up the sky. The illegal firework no doubt thrilled the teenagers who had managed to acquire them.

"You like him," I said as we rocked forward and back in a rhythm we sensed even though we could no longer see. The lights were off in the house. Charles and May had gone to bed. The stars gleamed above us because even if the entire town had been lit from stem to stern it wouldn't have given off enough light pollution to diminish the starlight. I had to admit I preferred the stars to the fireworks. Their soft twinkling had calmed the rush caused by seeing Jacob Walker.

"Just to be clear, I do not *like* like him," Lu said. "There's a harmonica player in Arkansas. Her name is Calliope Jane. On record album credits anyway. I'm her Charles. Have been asking her to move to the mountain for years. Pretty sure I'm wearing her down 'cause unlike May she has not been married before. I think I'm convincing her it could be good. That we could be good together."

In the dark, I could feel Lu's ache. Her heart. Her soul. I could feel her love for Jane and how good they *would* be as a married couple on the mountain. My eyes burned a little. I'd like to see a Jane have a happy ending. It was too dark for anyone to see. Except I knew that Lu felt my emotion as I felt hers.

"He's been good to May and Charles since he came. He doesn't sleep here often. He's in the woods a lot. But you saw how that ointment relieved Charles's pain. And Jacob insisted on helping him apply it before he left," Lu said.

"You trust him with May and Charles," I said. It wasn't a question. I could hear it in her voice. The ease. The comfort.

"And I trust him with you," Lu added. "Jane is my heart, but you're in my bones. And I think Jacob could be there too. With time. Something whispering inside me says it's all up to you. But whenever we're all together those whispers are loud, Mel. It's been the music for me forever. I'm not much on gardening or stirring up recipes. But May's always said there's magic in the music. If that's so, then there's magic in me."

"No doubt of that," I said. I knew Lu was magic. I'd known as long as Sarah had known because Sarah's knowledge was in me. "It's Walker I'm not certain about."

"*Walker.* Huh. So it's like that, is it? That's just your nerves talking. In my experience, there's always one who does the asking and one who has to deliberate. Just don't deliberate too long."

I made a noncommittal noise in the dark.

"I haven't been drinking Granny's valerian tea," I said to change the subject. "I've still been dreaming Sarah's memories. I think there are things she knew that I need to know too."

Lu had stopped rocking. I felt her stillness beside me.

"You're going to wear yourself out," she said. "You're tough. I'll give you that. But even you need sleep. Have you told Granny?"

"I don't want to worry her any more than I already do," I said. "I'll be careful, but I'm sure this is what I need to do."

"Stubborn," Lu replied, but her rocking had resumed. She wasn't wrong. And I couldn't help feeling it was good to be known so well again, warts and all.

I'd enjoyed my time with Lu too much and I'd waited too long to head home. It had been hours since the last firework had lit the sky and no cars had passed May's house in a long time. The town had only a few streetlights, so Lu loaned me a flashlight. It wasn't far from May's bungalow to Granny's house. I carefully carried the birdhouse under one arm and aimed the beam of light on the sidewalk. I'd traveled less than a block before I noticed the tall, lean silhouette of a hatted man following me. He kept his distance, but he didn't skulk or hide. His strides were lazy and slow, his long legs easily keeping up with my paces, which increased in rapidness the farther I traveled from Lu.

My phone was in my pocket. I could have called Lu. I could have called Granny. But I didn't want to worry either one of them. And I most definitely didn't want the man behind me to know he had scared me.

He had.

And I was certain the distinctive figure following in my footsteps was Reverend Moon.

He had a gangly way of walking, his long arms thrown out in front of him, then falling back behind. His boots scraping on the ground. Swoosh. *Scraaaaape.* Swoosh. *Scraaaape.* His swinging arms combined with the length of his legs created a spidery gait, made even more disjointed by shadows thrown oddly from widely spaced streetlamps.

I didn't run.

I forced myself to walk as normally as I could.

I passed the fire station. In the dark, its bunting was less festive. I knew there were volunteers who would rush to the station at a moment's notice from all over Morgan's Gap. There was a single hook and ladder truck housed in the station that they took great pride in keeping polished and prepared.

But the station was deserted and quiet now. No one was nearby to help me.

Moon was worse than all my other Sect stalkers combined. Because we were all alone in the dark heart of the night surrounded by a sleeping town. How long had he waited for me to leave May's? Had he listened to Lu and me share our secrets on the porch? I hated the idea of him listening to her talk about her Calliope Jane. I hadn't yet met the harmonica player, but if Lu loved her then I loved her, and I didn't want Moon anywhere near either one of them.

My flashlight threw a meager halo in front of my shoes. I longed for the families with sparkler-waving children I'd seen earlier in the evening. At the edges of my consciousness, I thought I could almost sense Lu settling down for the night and Walker threading his way into the nighttime wildwood. But that was wishful thinking. I wasn't Sarah. I wasn't special in any way. I didn't really believe in a mystical connection between the three of us. I was alone. If Moon tried to do anything other than intimidate me, I would have to handle it myself.

I tightened my grip on the flashlight. It was nothing but plastic beneath my fingers, its housing flimsy and light. Not a weapon by any stretch of the imagination.

Finally, Granny's house was in sight. I experienced a rush of relief until I glanced back and realized that Moon had closed the distance between us. For a second, he was perfectly illuminated by a neighbor's porch light and his gaunt face was contorted into a grimace of such fury that I almost dropped my flashlight. His expression didn't match his eerily graceful insectile movements. Had he gotten angrier as I hadn't acted afraid? I hurried then. Toward Granny's house. Toward a door I could slam and lock against the hatred that seemed determined to hunt me down.

I thought Moon would stop. Surely he would stop. At the corner. Across the street. At the curb. At her front stoop. When I finally made it to the door, I didn't look around. I imagined him at my heels, his spidery arms reaching to grab me from behind. I fumbled one-handed with the knob and as the door opened I dropped the flashlight. I didn't take the time to retrieve it. I rushed in and closed the door behind me. The flashlight rolled, its beam of light making crazy flashes across the front windows. Then, it stopped. Perhaps it had come against a rail or a flowerpot. Or maybe Moon had followed me all the way up onto Granny's stoop. It was easy to imagine the rolling flashlight had come up against his booted foot.

As I locked the door, I could have sworn I sensed Moon's presence.

We stood there, me on one side of the door and him on the other, for a long time. This wasn't a face-off. I knew that I wasn't the one keeping him at bay. This was Granny's house. She would wake up. She would come downstairs and send him away. He was waiting for that.

But if he was, he waited for a banishment that never came.

Granny had been more and more tired lately. She'd been sleeping in and looking worn.

I don't know how long I had stood there, but eventually I forced myself to place the birdhouse on the entryway table. I made myself walk away from the door. I went to the front room and moved the curtain aside, slightly, carefully.

The flashlight's beam had dimmed, but I could see the front porch was empty. If Moon had actually been there, he was gone.

Jacob left his Jeep hidden behind a copse of mountain laurel. There hadn't been any fireworks in the distance for some time. Even the teenagers with illegal rockets had gone to bed. He'd often used the natural tunnels created by the winding branches of laurel to make his way into the wildwood, undetected by man or beast. Tonight, he did the same. Crouching down, crawling at times, silently progressing toward the interior of the woods. The ground beneath his feet was worn smooth by the padded paws of bears. They also liked the cover of the laurel tunnels, so he kept a keen ear alert for any hint of shuffling, snuffing sounds that might indicate he wasn't alone.

Intent on his mission, he was taken by surprise when a sudden overwhelming urge to backtrack, jump in the Jeep and head back to town claimed him. The need to go back was so strong as he exited the mountain laurel thicket he had to grab handfuls of the leathery leaves on either side of the "tunnel" opening to stop himself.

Several deep breaths later the compulsion was gone as if it had never been.

Jacob was a man who trusted his instincts. Without letting go of the mountain laurel leaves, he dropped his head back, loosened his focus for a few minutes and opened himself up to whatever his intuition might have to tell him. Stars winked above him. The forest was silent around him. The earth was solid beneath him.

And whatever had caused the urge to go back to town was definitely gone.

But the problem of Mel Smith was still very much on his mind. When he'd left her and Lu, they'd been watching the stars come out from rocking chair perches on May's front porch. Lu Rey was downright sneaky with her interrogation technique. She'd used the dark front porch and the mesmerizing movements of those chairs on him once or twice since he'd been back in Morgan's Gap. Just imagining her and Mel having a heart-to-heart made a nervous sweat break out beneath the curls on his forehead. He'd managed to come out of those conversations with Lu with his secrets intact. Would Mel be able to do the same? And why couldn't he tamp down the thrill that maybe, just maybe, one of her secrets was how she thought about him?

He had a job to do. And it didn't include making Mel smile. The need to do that was entirely personal. In the pitch black of the wildwood, broken by only the familiar mating dance of lightning bugs all around him, he could admit that he was already addicted to the way she'd freeze, and her hazel eyes would go wide and her lips would curl. When she was caught off guard, she would warm—for him— for those few surprised seconds. Her mouth plumped and softened like a mirage. Eyelashes came out of nowhere. Then, her face would stiffen as if she'd remembered the world and everyone in it wasn't to be trusted.

He was a professional. He wasn't here to make friends. But it had happened. Charles was definitely a friend now. So was Lu. He hadn't told her much during their porch conversations; he wasn't free to converse, but he had listened to all of her stories and many of her songs. They'd shared an easy camaraderie that might survive the summer.

Mel was different.

They couldn't form an easy friendship on a foundation of lies. She was too damaged and he was too driven. There wasn't any room in their lives for connection. And yet, addiction didn't really leave a man room for common sense. That curl of her lip. Those startled eyes.

Most of all, his stupid ego. He wanted her to know him. Really know him. And he wanted to get to know her, damage and all.

And that wasn't okay.

He had grim work ahead of him. There was no time for anything else. He only wished the instincts he'd always trusted didn't place Mel Smith's face in his mind every time he tried to listen to them.

Eleven

*S*trangers *might have seen* the trio converge on Granny's house with baskets and bags full of ordinary things only to think they had been invited to tea or a sewing circle that Monday morning.

Sadie would have chuckled if the situation was less dire. Her lover, Kara, had an aversion to needles, and their best friend, Joyce, would surely bring a bottle of her famous dandelion wine. Most folks from Morgan's Gap would be familiar with the odd comings and goings of the only active trio since 1973. They'd know something was going on besides steeping and stitches when they saw the three of them gather. Especially at Granny's house. Wasn't a soul in the county who didn't know about Granny, and most had been helped by her at one time or another.

Sadie parked her red truck on the street, leaving Granny's driveway open for Kara's van. She grabbed the gallon jar of dried beans that had ridden shotgun beside her and carried it, cradled in her arms, toward the house.

"Not like a baby shower, is it?" said Kara. She lifted a basket from the back of her van and Sadie couldn't help but smile even though her earlier chuckle had died before it could bubble up from her chest. She'd given Kara the basket at least ten years ago and in spite of constant use it was still beautiful and strong. Fitting for the strong, beautiful woman who used it.

The trio was often called in "for luck" at showers. Both for babies and for weddings. They were invited for blessings at birthdays. And for housewarmings and graduations. Some saw it as harmless mountain tradition, and besides, a wisewoman or three lent gravitas to important occasions. But some folks were superstitious enough to feel some truth in their little rituals and in the singsong poetry that often accompanied them.

"It's all serious business. We'd best not forget that," Joyce said. She'd pulled her newish sedan in behind Kara's van and they'd waited for her so they could go in together.

"She didn't sound good, did she?" Sadie asked.

They had promised to help. And they would. To the best of their abilities. But an ailing Granny didn't bode well. Kara reached for Sadie's arm on one side and Joyce did the same on the other. They would cross the threshold in one stride. They fell silent while the entry was accomplished. One stride. One intent. Together.

For luck.

To bless.

To grow.

And this time to heal.

"And the bees seem more industrious than ever," Sadie said as she took her turn washing her hands in the bowl of herb-infused water Joyce had prepared. Granny was worse off than they'd expected. She was already in bed when they arrived and the house had been chilled—nothing baking, nothing steaming to welcome them in.

After they cleansed their hands, Joyce pulled a dark green glass bottle of the expected wine from a grocery sack dotted with a cheerful ladybug print. She uncorked the top with practiced ease and poured them all a juice glass of wine. They drank to fortify their nerves. A slightly bitter, slightly alcoholic brew, the wine tasted like summers past—grassy and fresh.

"Mel was embarrassed. Not accustomed to asking for help," Granny said from her place on the bed. She'd declined her portion of wine, which immediately made them all look at each other as they quickly drained their own glasses. "But she has the remedy book. All the help she needs can be found there."

"So many dead bees," Sadie said. Her throat tightened. When she closed her eyes, she could still see the piles of writhing bodies on the grass. "But I think she felt their sacrifice."

Kara stopped her own preparations to softly grip Sadie's shoulder in support. They'd grown up together. Ever so slowly and naturally becoming more than friends when they hit their thirties and realized the reason they'd never married and started families with anyone else. Joyce had known long before they had that they were a couple within the trio. She'd been giddy when they had shyly made it official.

"There's great strength in her. Tremendous potential. But so much anger and pain. Sarah got through to her. But now that Sarah's gone it's up to her to reach out. To want to connect," Granny said.

"You're expecting a lot from the girl. To bring us all together when she's been determined to be on her own her whole life," Joyce said.

Sadie blinked. Joyce's mistake had instantly dried her eyes. Mel was a tough young woman but Sadie had seen the hidden hunger buried deep in her eyes. She was lonely. She trusted no one. But she longed to be able to. Her rapid connection with the bees proved it.

"She doesn't want to be alone. She just doesn't know how to be together," Sadie corrected.

Granny nodded. "She cared for Sarah but she didn't know how to accept care in return."

"And you've worn yourself out trying to reach her," Kara guessed.

"We can't do this without her," Sadie said.

Kara and Joyce already suspected her concerns. She could feel their worry. But, in spite of the connection they shared in their minds, she needed to finally voice them aloud.

Promise or not, they were only aging aunts more used to blessing babies than fighting murderers and corruption. They were more tapped into the energy of the wildwood than anyone, but even she hadn't been able to save the bees. That, more than anything, made her worry about what Granny was attempting to do. It was one thing to wish a newborn well and nudge a little success and happiness their way. But the Sect community had been a kingdom unto themselves for so long with Reverend Moon as their dark prince. How could a wisewoman's stirrings and whisperings really change that?

"We aren't alone. Even without Mel, we aren't alone," Granny corrected.

"But there's still time for her to come around."

For weeks, I'd found Granny in the kitchen when I returned from deliveries. Today, she wasn't there. Then again, I returned later than usual these days because I always made a detour by the park. At first, it was to bring water to the bee balm, but after finding it flourishing and the soil damp, I returned out of curiosity. This morning, I'd finally caught someone watering the plant and I was still pondering the discovery. He hadn't seen me. I'd kept far enough back behind the crooked lichen-covered trees to avoid his notice.

Walker had poured a small bucket of water around the base of the bergamot and then he'd crouched down to sit on his heels. I couldn't tell if he said anything. I could only watch as he reached out to touch one blossom after another with gentle hands. *Jacob.* I held my breath. All the way across the park, it was as if I felt the petals that trembled after he brushed them with his fingers. After a few moments, he rose and walked away. I had waited until he disappeared around a corner before visiting the plant myself. It had obviously taken root. And a fat bumblebee had even landed on a vivid red flower while I was there.

Caring for the bee balm he'd helped me plant was such a simple gesture, but it threatened to make me feel even warmer toward the man. His care. His concern. The tattoo of the tree I'd glimpsed so like the one on the cover of the remedy book. He'd been at the apiary. Maybe he understood a little bit of why I'd needed to apologize to the bees.

After that, the entire park had seemed greener. The grass less patchy. Even the poor trees had seemed less stunted than before.

When I returned to find Granny mysteriously out of the kitchen, her cat was on the counter, but even his usual the-world-owes-me-more-than-kibble manner seemed rattled. His tail twitched aggressively and an aura of floating hair showed all around his body as if his un-settled demeanor had caused him to shed more than his regular copi-ous amounts. I'd recognized Sadie's truck parked outside, along with Joyce's sedan and a van I wasn't familiar with.

"What's up, Cookie Cat?" I asked. Turns out, Granny never called him by name. In fact, she'd changed the subject whenever I brought it up. So rather than trying to play Rumpelstiltskin I'd opted for CC. He didn't seem to mind any more than he minded anything and every-thing else. I sat the nearly empty delivery basket on the counter beside the huge disgruntled tabby, but before I could risk life and limb to soothe him with a pet, he jumped down and fled the room. Since he usually dodged my attention by hiding behind Granny, I assumed he'd gone to find her.

"Where has she gone off to, then?" I grumbled. The old cat had seemed to settle around me recently. His rejection stung even though I'd never admit it.

But then CC's head poked around the corner of the door he'd used for his rapid exit with a yowl that startled me. I always saved Lu's shop for my last stop so I could linger and visit awhile. I wasn't prepared to transition from music and laughter to whatever was going on in the oddly silent kitchen that had obviously disturbed the cat so much he was complaining to me about it.

"Traumatized by a cold stove?" I joked, but it was the most natural thing in the world to leave the kitchen and follow the cat as if he knew where I needed to be better than I knew myself.

The kitchen wasn't the only room in the house that was silent and chilly. When I'd left that morning with a basketful of tea, tisanes, balms and powders, Granny had been in the pantry. We had barely spoken, as was our early a.m. routine. But now the emptiness of her kitchen radi-ated outward until the whole Queen Anne seemed lifeless and dull.

CC's feet were the only sound and he padded them lightly as if he tiptoed up the cherrywood staircase on purpose, whisper soft. I fol-lowed his lead, placing my feet quietly, the whole time straining my ears trying to hear evidence of what the old wisewoman was up to.

We ended up at Granny's bedroom door where we didn't surprise several visitors who acted as if our arrival was expected. Cookie Cat sashayed into the room and jumped up on the bed to lie on a crocheted throw beside Granny's pillows. I stopped at the doorway, blinking. My hostess was bundled under a colorful patchwork quilt. Her face was starkly pale against the quilt's bright floral pattern, created by thousands of hand-stitched cotton pieces.

"You've met Sadie and Joyce. This is another friend of mine. And yours too, of course. Kara...this is my Mel," Granny said. I'd seen Kara before. Morgan's Gap was a small town and I was already accustomed to many of its faces even if I didn't know them by name. Unlike Sadie, Kara wore dramatic makeup and her hair was a wild shock of bottle red. But it was her clothing that most drew the eye. Kara loved what Sarah had called "hand work." Crocheted vests, patchwork skirts, knitted caps—even in the summer. She always made me smile whenever I saw her unconventional look on the street.

"Everything is going to be fine," Joyce said. She was placing a black lacquered tray decorated with a Japanese pagoda and vivid cherry blossoms across Granny's lap. On the tray was a china cup filled with steaming liquid and a plate of dark brown, buttered bread.

"What happened? What's wrong?" I stepped over the threshold with every intention of claiming a place among the strange group. Granny and I hadn't spoken much since I'd messed up with the bees. I hadn't explained to her that I was planning to stay with her. At least until next semester. Every time I thought to bring it up, she had looked too tired for conversation.

I knew I'd failed some kind of unspoken test at the apiary. I didn't think my apology at the park negated that.

Granny was propped up to access her snack, but she was obviously weak. I'd known she was old, but this was the first time she seemed ancient. She carefully picked up the cup with both hands and sipped the slightly green liquid, and as she swallowed the lines on her face stood out in sharp shadows against her pallor like chiseled clay.

Sadie was arranging a kaleidoscope of dried beans on the top of an antique bureau while she murmured inaudibly under her breath. Her black skinny slacks and gray flyaway sweater were too businesslike for the giant mason jar in her arms that held the multicolor beans she fished out one by one for her seemingly inane task. She wore tiny studs in her ears that turned out to be glass honeybees when I looked closer. I thought about her entire body covered in pulsing bees and shivered. The pattern she created from the beans reminded me of the mandalas I'd seen on silken scarves sold by sidewalk vendors in Richmond.

Kara wore an outfit like the women who sold those scarves along-side handmade jewelry or artisanal soap from colorful pop-up stalls at weekend flea markets. Her skirt was tie-dyed and voluminous, swirling around her bare ankles in a riot of blues and purples and greens. Her top was a chunky sweater knitted with what seemed to be leftover skeins of yarn of every shade. She was adding more dried herbs to a smoking porcelain bowl by crumbling them in her fingers. Gems set in silver rings on every finger sparkled as a pungent, but not unpleasant, aroma filled the room.

"No, dear. Three for the task is all I need.

"Three to strengthen.

"Three to recharge.

"Three to protect," Granny said. She'd swallowed all but the dregs in her cup and Joyce accepted it when Granny gave it to her. She didn't set it aside. Instead, she looked at the stuff left in the bottom of the cup and tsked like she'd seen something worrisome.

Three. Three. Three. The number echoed in my mind like something I should note, but then I was distracted from the echo by something else Granny had said. Protect?

"What's happened?" I asked again. My question came out as a croak. Not cool, but until now I hadn't realized how much of my guard I'd lowered with Granny since I'd come to town. I stood nervously several feet away from the sick woman, pretty sure I should turn around and run away instead of experiencing the concern that was constricting my throat.

"She expended too much energy to call you h—" Kara said.

"*Here*. To call you *here*," Sadie interjected. She flicked her eyes at Kara and then away too quickly for me to interpret the silent communication that seemed to pass between them with the glance.

"I came because Sarah told me to. Before she died," I corrected.

Sadie turned from her finished bean art with an empty mason jar in her hands. She'd taken thousands of dried beans from the jar to create the pattern on the bureau near the bed where Granny lay. I followed the beans around and around until I grew dizzy. I had to look away or risk being sick on the bedroom floor.

"One of the reasons," Kara nodded. "Our lives are nudged by millions of choices every day. Coffee or tea? A coat or a sweater? One lump or two?"

"Some of us learn to nudge the nudges," Sadie said.

"You took more than a nudge. And that kind of a shove doesn't come cheap," Granny said. She laughed with a sudden hoarse bark that shook her shoulders and rattled in her chest.

"Maybe you should see a real doctor," I said. I stepped toward the bed, but Joyce gracefully rose from the chair beside the bed and met me halfway.

"Instructing a novice at her age has taken a lot out of her these last few weeks. She needs to detach and rest," Joyce said. "Before we all come together for Gathering at the end of the summer."

She still looked like a Sunday school teacher, but one with a little "dancing in the pale moonlight" behind her gentle blue eyes.

"Gathering?" I asked. I stayed where I was. Who was I to challenge the edict of these older women? Guilt gnawed at my stomach at the very idea I was the one to blame for Granny's illness. I'd failed to protect Sarah. I'd failed the bees. And it turned out my epic stubbornness might be hurting Granny too.

"To celebrate the end of summer and the final harvest before the fallow time of winter. We gather. All of us on the mountain and from the mountain," Sadie said.

Granny nibbled on the bread from her tray. "This year you'll feed the yeast in the wildwood before we bake the bread," Granny said. The other three suddenly looked at the woman lying on the bed as if she'd surprised them. "This is the rye from last year. We commune with the baking and the breaking of the bread at Gathering. And some loaves are taken home by each of us. It helps keep us connected to the wildwood and each other." Her eyes were unfocused as if she was remembering a hundred years of Gathering in days long past.

"Fresh is best. We can help her now, but Gathering will be what she most needs. To commune with the wildwood is the best way to recharge," Joyce explained.

"It's time. Time for you to move to the Ross cabin. I've done all I can do for you here. I would have liked more time to prepare you for the end of summer, but..." Granny sighed and closed her eyes. The three other women in the room trained their eyes on me and I suddenly had to look away from their intense curiosity. They must see me as an interloper. A newcomer who didn't even fully believe in the wisdom they practiced.

Wisewomen.

Witches.

I'd been happy to help Granny. To dabble in recipes and remedies. The days and weeks had passed, but I'd barely begun to scratch the surface of this town's secrets, and suddenly I was faced with a much more serious choice than I'd expected. Was I going to take this as deep as it seemed to be leading me? Just when I'd decided to stay with Granny, I was to be sent away, deeper into the wildwood and its strangeness, all alone.

"It would have been sacrilege. The way your friend's mother was killed. The murderer didn't only take her life. He or she tainted the locust tree…"

I hadn't mentioned the Sect women following me after I'd confronted Moon on the street. I hadn't told anyone about the Sect man almost running me down. Morgan's Gap seemed warm around me. Wrapped in the hug of small-town ways, my occasional nervousness had been easier to shrug off.

But then Moon had followed me home.

My heart thumped in my chest and the cool wash of adrenaline flowed beneath my skin. I was being sent into the wildwood where the Ross women lay sleeping, marked by the twisted, twining roots of black locust trees. I could hear the cree-cree of the straining rope that had held Sarah's mother's body. Another Melody. Dead and gone. Murdered.

There was death and danger in the wildwood.

There was also life.

Which way was I being nudged to go?

Twelve

T *he days were already* shorter. The leaves had the slightest hint of drying around the edges, but it was enough to cast a golden-brown hue over the entire forest as if a determined army of fairy decorators were manically gilding everything before autumn could take away their palette. In Richmond, I'd barely noticed the seasons, especially since Virginia seemed to have only two—a long drawn-out summer that was by turns mild to blazing hot and a winter that hit hard and fast and was unrelenting for two to three weeks around the first of the year.

But on the mountain autumn approached with a tangible taste in the air. The higher elevation and the abundance of trees was part of that flavor. Summer was mossy and verdant and sweet. Fall was ripe and lush and slightly bitter like a strong cup of espresso left out in the night until it settled and chilled to a thicker, darker brew. You could see autumn coming in the lengthening shadows and the shortening of midday, which gave rise to an age-old instinct to gather in and huddle close against the encroaching darkness.

My move to the Ross cabin got a later start than I'd intended because I'd wanted to complete one more delivery for Granny before my rounds became a weekly rather than a daily routine. Those lengthening shadows greeted me when I pulled up to the house and I second-guessed my decision to follow Granny's instructions. Of course, Sadie, Kara and Joyce wouldn't have listened to any argument. Their love for Granny ran true and deep. Her word was law. And they were a force to be seen when deployed on her behalf.

I was here.

The ancient minivan I'd borrowed from Kara was packed with supplies.

I tried not to think of Reverend Moon stalking after me on a shadowy street. Or how easy it would be for the Sect to find me way out here all alone. I refused to be scared away. I'd thrown a Louisville Slugger I'd found in Granny's umbrella rack in the back of the van with the rest of my things. I'd borrowed it without compunction because (1) I would absolutely use it, and (2) in Granny's houseful of oddities, she'd never notice it wasn't around.

I exited the van. The sound of wind rustling the drying leaves was my welcome. The forest sighed with wafts of musty leaf decay that also heralded fall. But it was rich and pleasant. I breathed in the scent of the wildwood, thinking of Sarah and Granny and, yes, the biologist. This was Jacob's wildwood too. Jacob of the mossy eyes and mysterious intensity.

I retrieved an overnight bag from the backseat and picked up a box of kitchen essentials. I'd left my laptop in town. My phone barely worked this far out. Internet would be impossible without a satellite provider. Melody Ross must have seen no need to be online. Even without the laptop, I would have to make numerous trips to haul everything Granny had sent with me inside—blankets, sheets, towels and more.

The elderly woman had obviously never lived out of a backpack. I had closed out the apartment in Richmond with a couple of phone calls. What clothes and keepsakes I hadn't been able to part with had fit in a few bags and boxes that now sat in a closet at Granny's house.

Granny had also packed me a tin of her valerian tea. I set it on the counter with no intention of brewing it. If dreams came, so be it. I needed to be open to whatever clues Sarah's memories revealed about what had happened to her mother.

Eventually, if I was going to live this far out, I was going to have to buy a car of my own. Kara and Joyce were going to come and pick up the van tomorrow. I hated I'd had to inconvenience them as much as I had. I wouldn't need much cash, but as a barista I hadn't been able to put a lot of money aside. My savings would be depleted sooner rather than later. A cheap car. A very cheap car.

That would be a problem for another day.

For now, I carefully climbed the creaky front steps and tried to ignore the sound of the porch swing's chains. I balanced the box on one bent knee to fish the key to the cabin's front door from my jeans pocket.

A flurry of faded brochures and pamphlets fell when I opened the screen door. They'd been left sandwiched between the screen and the glass of the front door. I saw the logo of a natural gas company on several of them. And the "No Pipeline" slogan on several others. It seemed representatives from both sides had been busy visiting the community, even all the way out in places like this.

I would take my box inside and then come back to scoop up the trash.

Granny had assured me that she and her friends had kept the inside of cabin clean and tidy. I had to lean against the unused door to make it open, but I was met by the fragrance of lemon furniture polish and a trace of bleach. The air was slightly too warm and stale from being mostly undisturbed and there was that expectant feeling of a vacation home inhabited infrequently—ready, waiting.

At that, I paused.

The hair on the back of my neck stood up. I reached quickly and felt for a wall switch. Granny had said the electricity had never been turned off. Relief shamed me when an overhead light fixture with an old-fashioned amber glass globe illuminated the room. But the relief was short-lived. I had braced myself, but not enough. Of course, I knew this place from my dreams. I'd seen this living room and the kitchen beyond before. I had descended those stairs with my heart pounding in my chest.

More evidence that my connection to Sarah had been real and deep and impossible to define in ordinary ways.

My load was heavy and I wasn't backing out now.

I pushed myself forward into the great room and over to the kitchen counter where I deposited the box of supplies. The living room furniture was covered with plain white sheets. I dropped my bag to the floor and reached to uncover the couch and two armchairs. Only a little dust was disturbed and with it a stronger bleach scent from the sheets themselves. I folded them and found the hall closet after opening a closet lined with wire shelves first and a small, dated bathroom second. I guessed the closet with wire shelves was a pantry. It was closest to the kitchen and held an impressive store of canning supplies—brand-new and ready for use—empty jars, lids and rings. There was also a large pot on the floor with an interior metal basket meant for boiling the jars to sterilize and seal them.

I was supposed to find an abundance of ripe blackberries in the garden and turn them into preserves. My cottagecore duties continued, but, as usual, there was more to every seemingly simple chore than met the eye. A wisewoman's goal was to nurture the connection between man and nature. And to use the connection to help and heal her community. The bees had shaken me with how deep that connection could go. But canning blackberries I could handle. Hopefully. Granny had gone over the instructions with me several times to clarify the faded recipe in the remedy book. I had brought sugar with me along with my groceries from town.

The hall closet was empty except for a box filled with framed photographs. I shied away from those for now and forced myself to continue exploring.

Unlike in my nightmares, Sarah's mother's old room was completely empty. I was glad. It was bad enough the layout of the cabin matched my dreams. I closed the door of the empty bedroom, trying not to shiver at Sarah's memory of that morning.

It was late afternoon by now. I flipped on every light I passed. I was alone. There was no one to witness my need to keep the shadows away. But the hair on the back of my neck refused to settle and my pulse continued to race.

Facing my fears. No big. Why did it feel like playing Russian roulette? The next door or the next might prove my nightmares real. The stairs were especially chilling. Granny had told me the spare bedroom was up there. Neutral territory where I planned to sleep. But I would have to walk past Sarah's old bedroom to get there.

Ready. Waiting.

Every floorboard creak and every door sigh only contributed to my mood. The cabin was both too quiet and not quiet enough. Granny had advised me to flush the taps before use and to open the windows at night for fresh air and natural air-conditioning. There was also an oscillating fan in the van to dispel the heat that could accumulate upstairs from the tin roof.

I could have gone out to the van for the other supplies. I didn't. It would be a retreat. I knew it and refused to give in to the impulse. Sarah had been my home. And this cabin had been Sarah's. I wouldn't be afraid here. I squared my shoulders and took a deep breath to calm my racing heart. Then I took each step more firmly than the one before until by the time I reached the small landing I was walking more naturally. Only then did I blush because I'd been creeping around on tiptoe like an intruder before.

I was invited.

I was welcome.

The Ross cabin, Granny had assured me, was mine for as long as I would have it.

To my left, Sarah's bedroom door was open. Unlike her mother's room, there was still an iron bed, painted a cheerful sky blue. And hanging on the walls were dozens of paintings, crinkled and aged, the sort a young girl would create at school. A sudden, ferocious grief scalded my throat and burned my eyes. At the same time, I rushed forward to lay my hands on her creations as if I could infuse them with my life and breath and create a bridge between this living Sarah and the dead one I'd lost.

They didn't connect me with my Sarah, of course. Every poster was filled with flowers and plants and the life she'd known before her mother's murder. The Sarah I had known had been more muted and darker than the Sarah who had painted these.

My hands fell away and my eyes dried. There were no other belongings left in the room. The shelves were empty. But I still went to the bare bed and looked under the faded pillow. Somehow, I was surprised not to find the crochet mouse charm I'd held as Sarah in my dreams. Its place was empty save for a dusting of lavender. The floral dust trailed to the edge of the bed, but there was no charm on the floor.

Maybe Granny or one of her friends who had helped keep the cabin clean had taken the charm away. The missing charm made my chest feel tight, but the room bothered me less because it wasn't *my* Sarah's room. I closed the bedroom door in respect for a young girl I'd never actually known.

After that, it was easier. I found the spare bedroom on the other side of the landing. A slanted ceiling made it small, but floral wallpaper and another iron bed painted white made it cheerful enough. I opened the window and a deep woodsy scent freshened the room. It came from the wildwood path I could see directly below. In the late afternoon sun, the backyard wasn't exactly like the one from my nightmares. Butterflies stirred the blossoms they favored and peace seemed possible.

Not that I'd found peace yet. There was no Internet here. No streaming. I couldn't pop out for a bagel or a new book. It was intimidating. All I had was my own company and mundane tasks to keep me occupied. The isolation magnified my nerves. I tried not to search the surrounding woods for faces. No one would follow me here. Who would want to spy on me sweeping out a cabin or stocking the fridge? I would get used to the hush and the remote location. Eventually I would stop seeing kerchiefs in every shadow. I would replace Sarah's nightmare images with current happier ones.

Finally, after more windows were opened, my bed made, and towels hung, I put the groceries away in the harvest-gold refrigerator and pantry by the light of the setting sun...and every bulb in the house. The Ross Remedy Book sat on the counter, back in the place where its pages had once been ripped and flung. More than anything, restoring the repaired book to its rightful place helped me to settle. It looked at home, as if I'd clicked a difficult puzzle piece into position. The picture hadn't been completed yet, but the possibility of completion was within reach. Only a few more pieces to go.

Tomorrow, when the sun was high, I'd visit the garden.

Sarah had been sent to retrieve the pan. The same one had been used to feed the yeast for so long no one knew if it had been shaped to fit the crook in the old oak tree's roots or if the crook had grown to provide a perfect place for the pan after generations of Ross women had welcomed the wildwood to enrich the rye bread broken at Gathering.

Sarah's mother had added a fine-mesh screen over the customary linen cloth to discourage creatures bigger than pollen and spores and beneficial bacteria from invading the mixture, so Sarah had to dust off only a few early fallen leaves.

Her mouth was already watering at the thought of the fresh brown bread, heavy with seeded texture, and its darker crisp crust just perfect for a slathered dollop of creamy butter. She leaned to carefully pick up the bent pan, transferring it from the fitted hug of the oak's roots to her arms.

"You there, girl. Why are you skulking around that tree?"

Sarah knew the voice. She'd heard it before preaching truly scary things on Main Street—hate, separation and suffering—the sort of things that were the opposite of all she'd been taught.

"Fetching the yeast for my mother is all," Sarah answered. She tried to keep the fear from her voice because her mother had once told her Reverend Moon was drawn to fear the way raccoons were drawn to hornet larva. One whiff of that squiggling vulnerability and he'd dig and dig until he found more.

"Heathen practices. Communing with the trees and the plants as if they were your Savior," Moon hissed. He'd come out of the trees behind her,

skirting the wildwood garden rather than walking near it. The old oak was off the path in its own smaller clearing. Moon invaded it, his every step wrong in a way that made her throat tight and her hands on the yeast even tighter. Protective. He was in the wildwood, but he wasn't. He wasn't welcome or accepted. If the leaves and vines could move quickly, they would have curled away from him to avoid his blight.

Sarah lifted her chin, but she also edged toward the path that led back to the cabin and her mother. She was only ten. Old enough to be given the honor of fetching the pan. Not old enough to stand against Reverend Moon all alone.

"Better to take that pan and throw it in the fire, girl. Better it burn than your ssssoul," Moon spit when he spoke, so full of anger he shook with it and it bubbled up in spittle on his lips.

She already had a white-knuckled grip on the pan. He was a threat to the yeast, the bread, Gathering and everything their communion with the forest meant to the wisewomen from the mountain.

He'd come way closer than she liked and his body was poised as if he was going to pounce and wrestle the pan from her fingers. He was a big, bony man. At least six feet tall. And his black wide-brimmed hat made him seem even taller. It shadowed his face until his eyes looked almost like empty black holes and his teeth were gritted so she could see the filthy tobacco stains that made her shudder.

"I found the blasphemous trail that leads my flock astray. No telling how many have been drawn here by this abomination and the evil worked with these devil weeds," Moon said. He punched at the garden, gesturing with a fisted hand. To her, he was the abomination. The garden was peaceful in all of its familiar tangle. In it, she saw only help and healing not evil.

She planted her feet in the ground, digging into the undergrowth with her heels. She could tell by the fist he continued to shake this wasn't going to end with her easily walking away. Her mother had trusted her with this sacred chore for the first time and Reverend Moon wanted to ruin it.

"Take the pan to the house, Sarah. The ladies have the kitchen ready." Melody Ross came up the path like she always did. As much a part of the wildwood as the trees themselves. She left the path to come and stand beneath the old oak with Sarah and Reverend Moon, but unlike Moon her steps were comfortable and careful. She didn't hate or hurt the forest. She noticed. Every leaf. Every fern. The wildwood wouldn't curl away from her. Ever.

"I want nothing from your kind. I came to warn you. Stay away from my women. Don't taint them with your potions or poison them with your balms," Moon growled. He loomed over Sarah, still, but even though her mother wasn't much taller than she was, Moon seemed smaller than he had seemed before. His broad shoulders had rounded in on themselves and his fists looked less threatening.

Her mother reached to place her hand, palm flat, against the oak tree and she seemed to grow even taller, as if the old oak lent her its height through its rough gray bark.

"Okay, Mama," Sarah said, as if Moon hadn't spoken.

Spurred on without another glance or word, Sarah walked away. The yeast was too important to risk and she was its caretaker. She didn't run. Predators chased, and Moon was always hunting for prey. The wildwood had fallen silent. No insects whirred. No squirrel chattered. No birds sang. Even the breeze had died. She held her breath, feeling a million eyes on her, hidden in the branches and bows above and the bushes and briar patches beneath. And none so icy as the gaze of Reverend Moon drilling into her back and freezing her spine.

Suddenly, Sarah stumbled on a tendril of creeper. Her mother had taught her how to walk in the forest. She was never clumsy or awkward in the wildwood. She paused and looked nervously back over her shoulder, afraid that Moon would decide to pounce after all.

But Moon had stepped back several strides from her mother and the oak tree. He was half turned toward the way he had come.

"Take care not to get lost on your way home, Reverend. The wildwood can easily turn you around if you aren't careful. If you aren't wise to its ways," her mother said. "This ground has been sanctified by Ross women for generations. Trespass leads to misfortune."

Reverend Moon no longer had fists. His hands were limp at his sides.

But when Melody Ross began to hum he jerked backward from her as if a puppet master had pulled his strings. Sarah recognized the tune. Her mother had once told her it was ancient. Written long ago and far away. It had come across the ocean from distant lands with the first Ross who had settled in Morgan's Gap. Her mother softly sang the words to the chorus in a language few had spoken or heard. It was a lullaby of sorts. Meant to put babies, and maybe even gardens, to rest.

Reverend Moon hurried away mumbling a much clumsier rhyme that had no real faith behind it at all.

He crashed through the forest the way he'd come—twigs snapping, branches scratching, bushes scrambling.

Finally, the first bird sang, heralding his absence.

"Well, why are we dawdling? It's time to make the autumn loaves!"

Sarah was allowed to carry the pan all the way back to the cabin. An honor her mother didn't revoke because of Moon's interruption. She was glad to have her mother behind her on the path, in between her and Reverend Moon. Yet, it was the wildwood that sheltered them from Moon and others like him, a living wall they would tend forever.

Thirteen

I slept for several fitful hours before I was startled awake. I'd met an older, more horrifying Reverend Moon in person, so it wasn't the lucid dream that woke me. There was no need to reach for a light because I'd left the bedside lamp on. To read by. Or so I'd told myself. Even though the remedy book had been closed on the table long before I closed my eyes.

My whole life I'd slept through city sounds at night—sirens, car doors, neighbors shouting and stray-cat fights. Whatever had disturbed me had been strange to my sleeping senses. I'd placed the baseball bat under the bed. It was there if I needed it, but I wasn't going to scramble for it every time an insect whirred.

I sat up as an owl called from deep in the woods outside. Its echoing cry drew my attention to the window. I clutched the blanket and stilled so I wouldn't disturb the small gray-and-white mouse that sat on the ledge, silhouetted by moonlight but illuminated enough by the lamp's glow that I could see its crinkled whiskers and the twitch of its pink nose.

The owl called again and the mouse turned slightly toward the sound. It didn't duck or run for cover. It simply settled on its haunches before turning back to look at me.

Did it understand that the owl couldn't get through the screened window?

The cabin had been empty for a long time with only the occasional cleaning, but I hadn't seen any mouse droppings or any other evidence of rodent infestation. Maybe a solitary mouse had found its way in to shelter before the weather grew colder?

"Did you wake me? Or was it the owl?" I asked, thinking my voice would startle the little creature away.

The mouse only looked at me and I was suddenly reminded of the way CC looked: Knowing. Aware. As if complex thoughts were going on behind his furry face.

"If you don't make a mess, you can stay. Keep me company until Gathering," I said. I drew the line at confessing to the mouse that my sudden need for lights was embarrassing. Concerning my mental health, a fear of the dark was probably no more worrisome than feeling compelled to talk to a mouse.

"Not on the bed, of course. That's off-limits," I continued.

And then I thought of Sarah's charm. The crocheted mouse that had disappeared. Oddly enough, the mouse on the windowsill was also gray and white with a pale pink nose. But it was its crooked whiskers that most reminded me of the clear nylon thread that had created whiskers for the crochet mouse. Sarah's pocket and her clutching fingers had crimped that thread. I knew that. I'd seen and felt it in my dreams.

The mouse on the windowsill had real whiskers. I watched as it slowly began to clean its face as if it regularly chatted with houseguests at midnight. Real, crimped whiskers.

"Charm," I breathed out as I fell back on my pillows, but I fell asleep before I could decide if the idea was any crazier than sharing Sarah's memories.

The next morning dawned cool and bright. I flicked off lights in every room. It was probably the glow from the cabin that had disturbed the owl the night before. Maybe acting as a beacon to the mouse. I vowed to use only a normal amount of light tonight. I'd slept deep and hard after the interruption. No more nightmares. Maybe living here in the wildwood air would be good for me like Granny had said.

I checked more carefully for mouse droppings and found none. I wiped down the kitchen anyway. From the tops of the knotty pine cabinets to the crooked plank floor, I found only one living thing— a long-legged spider I quickly banished out the front door with an express ride on a dustpan I'd found on the pantry floor.

Maybe I'd dreamed the gray-and-white mouse so like the crochet charm I'd also dreamed. If so, I hadn't dreamed anything else for the rest of the night, which made me less worried about rodents than I probably should have been. Sarah's charm had been stuffed with garden herbs to keep the nightmares away. If I did share the cabin with a mouse, and if he kept the nightmares away, I would consider myself charmed as well.

It was well after lunchtime before I realized I was putting off the inevitable first trip back to the wildwood garden. Granny had given me instructions for which recipes I needed to learn before Gathering. I'd brought some ingredients with me—sugar, flour, baking soda and salt. But I would need to harvest the rest. I changed from flip-flops to sturdier canvas sneakers and grabbed the basket I knew I'd find waiting by the back door.

How many times had Sarah or her mother hooked the large container woven from willow branches on the crook of their arms before heading out to the wildwood path at the edge of the lawn? I tried to imagine happier times rather than the torn and bloody pages of the remedy book soaking up dew as I marched off on my mission.

But it wasn't only a garden I meant to visit.

It was a murder scene and a cemetery, and the ground, while not hallowed by priest or preacher, seemed sacred from the many generations who had turned the soil and planted the seeds. They had harvested and brewed, and from what Granny had said, fed the yeast, baked the bread and gathered in communion as a community of wisewomen. Year after year, for as long as anyone could remember.

I was supposed to be a part of that community this autumn. My head filled with the remembered hum of angry bees with that thought. I wasn't as alone as I'd been when Sarah had died, but I couldn't quite accept the totality of connection the wildwood seemed to want from me. Unlike the remedy book puzzle piece, no matter how I twisted and turned I could never fit myself into place.

Even though I'd been isolated for hours, I wasn't surprised to find Tom in the garden. Granny had told me to get used to his coming and going. And Sarah's memories of him were warm. He was a person she had trusted. The woods had welcomed me onto the path with the fussing screech of angry squirrels and a song of mingling birdcalls I was too inexperienced to separate and identify, but Tom was such a frequent visitor that the wildwood didn't fall silent at his passing.

"Oh, I see you beat me to it," I said. The older man was spry and quick and he was picking plump handfuls of blackberries from the bushes that lined the north edge of the garden and depositing them into a white five-gallon bucket that was stained with the evidence of having been used for just such a chore before.

"For you," Tom replied, gesturing with his equally stained hands, more purple than red, toward the bushes, drooping and heavy with fruit.

I'd never seen such blackberries before or such abundantly filled bushes. Each briar-spiked vine held dozens of giant berries. I stepped forward and leapt the creek to help Tom with the harvest. We worked silently until my fingers—and my lips—were as stained as Tom's.

The first bite had shocked me with a taste so rich and juicy and full of darkly sweet flavor. The wildwood blackberries reminded me of dewy midnights and morning mist and mountain fog. There were deep woodsy notes behind the berry tang I'd never tasted in blackberries purchased from the grocery.

"Not bad for my first taste from the garden," I commented. Tom paused in his picking and looked at me. I knew to expect his scarred face, but I still inwardly cringed at whatever grievous injury had caused the slash across his nose and mouth. The medical treatment he'd received hadn't prevented the cruel curl of his lips that made his speech so difficult. For him to utter and listeners to understand.

"Jam even better," he croaked and his smile would have been a horrible thing if the beautiful berries we labored together to pick and preserve hadn't colored it.

Finally, after over an hour of filling the bucket and partially filling my basket as well, we had divested the bushes of every last blackberry. Tom picked up the heavy bucket and gestured toward the path, telling me wordlessly to lead the way. I hadn't been surprised to find him here, but I was surprised by how easily I'd settled into working with him. I felt completely comfortable with him at my back as we returned to the house. The screeching squirrels had gone back to their own harvest, assured by our interest in the berries that we weren't after their walnuts or acorns, so only birdsong soundtracked our hike back to the cabin.

I led the way into the kitchen and watched Tom, more at home than I was, carry the bucket to the sink where he upended his load of berries and turned on the spigot.

"Thank you for your help," I said.

He'd been a friend to Sarah's mother. That's all I knew. That and his care of the garden even after Sarah and her mother were gone. His clothes were faded, but clean. A checkered flannel shirt tucked into blue jeans held up by a worn leather belt. His boots were also leather and worn with extra-long laces wound around the shafts as if to help hold them together. He turned from the sink, still holding the empty bucket. And I guessed I also knew the look in his eyes. Haunted. Lonely. Maybe a little bit mad.

Jacob Walker had warned me of danger on the mountain. Wild animals. The Sect. A murderer who had never been caught. But I swear I saw no harm in Tom. At least none intended toward me.

"Always," Tom hoarsely whispered.

And I wasn't sure if he meant he'd always help me or if he'd always be here, year after year, to pick blackberries, no matter who was here to can them.

"Come back for a jar of preserves when they're ready," I said. And then my cheeks burned because he looked taken aback, as if the berries were as much his as mine and of course he'd expect some jam.

Fourteen

*B*efore *I came to* the mountain, a triple espresso half-caf latte was the height of my culinary achievements. Sarah was the cook and even she preferred pizza to almost anything else.

I carefully set up the kitchen for preparing blackberry preserves the same way I would have set up a mad scientist's laboratory. Canning was easily as alien to me as test tubes and beakers full of mysterious chemicals.

When I'd cleaned the kitchen last night, I'd found a large copper-bottomed kettle in the cabinet by the stove. I'd scoured it well so it was ready for the washed berries I scooped into it from the sink. The remedy book was on the counter, propped open with a large wooden spoon I'd also found so I could refer to the blackberry jam recipe.

The instructions called for a three-to-one berry-to-sugar ratio. I measured carefully, noting that someone in the past had crossed out and scribbled over a higher sugar content. There was also an added note about substituting honey for sugar if preferred. I shied away from thinking about honey. Because bees. Even if my apology had been accepted, I didn't know if I should go there.

I used a fork and a large glass mixing bowl to mash several cups worth of berries, but other than those, the recipe called for whole berries. Of course, they were so plump and full of juice that none would be left entirely intact by the time the process was complete.

I measured the lemon juice as carefully as I'd measured the sugar. My pulse quickened as I worried about spoiling the gorgeous berries from the garden. They were precious in that there would be no more until next year, so the pressure was on. But even more so because Granny was sick and Sarah was gone and somehow this yearly tradition had fallen to me. Mel Smith. Not exactly the Betty Crocker type.

Granny had warned me about the need for constant stirring as the sugar, lemon juice and berry mixture began to bubble. She'd also prepared me for the foam that would rise to the top and need to be constantly skimmed off and plopped in the nearby sink. This was the thickening process, and while I worked on stirring and skimming, the giant canner was on another burner beginning to steam sterilize the jelly jars.

When the blackberries were thickened, I would spoon the preserves into the jars, wipe the necks, and place on the lids specially made to seal vacuum tight to the hot jars. Then I would apply the rings, screw them tight and ensure the seals were completed by submerging the filled jars in a bath of boiling water.

The preserves would keep for months through the winter if I did the task right.

I worked through the afternoon and into the night. The kitchen was filled with heavy, sweet-scented steam and my hair was a damp riot around my face by the time I canned all the berries we'd picked. It took several batches of berry mixture to use all the blackberries and the jars

Granny had provided. As the last jars cooled on the counter to the tune of lids pinging as they sealed, I read the part of the recipe that had been crossed out and was glad I hadn't needed to deal with melting paraffin wax and pouring it into the jars over the jam to create a seal.

Apparently, even the Ross Remedy Book was updated from time to time to avoid botulism from tainted food.

Finally, rows of preserves so deeply purple they were almost black lined the kitchen countertop. You didn't have to be a witch to appreciate a job (hopefully) well done. Canning wasn't sorcery. It was stained fingers, stiff shoulders and frazzled hair. But, I still remembered the first taste of blackberry from the wildwood garden and I knew my afternoon hadn't been spent on a mundane chore.

Much of the garden would sleep or even die in winter. Granny had explained the blackberry preserves would be handed out at Gathering for the wisewomen and their families to have during fallow months when nothing much grew in the wildwood. Along with frozen rye bread and dried roots and herbs, the berries I'd canned would maintain their connection with the wildwood.

Magic? Or community? Or a little of both. I'd always been apart, finding strength in being separated from others. Now I wasn't so sure. Preserving the blackberries was my first major test before Gathering when I would suddenly be thrust into an entire group of women who believed... What did they believe exactly?

It had been a long time since the last lid had tinged when a sudden movement intruded on my satisfaction over the clean, cooling kitchen and trepidation over the coming Gathering.

The mouse was back.

The tiny creature climbed to the top of one jar and sat back on its haunches the way it had the night before. It washed its face nonchalantly as I watched. Unbothered by my presence.

"Well. Charmed, I'm sure," I said. But I missed the sarcastic mark. Truthfully, I *was* charmed. The mouse was as brave and bold as I'd ever pretended to be. I knew I should shoo him off the shiny golden lid, but I also knew the warm jar was probably a pleasant seat.

And I could always wash it later when the mouse had moved on.

"You seem to be very clean for a mouse," I noted.

He paused his facial long enough to look at me and blink. His whiskers twitched and I thought about standing up and offering him the pocket of my sweater as an alternative resting place. I didn't. The fanciful idea that he was in any way related to the crocheted charm Sarah had carried with her was ridiculous. Brought on by exhaustion, nerves and the almost make-believe quality of the steamy kitchen.

"Not sure if CC is coming for Gathering, but I'll let you know," I said. I wasn't sure if wisewomen had familiars like witches. There might be a clowder of cats at Gathering for all I knew. Of course, by the end of the month, I was sure the mouse would have moved on. I kept a clean house. There would be no crumbs for the creature to scavenge in my kitchen.

Mine.

I stopped at the thought. My face was too warm and I had to take a deep breath. I let it out slowly, and with it any thoughts of permanence. Claiming a space of my own seemed presumptuous. As if I'd borrowed a bubble of peace that was almost surely doomed to burst.

Fifteen

Sarah had scrubbed the *kitchen down after the last pickles were safely sealed in their jars. Now she sat with carefully washed hands, a pen and the Ross Remedy Book open to the first blank page. Her notes along with all the edits she'd made as she perfected her first recipe were stacked at her left elbow. The final batch of pickles was lined up in a proud line on the counter across from the book.*

The small, woody cucumber plants that grew in the wildwood garden had originally been cultivated from a wild species more than a hundred years ago. The cucumbers themselves were fully mature at three inches long with tough, nearly black peels and firm dark green flesh. Their flavor was grassy and bitter and the Ross women had mainly used them in digestive remedies and ointments meant to combat eczema.

But, for as long as Sarah could remember, from her earliest days of toddling to the garden, needing her mother's hand to stay on her feet, she had been fascinated by the toylike miniature cucumbers. Melody Ross believed fascinations lead a wisewoman to where she was meant to go. So as soon as Sarah was old enough to begin experimenting in the kitchen with herbs and spices and the pickling process, she began to come up with the recipe that would be her first contribution to the Ross Remedy Book.

Wildflower honey to offset the bitterness of the peel that she wanted to keep for its crisp crunch.

Dill for vitamin C and to fight infection and for the whimsy of its anti-witchcraft mythology. (Her mother had explained that dill weed hadn't been allowed near the garden until 1955.)

A hardy variety of mountain peppercorn you couldn't find in a store. Piney with a hint of spice that lingered on the tongue long after the pickled bite of cucumber had been swallowed.

Her mother had never interfered with her pickle project, but now that she thought she'd arrived at a final recipe, Melody Ross stood beside a single open jar. Sarah hadn't tried a bite yet herself. Because the ultimate judge of whether her recipe was worthy of being written into the Ross book would be her mother.

Sarah placed both of her palms on the counter to steady her hands. Her whole body seemed to tremble with excitement and nervous anticipation. Her mother had already examined the appearance of the pickle jars. When she'd tilted the jars to the light, playful peppercorns floated in clear liquid, falling down and around the pickled cucumbers with a spicy snow globe effect.

But now the jar was open and her mother had speared a pickle with a long handled fork. She pulled it out and held it up, looking closely at it before she lifted it to her mouth and snapped off a bite with her even white smile. The crunch was audible and Sarah's mouth spread into an answering smile when her mother closed her eyes as she chewed and swallowed.

"Better than I imagined those tiny cucumbers could ever taste," Melody Ross proclaimed.

Sarah jumped down from her stool and grabbed the fork from her mother to take the rest of the pickle into her own mouth. The perfect balance of flavors and textures exploded as she happily chewed.

"You've done the wildwood proud," her mother said. But her smile eased

and she placed both hands on Sarah's shoulders. "Our family has been given a sacred responsibility. We're ambassadors between nature and humankind. It's okay to be joyful, but we need to be solemn as well. And give thanks for all the garden gives us."

"I know, Mama. I'm very serious about my pickles," Sarah said. "I always knew. From the first time I picked one and held it in my hand."

"The wildwood tells us everything we need to know. It gives us everything we need. We just have to listen to its whispers," her mother said. "And heed its warnings."

Her mother's hands gripped her shoulders a little more tightly.

"People are growing too distant from the land. They take what it has to offer—wood, coal and water—and give nothing back. There are fewer of us living in harmony with the mountain. And there are people who want to destroy that harmony because they want to usurp nature and be above us all. When you write your first recipe in the Ross Remedy Book, it's a rite of passage, Sarah. It means you want to accept your place as an ambassador, a caretaker. You'll become a wisewoman. There's pride in that, but there's also weight. It's a load you'll carry the rest of your life. It isn't easy. And it can even be dangerous. I've taught you to honor the wildwood with every step and every breath, but it's up to you whether you accept this sacred duty."

Her mother spoke in a ceremonial rhythm Sarah instinctively recognized. She was only nine years old, but she understood because the never-ending cycle between her family and the garden had always been a part of her life. She thought she might know who some of their enemies were and her heart pounded because she was old enough and smart enough to fear them.

But she was also a Ross. Melody Ross's daughter. She would be brave.

"I accept," Sarah said, with her back straight and her chin high. She reached for the pen and sat down in front of the open book. Her mother came to stand behind her, holding her shoulders in support as Sarah began to write.

Sixteen

I found Sarah's recipe in the remedy book, easily paging to the place where she'd written it so many years ago. The book was so thick and full I hadn't noticed Sarah's handwriting before. That was the simple explanation. Her careful, rounded script had simply been hidden among dozens of unfamiliar, even archaic styles. But part of me wondered if the book had revealed it to me now. That it had somehow become synchronized with my dreams.

I ran my fingers over the ingredients and traced the loops of her signature at the bottom of the page. I'd never made pickles in my life, but the blackberry preserves had boosted my courage and the spicy flavor of Sarah's pickles still lingered in my mouth after the dream.

Tasting Sarah's contribution to the Ross Remedy Book was suddenly imperative to me. I'd never practiced any religion with conviction. There had been foster homes that had forced me to attend Mass or a Protestant Sunday school. I remembered one summer in particular when Sarah had cried every day when we'd been compelled by self-preservation to a Bible school in order to earn dinner for a week.

I'd gone through the motions, watching the clock and disbelieving everything I was told. No one would save us. No person or deity. Only we could save ourselves.

But this symbiosis my namesake had believed in between her family as caretakers and the wildwood as provider appealed to me somehow. Maybe because Sarah had believed in her mother and the wildwood with every fiber of her being even after the relationship between the garden and her family had seemed to fail.

In learning from Sarah's book, was I reestablishing a connection that had been lost? Had that been what Granny intended? Initially, I'd seen this as therapy. A working country vacation as a break from the city after all I'd been through. A sort of personal rehabilitation following grief and loss. The more I dreamed about Sarah's past, the more I believed there might be more to this summer than that.

Over the next two weeks, my daily trips to the garden were no less momentous, but I got on with them alone. Well, mostly alone. The little mouse had become my constant companion and for some reason I couldn't chase him away. The first time I noticed him in the woods I automatically assumed he had to be a different mouse than the one I was used to seeing in the house. But his crinkled whiskers and gray-and-white coloring were too distinctive to mistake. I saw him nibbling sunflower seeds from the wilted head of a tall-stalked flower while I was gathering walnuts. Then, I saw him napping in a milkweed pod that had busted open to release its seeds, leaving a soft bed of silken threads for a mouse smart enough to claim it. On that day, I snipped flowering mugwort while the mouse slept and then I gently tapped his bed to wake him when I was finished.

He would follow me back, or he wouldn't, but I was compelled to let him know.

Sure enough, after I'd bundled the mugwort into bunches and hung them upside down on a clothesline I'd strung through the kitchen for drying herbs, the mouse appeared on top of the armchair nearest the kitchen.

"Is there a tiny pet door I haven't been told about?" I asked.

But of course his only answer was a twitch of his crinkled whiskers.

"Good thing I'm scheduled to go to town tomorrow. You're not much of a conversationalist," I said.

I had more than a basketful of garden stuffs to take to Granny. Some for her own "edification," like the peach cordial I'd retrieved from a root cellar she'd stocked last spring with ancient-looking green glass bottles corked with red wax. Some for her soap and moisturizer preparations, like dried lavender, and the mugwort for menstrual tea. Some I'd prepared for sale myself, like the walnuts I'd cracked until I'd replaced the blackberry stains on my fingers with a new blackish-green tint from their hulls.

I'd already been to town once to make Granny's rounds. She was showing improvement. Her color was better. Her cough had cleared. And I was glad. Only disappointed that Joyce had been right about my removal. I hadn't meant to be a burden or a drain. But I had been and it hurt my pride.

After I'd finished hanging the mugwort, I packed the willow basket and a wooden crate I'd also found in the cellar. The pantry held the blackberry preserves and the pickles I'd made after that. Sarah's pickles. I'd known how they would taste from my dreams. But still, the first crisp tangy snap between my teeth had brought tears to my eyes. They would be shared at Gathering not sold in town.

When a knock sounded on the cabin's front door, the mouse disappeared from the top of the armchair as if he'd poofed into thin air. But he reappeared on the counter beside the crate as if he'd joined me to face whoever was at the door as a united front.

"No worries, then," I said, rolling my eyes at the diminutive backup.

I dusted off my hands and went to the door. Mindful of murderers, I peeked out the window before I turned the knob. I'd halfway expected it to be Tom, returned for his share of jam, but it wasn't. The door still required a tug to open because I mostly entered and exited through the back. And, of course, my tug was too fierce, causing the act of opening to be a sudden and dramatic whoosh. Jacob stood on my front stoop. He stared down at the red galoshes I hadn't yet had the heart to move.

"Oh. Hey," I said, as lame as extra casual can sound after an awkward ta-da. I wasn't sure if it was because of Lu or because of the bee balm, but my brain was rebelling against any idea of keeping the biologist at a distance. With a brush of his fingers on the bergamot's leaves, he'd become "Jacob" to me.

Then, I saw he had a bundle of damp greenery filling the wide brimmed hat he held in this hands.

"Granny might have a hard time gathering peppermint these days. I thought I would lend her a hand," Jacob said. "There are several places along the creek near the garden where water mint and spearmint have naturally hybridized."

It had been weeks since he'd warned me away from the wildwood, but a goodwill gesture seemed extreme. Opposite end of the spectrum from get out "while you still can." There was also a world of difference between stopping to loan me a shovel in town and bringing me a present all the way out here. I thought about him caring for the bergamot plant—the watering, the caressing of each petal as if he encouraged it to grow. I didn't open the screen door as quickly as politeness dictated I should and we stood at an impasse while a hummingbird flew around the boots, fooled by their vivid shade into looking for a flower that wasn't there.

"I also noticed the blackberries were gone," Jacob said softly, as if I were a deer he feared he might frighten away.

"Tom helped me pick them. I made preserves. I think the Ross recipe is a sort of jam preserve hybrid actually. I took a jar to Granny last week, but I haven't heard her verdict on how I did." I nudged open the screen door and held it wide enough for Jacob to get the idea. He stepped inside. The cabin's great room immediately felt even smaller than it had seconds before.

"I sometimes collect things for Granny. Peppermint. Or Saint-John's-wort. I always keep my eye out for chanterelles," Jacob said. "She's done a lot for...the people on the mountain. She usually won't accept much in return."

Granny and Jacob weren't friends. But they weren't exactly enemies either. I'd been right in thinking that a healthy dose of respect ran both ways between them. Tempered by condescension. Granny for Jacob because of his city education. Jacob for Granny because of love potions and whatnot.

Verdict was out on what Jacob thought of me. As a wisewoman's apprentice. Or otherwise.

"Let me get you a jar of blackberry preserves. I made several batches. Tom and I gathered a five-gallon bucket of blackberries and then some," I hurried over to the pantry to grab a jar, both to fill the silence between us and to put some distance between his body and mine. He'd brought the outside indoors; the scent of moss and trees and forest breeze rode in on his clothes or on his skin or in his hair. One whiff had made me want to lean closer to discover where the woodsy scent clung softly to his rugged frame.

"Mel. There's a mouse on your counter and it just bared its teeth in my direction," Jacob said calmly.

He walked toward the kitchen. And sure enough Charm was braced on all four feet with a snarl twisting his little face like I'd never seen. Charm? Yes. It suited him. He was no ordinary mouse.

"This is Jacob. He's brought some peppermint for Granny. Behave," I said as if the mouse was a guard dog I had to tell to stand down.

Charm lifted his pink nose in the air and sniffed dramatically, once, twice, three times before his snarl and stance slightly eased. Slightly. He still looked angry even though the forest scent of Jacob had apparently soothed him.

"You have a pet mouse?" Jacob asked. He didn't come closer and I was suddenly struck by the idea of the self-possessed man held off by nothing but an angry mouse. The man made me unaccountably nervous. I liked that Charm made him nervous in return.

"This is Charm. Charm, meet Jacob Walker. He protects the forest from little old grannies and their friends," I said.

I reached out with the jar of preserves at the same time to soften the edge of my teasing. Jacob met my eyes, but he didn't lift his hand to accept the gift. Instead, he took his hat over to the sink to tip the peppermint out into the basin before placing it back on his head. No wonder he always smelled so fresh and woodsy and *green*. He moved back to the opposite side of the counter, but he still didn't accept the jam. Either because of the mouse or because of me, I couldn't be sure. I lowered the jar to the counter and left it there for him to take or leave as he chose.

"Wisewomen love to pass as nothing but grannies, beekeepers and Sunday school teachers. You and I both know better. Don't we?" Jacob asked.

Bees. Would I ever stop flushing when I thought of my failure that day at the apiary? I ignored the remembered hum in my head and pretended my cheeks weren't warm. "Since the last time we spoke I've learned to make jam and pickles. Dangerous dabbling in the black arts, I'm sure. I'm surprised people risk eating the preserves," I joked. But it was an act. I knew deep down those blackberries *had* been special. And the rye bread made with wildwood yeast would be even more special still. Did Jacob know? There was a gleam in his eyes that said he did. Maybe better than me. Maybe even better than Granny herself. The little tree tattoo on his wrist was covered by the cuff of his sleeve today. But I knew it was there. Was it as simple as a nod to his profession or did his beliefs run deeper than science could explain? He'd scoffed at Granny's practices, hadn't he? Or had his warnings been an indication of the opposite, that he took the wisewomen's beliefs seriously?

He still hadn't picked up the jar of preserves from the counter where I had left it.

Of course, he'd have to brave a pretty ferocious looking guardian to do so.

"Charm? You should rethink that. Tiger. Fang. Something less cute would suit him better," Jacob suggested.

"Thank you for the peppermint. I'll take it to Granny tomorrow. I'm headed to town to make rounds in the morning," I replied.

"Good. You shouldn't be out here by yourself all the time," Jacob said. He leaned back against the armchair with one hip. A growl came from the mouse on the counter, but then died down when the biologist's sudden movement stopped.

"I'm not alone," I said. Jacob cut his eyes to the mouse and back to me. He cocked a brow that said not everyone would respect Charm's jurisdiction. "Charm, Tom, you...I'm right in supposing you're one of the ones that keep the paths smooth around the wildwood garden. Why haven't you stopped to chat before now?" I continued. I hadn't seen him in town either. Which was strange considering how often he'd just shown up wherever I went before.

This time Jacob froze for reasons having nothing to do with the mouse on the counter. He slowly lifted his chin to meet my inquisitive gaze.

"That day we planted the bee balm I didn't know why I felt the need to drive to the park, but I wasn't surprised when I found you and Lu there," he said. "I'm used to following hunches and nudges. But afterward, I felt like maybe you were uncomfortable with me...showing up too often."

I wasn't sure if I was getting more comfortable with hunches and nudges or not. But I certainly wasn't going to admit to anyone other than my own deepest thoughts that I was nervous. "I'm here. I'm staying. There's no reason to avoid each other, is there?" I asked.

"No. No good reason," Jacob said. His eyes were darker than ever inside the confines of the cabin. The shady hollows under pine boughs—green, but nearly black. "I guess I better get back to work. You don't have to tell Granny the peppermint is from me. She might like it better if it isn't."

This time Charm didn't growl. Maybe because Jacob pushed off from the chair straight for the door. I trailed after him, having been in the mountains long enough to know that there were several rounds of goodbye and one of them had to be at the door.

"See you," I agreed, as if we'd somehow made a date because we hadn't vowed to avoid each other forevermore.

Jacob's accent was as Appalachian as Sarah's, but he didn't linger for goodbyes on the porch like I'd expected. His leaving was as definitive as his showing up had been. Sudden. A rap on the door. A boot heel on a step. There. Then gone.

Had the peppermint been a nudge he couldn't resist, a favor for Granny, or an excuse to see me again? The jar on the counter seemed to mock me after I'd closed the door.

He might have helped me plant the bee balm, he had carried it water regularly afterward and he had brought the mint for Granny, but, almost to spite the pull between us, he was keeping his distance.

He still wanted me to go away. He thought I didn't belong. The cabin seemed hollow when I turned back inside to finish my prep for tomorrow. Charm had disappeared. The sun was setting. And everything I placed in the crate seemed to make a thunk that echoed down the hall.

Charm had been confused by the man—his wildwood scent, and the rush his mistress felt. He was the now-living link between the new wisewoman and the garden and every day he was more in tune with her thoughts and feelings. But she wasn't sure about the man and that made Charm unsure as well.

Charm now had a name. It was the same name another had called him before he morphed into skin and bone, before blood pumped and air flowed in and out. He liked it okay. The name. Especially because his mistress had claimed him with it instead of chasing him away. He couldn't run away. Wouldn't. Even if he did have four feet for running. He wasn't made for "away."

He didn't remember his making, but he knew his purpose.

And his new mistress had accepted and strengthened the bond he created between her and the garden by accepting the bond between him and her. Contentment wasn't a thing his mistress knew. So he stayed watchful and wary like her. Tomorrow she would go to town. He felt her intention even if he didn't fully understand her plans. He didn't have to. He was a link, a living conduit for the wildwood garden to connect with one of its people. There were others like him, but different—bird, cat, cricket, mink. Living links from wisewomen to garden and back again.

Charm climbed into the crate and instinctively fashioned a soft nest for himself out of dried lemongrass. His mistress was sleeping. It was no longer his job to keep bad dreams away. There were things the wildwood needed his mistress to know. The garden had been tainted by someone who kept themselves apart, someone who didn't understand the power and peace of interwoven existence. A killer who despised the laws of nature because they wanted to rule over everyone and everything themselves.

This knowing by his mistress would be dangerous, but Charm had been made brave enough to stand by a champion's side. Because the ultimate danger of desecration was to the wildwood garden itself.

Seventeen

S adie picked me up early the next morning. The sun was still sleepy beneath a horizon that held only a hint of pink. I carefully put the crate and my willow basket in the back of a dented cargo van so I wouldn't disturb Charm's sleep. There was barely enough room. I could see why Sadie used a van for market days instead of her truck. Willow and birch branches were tied together with twine in large bundles beside a variety of baskets in varying stages of completion. There were also tools for cutting and trimming and shaping the branches.

"Did you make the willow basket I use to gather from the garden?" I asked as I climbed into the passenger seat.

"That was one of my mother's baskets. I was only stripping and trimming branches at that point, but I took over when her stroke made it impossible for her to go on. She still comes to the farmers' market with me on Saturdays and Sunday afternoons. But I do all the weaving myself now," Sadie said. "Granny has several of my baskets. Most people couldn't tell them apart since I learned on my mother's knee. But I can tell. I remember every one I've made."

The console lights illuminated her calloused fingers on the steering wheel. Her baskets were utilitarian and works of art at the same time. I liked that she never forgot one. Wondered if there was some kind of sensory memory involved with the twining and turning. Each one was different, like snowflakes, because of the natural materials she used. I decided to visit Sadie's stall in the market so I could see her weave sometime soon.

It was still dark enough to need headlights as we headed down the long, winding drive. The sagging barn and outbuildings were nothing more than hulking shadows. Morgan's Gap was as sleepy as it had ever been, but after my time spent alone in the wildwood, the streets seemed louder even with the first light of the morning sun. Sadie dropped me off without coming inside. Baskets and bees were only her side hustles. She had to get to her day job at the post office. Granny was out of bed and in her kitchen once more when I let myself into the house.

"I have today's basket ready for you," she said and her rosy cheeks made me smile.

"Come on. Don't just stand there. Joyce isn't around to fuss and there's no harm in a hug."

She gathered me into a big embrace before I could protest, but the strength in Granny's arms caused my grumbles to die unuttered on my lips. The old wisewoman was obviously doing much better than she'd been doing last week.

"Well, Joyce was right about me moving out. You've been improving and now you look great. The best I've seen," I said. Besides the rosy cheeks, Granny's eyes were clear and bright and her back wasn't stooped. She stood with her feet planted wide apart and her hands on her hips, claiming every inch of her barely five feet with a wide grin on her face.

"I overdid it. That's all. And I would have continued to overdo it if you were underfoot," Granny replied.

I plopped the long rectangular crate on the counter and placed the willow basket I'd brought with me on a nearby stool. Granny began going through the things I'd brought, sorting and mumbling and exclaiming in turn.

The delivery basket was on the kitchen table. I ran my fingers over the handle that had been woven with thin branches and noted how the ends of those branches were wound around thicker branches that formed the basket itself. I went on to examine its contents and the accompanying list that indicated where each packet, parcel and bottle should go.

Until a startled exclamation called my attention back to my companion.

"Seems you've got a hitchhiker," Granny said, after her initial wordless surprise. From the interior of the crate, she lifted Charm by the scruff of his little neck, crinkled whiskers twitching this way and that.

"Where's CC?" I asked, suddenly afraid Granny's cat didn't have a penchant for only cookies.

"I don't think you have to worry 'bout that, hon. Cat won't be bothered. They're the same creature, more or less. This is very good. You're getting on better than I'd planned!" Granny said.

I stepped forward, still concerned, and Granny lowered Charm into my cupped palms. It was the first time I'd held him and my heart pounded at his soft fur and cool, bare feet. I brought him in and cradled him against my chest without thinking, not sure when he'd become a pet instead of a pest.

"The same creature?" I repeated, confused.

Granny perched on an empty stool before she answered while Charm didn't squirm or even try to get away.

"First, this lifestyle of ours is freely chosen. You can walk away from the wildwood at any time…in spite of what your Mr. Walker might say," Granny explained.

"He's not mine," I interrupted.

"*Mmhm*," Granny said, but she shook her head slightly as if I was too obtuse for logical arguments. "I told you the Ross Remedy Book would teach you. And it has. You're well on your way. But I haven't told you exactly what's happening as you brew and preserve and consume what you harvest from the garden."

I looked down at the unusually quiet mouse in my hands. Charm looked up at me, content to warm his feet against my palms.

"It's a connection. Deeper than appreciating nature, isn't it?" I asked. "And the reason Jacob warned me away is because you can leave whenever you want to, but once you're connected the desire to leave is gone."

"If I tried to leave this mountain, my heart would rip in two," Granny said matter-of-factly. "I suspect Jacob Walker is the same even if he is much younger than I am."

"What does Charm have to do with it?" I asked.

"Your little 'mouse' is what some might have called a 'familiar' at one time. They improve our connection to the wildwood. Think of him as an emissary. Between you and the forest, the garden, the mountain itself."

"And you think he's a sign that I'm learning what I need to learn?" I said.

"You're forging and accepting the connections between yourself and the wildwood. Faster than I've ever seen. Most of the wisewomen were born and raised around here or in neighboring communities…"

Granny trailed off as if she'd stopped herself from saying more. Then she jumped up and went to the cupboard. She brought down a vintage canister with a glass top. From inside of it she scooped out a spoonful of pine nuts and sprinkled them on the counter beside the crate.

I moved to carefully place my hands beside the pile. Charm raised his nose into the air and sniffed before he jumped off my hands to accept the offering.

"Those came from out by your cabin. You should make sure he gets plenty of food from the wildwood. Nothing from the store. I imagine he would refuse it, but just in case, don't offer," Granny instructed.

"That's why CC mostly eats your cookies," I said.

"Cat eats anything and everything, but I make sure he gets plenty of what he needs," Granny said. "Your mouse is smaller. Outside things might harm him. Especially while he's new."

"He...he reminds me of a crocheted toy Sarah used to carry in her pocket," I whispered. It was one thing to name a mouse Charm; it was another to voice a crazy theory out loud.

"Sarah's mother was powerful. So powerful. Her connection to the wildwood was stronger than any I've known. If she made that crochet mouse and if she charmed it, there's no telling what the garden would allow it to do. When needed. This isn't any kind of science man has ever understood. But it's as real as you and I standing here. We don't have to understand it. We only have to feel it and live it," Granny said. "Trust your instincts. They've brought you this far."

"Trust isn't exactly my strength," I said. I hadn't told Granny about the pull I felt toward Jacob and Lu. I wasn't ready to admit it out loud. I think my heart was more than ready for connections my head simply wouldn't allow. Charm had cleaned up all the pine nuts and now he sat back on his haunches to clean his face. Pretty as you please.

"You don't have to learn to believe in the power of the wildwood.

You're already there whether you admit it or not. But you do have to learn to trust in its power and in yours. And that might take longer than we've got," Granny said. "You're a prickly thing. I'm surprised the wildwood didn't send you a porcupine."

Outwardly I laughed, but inwardly I cringed. I knew my growly little mouse could be as prickly as me. I was wearing a belted cornflower blue sweater with huge pockets. I'd already placed the customer list in one. Now, I leaned toward the counter and opened the other. Charm finished cleaning his face and paused. He looked at me as if he needed to meet my eyes to understand what I wanted. Then, he scurried over to the edge of the counter and leapt into the hiding space I'd offered.

It was both crazy and completely natural. As normal as anything else that had happened since I'd come to this town.

Charm slept in my pocket all morning while I made Granny's deliveries. Until I stepped into the beauty shop on my next to last stop and found it deserted. Usually, every dryer was occupied by women in rollers like this was 1965, but today, there was only one client in Betty Rutherford's chair. The stylist most people around here referred to as a beautician was blowing out this particular client's hair with a huge round bristle brush and a chrome hair dryer that was surely retro.

"Oh, come on in, Mel. I've got to finish with Vee and then I'll pay you for the moisturizer," Becky shouted above the hot whir in her hands.

Vee was as retro as the hair dryer. She was dressed in a polka dot dress with a fitted shirtwaist and a full skirt. Nipped around her tiny middle was a white patent leather belt that matched the kitten-heel pumps on her feet. A matching designer handbag rested on the table beneath the mirror. Her legs were that telltale too tan that indicated opaque hosiery. High above that her face was perfectly made up, but not exactly stylish, with nude gloss and pale eye shadow that washed out beneath the feathered bangs so frosty Becky must have just rinsed out the bleach.

The capri jean bibs I'd made by whacking off the length of an old pair of overalls I'd found in the cabin's attic were decidedly less of a put-together ensemble. She suddenly reminded me of a doll who had been dressed for this occasion. With a faded black T-shirt and canvas high-top sneakers on, I felt more comfortable than I had any right to be in Vee's presence.

But the woman, who appeared close to my age beneath the hairspray and lip gloss, smiled and I smiled back, more at ease. Her appearance might be a little plastic, but she was a person beneath it all. Suddenly, I had the impulse to give Vee a jar of the blackberry preserves I'd canned. I followed it, reaching into my basket and pulling out the jar before I could second-guess my instincts.

"Biggest blackberries you've ever seen," I said.

"Oh. Th-thank y-you," Vee stammered. She hesitantly took the jar I thrust toward her and cradled it in her hands as if she wasn't quite sure what to do with it.

"There. Now. Isn't that nice?" Becky said, turning the salon chair so her client faced the mirror. The *i* in "nice" was longer than it should be, drawn out as if she too thought Vee would be more comfortable in jeans. Our gazes met in the mirror above Vee's head and I blushed because there was a warning there. I might seem like someone who hadn't been taught social graces. *True.* But I wouldn't hurt someone's feelings by commenting negatively on their appearance. Vee must have spent hours getting primped and "perfected," but she leaned forward without commenting on her own appearance as if what she looked like didn't matter at all to her. She fumbled open her purse and quickly shoved the jam inside, then she snapped the clasp as if she was in a hurry to hide the gift.

While Vee was focused on putting the jar in her bag, Becky frowned down at her client's hair. She obviously disapproved of her own work. So why hadn't she suggested a different style?

The answer opened the door to the hair salon and walked in behind us. I saw everyone's reaction to the man's entrance in the mirror. The buffer didn't lessen the impact. Becky looked like she might vomit. Vee looked like she might faint. She pushed the handbag away, guiltily, as if the blackberry preserves were contraband she didn't want to call attention to. I looked confused and the man...He looked as plastic and polished as the woman in the chair.

"Time's up. We have a luncheon, remember? Enough spoiling for one morning," the man joked. No one laughed for the beat of several seconds and then Becky and Vee laughed in that high-pitched fake way that's freaky and frightening at the same time.

Why were they afraid of this man? Both of them. I tightened my grip on the basket and planted my feet. I'd had the same reaction myself too many times before to stay calm and detached. Every time I met a new foster parent. Every time a teacher took advantage because they knew there was no one at home who cared. Vee and Becky saw the man as a threat in some way. I was going to run with their assessment.

"She's all ready for you, Hartwell. Aren't you, Vee? Pretty as that picture of Jackie O. in the old *Life* magazine," Becky said. Her voice was oddly breathless as if she was in a hurry to appease him. I glanced down to see the magazine she referred to on her station. I hadn't noticed it before. Was the luncheon some kind of cosplay event? But, no, the man's charcoal suit was modern with small lapels and a single button paired with straight-fitted trousers that hit right above his polished black loafers.

"Hello. I'm Hartwell Morgan. I see you've met my wife, Violet," he said. He enunciated his wife's full name as if *Vee* was presumptuous on Becky's part. "And you are?"

He reached out his hand and I froze, wanting to recoil, but somehow sure my distaste would hurt Violet Morgan. I followed Becky's lead in some instinctive steps I didn't want to dance around male ego.

"Hartwell is the mayor of Morgan's Gap," Becky rushed to say. "His family founded the town."

Violet had gracefully risen from the salon chair on the opposite side without speaking. Her smile was gone and she stood, carefully poised, like a pretty robot waiting for programming.

Hartwell looked down at the basket in my hands, but he didn't curl his lip at my bibs in spite of the strict old-fashioned beauty standards he apparently had ordered for his wife. The lip curl didn't happen until I spoke, finally tired of a tension in the air I could only partially understand.

"I'm Granny's apprentice, Mel Smith. I'm living at the old Ross cabin. Do you know it? Outside of town," I said. I threw the information at him to see how he would react, but I felt movement in my pocket and a hum that indicated Charm was upset. Maybe I shouldn't have been so bold, especially with a man who made the hair stand up on the nape of my neck. I was glad the woven material of my sweater muffled Charm's growl. No need for both of us to antagonize the mayor.

Violet flinched, but only slightly. I might not have noticed if I hadn't been facing her and trying to decide if the strand of pearls around her neck was uncomfortably tight. Had she been the one who had been behind the movement of the curtain in the mayor's house the day we'd planted the bee balm? Or had it been her husband? Something about the idea of Hartwell spying on us in the park sent a chill down my back.

"Yes. I know it," Hartwell replied. He lowered his hand. Either deciding I wasn't going to shake his hand or determining he didn't want to shake mine. "Apprentice? Potions and poultices? Salves and tinctures? Y'all wasting your time when there's a pharmacy on hand." Hartwell let out a bark of laughter that was way too loud for the empty shop now that the dryer was silent. No one joined him. He stopped laughing and jerked his head toward his wife. An unspoken order for her to titter nervously once or twice? Because that's what the poor woman did and the sound was like broken glass against my ears— pained, sharp and nothing funny about it.

"I was just telling Violet how much I like the moisturizer Granny makes. My skin is so smooth and it smells like peppermint," Becky said.

"My wife gets her moisturizer from the finest department stores. She doesn't need that old hippy's wares," Hartwell said. Then, ever the politician, he caught himself. "Not that I don't support small businesses because I certainly do. Isn't that right, Violet?"

"Yes, Hartwell," Violet responded. She was a doll. A beautiful, miserable doll, and something about her eyes was hauntingly familiar, an expression I recognized but couldn't place.

"And we appreciate your support, Mayor," Becky said. "You were missed while you were away." To me, Becky continued, "He had a big energy conference in Richmond."

"And many important meetings before and after that," the mayor interjected.

Violet hooked her hand in the crook of Hartwell Morgan's proffered elbow as if directed by some cue I hadn't seen. Becky placed the white patent handbag over her client's other shoulder. Violet grabbed the bag with her free hand and pressed it close against her hip. Something told me Hartwell Morgan would be angry if he knew I'd given his wife the preserves, but the way she clutched the handbag close made me think she was happy to have them in spite of his certain disapproval. I hoped she was able to enjoy the decadent, natural sweetness of them later when she was alone.

Becky followed them out. The mayor kept his eyes on mine all the way across the shop and out the door until it closed and he finally turned away.

"God. That man makes me a nervous wreck. He has to have things just so. I'm glad they had a lunch date. Sometimes he makes me rewash and style her hair until he approves," Becky said. "I'm always glad when they go to a Richmond salon instead."

"She seemed nice before he interrupted," I said.

"She's as nice as she's allowed to be," Becky said. "He keeps a close eye on everything she says and does. Even when he's away, he has folks look after her. He wants to be governor someday."

"It's not the sixties anymore," I said. Charm had quieted and I was free to use both hands to fish Becky's moisturizer out of the basket. The recyclable glass bottle was wrapped in brown paper tied with twine. No fancy packaging or labels for Granny. She *was* an old hippy after all. I chuckled at the narrow-minded description that didn't nearly capture all that Granny was.

"Haven't you figured out that Morgan's Gap is fifty years behind the times? Besides, Hartwell Morgan definitely doesn't believe in women's rights. He might be against Granny's herbal wares, but I wouldn't be surprised if he encourages Violet to take pills that keep her calm and quiet. There are times when she's not right. Even when he's not around," Becky said.

"Something stronger than valerian tea," I added.

My throat tightened and the room had gone suddenly cold because I'd realized what had bothered me about Violet Morgan's expression. She didn't wear a scarf or homespun clothes, but her eyes had been eerily like the eyes of the Sect women I'd seen with Reverend Moon—herded, kept, all their individual needs and desires unspoken and unseen.

Eighteen

I wasn't ready to head back to the cabin when my deliveries were finished, but I was still nervous about CC in spite of what Granny had said. So, while she took a nap after a quick soup lunch that nonetheless seemed hearty and sweet for someone who had been eating alone a lot, I sat on the swing of her front porch. It wasn't too cool with the afternoon sun still warming every spot it could reach and the occasional passing car was a nice change from seeing no one for days.

Charm joined me, nosing in corners for dead beetles and squeaking with pleasure when he found a stray acorn. I read through the instructions for cultivating wild yeast and baking bread. Again. My dreams were good for learning; I wanted to get it right.

For Sarah. For Granny. For Kara, Joyce and Sadie for that matter. I couldn't bring myself to think *for the wildwood* but the words were there, a secretive whisper in my heart. Maybe grief had driven me a little over the edge. I was grasping at a belief system that had to be more folktale than reality. But, when a little tame mouse was nibbling an acorn several inches away from your feet, it was hard to remain a skeptic. Truth was, I wanted to accept what these women seemed to be offering me—a place among them. I'd never had a mother. Had never allowed myself to think of the nameless, faceless person who hadn't wanted me. Now, I had four older women who truly seemed to care. About me. And that seemed more magical than anything found between the remedy book's pages.

When the turquoise Chevy pulled into the driveway, I closed the remedy book and stood to stare. Smoke poured from the exhaust and the engine roared in protest as the driver applied the brake. I knew who it was before he opened the door and jumped down. The rusted metal hinges screamed, but Jacob Walker slammed the truck's door and walked around the hood as if he reclaimed junk trucks from wildflower fields on the regular.

"Granny called. Said you needed a vehicle. Figured this one might do no more than you'll need to drive it. Of course, I'd say it's been ten years since she's been down by that barn where it was parked. I had to clear out two hornets' nests and an abandoned trove of hazelnuts some poor squirrel had forgotten and left behind," Jacob said conversationally. He paused at the stoop and looked up where I stood. The porch gave me a height advantage for the first time since we'd met.

"Sadie gave me a ride this morning before work. They were all going to decide who would get the chore of taking me back tonight," I said.

"I left my Jeep and toolbox out at your place so I'll ride back with you, if that's okay," Jacob said. He wasn't dressed in hiking clothes today. Instead, he wore a pair of jeans and a black canvas jacket. The tough, ripstop kind you'd see on a mechanic or a carpenter. A tight gray V-neck T-shirt hugged his chest beneath the jacket and square-toed work boots covered his feet.

"So you're a mechanic as well as a biologist." I didn't step back to invite him onto the porch. I didn't step down to join him on the walk.

I enjoyed the view from above and hoped Charm wouldn't launch a growling attack onto Jacob's upturned face from a porch rail.

"I know the basics. Got it going and onto a flatbed tow truck and we brought it to the garage in town. Joseph went over it from hood to bumper. Replaced all the belts and hoses. New tires. Well, fairly new. Greased it up. Fresh oil and gas. He says it'll run a few more years. I figure it'll get you through the summer at least," Jacob said. He'd eased back on his heels and jammed his hands comfortably in his pockets, seemingly in no rush to join me.

"I can't even believe it runs. It looked like nature had completely claimed it. How much do I owe?" I asked.

"Joseph owes Granny. She saved his life when he was born. Breech. She used to midwife a lot back then. Delivered most of the town that age. Joseph figures he wouldn't be here if it wasn't for her expertise." Jacob had taken a couple of strides forward. But he was still far enough away to be completely normal and not at all remarkable.

"Maybe I'll take him some cookies the next time I'm making my rounds," I said. For some reason an unremarkable distance for others was notable with Jacob Walker. A few feet felt like a few inches.

"Your mouse came with you," Jacob said. Sure enough Charm had finished with his acorn and now he stood at the top of the stairs.

"At least he isn't growling," I said, although I didn't think we were in the clear yet. I noticed distinct tension in the creature beside me. His nose didn't twitch. His body was still.

"I could introduce you as a friend. You don't smell like the wildwood today. He might be confused," I said.

"Probably smell like axle grease and engine oil today," Jacob agreed. "Half a dozen of us worked on the truck all day. Joseph called in a bunch of favors. Then again, lots of folks around here would do anything for Granny. She's backwoods royalty in these parts." Then he smiled up at me and I saw nothing but mossy shadows in his eyes even if he was in town. "We are friends, Mel. You can tell him that."

I wasn't sure if Charm would listen or believe me. I also wasn't sure Jacob Walker was my friend, but he had definitely done a huge favor for me today. Or for Granny. But either way I was the beneficiary.

"Be nice to Mr. Walker, Charm. The wildwood likes him. That should be enough of a character reference for you," I said. Yet I knew my prickly familiar was taking the lead from me. I liked him. Couldn't deny it anymore. And liking him made me nervous.

"We're having chicken and dumplings for dinner. It's been simmering on the stovetop all day. You're welcome to have a bowl before y'all leave for the cabin," Granny said from the front door. "And you don't fool me, Jacob Walker. I know you see me as more of a meddling vagabond than a queen."

In spite of Granny's dig, Jacob accepted the invitation and was on the porch and through to the bathroom to wash his hands before I could note anything but a whiff of gasoline in his passing. It was Granny who paused in the hallway on the way to the kitchen. I'd scooped Charm up to pop him back in my pocket and followed the two of them inside.

"I like him too. But he went away for a long time. Came back different. Like him, but wouldn't trust him as far as I could throw him," Granny muttered as if she could read my mind.

After that, dinner was a subdued affair. None of us talked much. The food was warm and plentiful, savory as only butter-filled southern fare could be. The chicken was tender and the dumplings turned out to be flaky homemade biscuit dough Granny had dropped in the gravy, dollop by dollop, to boil. I wasn't sure what Jacob usually ate, but he hadn't forgotten how to do justice to a home-cooked meal.

I ate what I could so I wouldn't hurt Granny's feelings, but my stomach was tight with nerves. Granny didn't trust Jacob Walker. That shouldn't have been a problem for me. I never trusted anyone. But I found it suddenly was. I might still be prickly, but I was drawn to Jacob for reasons way beyond his messy hair and his mossy eyes. I was afraid there was wildwood magic to blame for how I wanted to relax in his company—and Granny really wasn't going to like that.

When Charm crawled out to sit on the arm of my chair, I tried to act as if I always fed a pet mouse at the table while a big fat cat stared and stared. No one else seemed to mark Charm's sudden ease with a handsome dinner companion he'd previously greeted with only growls and teeth.

The cab of the turquoise Chevy smelled like oil and gasoline and maybe a hint of squirrel cache. But someone—Joseph or Jacob—had hung a tree-shaped air freshener on the rearview mirror that attempted to dispel the less pleasant odors with a touch of fake pine. Someone had also washed down the console and the vinyl seat cushions and vacuumed out the floorboards, where only a little of the passing road showed through rusted-out places.

Jacob gave me the driver's seat with a show of confidence I didn't feel myself. I knew how to drive a manual transmission, but I'd learned in a cheap little hatchback that had been my and Sarah's first car. It hadn't been nearly as high off the ground and its gearshift had been easy to manipulate.

I learned the stubborn shifting required of the old Chevy with Jacob's help by the light of the setting sun. The knob of the shifter vibrated under my hand and I tried not to notice how warm and strong Jacob's hand was over mine as he demonstrated how to manhandle the truck into gear. Depressing the clutch took the remainder of my strength and the steering wheel was so loose and crazy that the ride back to the cabin was too much of an exhilarating jounce for conversation. Not because of Jacob's hand. His touch was impersonal and instructive. Nothing more. But I was more than ready to jump down and get out of the truck when we finally arrived.

"... *wouldn't trust him as far as I could throw him.*"

I'd left the porch light on to welcome me home. It currently illuminated Jacob's Jeep in the driveway and a veritable flock of moths attracted by the glowing halo in the mountain dark.

"Come in and get a jar or two of jam before you leave," I said. I wasn't sure if I wanted him to clear out as soon as possible or linger for a while. Charm was asleep in my pocket and didn't get a vote.

"I'd like that," Jacob said.

I unlocked the front door and reached for the switch.

Nineteen

On the counter that had been empty, a cardboard box sat. It was the box filled with photographs in frames that had been in the bottom of the hall closet. I'd planned to go through it eventually, but I'd been conveniently too busy since the day I'd moved in. Sarah would be in that box. The Sarah I'd dreamed about. The Sarah of the cheerful school art in the upstairs room. That Sarah made me nervous because she wasn't the Sarah I had loved and the difference made me wonder what other information from the past I was missing.

"What's wrong?" Jacob asked. I'd paused inside the front door and my frozen body kept him from entering.

"That box wasn't there when I left this morning," I said. I forced myself forward so Jacob could see the box and the frames set up all around it in a jumbled tableau. "I must have left the back door unlocked."

"Or someone has a key," Jacob said.

My spine tingled as adrenaline spiked at his suggestion. A faceless intruder had come into the place I had claimed as my summer home and been so bold as to rummage through closets without putting things back the way she or he had found them. This was way more intrusive than the natural gas company's flyers left on my front door.

Jacob went quickly past me and over to the back door. The knob turned easily when he tried and he opened the door to the darkness of the backyard. Beyond the yard, the forest was even darker. The sun had fully set. Early autumn crickets sounded in a chorus that was too cozy to be the backdrop of a break-in.

"Why would someone come in uninvited to look through old photographs?" I wondered. I went to the counter so I could look at the pictures that had been taken from the box and propped on the stands of their frames. They had been arranged facing the door as if someone was trying to show them to me when I came home. "Not only looked through them. Left them out for me to see."

"I guess it could have been any of Granny's friends. They might have keys in order to come in and clean," Jacob suggested. He closed the door and reengaged the lock. He also slid the dead bolt home. Then he came over to look at the photographs too. There were snapshots of a younger Sarah. The lighter, happier one I'd never known. She smiled from the photographs with a rambunctious twinkle in her eyes to go with a wide-open grin. There were also several photographs of Lu as a young girl. I'd seen her like that in my dreams. More serious than Sarah, but still lighter and easier than the woman I knew today. I couldn't separate Sarah's love for her best friend from my own heart. I'd loved Lu right away because of those dreams and now I saw her exactly as she'd been in those days. My dreams were accurate right down to the gap between her two upper front teeth.

"I don't think any of them would come without letting me know. Besides, I saw most of them in town today," I said. "What about Tom? He might have a key."

One of the photographs was of Tom and a curly-haired woman I recognized as well. Sarah's mother. Alive and even more twinkling than her daughter. She looked at the camera boldly, as though inviting the photographer to join her on an adventure. And Tom looked at her, his eyes gentled by admiration, his face undamaged and handsome although it had already been made craggy by the sun.

His look made me blush. It was open and honest and raw about his feelings for Melody Ross. No wonder he still took care of the garden so long after her death. This photograph revealed his love for the young wisewoman. A love I suspected lasted to this day.

"Tom keeps to the woods mostly. You won't find him in town or near houses very often if he can help it. He's shy," Jacob said. "From the looks of his face, he has reason to be. No one knows exactly how or when he was hurt."

The other photographs were all of Sect women.

Dozens of them. The homespun dresses and kerchiefs on their hair were exactly the same as the ones I'd seen on the women in town with Reverend Moon. But their expressions were not the same. These women smiled and laughed. Many showed the signs of pregnancy, but unlike the women I'd seen, they didn't seem afraid.

The difference between those women in town and the women in these photographs was Melody Ross. She was in many of them. Hugging the Sect women. Holding them. Touching a shoulder here. Or laying a hand on the top of one's head there.

No wonder Reverend Moon had come through the wildwood to see what or who was luring his flock away. These photographs lent credence to my dream. The Sect women—some of them little more than girls—had come here for Melody's help and she had given it. I shivered in admiration when I remembered Sarah's mother facing the wildwood and sending Sarah and Lu back to the house. I'd met Reverend Moon now. I'd confronted him in real life.

These photographs of the Sect women with Melody Ross told a story of courage—on their part and hers. Sarah had always thought I was brave. Her mother had been more courageous than I had ever been.

One photograph had been placed in front of all the others. The woman in the photograph seemed to be wearing a Sect dress, but she'd removed her head covering. She had a curly chestnut mane. Similar to my own. But the photograph didn't show her face. She was looking down at a tiny swaddled infant in her arms. I picked up the frame and opened the back, but there was no writing on the back of the photograph. The woman was a mystery.

Someone had wanted me to see these photographs and that someone had placed this one in front.

"Until you figure it out, keep the dead bolt locked. Especially when you're sleeping," Jacob suggested. "I don't like the idea of someone coming and going without your permission."

"I like it less than you do," I said. I placed the photographs of the Sect women back in the box. But I decided to keep the one of Sarah and Lu out, as well as the one of Tom and Melody. These were happy photographs. They belonged on display. I carried the two frames over to the sofa table and arranged them. But the action gave me time to have an extremely uncomfortable thought.

"... *wouldn't trust him as far as I could throw him.*"

Granny hadn't tried to stop me from taking Jacob with me to the cabin to retrieve his vehicle. Jacob's Jeep was in the driveway outside. He'd been down at the barn to get the old Chevy, but at some point he'd been here at the cabin alone.

Was he the one who had come inside, poking around? He picked up the box while my mind raced . . . and he carried it back to the hall closet. The door was slightly ajar. He kicked it the rest of the way open with his foot and placed the box exactly back in the place where it had been. Had the slightly open door clued him in to where the box belonged? Or had he been the one who found it there, so he knew where it should be returned? The idea he would pretend ignorance made me slightly sick. I'd warmed to him more than I should. The two of us had enjoyed a relatively easy camaraderie all evening in spite of Granny's awkwardness. So much so I hadn't even thought twice about us being out here all alone.

Charm stirred in my pocket, no doubt woken up by my sudden fear. My hands had closed into fists and my back had gone stiff. Jacob was no slouch. He wasn't muscle-bound, but if he wanted to harm me he probably could no matter what I did to defend myself.

Damn the nightmares that allowed me to easily call up the vision of Sarah's mother hanging in the black locust tree.

I had allowed myself to be caught completely isolated with a stranger. He'd helped plant the bergamot, and later, he'd tended it, but that didn't mean that I knew him. I thought the accident that killed Sarah had been caused intentionally and I knew for certain that Melody Ross had been murdered. Maybe even in this very room.

"I'm sure there's an innocent explanation. No one around here bothers much with locked doors. Crime is low and people generally look out for each other," Jacob said. He headed toward the door as he spoke. I wasn't sure if he noticed my unease, but I didn't care. I edged back from him as he passed, completely uncomfortable with the rapid rise of suspicion tightening my chest.

"Crime is low except for the occasional murder," I corrected.

Jacob paused parallel to my position. He looked down at me and I was pretty sure he noticed my clenched fists and my stiff posture. My eyes were narrowed and there was the distinct sound of a growl coming from my pocket.

"I didn't notice anything earlier today when I came for the truck," he said. "But, of course, I didn't come inside."

"Of course," I said, not at all sure he was telling the truth.

"You're right to be careful, Mel. I'll get that jam another time," Jacob said. "Lock the door behind me. Dead bolt and all."

I walked to the door on leaden feet to turn the lock and slide the bolt above it home behind him. The bolt wiggled in its slot, not nearly as sturdy as I would have liked it. I would fix that tomorrow. I wouldn't allow the fog of fear currently threatening to cloud my mind to stop me from taking practical actions. Jacob or not, someone had intruded. Now that I had a vehicle, I could easily run into town for a better bolt. Sarah and I had lived in Richmond apartments with lazy supers where we'd had to install a half dozen locks because of dangerous neighborhoods. The hardware store wouldn't be open tonight, but I would be there when the doors opened tomorrow morning.

The photographs on the sofa table mocked me when I left the downstairs lights on before climbing up to my bedroom.

Jacob Walker's Jeep rolled to a stop near the barn where the turquoise Chevy used to sit. Headlights went black. There was no moon and the stars didn't illuminate much when the Jeep's door opened to allow a graceful silhouette to exit. Several doe in the field opposite the barn were spooked when the silhouette paused and mimicked the exact sound of a screech owl, once, then twice, before it made its way back up the road toward the cabin. The deer flashed the whites of their tails and then took flight, disappearing into the forest as if pursued by a dangerous predator. But the silhouette didn't give chase. It had another job to do.

Sarah had a willow basket full of blackberry jelly hooked over her left arm. Her right arm was hooked at the elbow with Lu and they skipped together up the sidewalk of Main Street, dodging pedestrians and avoiding cracks with the absolute certainty of eleven-year-olds that their mothers' backs were depending on the careful placement of their feet.

Her mother had dropped them off to deliver the jars she'd canned the day before.

"Fresh is best, but canned will do very well in winter," Melody Ross always said.

Apparently, lots of folks agreed, because they had jars for almost every woman in town. While they delivered jam, her mother was to visit Granny, an old midwife who had agreed to give Melody lessons in the art of delivering babies.

More and more Sect girls were making their way through the wildwood to the cabin, and her mother had told Sarah they couldn't turn them away.

"They're desperate. Too scared to run away. Too traumatized to want their daughters to face the same fate. We have to help them, Sarah. As women. As human beings. The wildwood has led them to us, and now it's up to us to do the rest," her mother had said.

It was a secret. One they kept as they kept the exact date of Gathering and all the knowledge in the remedy book. To themselves and a select few of like-minded individuals. Lu and her mother knew. Granny and her friends knew. Tom knew. Mad Tom they called him. Because he lived way out in the woods, moving from caves to hollowed-out trees and dugouts he cut into the hills himself. Melody Ross didn't call him Mad. Never. And so Sarah didn't either. He was their friend and always had been.

Lu started singing. Sarah was glad it was a hymn everyone knew. She loved Lu's special songs she made up all in her own head. But people always took notice when she and Lu sang along to a new tune. One folks had never heard before. They couldn't know Sarah learned it instantly right from Lu's mind, but they seemed to suspect.

They skipped and sang about flying away from shop to shop and house to house. There was no payment exchanged for the blackberry jam. Every year, the supplies to can it up just arrived—bags of sugar from Mrs. Fields, lemon juice from Granny's friend Sadie, new seals from Granny herself. Like the bread at Gathering, the blackberry preserves were a sharing between the wildwood, Melody Ross and the women of the town.

Some of the women were no longer practicing the old ways, but their grandmothers and great-grandmothers had, and maybe, Melody said, their daughters would carry on the tradition again. The connection needed to be kept and preserved for later use like the blackberries themselves.

Jessica Morgan was like that. An elderly maiden aunt from the founding family of the town, Jessica had accepted a jar of blackberry preserves from the wildwood every autumn for as long as Sarah could remember. She lived in a tiny cottage behind the courthouse on Main Street. And this year Sarah and Lu approached it with no trepidation. Miss Morgan taught Sunday school at the Presbyterian church, and both Lu and Sarah had attended Bible school there on occasions when there was a fun theme during a rainy summer day.

Sarah didn't pay much mind to the shiny convertible sports car in the bricked drive when they walked up to the door. All the Morgans were rich and it wouldn't be a big deal to see Jessica Morgan's brother or nephew come to call. But Lu slowed and stopped, tugging on Sarah's free arm to make her pause.

"Maybe we should bring the jam back when Miss Morgan is alone," Lu said.

Sarah might have agreed if she'd been delivering some of her mother's other wares. She'd seen townspeople become outright ugly about love potions or sleeping tisanes.

"I don't guess there's any harm in blackberries, Lu. Even rich people like biscuits and jam," she argued.

Lu didn't seem convinced, but she let Sarah loose and followed after her to the side door.

"Always go the back or to the side doors, girls. Back-porch friends are best," Sarah's mother had taught them.

But, this time, instead of the door being answered by the familiar stooped form of Miss Jessica Morgan and the walker she used to get around now that her joints were stiffened by arthritis, the door was flung wide by Hartwell Morgan, a teenager just mean enough for both girls to fear.

"Little bitches come to call," Hartwell sneered. "Or is it witches? I've heard that might be the truth of it. Don't you know Halloween is a month away?"

Hartwell was older than them. He'd left the elementary school two years before and now attended the combination middle and high school that was situated over Sugarloaf Mountain and halfway down the other side to be shared with the next town over. He stepped through the open doorway and loomed over Sarah as if he dared her to back away. She refused. Acting like her feet were glued to the ground even though his expensive leather loafers had toed up to her cotton sneakers and she didn't like his nearness, not at all.

"We aren't trick-or-treating. We've brought Miss Morgan her jam," Sarah said. There was no reason for her heart to pound and sweat to break out on her upper lip. There was no reason for Lu to grab ahold of her arm like she was going to haul her away. Hartwell wasn't kind. That was true. He was a bully for sure. But they were standing in front of God and every-body in the middle of town and, Morgan or not, Hartwell wouldn't actually hurt them.

"My aunt isn't feeling well today. Maybe she's been eating too much hippy trash. Your mom even have a business license for the junk she sells out of the back of her car, little girl?" Hartwell asked. Sarah didn't like the way he sidled closer or the way he leaned down to press his face near hers or the way little girl *caused his hot breath to flow over her cheek.*

"Come on. Let's go," Lu insisted. This time she didn't wait for Sarah to argue. Not that Sarah would have anyway. She allowed herself to be pulled back down the footpath to the public sidewalk, glad that Lu forced the retreat before she humiliated herself by running away.

Because when he'd leaned close to her Sarah had seen something in Hartwell's eyes that said he would hurt her even in the middle of town . . . and no one would care like they should because he was a Morgan and she was just the child of a hippy, a witch, a woman who had never been married to an important man.

"When I run this town, things will be different," Hartwell shouted after them.

"You're crazy. Morgan's Gap will always be exactly the same," Lu yelled back, but it took several blocks between them and Miss Jessica's cottage before they were comfortable enough to slow down.

Twenty

I didn't sleep well. The sun had already risen by the time I had dressed and headed down for breakfast. I was getting used to a caffeine-free lifestyle, but on mornings like this, after fear-fueled dreams, I would have appreciated a cup of coffee.

I settled for the chicory root blend that had been a gift from Lu's grandmother and stood looking out the window in the back door, toward the wildwood. The yard was empty save for a woodpecker that passed through with a brilliant flash of its scarlet head and a flutter of white-tipped wings.

I'd known Hartwell was bad news two seconds into meeting him. I hadn't needed Sarah's memories. They were merely confirmation. Poor Violet. I wished she could run away as easily as Lu and Sarah had run all those years ago.

Charm was nowhere to be seen. He hadn't been in my bedroom and he wasn't on the kitchen counter or the back of the armchair he preferred so much that I'd placed a chenille throw there for him to use as a nest. Sometimes he disappeared for hours only to reappear with no indication of where he'd been.

The sound of a car in the drive broke the silence and I jerked wide-awake in a flash of trepidation that shamed me. I couldn't expect danger from every sound and visitor. That was no way to live.

Out the front window, I could see Lu's four-wheel drive station wagon settling behind the Chevy. Her car was instantly recognizable from all the festival and concert bumper stickers that covered not only the wagon's bumper but every inch of its backside. Along with the event stickers, there was a "Coexist," a pagan spiral symbol and a rainbow flag.

Then there was Lu herself. She exited the wagon with purpose and a hardware store bag in her hand. But she still paused and lifted her face to the sun coming over the tops of the trees behind the cabin. She breathed in deeply before slamming the car door and turning toward the porch. The familiar strips of colorful ribbon twisted into her hair, her bright red peasant blouse and her wide-legged jeans more than cheered me. Lu was all that was right with my world when everything else was wrong.

I'd already moved to open the front door and welcome her, all my fears that had lingered from the night before dispelled.

"Jacob called me. Out of the blue. On the shop phone. He said you needed a new dead bolt and that you might not be comfortable with him bringing it to you." There were questions in her eyes and in her voice, but she didn't ask them. She held out the bag and I took it. I rummaged through what she'd brought while she stepped inside, carrying with her the scent of morning dew and that hint of wood shavings that always lingered around her. The bag held a new brass bolt much larger and sturdier than the old one that was loose on the door and the screws and screwdriver needed to install it.

"Old Sue is running again," Lu continued, pointing back at the Chevy in the driveway.

"Jacob took it to the garage in town. They made it roadworthy for me," I explained.

"Huh. *Jacob* sure is taking a sudden interest in being neighborly," Lu noted. "And I've never known him to show any interest in anything that isn't a plant or a tree."

She arched one eyebrow high and I ignored it along with the quirk of her lips that seemed to be too knowing by far. My life was too confusing to add the complication of a friend's matchmaking to it.

"When we came back here last night to pick up his Jeep, someone had been in the house," I said. To bring her up to speed. Not to change the subject from the biologist who had done yet another considerate thing for me. He'd noticed my discomfort. He'd left and then he'd sent Lu with the new lock instead of coming himself where he wasn't exactly welcome. Had he known Lu was the one person in Morgan's Gap I completely trusted?

"Did they break in?" Lu asked, looking around to see if there had been any damage to the doors and windows. Her mouth had settled into a firm line and her eyes were no longer crinkled and teasing.

"No. And that's part of the problem. Either I forgot to lock the back door or they had a key," I said. "They had been through the closets and left a box of photographs on the counter. I won't feel comfortable sleeping unless I use the dead bolt and the one on the front door needs to be replaced."

"You stayed here after that?" Lu asked. She'd put her hands on her hips and I suddenly wondered if she'd pull me away from the cabin in the same way she'd pulled Sarah away from Jessica Morgan's cottage.

"This is my home, for now, Lu. I'm not going to be frightened away," I replied. My home. There. I'd said it. I held my breath for a few seconds, but the universe didn't dissolve and take it all away.

"You're nervous for good reason, but too stubborn to leave," Lu said.

"And nothing I say is going to change your mind." She lowered her hands from her hips and let out a long-suffering sigh. Her exasperation comforted me. I felt a smile relax my lips. I hadn't really known her that long, but Sarah's memories made it seem longer. Not sure why she acted like she felt the same, but I suspected it had something to do with the same reason the trio could finish each other's sentences.

"You're not wrong. I am stubborn. Sometimes it comes in handy," I confessed. My smile must have been contagious. Lu's mouth tried to curve softly at the edges, but the expression wavered as she looked around.

"This is the first time I've been to the cabin since the murder. I've missed every Gathering since then," Lu admitted.

"Oh, Lu…" I began. I didn't know exactly what Lu believed about the wildwood or the wisewomen who practically worshipped it. I only knew she'd brought the bee balm to the park based on a compulsion without batting an eye. "Granny says she brewed me here. And I've been dreaming. Lucid, vivid dreams that aren't actually dreams at all. Somehow Sarah's memories are alive in me. I…I feel like I've known you forever," I whispered. Sharing all my secrets with her left me feeling shaken and vulnerable, but wasn't that what connection was? Lowering your defenses. Being brave. Accepting the risks along with the benefits. My hands were shaking, but I immediately felt lighter. Especially when Lu's smile firmed and widened.

"I loved her, you know. When she was sent away, a part of me left with her. And when I started to tour and perform I looked for her face in every crowd," Lu said. Tears filled her warm brown eyes and I had to blink away the sting of answering tears in mine. I'd loved Sarah in a different way, but we had both lost her. I hadn't stopped to consider how horrible it was that Lu had lost her twice.

"There are photographs. And some of her artwork from school

is still on her bedroom walls upstairs," I said. "I've been meaning to box them up. It seems sadder to leave them there, somehow. I've been waiting for the right time. You should look and see if there's anything you'd like to take."

Lu nodded, then stooped to look closely at the photographs on the sofa table. She and Sarah were laughing at the camera and Sarah's arm was tossed around Lu's neck. Sarah had barely mentioned Lu to me, but I knew now it was because losing Lu must have been too painful for her to talk about on top of everything else.

Sarah hadn't dated much, but when she did, she dated women. Lu had been her first love. I'd felt the beginning of that love when I'd dreamed. Who knows what lifelong relationship they could have had if the murderer hadn't interrupted?

"I need to ask you something." I suddenly remembered the photograph of the Sect woman and baby the intruder had left out for me to find. The one that had been in front as if it was more important than the rest. I went over to the hall closet and pulled out the box. I'd left that photograph on top, subconsciously intending to look at it again.

"This was set up on the counter when I came home last night. Do you recognize the woman?" I asked. Lu had been here often as a young girl. She must have seen some of the Sect women come and go. The photograph didn't fully show the woman's face, but maybe there would be something about her that jogged Lu's memory.

She straightened and came over to take the framed photo from my hands.

"I think this photograph is older than I would remember, Mel. See how the color has faded around the edges. My baby pictures look like this in my mother's albums. The ones she took with a camera instead of a phone." She opened the frame the way I had to check the back for writing, but then she lifted the photo from the frame. She tilted it toward the light and then showed me the pale imprint of a date and time stamp on the development paper that had been used. I was too used to digital prints. I hadn't thought to check. I had no baby photographs of myself for reference.

"Yeah. As old as I am. If I ever met the woman or the baby, I wouldn't recognize them from this photograph," Lu said.

I was the same age. If Sarah's mother had helped this woman, she had helped her the same year I was born.

"I'm not much of a detective. I didn't even notice that date." I put the photograph back in the frame and then put it back in the box. On top. In case I wanted to look at it again. I was drawn to it. Probably because it had revealed a part of Melody Ross's secret life to me. Living out here by the wildwood. Helping the Sect women who couldn't go to anyone else for help.

"It was nighttime and you were upset," Lu said. She squeezed my shoulder before pushing the box back into the closet and shutting the door. When she turned back to face me, her serious expression had been replaced by a smile. "Plus Jacob Walker was in the room being all neighborly and helpful."

"At that point I thought he might have been the one to break in," I said, although her teasing had hit a little too close to home.

"He was ahead of me in school, but I remember him as a good guy. A quiet guy, not rowdy like some of the others. And his father was a friend of Granny's before he died. Not sure about his mother. They moved away from the mountain," Lu said.

"Was his mother a wisewoman too?" I asked. My pulse quickened at the thought. It would explain so much—Jacob's comfort in the forest and his obvious connection to it. "I'm surprised she left."

"She was an organist at the Episcopal church. But she came to Gathering every year I can remember before she left town. That much

I know," Lu said. "If she was, would that help you to consider Jacob a friend?"

I could easily imagine Jacob learning about nature at his mother's heels. He'd probably grown up in the woods. No wonder he loved the forest and knew so much about it. But, why had his mother moved away?

Friendship was too soft, too easy to describe what I felt for Jacob. So I didn't answer. "I can never figure out if Granny disapproves of Jacob going away to school or of his coming back," I said.

Lu laughed. Like her singing voice, her laugh was rich and ringing, filling the room and a person's heart at the same time. "Granny thinks everything we need to know is left in the bottom of a teacup after we drink."

I thought about the three of us planting the bee balm together. Three. Three. Three. Granny placed such importance on the number and I'd seen that emphasis in the remedy book as well. Sexual attraction aside, if I trusted Jacob, would the pull between us feel more like the pull I felt to Lu?

"Things are complicated right now. Too complicated for me to fall into a 'friendship' with Jacob Walker," I said. "And I might not be far from digging into my tea leaves for answers."

"I was raised in the wildwood, Mel. I never went away. The idea that Sarah would somehow share her memories with you doesn't shock me. I always believed she would come back. And she has. Through you and with you," Lu said. "I'm not a wisewoman. Not like Granny. But I've lived side by side with the old ways my whole life. You felt like a sister to me from the moment you walked into my shop."

We both stepped into the hug at the same time and Sarah's spirit was there with us. Kept alive because we would always love her, but also because we were in her wildwood, a part of it as much as she had been. Lu might not share Granny's exact beliefs, but she worked with wood from the forest every day. She inhaled the sawdust and brought the walnut's song to life with her own two hands. In her own way, she was as much a part of the wildwood as Jacob. Like Granny, her craft was as much mystical as practical.

"I'll go upstairs," Lu said into my hair. "There's a painting I remember. Of fairies flying around the blackberry bushes. Sarah was always chasing fairies. With Sarah you could never tell where a game ended and real life began." Lu stepped back, but her hands gripped my upper arms and it was that warm, firm hold that punctuated her next words. "My mother used to say she was a changeling. Left here by the fae. And she really was. Special in a way I won't forget," Lu said.

"She was. Even after her mother was killed, she was singular. Different. I saw the possibility of another world in her eyes. One I'd never known. One with more sunlight," I said, remembering. Lu had a faraway look in her eyes. For a moment, we were both seeing Sarah and maybe striving to feel whatever mystical gift she might have tried to bequeath to us.

But, in the end, we were left slightly sheepish with only ordinary dust motes settling around us. No fairies at all.

Lu went upstairs. She was gone for a long time. I waited patiently. I'd said my goodbyes to Sarah. I continued to say them every day. When the other woman came back downstairs, she held a watercolor painting in her hands. I hadn't looked very closely at the artwork on Sarah's walls, but this one had been created with a little more time and skill than the others I'd seen. She must have painted it just before she left the mountain.

"I'd like to keep this one, if it's okay," Lu said. She handed me the painting so I could see what I was giving away.

"Of course. I'm sure she would have wanted you to have it."

The blackberry bushes had been painted in enthusiastic splashes of purplish-black and green. The fairies were holding hands and hovering above the thorns. They looked out of the painting as if mischievously waiting to be chased by two girls who were out of frame.

"It's time for me to go to the garden again. I need to visit her there, alone, if you don't mind," Lu said over my shoulder. I placed the painting on the counter for her to take with her when she left.

"I'll stay here and fix the bolt on the door and then we'll have some lunch," I said.

I understood why Lu needed to say goodbye, but I also suspected she needed to reconnect with the garden and the forest in ways she hadn't been able to accomplish at a distance or through her music.

It was almost time for Gathering. All the wisewomen would come together for the baking and the breaking of the bread. It wouldn't be only a few old women like Granny who would come. There would be women like Lu and like me. There would be children. And maybe it would mean more to some than others, but I was responsible for treating the process with the respect and even reverence it deserved.

Because of Sarah, but also for myself. I'd been a survivor my whole life, but I hadn't stopped to figure out what I was surviving for until Sarah had died. I'd experienced a deep and peaceful satisfaction in following the recipes in the Ross Remedy Book. I didn't know if it was the careful processes that took me away from the pain or if it was the connection to the past and the wildwood and the women that had come before me when I'd never had any connection at all.

What I did know now that I had found Granny, the trio and Lu was that the pain I carried wasn't only the pain of losing Sarah. It was pain at the injustice that had left me alone, targeted and hurt as a child, and as an adult, by hate and ignorance and corruption.

It felt as if I was fighting that injustice. Which was crazy. I was making jam and bread. And yet, the truth of the fight pounded in my heart when I realized that jam and bread from the wildwood was life, the simple power of life itself. By sharing what I made, I was sharing the ongoing cycle of life with others.

The pagan symbol on Lu's station wagon was a spiral. Ongoing. Eternal. And what was survival really but the desire to go on?

The old bolt came off the front door easily. But it took me a while to replace it. The wood was still solid enough that I had to wrestle the screws into it. When I was finally finished, my stomach was already protesting the single cup of hot chicory brew I'd had for breakfast.

On the back porch, there was an ancient metal furniture set painted a pale green. I carried a platter of grilled cheese finger sandwiches and a covered pitcher of lemonade outside and sat on the glider. I gently pushed it to rock forward and backward while I watched the path for Lu to return.

"We used to sit there and break beans for Melody," Lu said. She'd stopped at the end of the path to look at me before she'd come forward into the yard. My hair was untied. It curled all around my face. Maybe I'd reminded her too much of Sarah for a second. Curly hair was a mountain thing. I saw it often in Morgan's Gap. Ross blood, Granny said, showing up in people generations after it had been sown.

"Sarah used to buy fresh green beans at the market in Richmond. She taught me how to break them. They really are better fresh than they are frozen or canned," I said.

Lu came over and sat down on the other end of the glider. I passed her the platter of grilled cheese and she took a sandwich. Then, I returned the platter to the table and poured her a glass of lemonade.

Her eyelashes were spiky and there were tearstains on her cheeks.

The first trip to the garden was the hardest. After that, I'd found there was comfort in it. I'd decided the tradition wasn't macabre, as I'd originally thought. It was soothing. All the Ross women resting in the roots of the black locust trees seemed fitting. The garden thrived and died and thrived again. Its cycle was a perpetual memorial.

"I thought I should visit the garden before Gathering, but I'll be back for the breaking of the bread. Sarah would want that. She wouldn't want me to lose that connection especially now that she's gone," Lu said.

"I'll begin cultivating the wild yeast tomorrow," I said. "I've studied all the instructions and I'm going to start a little early so I can redo the culture if I mess up." My voice must have betrayed my nervousness because Lu drained her lemonade and stood. She placed her empty glass on the table and then reached to take my hand in both of hers. They were calloused from her work—bumps on the pads of her fingers where she plucked the strings, rough skin on her palms from where she sanded the wood into a high gloss. She didn't comment about the scars on my fingers. She accepted them as if everyone she knew had been scarred in one way or another. No big deal.

"Sarah would be so happy you're here. Taking up the old ways. Continuing on with traditions stolen from her. You were her family. Nobody better to bake the bread. Nobody," Lu said. She squeezed my hand tight and then she let it go, but the warmth of her confidence in me lingered well after she was gone.

Sarah's shoulders and forearms and even her fingers ached from hours of kneading dough. It might be a few more years before she had the same muscular forearms her mother had from years of doing the same, but this year she hadn't given up. She'd kneaded long into the evening after older, more

*experienced women had quit. And even after a quick shower at the crack of
dawn this morning her skin still smelled yeasty and sweet.*

Or maybe the scent was stuck in her nose.

*It was joined by the scent of baking bread—rich rye dough becoming
golden brown with crusts toasted dark. They'd baked all day yesterday and
all through the night. There were loaves in the oven of the cabin's kitchen
right now. Even as they wiped the dew off the tables and spread the old
scarred wood with bleached white cloths.*

*All who could come to the Ross cabin to help had set up long, low tables the
night before. Dozens of them covered the backyard in rows, surrounded on
three sides by the wildwood and backed by the cabin itself. The setup allowed
people to come through the house if needed or from the path that led from the
driveway around the end of the cabin. By the end of the day, there would be
a hundred vehicles or more parked along the drive and spilling over into the
fields by the barn, freshly mowed by Mr. Brown for the occasion.*

*Her mother traded the hay from the fields for the labor. In Morgan's
Gap, most people were "doing all right," but few had extra money. Growing things, making things, raising things...All to make ends meet...while
working at whatever jobs they could find even if it meant driving down the
mountain to larger towns and cities was a way of life.*

But today was the first Sunday in November.

*Gathering didn't need balloons or streamers or any decorations. Her
mother had explained to her when she was still a little girl that the wildwood provided a blaze of color for Gathering. It provided the yeast and the
grain for the bread. It provided the apple blossom honey they gleaned from
the hives that sat in a small clearing near the Hall's orchard. It even provided the fresh churned butter because of the hay Mr. Brown's cows ate.*

And, of course, Sarah's favorite blackberry jam.

*Folks carried out platter after platter of toasted brown loaves. It was
easy to forget sore muscles when people were laughing and talking and your*

mouth was watering. Other tired hands patted her shoulders or ruffled her curls. Some even praised her work, noticing that she was no longer one of the young'uns that ran around their legs. There were dozens of kids too young to help. Oh, maybe they would be interrupted now and then to fetch or carry before they were absorbed back into their games of hide-and-seek or tag. They flitted like the fairies she used to pretend to be, in and out of the forest paths and, with them, the occasional flash of an animal.

"You missing those days?" Lu asked with a grin. Like Sarah, she was just past the point of playing in the woods with the little ones. She carried a crock full of butter that had been chilling in an ice-water bath for several hours. It was covered by a wooden lid that fit snuggly down into its opening to keep the bugs out. The same crock had probably been cooled in a springhouse before refrigeration and ice came to the mountain. There were still some in use, built to last of rock that had become moss covered because of their proximity to cold water bubbling up from deep in the ground.

"A little. If I move my back just so," Sarah confessed. She twisted her neck to show where the stiffness from hours of kneading caught between her shoulder blades.

"Your mom made twice as many as we did. I don't think I'll ever be that fast," Lu said.

"We can manage if we work together," Sarah said. The cool morning air made the heat in her cheeks too noticeable, so she turned away from Lu to help arrange the platters of bread and baskets of jam on the table. Jars of honey glowed golden in the warmth of the rising sun.

She and Lu had been inseparable for a long time. It was only recently she'd noticed a nervous flutter in her stomach whenever Lu touched her hand or cut her eyes a certain way, but it was related to the way her spirit swooped high when Lu sang or laughed or picked out a tune with her nimble fingers on the mandolin.

There were other wisewomen paired together. Enough that the idea wasn't unheard of for Sarah. She'd never chased boys the way some of the other girls had done, not on the playground or through town. She'd never once wanted to catch a boy's eye. It had always been Lu for her. And she was pretty sure it always would be.

But she wasn't sure how to figure out if Lu felt the same.

"Let's get started," Sarah's mother said loudly from the open door of the cabin. She came forward with the stump that had been fashioned into a knife holder. It had been polished by a hundred hands by now so its patina matched the patina of the wood-handled knives that had been sharpened on the whetstone so many times their blades were nearly as thin as paper when they were pulled, one by one, from the slots in the block.

Each woman who had helped make the bread took a knife. And although there were a few smiles, including the one shared between Sarah and her mother when Sarah pulled out a knife for the first time in her life, all the laughter had died. This part was solemn. A quiet before Gathering truly began.

The loaf Sarah cut into was one of the last loaves to come out of the oven. Steam rose up from each slice, so thick and fragrant Sarah could taste the flavor of the rye on the back of her tongue. A line of people had formed, but every woman who cut the bread took the first piece for themselves. Soon the scent of melted butter and warmed honey joined the scent of rye in the air.

But Sarah ate her first slice plain. The whole grain rye was thick and firm between her teeth and heavily rich against her tongue. She chewed and swallowed the first bite slowly, savoring the fresh-baked goodness, but also savoring, as her mother had taught her, the connection to the wildwood. She closed her eyes as she swallowed and she saw a thousand moments from planting to harvest to baking, from seed to plant to table, from dirt to loaf.

The laughter resumed, calmer and quieter than before, as if the whole Gathering had also appreciated a moment of acknowledgment and gratitude during those first bites.

Sarah served hundreds of slices. So many that the faces of all the townsfolk blurred in front of her. But Lu was by her side, slicing and serving along with her throughout the morning, and the constant movement actually worked much of the soreness away. It was after nearly everyone had been served and the platters were filled with extra slices for anyone who would care for another, or five more for that matter, when Hartwell Morgan made an appearance.

He came into the backyard as if he owned it and many of the people at Gathering stopped to stare. He swaggered forward without acknowledging the audience, either because he was used to people gawking or because the onlookers were beneath him. It had been a year since he'd refused to allow Sarah and Lu to deliver the blackberry preserves to his aunt. In that time, he seemed to have grown another few inches taller and broader, filling in his formerly gawky teenage frame.

They'd never refused to serve someone at Gathering.

When Hartwell walked up to her table and stood directly across from her, waiting, even though there were plenty of slices he could have taken without waiting to be served, Sarah froze. Not like a deer in headlights. She wasn't afraid. When Lu had pulled her away, she hadn't been afraid and that had been in town. Here, in the wildwood, she had nothing to fear. This was her place, the Ross family place, a place they had claimed a century ago.

And a place that had claimed them.

From the corner of her eye, Sarah saw movement in the trees and among the trees. Children? Animals? The leaves and vines and branches themselves? It didn't matter which because they were one and the same.

Isn't that what Gathering proclaimed?

"Smells good," Hartwell said.

Sarah had been going through the motions of cutting and serving for hours, but suddenly her hands wouldn't obey. She'd been taught to obey her instincts. To listen to the wildwood whispers that directed her in the way she should go. The movement at the edges of her vision had expanded. Now it seemed that all three sides of the yard surrounded by the wildwood shimmered, and behind Hartwell Morgan's back a fox had appeared out of the forest shadows to stand with its four feet planted apart on the path and its bristly snout down.

Hartwell smirked expectantly and looked from her eyes down to the knife in her hand and back again.

But his smirk disappeared when Sarah raised the knife high and brought it down hard, driving the point into the table.

"Sarah!" Lu exclaimed. The thin, sharp blade had slid easily into the wood without breaking, but the weight of the wooden handle caused it to sway back and forth long after she'd taken her hand away.

"You'd better think twice, Hartwell. Might as well eat a handful of twigs. This bread might not agree with you." A boy Sarah had served earlier had stopped Hartwell's hand by the wrist. Sarah didn't know if Hartwell had been reaching for the handle of the knife or simply reaching for a slice of bread. The boy was Jacob Walker. She recognized him from school. He was a grade or two above her and a grade or two beneath Hartwell. He wasn't as tall as the older boy, but he was more muscular. He easily held Hartwell's wrist even when he tried to pull his arm away. "I'm telling you. Shits for days. These hippies have iron asses."

Hartwell laughed. Jacob met her eyes and his didn't hold a trace of humor in spite of his crude joke. He'd thanked her for his slice. He'd slathered it with blackberry jam and butter. She'd seen him eat it down to crumbs and then lick those from his fingers.

"What are you doing here, Walker?" Hartwell asked.

"My mother made me come. So I came. Now, let's get out of here," Jacob said. His face mirrored Hartwell's sneer. But the expression seemed weird on his face. Unlike the sneer that had already left its mark on Hartwell's face in soft lines that would probably harden in the years to come.

Sarah waited for Hartwell to refuse. She braced for uglier. What would she do if he tried to spoil the bread or ruin Gathering? The fox on the path hadn't moved. Now Sarah noticed her mother stood much like the fox, feet apart, chin down and eyes on Hartwell.

But Jacob Walker was lightning on his feet and he wore a jacket with the school's mascot emblazoned on the back identical to the one Hartwell Morgan was wearing. Unlike Hartwell, he'd earned his place on every team.

"Scrimmage?" Jacob asked. The whole Gathering heard it as the dare it was.

"Hell yeah," Hartwell jerked his wrist from Walker's hand as he turned to leave and this time Jacob let him go.

He nodded at Sarah and her mother when Morgan's back was turned. Then he followed the older boy away, looking like the older one himself by a half dozen years.

Twenty-One

I *wanted to thank Jacob* for calling Lu, but I was still wary of him. He was part of the mountain I was growing to love and not part of it at the same time. Granny's distrust matched my own instinctive surety that there was something about him I didn't understand. Unfortunately, that surety warred with another from somewhere deeper than head or heart or bone, a whisper that reminded me of fingers on petals and a tree on his wrist, of his care for the bees, and, of his evident care for *me*.

Reverend Moon and Hartwell Morgan had featured in my nightmares multiple times. Had one of them been the faceless man in the shadows the day that Sarah had made apple butter for one of the last times? I'd met both of the men in person now and I could well imagine either one frightening the Sect girl who had run away after the bee sting.

They frightened me too, but hadn't I learned by now that running away didn't solve anything?

It was Saturday and I'd decided to go to the farmers' market in town. I wanted to see Sadie's weaving and maybe even buy a new gathering basket of my own. I wasn't going to seek out Jacob, but if I happened to see him there was no harm in saying thank you.

I also figured the market would be the best place to ask questions and generally nose around. I'd noticed people were wary of strangers, but my affiliation with Granny was softening that natural distrust. The more they saw of me, the more people were likely to let me in on the "gossips and goings-on" as Granny would say. This mountain community had secrets, which meant there were individuals who might spill them.

I was becoming a part of the Morgan's Gap community, but, for all my time and effort, I didn't feel any closer to understanding why the Sect people watched my comings and goings. I'd grown used to seeing homespun dresses flash around corners or hats disappear around trees whenever I walked around town. The constant creeping wore on me. I encountered enough disapproving glares that I dreaded them even when none were around. But I was too busy to let their vaguely threatening surveillance slow me down.

Gathering was only a couple of weeks away.

That morning I had pasteurized the whole meal rye flour Granny had given me from a local mill by placing the bag in a low-temperature oven for forty-five minutes. While the flour was baking, I had scalded the bowl and the screen covering with boiling water and set aside some of the boiled water to cool. Once the flour was pasteurized, I placed it in the bowl and added enough of the sterilized water to make a thick mixture.

This process created a growth medium in the bowl just as Ross women had been doing for generations. Charm rode on my shoulder when I carried the covered bowl out to its place in the roots under the oak tree near the wildwood garden. I pushed away the image of a disapproving Reverend Moon that haunted the spot and focused instead on my purpose. The bowl fit perfectly in the root stand the tree had seemed to grow for it.

The mixture would be slightly sheltered there from the elements while still being open to the microbiology of the forest. I'd left it there, but I needed to check on it each day until a stinky brown liquid formed on top. Once that happened, I'd pour the brown liquid away and add fresh rye flour and water to encourage the beneficial microorganisms to flourish. And I'd repeat that process until yeast bubbles began to show, continuing again and again until a frothy, bready scent indicated that my cultivation of wild yeast had been successful.

Please, please, please.

The rye bread was more important than the blackberry preserves or the dried herbs. It was much trickier than the pickles or the soaps. I felt like I was prepping for a final exam, only this one would be graded by a crowd of people I had known for only a short while. A crowd who would decide if I was who I had decided to be even before I could be certain myself.

Granny had faith in me, but my faith in Granny was a fledgling thing, not nearly as confident as it should be. I had more faith in the Ross Remedy Book mainly because Sarah had believed in it and the strong foundation it represented. The book had become my constant companion. So much so that I spent as much time analyzing the scribbles and sketches and doodles in its margins as I did reading the recipes. And that was something because many of the recipes were written in archaic English and tiny scrawls I could barely understand.

The entire book was illustrated. Trees, plants, seeds, animals, mushrooms and other fungi—some artwork was beautifully rendered in exquisite detail, some was obviously the work of a moment to scribble in a random thought or a likeness.

I especially loved the foxes and looked for them like a quirky game of *Where's Waldo*. There were dozens throughout the book and each one was sketched with precision that captured every whisker and every strand of fur. I wondered if the fox had been someone's familiar and after that I took particular notice of all the forest creatures that had been sketched. There were thousands. Squirrels, raccoons, rabbits and turtles. Owls, crows, bullfrogs and weasels.

Not so whimsical were the anatomically correct hearts that also showed up with startling frequency. Not so strange in a book full of medically helpful natural remedies maybe. But still somehow out of touch with the usual style of doodles and entries. There was also a strange fascination with the moon. Every phase. Every stage. Drawn over and over again by what seemed to be the same hand. I might have been wrong, but I decided the moons and the hearts had been drawn by the same person, their strange obsession threatening to overwhelm the pages.

I liked the familiars best. So much so that I began to doodle Charm in practice on spare sheets of paper. Granny had given the remedy book to me, but I wouldn't dare to make a mark in it. Not yet. Besides, I couldn't be sure Charm belonged. Not when I still wasn't sure if I belonged.

Currently, Charm perched on top of a satchel handbag Sarah had given me several Christmases ago. I understood the gift better now than I'd understood it then. On black denim fabric, embroidered foxes cavorted—running, jumping, standing up on their back legs and leaping over unseen obstacles. I imagined that Sarah had liked the foxes in the remedy book too. I'd tossed the satchel onto the passenger seat without realizing that Charm had hitchhiked inside of it, but he seemed no worse for wear. His whiskers were exactly as crinkled as ever. His nose a shade of pink too bright for nature and much more like a skein of yarn. He twitched it at me while I wrestled the truck to town, only occasionally cursing at a stubborn gear or the steering wheel's loose handling.

Someone had painted "farm use" on the rear tailgate with black paint, but I planned to ask Granny about the truck's legalities. I figured even in Morgan's Gap I would need tags and an inspection sticker, although I laughed at the idea the old smoking relic would pass any kind of fair inspection.

I made it into town and pulled into a free parking spot near the farmers' market. All the parking meters were covered with knitted covers like colorful scarves gone rogue and I wondered if they were official or if one of Granny's friends had decided to make parking free for the day with an impromptu yarn bomb display.

The covers made me grin, as did the chaotic atmosphere of the street and the market pavilion. Like a barn, the pavilion had a bright red metal roof, but it was open on all four sides so the rows of booths under its shade were visible. More shoppers than I would have imagined walked up and down the aisles. I noted the plates on the vehicles as I passed. There were some from as far away as North Carolina and West Virginia.

Charm tried to climb onto my shoulder, but I transferred him to the pocket of my jean jacket instead. I wasn't sure Morgan's Gap was ready for a pet mouse familiar even on a market day.

Once I had entered the circus of people and wares, browsers and artists, craftsmen and customers that made the open marketplace seem like a big top under its red metal roof, I knew no one would have noticed a mouse on my shoulder. Not when there was so much going on and all sorts of other distractions.

I passed a fiery kiln used by a glassblower who was shaping a multicolor swirling blob on the end of a long metal pipe. He blew into the end of the pipe at intervals only he understood while a small crowd oohed and aahed over the hollow glass sphere taking shape. Spheres he'd already completed were hung on a nearby rack by gossamer nylon threads. The colorful glass tossed a prismatic rainbow over passersby.

"Only twenty dollars," a young woman said, noticing my interest.

My low-key lifestyle rarely required me to tap into savings, but I was acutely aware I no longer earned a steady paycheck. I couldn't afford pretty baubles no matter how much I could imagine the amethyst sphere brightening the cabin's kitchen.

"Maybe next time," I said, tapping the one I most liked with a fingertip to make it gently spin. The woman wasn't a pushy salesperson. She smiled and nodded and spoke to the next potential customer stopping by.

Thankfully, Sadie's booth was nearby so I wasn't tempted by anything else before I found her. She sat in the middle of four tables that held completed baskets. Like some of the other artisans, she was weaving a basket as a means to draw attention as well as add to her stock. Arranged all around her chair in neat, easily accessible containers were the supplies I'd seen in the back of her minivan, as well as a tub of water she used to soak the branches to make them supple and easier to maneuver. Her gloved hands moved so quickly it was hard to keep up with what she was doing. Had her mother slowed down the process for teaching or had Sadie simply picked up the technique by some superhuman means of observation I didn't possess?

My heartbeat kicked up a notch when I noticed the honeybees that came and went while Sadie worked. She wasn't wearing her earrings today. But actual bees would occasionally rest on her lobes in between flights as if they were comfortable there. Sadie never shooed them away. After a while, I accepted that there would be no overwhelming buzz in my head and no repeat of my previous mistake. Either because there were only a few bees or because I was gaining a little more control of myself—the gardening, the canning, the constant immersion of myself in the wildwood. And, of course, Charm. I had my own familiar now. I didn't need to borrow Sadie's.

"There's another chair. Mom wasn't feeling well today. Come sit with me awhile," Sadie said. I'd seen the other chair. A quilted pad covered its seat and its back was a rounded Windsor meant to hold a much larger woman than me. I sat, but the chair made me feel like a child even though my legs touched the ground.

"This one will be too small for you. I like to keep smaller ones on hand for people who want to use them for storage or decoration. Or for children," Sadie said. The bottom of the basket she was weaving was round. The staves on the side were longer branches that had been woven into the base. Sadie was currently weaving the sides of the basket by twining soaked branches in and around and out the staves. Around and around. When one branch was finished, she reached down to pick up another to begin the next row. Again and again. It was soothing to watch and satisfying to see the basket take shape. She used only three tools—and she told me about them as I watched. A bodkin looked almost like a screwdriver. It had a sharp metal shaft that narrowed down to a point and was used to create slots to begin the cross-shaped base of the basket. There were small clippers used to trim the length of branches and a knife used to sharpen the edges of any branches that needed to be inserted into slots the bodkin had made.

"I don't kill trees for my materials. I take trimmings from anyone who offers. I rarely have to ask. I hunt for deadfall in the spring. There are always trees that are felled by ice and snow over winter," Sadie murmured. It almost seemed like a crooning lullaby she was singing to the developing basket in her hands. A reassurance that its life hadn't begun with death.

"Willow and birch," I noted.

"Willow and birch are my main materials, but I'll work with most any, really. Oak and ash are pretty," Sadie said. "You can choose whichever of the larger ones you like. Picking a basket is more complicated than material, size or shape. It's more personal. You'll know which one when you touch it. Try," she continued. She nodded toward the stacks of baskets on the tables. So many I was overwhelmed at where to start. But I rose at her direction anyway.

I'd known they would be expensive, but I swallowed hard when I saw the tiny sticker price tags on the larger baskets that would be right for my needs. I was glad I hadn't splurged on the glass orb. This was a business expense, but it would put a noticeable ding in my savings.

"Don't worry about the cost. Granny says you've more than earned the price of my best basket with all the work you've done for her since you came to town. Plus caretaking at the cabin," Sadie said as if she'd read my thoughts.

At that, I allowed my hands to trail more firmly over the baskets. I'd been afraid Sadie was going to try to give me one. I could accept one as payment better than I could accept one as a gift. The oak and ash baskets were made differently than the branch baskets. Their sides were woven with split strips so their color was pale and bright, but it was the branch baskets that seemed sturdier.

Again and again, I was drawn back to the willow.

One in particular seemed to get stuck in my hands. Sadie had woven it with very narrow branches that were almost vines. Because of the size of the branches, it had taken many more rows to complete the entire basket. I turned it over and over again, loving the smooth feel of it against my palms. Its color was dark brown, but with a greenish tinge like the moss I'd seen on the wildwood floor. And Sadie had created a pattern with the green and brown variations of the branches that reminded me of the bean kaleidoscope on the dresser.

There was no price sticker on this basket. From its beauty and its size and the strength of its handle and construction, it was worth too much for me to take. But when I tried to place it back on the table, Sadie interrupted.

She had risen from her chair without me noticing. I'd been so focused on the basket in my hands.

"That's the one. I knew it. I knew it was special when I made it. Never put a price on it. I knew it was for someone. Just didn't know who. Now I do. Don't you dare try to set it back down. It's yours. Was yours before you touched it," Sadie said.

My eyes burned. It was crazy. I hadn't known I was coming to Morgan's Gap until the morning I got in my car with Sarah's ashes. There was no way Sadie had woven this basket for me and yet my hands and my heart believed it.

"I hope you'll use it for years to come," Sadie said. She patted the side of the basket and then she patted my cheek. "Now go use whatever money you were going to spend on a basket. I have to get back to work."

I turned from Sadie's stall, blinking back the salty moisture burning my eyes. I wasn't used to presents. And certainly not presents handmade with such care. Accepting the gift meant I also had to accept that I was important to Sadie. Hard, but doable. That Sadie had become important to me was harder. I could fight back the tears, but I couldn't deny the cause of them.

Caring made me vulnerable.

I hooked the basket in the crook of my arm the way Sarah always hooked the basket in my dreams. I slowly walked away as Sadie began to weave the small basket again. It was difficult to feel Sadie's support and also, somehow, wonderful. With the basket on my arm, I was wholeheartedly taking my place in Morgan's Gap. I didn't go straight back to the glassblower's booth. There might be other, more practical things I should buy first.

Faces I recognized from my delivery days in town stood out in the crowd. Many spoke and remembered my name. Some blushed and hurried away. A few asked after Granny's health or asked me if I had any more blackberry jam. Soon I was moving from display to display as if I was part of the circus not a detached observer.

"He found you some chanterelles this time, Vee. I set them aside in case you made it by today." An older woman behind a table filled with wild foraged fungi of every shape and size imaginable handed a small nylon sack filled with bright yellowish-orange funnel-shaped mushrooms to Violet Morgan. Violet's hair and makeup weren't as perfect as they'd been in the hair salon. In fact, her hair was tousled and her eye makeup smudged. As if she'd been crying. But her clothes were as old-fashioned and perfect as they'd been before. She wore a dress with a nipped waist and full skirt and a shirtwaist bodice. For some reason imagining a closetful of nearly identical dresses made me feel a little sick.

"Hi, Mrs. Morgan. I hope you liked the jam," I said. It was a mistake. I'd been lulled by the mostly easygoing manners I'd encountered.

Violet whirled and looked at me with the chanterelles "he" had collected for her clutched to her chest. She didn't answer my question. She only hurried away and disappeared in the crowd.

"Oh, Lord. She scares easy," the woman who had given Violet Morgan her mushrooms said. "Mad Tom's the same way. He forages for me, but he doesn't like to talk much."

"Tom sent Violet Morgan the chanterelles?" I asked, dropping the offensive use of *mad*.

"Yes, but don't let on. That husband of hers hardly lets her out of his sight. She comes by once in a great while. Tom always leaves something with me she'll like. Chanterelles in fall. Running cedar around Christmas. Queen Anne's lace in spring. Not sure how they met, but it's harmless. They're both too backward to take it too far," the woman said. "Lord knows, Hartwell doesn't do a thing that makes her smile."

"I've met him. I won't say a word," I said. But I couldn't reconcile the eccentric woods dweller I'd met with a man who'd send secret presents to the mayor's doll-like wife.

Twenty-Two

I *didn't purchase any mushrooms* for myself, but I did end up buying several bags of homemade candy. I couldn't resist Lynn and her children. Andy, Randy and Sandy waved me over, and for the first time I thought that maybe Randy was the tallest, Andy the oldest, and Sandy the one whose shoes were always untied. Their carefully lettered sign said that proceeds from the sale of the candies they'd made would help the Humane Society. Sarah and I had always had a soft spot for orphans, animals or otherwise.

And sweets.

I savored a dark red cinnamon drop while I continued from booth to booth. I planned to make my way back around to the glassblower's spheres, but I was interrupted by the quiet appearance of Jacob Walker from out of the crowd. He didn't seem to notice me. I stopped in my tracks before I reached the booth where he had paused to look at hand-carved hiking sticks. People flowed around me without complaint as if I was a rock thrown into their stream.

The walking sticks were works of art. From here I could see the handles and knobs had been carved into all sorts of animals and the staffs had been made from carefully chosen saplings shaped by climbing vines. I wasn't surprised Jacob would be interested in the carver's wares. But the amethyst orb he held by its nylon thread did surprise me. It spun around and around as he idly twisted the thread in his fingers, catching and throwing the sun in a dance of purple to lavender light. There was no mistaking the one I'd wanted because each of the glassblower's spheres was unique.

An accidental nudge from a person trying to pass around me finally urged me forward. I'd intended to thank him if I saw him. I couldn't back down now because the actual seeing made my pulse a little quick.

He still hadn't seen me. With his free hand, he turned a walking stick this way and that examining its cleverly carved handle, which looked exactly like a running fox. I stopped beside him, noting that each bristle of the fox's whiskers and each hair on its back and tail had been perfectly rendered in the cherrywood. Two shiny obsidian chips had been glued into the proper places for its eyes. Like the fox sketches in the remedy book, this fox had been rendered with such personality it seemed like it might leap off the hiking stick at any moment.

"I'll trade you the walking stick for the orb." I had no idea how much the walking stick cost. I only knew that Jacob Walker was bound to have it. I could see the connection between him and the tiny wooden beast. It was graceful and quick and from the wildwood after all. Just like the man beside me.

He let the hiking stick slide back into its place in the table, which the carver had modified with several dozen holes to hold the shafts of the canes to display them. Then, he turned toward me, lifting the glass sphere so its purple prism fell across my face.

"I wouldn't have guessed you'd like colorful baubles," Jacob said.

I glanced at the slowly rotating orb and back at the man who always seemed too determined to read me.

"The cabin is plain. And if I stay I'm going to need to make it mine," I said. My chin lifted because he wasn't wrong and it annoyed me. I'd never collected things, colorful or otherwise. Because you either had to leave possessions or lug them when things went south and neither was a great option. Jacob made me think twice about why I was drawn to the orb and why I hadn't bought it right away.

And that was annoying.

"I don't need another hiking stick. I have a graphite one. Works great in rough terrain," Jacob said.

"But you want the fox," I argued. "Just like I want that."

I tilted my head toward the sphere in his hand. The crowd around us had somehow herded us closer together than we'd been before. He wasn't a huge guy. Not tall. Not broad. But he was...noticeable. The scent of woods and autumn air was perpetual around him. It had to be an aftershave and, yet, so subtle and natural. Not cloying like cologne. Maybe the wildwood scented my skin and hair and clothes now too and I didn't even notice it.

"If you want it, it's yours," Jacob said. He lowered the sphere to my hand and I accepted it without meaning to. When he released the string, the warm brush of our calloused fingers together was slight and fleeting. Again his fingers on bergamot petals crossed my mind.

"I wanted to thank you for sending Lu with the lock," I said. My voice sounded funny. I'd received too many gifts since I'd come to Morgan's Gap. And I certainly couldn't accept the sphere from Jacob, even if there was no way I wanted to let it go now that I held it in my hand.

"She's your friend. Seemed like she'd be welcome," Jacob said. Now that his hands were both free, he pushed his hair from his face and settled his weight back on his heels. He didn't step away from me, but he allowed more air to flow between us as if he needed the space. I immediately filled my lungs and regretted it when he did the same, as if we'd both been holding our breath.

"She is and was," I said, to cover the regret. "I feel better with the stronger bolt. I'm used to living in places that aren't exactly safe, but it's different in the country. The cabin is so isolated that—"

"You should go back to Richmond," Jacob interrupted. The space between us narrowed again. He leaned in, saying the words urgently, but quietly as if he didn't want anyone else to hear him warn me away. Again. It wasn't the first time he'd told me to leave. But it was more personal. We'd spoken several times. He'd seen me working and learning from Granny for months. He'd seen the fruits of my labor even if he hadn't tasted them himself yet.

"I'm staying." This time I didn't mean for only the summer. There was nothing for me back in Richmond. I was making a place for myself here. And I could no longer imagine a life without Granny, Sadie, Joyce and Kara. Plus the more I learned in Morgan's Gap and the more I dreamed about Sarah's past the more I wanted to know.

"I warned you the wildwood wouldn't let you go," Jacob replied. This time his deep, masculine whisper was warmer than it should have been. His eyes were warm too and I immediately recognized why I'd chosen the greenish-brown willow basket I held on the crook of my arm. Charm stirred in my pocket. He sensed my distress or my sudden stiffness woke him. One way or the other, his movement urged me to take a step backward.

"I still owe you some preserves, but the orb is worth more. If you won't accept the hiking stick, I won't accept this," I said, raising the glass sphere to the light. I couldn't help it if my proclamation sounded sad. I could already imagine the cabin lit by the sphere's purple glow when the morning sun passed through the glass. I didn't wait for Jacob to refuse. I carefully placed the orb in my basket beside the bags of candy, then reached for the fox handle.

But he stopped my hand with his. The full on contact of his grip startled. My breath caught and my whole body stilled.

"Gifts from the wildwood are tricky, Mel. Not sure if Granny has taught you that yet," Jacob said. "I haven't taken the preserves because I wasn't sure if you knew about the connections that are forged."

"I understand more than you think. I know I still have a lot to learn, but I'm not afraid of the wildwood or of sharing anything that grows in it with my friends."

"Are we friends?" Jacob asked. "Because I can never decide if we're completely at odds or so in tune it scares me." His grip eased as if he worried he might be holding me too tightly, but, although strong, his hand was gentle. *Scarlet blossoms stirring beneath his fingers.*

He seemed to be asking more than I could answer. There was more to Jacob Walker than he showed the world. Much more. Granny knew it. And didn't fully trust it. But he had helped with the old Chevy and he had sent Lu to help me the morning after the intruder frightened me. Even if I discounted the physical attraction between us and the slight animosity between him and Granny, he definitely didn't seem like an enemy. *He had helped me apologize to the bees.*

"I'm buying you the hiking stick," I countered, refusing to answer his question. Friend or foe, the fox was his like the basket had been mine when Sadie had woven it even before she met me.

Maybe I was beginning to hear the wildwood's whispers. Maybe I couldn't accept a gift without giving something in return.

Jacob let me go and I pulled the hiking stick from its slot. The carver rose from his stool where he was working on a cane with a handle shaped like something with wings. While Jacob watched silently, I shuffled my basket to pay. Then, I turned to hand the purchased stick to the person I knew it belonged to.

"Yeah. I reckon that's right." The carver nodded sagely before he spit a streak of brown chewing tobacco juice into a plastic soda bottle. Then, he went back to his stool and picked up his current project.

Jacob took the hiking stick with both hands and he gripped along its length as if getting to know it from handle to tip and back again. The fox's onyx chip eyes glittered and winked. A ripple of something flowed through me with the exchange—rightness. Another puzzle piece snapped into place.

"Granny isn't going to like this," he warned. And suddenly I wasn't sure how to handle the quirk of his mischievous smile.

Barter was common on the mountain. I'd dealt with it during my deliveries for Granny, often accepting fresh eggs, flower bulbs, baked goods and other offerings in exchange for her concoctions. I'd seen it going on all day at the market. But trading the hiking stick for the glass orb felt different. Like an exchange of gifts. And I didn't know what to say. I'd only known he had to have the fox and I had to have the sphere. Luckily, my awkward response to his smile was interrupted by the sudden rise of music in the distance.

Around us, the crowd had thinned. Neither of us had noticed. I'd been completely distracted by Jacob, the orb and the hiking stick. We both blinked and turned to see people had gravitated toward the far edge of the pavilion where a makeshift stage had been erected. Sometimes Lu presented educational workshops about her dulcimer making at the market, but apparently this one had given way to an impromptu performance.

I could hear Lu's rhythmic contralto along with her playing, the usual poetry in motion that made you hold your breath to keep from singing along when you knew you couldn't carry a tune. But there was a high, sweet soprano singing along with the old hymn Lu played. Clear and lyrical like a fresh mountain spring bubbling up from some throat I couldn't yet see.

"Trouble's coming," Jacob predicted in a growl under his breath. He reached for my arm as if he would hold me up again, but I slipped away, drawn by the haunting quality in the way the unknown singer trilled the sustained notes.

I had to weave my way through all the people who had dropped everything to stand and listen. I didn't blame them. Lu was practically humming under the song now, buoying the soprano notes on top of hers, giving the hymn a depth and resonance that made the old words seem more human than heavenly, voicing the ache of heart, and head, and bone.

I halted like everyone else around me when I finally saw the soprano singer. She wasn't up on the stage with Lu. She didn't have to be. She stood with her arms outstretched and her chin tilted high and the song came from some deep, tortured place inside of her that didn't show in her perfect doll-like appearance.

Violet Morgan had the voice of an angel, a fallen angel, with broken wings and only a song to keep her suspended for a short time from hell.

Jacob had chased me through the crowd. He stopped beside me. I looked away from Violet only because he put his hand on my arm. I started and partially turned until our eyes met.

"Come away. This won't end well," Jacob said.

I looked back at Lu, but she was absorbed in the moment of making music. Fallen or not, Violet Morgan's voice was sublime and Lu wasn't going to waste a second of the opportunity by looking at the crowd.

I didn't know Hartwell Morgan well, but I knew enough. If Lu wasn't lost to the music, she probably would have known better than to continue playing. I suspected Violet wasn't free to choose her own clothes or hairstyle or friends. She didn't talk much. She probably sang even less. I suddenly remembered the real fear in her eyes when she'd hidden the jam in her purse. And the way she'd snatched the mushrooms too.

"She might need help," I said. He didn't stop me when I stepped forward, but he did maintain his hold on my arm so he was forced to come with me. We stopped directly behind Violet and only then did Lu see me. She allowed the current verse to be the song's last, trailing off in a few subsiding chords. Violet followed her lead, dropping her clear trill to a whisper that made goose bumps rise on my arms and a shiver run down my spine.

But Lu hadn't ended the song soon enough.

"I've been looking for you," Hartwell Morgan said. His teeth were gritted in a smile that didn't reach his narrowed eyes. The crowd erupted in applause and Lu graciously accepted with the sort of humble gratitude only a genius displays. I suspected she would have pulled Violet up on stage to receive her share of the recognition—if she had been anyone but Hartwell Morgan's wife. It was obvious the mayor was livid. His cheeks were red. His eyebrows low and tight. He had grabbed Violet by the elbow and I could see where his fingers dug cruelly into the flesh of her arm. Her dimpled flesh seemed to cry out even though she didn't. Seeing her suffer his abuse in silence slammed into me with the force of a blow. And I wanted to hit back.

"Great turnout at the market today, Mayor," Jacob said. "Maybe you should say a few words."

I had been seconds away from throwing myself forward to stand in Hartwell's way. He had obviously been prepared to jerk Violet away and I wasn't at all sure what she might face once her husband got her alone. He seemed ready to explode.

Jacob Walker had seen what I had seen. And he had said the one thing that would perfectly distract a politician and protect his would-be victim. At least for a while.

Hartwell immediately released Violet's elbow and straightened his tie. He raised his arms high and waved at the crowd with both hands. The crowd obliged by continuing the applause that had begun for his wife. The red on Hartwell's cheeks faded. His smile became real as if he fed on the attention. Violet Morgan transformed back into the meek and tepid angel she'd been at the salon. Her smile turned small and obsequious. Her shoulders rounded in on themselves and her kitten heels came together. Hartwell patted her cheek before he jumped up on the stage Lu had quickly vacated.

She wouldn't lend the husband the same support she'd shown musically for the wife. If Lu had seen what I'd seen in the mayor she would have had to move or risk vomiting on his shiny black shoes.

Jacob somehow maneuvered me back into the crowd and off to the side. I didn't protest moving away from Hartwell as he began to speak. I didn't care what the man had to say. I'd seen enough of him to know he would never get my vote. Not for any position.

"To silence Violet's voice is a crime," Lu said. She'd zipped her dulcimer into a leather case and now it rode on her back. She held its straps with tight fingers. Like me, she was holding herself back. Unlike me, she didn't also have Jacob's hand on her arm. He didn't have to squeeze or manhandle the way Hartwell had. His presence was enough in addition to my own realization that any scene I made would only hurt Violet more.

"Don't, Lu. Leave it. You'll only contribute to Violet's problems," Jacob said. "If he gets enough adulation from the crowd maybe he'll go easy on her."

"She's like a different person when she's singing. I could hardly believe my eyes. Or my ears," I said.

"It's a crime," Lu repeated and this time she sounded choked up as if her frustrated fury was going to come out of her in tears if she couldn't release it with a fist to Hartwell's face.

"A crime it's almost impossible to fight without the victim's cooperation," Jacob said. His body was stiff beside me. He held the hiking stick with his other hand in a white-knuckled grip.

We stood there together, surrounded by the crowd, but alone in caring what was really going on. And our commiseration helped. Unlike my sudden, furious connection with the bees, my togetherness with Jacob and Lu gave the anger somewhere rational to go. We were a triumvirate of fury, contained, through all our efforts to keep the peace for Violet's sake.

As Hartwell continued to speak, there was movement in the crowd. Some people had dispersed and I was afraid a diminished audience would make Violet's punishment worse. But the thinning crowd only made room for Reverend Moon and a group of men dressed in similar black garb. They came to the front of the stage and clapped each time Hartwell paused for approval.

"Wonder where his flock is today?" I mumbled.

"Sect women aren't allowed to come to the market," Jacob said.

"Other women singing and laughing and running businesses might give them ideas," Lu said. "Let's get out of here, Mel. Before I vomit on someone's shoes."

I agreed. Violet looked even smaller beside the group of Sect men. She physically diminished herself by blanking her face completely and looking at the ground. Meanwhile, the Sect men continued to clap and shout "Amen" as if they owned the world. Maybe they did own this one. Hartwell laughed and nodded in their direction as if he knew them all and counted them as good friends and loyal constituents.

Jacob released my arm.

For whatever reason, it felt strange to step away now. And Lu looked between the two of us as if she suddenly sensed the strangeness as well. The three of us together could take Hartwell Morgan down. Even as I thought it, I doubted it. Political corruption was much more complicated than planting a flower. And yet, the whole park seemed to be improving. Every time I walked by, the trees seemed healthier. The grass seemed lusher. The bergamot ever in bloom.

"I'll come for those blackberry preserves soon if you don't mind," Jacob said.

"I've saved two jars for you," I replied. I should have told him I'd leave the preserves in town so he could grab them from Granny's house. I didn't. With an arch of one brow, Lu told me she'd noticed.

"Soon," Jacob said to my back as I followed Lu away from the crowd.

I returned to the cabin that evening with the riot of market still in my head. Lu had introduced me to a potter and I had impulsively spent more money than I'd meant to on three earthenware mugs. Three. It seemed extravagant. Not only in price, but also in the fresh hope that I would have someone to share tea with. When I'd lost Sarah, I'd seen a life stretched before me with only solitary sips. Now? I thought maybe a set of mugs was practical and possible.

My circle was growing.

Lu, Sadie, Kara, Joyce, Granny.

Jacob Walker.

Like my new basket, the mugs were swirled in a natural pattern of green and brown. The potter's stall had been set up like Sadie's, with his finished wares on tables, around a work station of a stool and a potter's wheel. His name was Matthew and as he shaped the beginnings of a clay bowl with his thick yet obviously sensitive fingers, he'd explained that his kiln was too large for the market. He fired his pieces at his home and brought them back to sell.

His wife, Grace, had wrapped my mugs in reclaimed paper bags with store logos I'd once frequented. They were crinkled, but serviceable, and I had been suddenly, fiercely happy to be using the bags for something a person had made with their own two hands. Not only because of the beauty of the mugs, but because the clay and natural dyes Matthew had used to make them had come from the mountain itself.

I'd placed my new basket on an empty peg by the back door. I'd washed my new mugs and placed them beside the sink to dry. The orb I'd gingerly taken and hung above the kitchen sink because I knew the morning sun would catch it there. Gingerly because it was delicate and because my feelings about it were as fragile as the glass. After that I went to clean up the stack of fresh pamphlets that had been left at my front door. The gas company and the "No Pipeline" activists had been all the way out to the cabin again. This time, instead of throwing them all in the trash, I kept the rainbow-colored "No Pipeline" bumper sticker.

What would become of the soil and the streams if the mountain was polluted? Pipelines leaked. I'd barely noticed the mention of it on the news before I came to Morgan's Gap because it had become a common story. But the construction horror stories had been more volatile. The land grabs and the right-of-way battles. The soil erosion and degradation of water quality. What would become of potters like Matthew and basket weavers like Sadie, the instrument makers and glassblowers and hiking-stick carvers, the foragers, gardeners and gatherers if the mountain was destroyed? On the news, the environmental costs had seemed distant. Here, in Morgan's Gap, with the people I'd met and the garden I'd tended, the cost suddenly seemed personal.

I saw Charm's little face in the window as I straightened from placing the bumper sticker on the rusted tailgate of the old Chevy. The window's glass reflected the sunset's glow, red on the horizon. I turned to see the wildwood trees outlined by the setting sun with an aura of light.

Charm must have been attracted to the light or maybe he was waiting for me. I went back to the house as if the little mouse had called me home. It felt comforting to join him and close the door against thoughts of the world intruding on the wildwood I was beginning to love.

Twenty-Three

*T*he *first heavy frost* crystallized on the mountain with a hush of white that glittered in the morning sun with a fairy-tale patina. I had settled into a quiet daily routine, but as I sipped steaming chicory blend from one of the heavy pottery mugs I'd purchased at the market, I stepped out on the front porch to appreciate how much more noticeable the frost was on fields and forest compared to city streets.

The air was more tangible than usual. It rested against my cheeks, lips and nose, a calm, cool thing that caressed when its crispness melted into moisture against my warm skin. I breathed deeply, taking in the fresh coolness and the way it enhanced the sharp scent of evergreen that was the top note of a forest that had mostly gone to moldering damp.

If the wildwood had been layered with scents in the summer, it was even more so now. The frost had only accentuated its richness.

I finished my chicory on the porch in spite of the chill, but my last sip was interrupted by the sudden flash of russet fur in the distance. I lowered my cup and narrowed my eyes to better track the movement near the trees at the edge of the wildwood. It was a fox, gamboling along the wood line, either on the hunt for mice or rabbits or playfully practicing its pounce.

I held myself still and silent as it traced the forest with its leaps and bounds until it had disappeared around the side of the cabin. But in spite of my stillness the fox, hyperaware of its surroundings, paused and looked toward the porch several times. Like the frost, the fox sighting was almost magical. The brush of its tail and the handsome sweep of its bristling ruff were so real and yet had almost a storybook quality when you'd never seen one in the wild.

I didn't breathe until the fox was gone and only after did I go back inside to get ready for my chores for the day.

Most blackberries were trimmed in late winter and early spring, but the blackberries in the wildwood garden needed to be trimmed in autumn, as soon as their leaves began to fall. Granny had told me how to go about it and when I'd suggested that maybe Tom would do the pruning she'd balked at the very idea.

"He'll know you're to do the trimming this year," Granny had said in that tone of voice that said there was no doubt about it.

I changed into jeans and a heavy flannel shirt with a lighter, long-sleeved T-shirt beneath. I'd switched over to boots from sneakers. A business expense ordered from the hardware store in town that moon-lighted as a mercantile for the farmers in Morgan's Gap. I laced them up tight over my ankles, thankful for the lug soles that could easily handle the slippery carpet of leaves on the ground. I'd also recently purchased some gardening gloves. I put those in the basket Sadie had made for me along with some serious hedge clippers Granny had told me to fetch from the old potting shed in her backyard.

The frost had mostly melted by the time I left the house. The air was slightly warmer, but I could still see my breath when I stepped onto the path under the trees. I paused and noted the footprints the fox had left in the dirt on the path that wasn't hidden by leaves. I wasn't afraid the fox would bother me. I had no Internet at the cabin, but in town I'd been able to read about some of the wildlife I might encounter in the Appalachians. Unless they were rabid, foxes weren't known to bother humans and the one I'd seen that morning showed no sign of disease.

I'd read to keep my trash contained safely so as not to attract black bears or raccoons. And I had no outside pets that might attract coyotes. So, while I still had much to learn about living in the country, I wasn't afraid to walk into the forest with my basket to take care of the garden.

At least not afraid of animals.

There were dangers on the mountain that didn't walk on four feet.

The break-in that hadn't required any breaking was always on my mind. As were my Sect stalkers. Just because I hadn't seen them outside of town, didn't mean I didn't expect to. I would be a fool to forget them and, no matter the beauty of my surroundings or the fairy-tale frost and fox, I was nobody's fool. My background had instilled in me the necessity of always looking and listening and bracing for what may come. So even as the nonmigratory birds began to sing around me, I was less relaxed than other gardeners would be.

To calm myself, I listened to the varied birdcalls as I set my basket down beside the twining vines of the blackberry bushes. I would learn to tell which birds were singing eventually; for now, they were an anonymous cheerful chorus. I picked up the striped canvas gardening gloves and put them on. As the garden prepared to slumber for the winter, the black locusts at its corners were becoming more prominent. I tried to imagine that the Ross women were resting in peace and that if there were such things as restless spirits they would at least appreciate me tending the plants they had tended when they were alive.

I knew Sarah would like me here. Although she'd be astonished at all I was trying to learn. At my decision to become someone besides a mere survivor.

There were sketched diagrams in the Ross Remedy Book that came after the blackberry preserves recipe. A Ross ancestor from way before Sarah's time had illustrated the care and tending of the blackberry vines. I'd studied them carefully and asked questions of Granny so it wasn't hard to trim the side and lateral shoots, which would give the plant's energy to the fruit. I also cut back the dead or damaged vines and trimmed the length of the longer canes.

"I thought you might leave after summer."

My earlier thoughts of diligence mocked me. I'd been too involved in my task. The soothing snip, snip, snip had lulled me. I straightened and turned to see Jacob coming into the garden clearing from the woods on the opposite side of the path. He must have gotten a very early start that morning to come from that direction because Granny had told me the forest stretched for miles and miles before it reached the Sect settlement on the other side.

"You warned me it would be hard to leave," I replied. "And I told you I was going to stay." I rolled my shoulders and puffed a stray lock of hair from my eyes. "I like the work. It's peaceful and necessary somehow."

"It's the continuity of it. It feels good to take up where others left off. Plus there's satisfaction in caretaking. Not only in seeing the results of your physical labor, but in the simple exertion of the labor itself," Jacob said. "It's one thing to work out in a gym—run around a track, lift weights. It's another thing to dig and plant, grow and harvest."

"Hike," I added. "You do a lot of hiking."

His sudden appearance had startled me, but now I was soothed.

Unlike my Sect creepers, Jacob's presence always felt right somehow. I wasn't quite sure how he fit in my wildwood puzzle, but I was certain he did.

"I'll admit I'd probably do it even if it wasn't a part of my job. I've always loved the forest even when I was a kid. Only now I have a good excuse to practically live here," Jacob said.

He'd stepped into the garden, carefully going around the raised beds and spiraling rows. I watched him approach and tried not to feel anticipation as he came closer and closer. He could have easily shortened and quickened his trip by crossing over the rows where the plants had dried and died down. He didn't. He strolled the long way around as if he was a monk enjoying a meandering maze. Watching him was almost a meditation as well and I had to blink to keep myself from being mesmerized by his graceful movements.

He might not jog or lift weights at a gym, but he was incredibly physical. You could see it in the way he placed his boots on the ground, sure-footed and certain. It was obvious in the way his body moved beneath his clothes, not an inch of spare flesh.

Finally, he came to the row of blackberry bushes and we stood together, hemmed in by the pile of vines I'd trimmed on one side of us and the wall of thorns on the other. I tried to casually accept his nearness.

"Granny told you how to trim?" Jacob asked.

He examined my morning's work and the pile on the ground.

"Yes. Granny said Tom would know it was for me to do this time," I explained.

"Did she give you those gloves?"

"No, I bought these. The thorns are intimidating. Especially on the older, woodier vines," I said. I held up both hands to show where the thorns had pricked the tough material of the gloves.

"Tom has tended the garden for a long time, but Granny wanted you to trim the blackberry bushes this year. I'm surprised she didn't tell you why," Jacob said. "May I?" He had reached for my left hand, but paused to ask permission before taking it.

The pause. The request. Suddenly, I had less of a problem with closeness than I'd had minutes before. I nodded. Just that. I didn't lower my hand or meet him halfway. I only nodded and waited to see what he planned to do.

Okay. I also held my breath when he reached to carefully pull the glove from my raised left hand, finger by finger. Once the glove came free, he tossed it into the basket on the ground. Then, he grasped my hand in his. I didn't pull away or try to step back.

"Do you trust me?" Jacob asked.

Our hands were between us. He wasn't crowding me. And he had asked permission to touch me. But my pulse was racing and the breath I'd held while the glove was removed came too quickly, now, between my lips.

"I don't trust anyone," I confessed and heat suffused my face when he looked up from my hand as if he was surprised by my candid reply. But was it candid? Deep down, deeper than logic, the memory of him tending the bergamot plant had stayed with me like a visual mantra repeated time and again. I did trust him. And Lu. I just wasn't ready to share that vulnerable truth with him yet.

"There's an old wives' tale about wild berries. I first heard it when I was a little boy running around this mountain like an Appalachian Mowgli. They said if you want cobblers and pies and to fill your larder with preserves you have to make a sacrifice to the bushes. That's why they have thorns. I pricked myself on purpose many a time back then. What do you say, Mel? Do you believe in old wives' tales? Are you willing to go there? Beyond the tea and tisanes? To ashes buried under black locust trees and sacrificing your blood to the blackberry briars?" Jacob moved his hand to hold my middle finger extended, but, like before, he paused.

He waited for my permission.

My breathing slowed as warmth settled in the pit of my stomach, from his touch, from his whimsy, from the intimacy of him knowing I was on the precipice of a new philosophy I didn't fully understand.

And from the certain knowledge that, understanding or not, I was going to let him prick my index finger.

He must have felt the release of tension in my shoulder and arm before I spoke. Because he moved my hand to the nearest vine and was already pressing the swell of my fingertip to its sharpest thorn when I breathed, "Yes."

The pressure was slight, but inexorable between his fingers and the plant. With my vulnerable finger caught in between. The thorn pierced my skin and blood welled, but there was only a fleeting sting before Jacob pulled my finger away.

He didn't ask my permission for what came next. I think it was an instinctive move on his part because his eyes widened above my hand with my shocked gasp as if he was as shocked himself.

His mouth hotly closed over the tip of my finger and he soothed the prick with his tongue. I managed to stay on my feet in spite of suddenly liquid knees and the loss of his slight support when he dropped my hand as if my blood had burned him.

I closed my bare hand into a fist to stop its trembling and watched as Jacob pressed his own fingers against his palm. He didn't make a fist. It was more like he was cupping a memory in his hand.

"Granny needs to tell you the stories. The wildwood isn't a soft escape from what you've known," Jacob said. "It can be a place of blood and pain."

"I wouldn't know what to do with soft if I found it," I said. The sting in my finger was already gone. My finger had a heartbeat. A fast one. But that was more due to the memory of Jacob's lips than the thorn prick. "I'm not looking for soft. I'm only looking for home."

Jacob opened his hand and ran his fingers through the thick waves of his hair.

"I'm sorry. I shouldn't have done that," he said.

I was too embarrassed to ask if he was talking about the prick or the taste.

"It's fine," I said. Talking about both. It wasn't. At all. I was trashed. By the intimacy of the thorn, his lips, sharing my blood, not the pain.

"Nature can be peaceful. But it can also be harsh. Granny knows. If you've decided to stay, you should know that too," Jacob said.

"I can deal with the thorns," I replied. I pulled the other glove from my hand and threw it into the basket to join the one that Jacob had removed. His gaze dropped to my naked fingers, but only for a second. His cheeks were ruddy when he looked back at me.

"I'm sorry," he said again. But before I could accept or reject his apology he turned away. He didn't hike down the path toward the cabin. He leapt over a dying zucchini squash bed and headed back into the trees from the direction he'd initially come.

I sank down to the walled edge of the squash bed. The world came alive around me. A blackbird sang. That one I knew already. The stream gurgled. Leaves floated to the ground. I turned my hand over in my lap. My finger was fine. The prick had been negligible. I wasn't sure why it still throbbed. I examined it for a long time, but it kept its secrets.

Twenty-Four

*M*y *Gathering dream hadn't* prepared me for the intensity of the labor involved with baking so much fresh bread. I settled into a rhythm of pull, twist, roll and slap. The cadence of the process soon echoed in my bones. The scent of the yeast was released from the dough as I worked, and deep within its sweet, pungent possibilities was the life of the wildwood from where it came. My mind was filled with visions of acorns falling to a moist carpet of soil, of tendrils bursting forth, of saplings reaching for the sun. The forest had breathed into the bread—morning mist and evening shadow—and I breathed the scent of the bread into me.

With each batch of dough, I became so in tune that I knew when it was ready to sit in a crockery bowl covered with a fresh clean cheesecloth to rise. I was a novice. But I wasn't. Because I had nurtured and tended. And now I communed with what we had done together—the wildwood and me. By the time I came to the last batch, I could feel the perfect moment from its springiness in my fingers.

I'd given my blood to the blackberry thorn. I gave my sweat to the rye dough. And the wildwood gave back to me. I was tired. Exhausted. But I was also replete with a whole summer of wildwood scents and sensations.

Only then, when the cadence eased and let me go, did I realize how extreme the physical exertion had been. I blinked and looked around the brightening kitchen. Sunlight hit the surface of the orb casting amethyst rays around the room.

Sarah had been much tougher than I was because the ache I'd experienced in her memory was nothing compared to the stabbing pain between my shoulder blades or the leaden weight of the overworked muscles in my forearms.

"I bake several loaves a week and Gathering still kicks my ass," Joyce grumbled when she noticed me rolling my shoulders. She'd come with Granny the day before and insisted the older woman not be allowed near the kitchen. Of course, Granny had stubbornly helped some "for old times' sake" before Joyce had succeeded in sending her to bed.

Kara and Sadie had arrived several hours after Joyce and Granny. Sadie had rolled her sleeves to reveal tight, toned arms ropey with the muscles she'd built from years of twisting and tying branches into shape. I shuddered to think what my back would have felt like by now if Sadie hadn't been there. Together, we'd worked through the night even after Granny had grudgingly gone to sleep. I wondered if Sadie had experienced the same visions of the forest I'd experienced while we'd worked the dough, side by side. Neither of us had spoken much through the wee hours of the morning. Had we been too focused on work for conversation or had we both been in commune with the trees?

"Fewer people come every year and I try not to be glad about that, but I can't help what my back thinks," Joyce said. She arranged cooling loaves on the counter in fragrant golden-brown rows.

"It's a shame. Lots of young backs in this town to take over, but there's no interest in it. That's why Granny overdid it apprenticing you. It's good to pass on what we know when we can. How it's meant to be," Sadie said.

"The natural order of things has been interrupted. No one wants to commune with the land. They only want the money they can make from it. More pavement. More mining. 'Ecotourism.' Thrill seekers don't really care about where they raft or run," Kara said.

"Some do," Sadie argued. "I'll take the outdoorsy types any day over the politicians and polluters. There are lots of hikers and river rats who love the mountain almost as much as we do."

"The more time spent in the wildwood, the better," Joyce agreed. "This year we couldn't even get a single church interested in making apple butter the old way. Oh, some of us made small batches and Kara made some cider, but it isn't the same."

I'd experienced an old-timey apple butter day in my dreams, so I was able to commiserate with the ladies more than they knew. My pang for the old times was just as strong as if I'd lived through them myself.

Charm sat on my shoulder and no one paid him any attention whatsoever. Probably because they'd all brought pets of their own. Granny's CC had claimed the back of the armchair Charm had vacated. Joyce had a long-eared hound on the front porch that looked like a cross between a Doberman and a bloodhound, all loose wrinkly skin and white teeth. Kara had a bright red cardinal. And no cage. He came and went through the front door whenever anyone opened and closed it as if he needed to stretch his wings.

And of course Sadie had her bees. Only a few. Nothing like the swarm that had engulfed her body when the Sect man had threatened her. But definitely unusual. Each one danced along her arm when it landed as if to communicate with her in the same way it would communicate with its hive.

Charm perched on my shoulder was nothing in comparison.

We had time as the loaves cooled in the kitchen to take turns freshening up. Even though my body was sore, I didn't feel like I'd been awake all night. There was a pulsing energy to my steps, as if I was a freshly sprouted sapling, and when I paused in a ray of sunlight on my way back downstairs I basked in its warmth as if my cells plumped from its nourishment.

I was closer to hearing the whispers of the wildwood than I'd been before. Outside, there was a breeze and Kara propped both doors open, front and back, so the air could flow and clear out the heat from all the baking. But what the circulating wind accomplished was to scent both front and back with savory rye so that from the driveway to the trees Gathering began before the first bite was taken.

When I made it back downstairs, I found Granny alone in the kitchen. She was sitting on a stool with the valerian tea tin open, and still full, in front of her on the counter. I hadn't gone so far as to dump any of it out. Not wanting to worry her and actively trying to deceive her were two different things.

"No wonder you have circles under your eyes," she said. Her forehead was more wrinkled than usual by concern.

"Maybe the dreams are coming from the wildwood. I need to dream. I need to listen," I said.

Granny placed the lid back on the tin and pressed it closed. "Each of us chooses our steps. Everyone's relationship with the wildwood is different. Some listen to the bees. Some share love with stitches. Some soothe pain with dandelion wine. You have a path too. A process that will be your own." She handed me the tin and I put it back on the counter by the stove. "It's there if you need it. Use it when you need to rest. We all need to rest sometimes. The wildwood won't mind. Even the garden is fallow in winter," Granny said gently.

I was relieved. That she finally knew I had opened myself to the dreams and that she understood. Even if she was still warning me to be careful, just as Joyce had warned her when she'd worn herself out with mentoring me.

I would still avoid using the tea, but I appreciated that she cared.

Even though I'd been warned, the trickle of guests that began to arrive after midday took me by surprise. For me, the Gathering dream was so recent that the dwindled number of people attending stood out in sharp contrast to the crowd Sarah had fed. But Granny and the other wisewomen seemed pleased. Just like in my dream, we cut and served ourselves the first slices. I ate mine plain to taste the rich whole grain. I marveled at the depth of flavor that exploded against my tongue. It was pure fantasy to imagine I could taste woodsy moss and gurgling creek and forest shadows baked into the bread itself.

Or was it? I'd seen the visions of what the yeast had fed upon in my own mind. I'd seen and felt the magic of its beginnings and the ardor that had embraced me during its making. As I chewed I felt the cadence again. Pull, twist, roll and slap. Only this time it was my heart being kneaded and worked and shaped into something worthwhile.

We were supposed to enjoy the bread as a gift from the wildwood, so I did. And only after we'd fully appreciated the first slices together did we invite the guests to line up to be served. One by one they slowly came by—people I'd met in town like Becky and Matthew and Grace. Lynn, the Humane Society volunteer, helped her three children choose what to put on their slices—Andy, Randy and Sandy weren't identical, but this time they didn't hold still long enough for me to spot the differences that would help me tell the towheaded boys apart. No one seemed to notice or care. We were all a convivial jumble. Friends, families and neighbors—talking and laughing and appreciating the day. They enjoyed crusty rye bread with fresh churned butter, apple blossom honey and blackberry preserves as the townspeople had in my dream, even though there were fewer of them.

And yet, more came than Granny had expected. We had to retrieve extra loaves from the kitchen time and again. During my deliveries, I had spoken to people about learning from Granny and baking the bread. I could tell by polite welcomes and conversations that some of the people I'd invited hadn't been to Gathering in a while.

"I forgot how delicious home-baked bread is when it's fresh," Becky exclaimed. "I haven't had this since I was a teenager."

"You're rejuvenating the cycle," Joyce said, once Becky walked away. She was no longer grumbling. There was a spark in her eyes I hadn't seen before. A hint of happiness. "Granny was right."

I had to tighten my grip on the knife in my hand because I almost dropped it in surprise. I'd already learned that Joyce wasn't the kind of person to throw around idle compliments. She'd been reserved with me. And she'd radiated disapproval over my impact on Granny's health. Making her happy was new. An accomplishment. My confidence grew every day, with every task I completed, but I still worried I might mess up again like I had with the bees.

But today, Joyce was pleased. All our guests seemed happy and that pleased me. We worked side by side and I glanced at her frequently to soak up her smiles.

Movement on the forest path startled me from the companionable glow.

Half a dozen Sect women came out of the trees. They had pulled the kerchiefs from their hair, but their homespun dresses were recognizable. They paused at the edge of the backyard until Granny calmly approached them with a platter of fresh-sliced bread.

"They risk so much. Anyone here might mention their attendance at the wrong time and place. Moon would be furious," Sadie said. For all her muscles and competence with her calloused hands, the beekeeper looked completely at a loss. If she could have swept up the Sect women in her arms and carried them to safety, she would have been happier. I could tell. She was a tender, a caretaker, someone who believed in sturdy structure and nurturing above all else. The plight of the Sect women left her feeling helpless.

"They need the bread more than any of us," Joyce said. She also looked at a loss. Her shoulders had drooped and her smile was gone. If she'd had a bottle nearby, I was pretty sure she would have gladly taken a restorative swig of her dandelion wine.

"You're rejuvenating the cycle."

How could any of us restore the connection between the wildwood and the town when there was such a blatant evil in the community?

Their initial tentative nibbles gave way to enthusiastic chewing as the quiet women enjoyed their bread. There was this at least. We could do this. The bread was a start. Granny came back with an empty platter. She asked Kara to take the Sect women another trayful because they didn't seem willing to come into the yard where other people were eating.

"I've been meaning to tell you. Sometimes they come through the trees for help. Melody never turned them away. Once they know the Ross cabin is occupied again, they might try to come to you," Granny said. "They live a harsher life than you can imagine."

I hadn't told Granny about the night Reverend Moon had followed me to her front door. I couldn't forget his spidery strides or the fury that had contorted his face in the neighbor's porch light. I hadn't told her about the other Sect people who had seemed to follow me around. I didn't want to worry her because of her health. I didn't want the trio to think I couldn't take care of myself.

"Can't decide if Mel should serve this one or not."

I turned away from Granny at the sound of my name only to see Jacob Walker stride into the backyard. Sadie had spoken before he'd appeared around the corner of the cabin like she'd sensed him coming. I wasn't even surprised. All of the wisewomen prided themselves on being in tune with the wildwood and today it really did seem to be whispering all around us.

"Well, he's not here to commune with you or me," Joyce chuckled. *Chuckled.* And not a sip of wine in sight. I was more used to scolding from the Sunday school teacher. But today, smiles and actual laughter tumbled from her butter-glossed lips.

Jacob had a cardboard box in his hands. He walked up to the table where I'd been serving and he placed the box on it firmly enough to make its contents rattle.

"Lu asked me to help carry the honey," he explained as Lu came from around the cabin with another box. "She was unloading when I pulled in."

"More than you'll need for this year, but Sadie says the bees have gone crazy this last couple of weeks. Producing more than she's ever seen," Lu explained.

"After ten years of diminishing bee populations, that's good news," Jacob said.

I'd avoided talking with Sadie about the bees since that day at the apiary. A rush of relief filled me to hear that the colony was thriving.

I sliced two thick slices of rye bread from a loaf that was still warm and held them out on a serving plate for the biologist. He looked me in the eyes as he took the plate from my hands and my cheeks heated.

Granny told me Gathering was a ritual held every year to commune with the wildwood. To reclaim our ties to it as a home and a life source. Many of the guests were casual nibblers who had come to what they saw as a social occasion or a silly old tradition. Even I wasn't sure what it meant to treat the wildwood as a sacred, sentient entity.

But something told me Jacob Walker did.

Like me, he picked up the first slice and bit into it plain. He closed his eyes and his skin flushed with what I thought was appreciation and pleasure. My mouth went dry. Did he taste the moss and the stream? Were verdant shadows exploding on the back of his tongue? And, oh Lord, why had I thought about his mouth and tongue.

His eyes opened at that very second and he watched me watch him swallow. No idea why I wanted that bite to have been kneaded and baked by my hands, but I did.

"Perfect," he said. And all the women around us looked from him to me and back again as if he'd said more intimate things.

"I'm not sure you should have any of her blackberry jam in public," Lu said. She didn't hesitate herself. She spread a thick slather of butter and preserves on a slice Granny had given her.

Jacob looked from Lu to me. He'd never come for the jar of preserves I'd saved for him. Now he looked at me as he reached down and dipped a spoon into one of the jars we were serving, and he spread a huge helping of the purple-black jam on his second slice. He picked up the slice and bit into it as if he dared anyone to interrupt, all while keeping his eyes locked to mine.

More people came and went while he chewed. There was conversation around us. But for the life of me I had no idea what was said. Everything else was a dim blur and the breeze, the beautiful bread-scented breeze seemed to swirl around us, and only the two of us, until I could almost make out the words it was whispering into my ear.

"What have you two been up to while I was sick?" Granny asked after Jacob had taken the second slice of his bread away. She was doing so much better. Joyce had forced her to slow down, not letting up on her nursing even after I'd moved to the cabin. But Granny didn't appreciate being continually kept out of the loop.

"He gave her that purple sphere she has hanging in the kitchen window," Sadie said. "I touched it and Red had to fly out the front door to cool his wings."

"He didn't give it to me," I began.

"Sadie works more closely with the wildwood than any of us. Day in, day out, holding its branches in her hands. And of course there's the bees always buzzing in her ears. A lot of time she just knows things. Sometimes better than we know ourselves," Joyce explained.

"We traded. The orb for a hiking stick," I finished.

"What sort of hiking stick?" Granny stepped toward me as if my answer mattered to her more than it should.

"One carved from a cherry sapling with a fox handle. He was looking at it and I knew it had to be his. He'd bought the glass sphere from the glassblower at the market after I'd decided to buy it. So, we traded. The fox for the orb," I explained.

"So much simpler than that," Sadie said.

"And infinitely more complicated for all its simplicity," Kara interjected. "Didn't you warn her about gifts from the wildwood?" she asked. The question was directed at Granny.

"It didn't occur to me. She's so prickly I didn't think I had to worry about it," she replied. She crossed her arms over her breasts.

"He warned me. He said it was a bad idea. But it felt right. Sarah would have called it a whisper. I listened." I crossed my arms across my chest too.

"He isn't trustworthy," Granny said. "His eyes don't match his words. He was born on the mountain. His mother was one of us. Then, they left. Now, he's back and I think he's lying about why he's here."

"Oh, we all know why he's here," Joyce said. She no longer chuckled, but there was still laughter in her eyes.

"Granny's wrong. And right. I'm not sure what's going on with him," Sadie said. "But I think I do know what's going on with him, Lu and you. I've lived with that sort of connection my whole life. It's too special to ignore. Even for someone used to ignoring connections."

"Well, you don't have to be a wisewoman to see the way he looks at Mel," Joyce continued.

"Jacob can't be a wisewoman," I protested, shocked at what Sadie had implied. We couldn't be a trio. Not when one of us was a man.

"The wildwood doesn't care about gender, Mel. Only the heart matters. And the blood," Sadie scolded. "When I was a girl, men like Jacob—and there aren't many, mind you—were called woodsmen. Special and rare. Like you. Like Lu."

While Joyce murmured what could be agreement or only more teasing, guests continued to enjoy the bread. We helped to serve people who came back for more slices even as we muttered about magic and mayhem among ourselves.

Calling Jacob Walker untrustworthy wasn't a fair assessment. I was sure of it. But I had also seen secrets in his eyes. Something didn't add up. And the attraction between us—Joyce was dead on about that—didn't completely negate my suspicions. As for any mystical connections, I wasn't ready to admit that yet. Not to them and not to myself.

It was almost anticlimactic when Violet Morgan slipped in late after most of the guests had already left. We'd sent many away with loaves wrapped in plastic to freeze and enjoy over winter. I was the one who took Violet one of the last slices on a plate and she accepted it without a smile. I was glad the Sect women had already disappeared back into the trees. I didn't think Hartwell's wife would give away their secret because she had so many secrets of her own, but I couldn't be sure.

"Your song was so beautiful. I thought I would cry," I whispered as she chewed.

"Sometimes I think tears are the only thing I have left that's mine," Violet said after she'd swallowed. I was surprised by her candor, but I shouldn't have been. Without Hartwell, and surrounded by wise-women, Violet was different than she'd been in town, both softer and harder. *Real.* No longer just a doll. And she obviously liked people who allowed her to be herself.

Granny interrupted. She came up to us and fished into one of her numerous pockets. But I was shocked by what she drew out of it to hand to Violet Morgan. Rather than a net bag of herbs tied with a thread, Granny handed the mayor's wife a recognizable packet of pills most women received from their gynecologist with a prescription.

"Thank you," Violet said. She palmed the packet and it disappeared so suddenly I couldn't tell where she had stashed it—pocket or purse, bra or belt.

"She is a prisoner and doesn't want to condemn a child to the same fate," Granny explained.

Helpless rage made me tremble. But I'd been a prisoner myself in many ways even in the city. For women and girls, all too often, the modern world was no different than the world had ever been. We had only gotten better at pretending we were free.

In Morgan's Gap, there were so many secrets, but some of them were imperative ones—women helping women to survive. I'd seen Granny go to the Sect women today. I hadn't noticed if she'd given them anything besides rye bread. But I thought she probably had.

I'd always been a survivor, but I was discovering that survival wasn't enough if you couldn't help others do the same.

The trio stayed to help me clean up. Granny watched from the sofa, proving that Gathering had almost been too much for her by staying out of the kitchen. Charm had leapt from my shoulder, disappeared in transit, then popped into existence on Granny's shoulder not one bit concerned about the fat cat on her lap.

I wasn't sure if I would ever get used to animals behaving in strange ways, but Granny didn't seem to mind the mouse at her ear so I let him be.

We washed all the loaf pans and platters and all the plates and utensils. Sadie dried the plates and handed them to Joyce, who placed them into a large padded container for the trip back to her house. While they dried and packed, I stored jars of leftover honey in the pantry.

"It is pretty. I might have to buy one of these for myself," Sadie said, gently tapping the amethyst-colored orb with one finger to make it spin. "Maybe one that isn't infused with Jacob Walker's energy."

"That's the third time you've set it to spinning in the last hour. Maybe you need some *energy*." Kara cut her eyes at Sadie and winked.

"It'll take me a week to recover from today. After that, we can talk," Sadie said. I hadn't noticed the flirtation between the two women before. Maybe they hid it in front of strangers, and I was finally considered a friend. Joyce was smiling at them as if she was used to their bantering innuendo.

"He saw you with it and bought it for you." Sadie leaned against the sink when she spoke and her eyes flickered furiously behind her lashes as if she was trying to see images that were coming to her too quickly.

"He didn't know I was there," I replied. But I suddenly wasn't sure. Sadie had known Jacob was coming before he appeared at Gathering. And the rest of the ladies in the room seemed to take her knowledge as certain.

"He bought the orb for you not for himself," Sadie insisted. She was back to washing dishes as if visions assailed her so often she wasn't fazed.

I went to the sink and reached up to touch the orb. It had stopped spinning. I was easily able to cup it in the palm of my hand. No visions came to me. Only the memory of Jacob Walker holding the globe by its nylon thread and how surprising it had been to see him with it—something I had wanted but hadn't allowed myself to have.

The temperature of the room seemed to increase by several degrees. I moved my hand away from the glass sphere. It was dark outside so the purple of the glass seemed darker as well.

"Granny probably has a love tisane in one of her pockets. If you want us to brew a little something up before we leave," Joyce said.

"Absolutely not," Granny said from the living room.

"I've never known you to resist when the wildwood is intent on a little matchmaking," Kara said. She had carried the container of dishes out to Joyce's car, but she'd returned in time to hear Granny protest.

"Never imagine you know what the wildwood is up to, woman. You're old enough to know by now that we can only ever guess and follow where our own hearts lead," Sadie said.

Kara came up to her and spun her around to pull her away from the sink into a hug.

"But Mel is still young. Plenty of adventurous mistakes left to make and that man seems like he'd be worth making a few nights of bad decisions," Kara said.

Sadie relaxed into Kara's hug with an exasperated laugh. Granny huffed up from the sofa, spilling cat and mouse off onto the floor. Charm washed his face like he often did to give himself time to decide what to do. CC stalked over to be let out the door. I had no doubt he'd wind up in Joyce's sedan, waiting for the ladies to join him.

"Too many mistakes made by the women on this mountain already.

'Wise' they call us. And maybe we are. But never 'wise' enough," Granny said. She was exhausted. Her curly hair hung limply on her sagging shoulders and she moved with a slight limp from a stiff hip she'd been complaining about all day.

"It's okay, Helen. The sun will rise tomorrow and you'll feel much better after a good night's sleep," Joyce said. It was the first time I'd heard someone call my mentor anything other than Granny. Joyce must have known her for a long time. Granny didn't protest when Joyce took her arm to lead her outside.

"Don't worry, Granny. I'm not looking for love. That's not why I'm here." I meant to reassure her, but she stopped. She turned and suddenly for all her tiredness she was fully alert, as she'd been at the beginning of the day.

"Of course that's why you're here. That's why we're all here," Granny said. My whole body paused between breaths, between steps, maybe between one heartbeat and the next.

Kara and Sadie both hugged me, one on each side. Tears pricked my eyes as I took a deep breath. I'd always thought I was helping Sarah, but I hadn't given her this. Such an easygoing camaraderie. Women who shared the same background and beliefs. I hadn't believed in anything strongly enough to share with anyone. Much less Sarah. A bug-out bag wasn't a belief. Being ready to run was believing in nothing at all.

Twenty-Five

I *fell asleep with the* glass orb in my hands. No one was there to see me try to privately sense the vibe of the man who had bought it. But when I woke to the sound of pounding on the cabin's back door, the orb fell to the rug and rolled several feet before it came to a stop like an embarrassing accusation in the middle of the floor. I could only be glad the carpet had cushioned its impact for several seconds before the pounding that had woken me resumed.

Charm was nowhere to be seen. He often disappeared. I never knew if he was traveling unseen behind the walls or under the floor or if he truly blinked out of existence to traverse some fairy pathways I couldn't imagine.

There was only me to answer the door so I walked softly, barefooted and clothed in only a summer-weight nightgown because I'd yet to shop for autumn clothes. But I didn't open the door until I'd peeked through the curtained window at the back of the house. The yard was empty under the stars. The forest was dark. And there was a Sect woman on my back porch.

I was afraid, but I wasn't nearly as afraid as she was. She was weeping. I was close enough to hear her through the door now and her sobs were horrible because they were gut wrenching but also so, so quiet, as if she knew better than to voice her pain.

When I opened the door, she fell back as if she regretted knocking. But she didn't run away, although she looked like she desperately wanted to. She was crying and panting and I suspected she'd run all the way here from the other side of the mountain. Her kerchief was missing. Her hair was a wild tangle around her face and her cheeks were smeared with dirt and tears.

Like the Sect women I'd seen in town, she was pregnant. Very pregnant. If Granny had been giving Sect women the same pills she'd been giving Violet Morgan, none had been dispensed to this particular Sect woman in time.

"Come in. Let me help you," I said. "Are you in labor?"

"No. No. Not yet. Soon. Very soon I think," the woman gasped. She allowed me to put my arm around her and lead her into the house. I helped her lower herself down onto Charm's armchair and I covered her with an afghan throw I'd washed by hand and dried in the sun. She gripped the soft crochet to her chest and huddled under it as if she wished she could disappear. Something her large belly wouldn't allow her to do even if the throw had been twice as large.

"I'll put the kettle on," I said. There were soothing things I could brew for her that wouldn't harm the baby. There were things I wouldn't brew for her now that might have helped if she'd come to me months ago. She was too far along for those.

While I waited for the water to boil, I fetched clean washcloths and a towel from the hall closet. I filled a dishpan with hot, sudsy water and took it to her. I didn't ask permission to wash her legs and arms and face. I did it because it needed to be done. She calmed while

I washed. This was a caring language between two people that anyone could understand, but especially between two women. I washed the dirt away and in doing so I helped her gather her courage and dry her tears.

"I can't have this baby in that place. I thought I could, but I won't. They can't make me. I'd rather die," she said. Her breathing had slowed. Her words carried the weight of conviction in every syllable. I knew this girl. I knew her because I knew myself.

The kettle whistled and I went to pour the water into a waiting cup. Nothing but wild spearmint leaves for now. I wanted to revive her enough for us to decide what to do. If the Sect came after her, the only weapon I had in the cabin was the old Louisville Slugger I'd borrowed from Granny's umbrella stand.

"What's your name?" I asked.

"Lorelei."

Her calmer voice sounded even younger than she looked. She drained the cup down to the dregs. I didn't look at the leaves. I didn't believe in divination. I never would. The future couldn't be foretold because our actions had to influence every second of every day. It was changeable. I had to believe that. Or my future would seem as hopeless as my past.

"There used to be a woman who lived here. I've heard the whispers. About women who pretended they'd lost their babies, but the babies lived and were sent away. For a better life. Off the mountain," she said.

"Life isn't perfect off the mountain," I said.

"Anywhere away from Reverend Moon is better," Lorelei said. It sounded like she might start crying again.

"So you ran away," I guessed. She didn't have a bag or even a coat. I'd been lucky to have those things when I'd run. I'd been lucky to not have to run alone.

"I couldn't make it all the way to town. And someone I know came here today. Saw the cabin wasn't empty anymore," Lorelei said. But then she froze. She'd calmed enough to notice her surroundings. Her hand grew suddenly slack and the cup fell from her fingers. I followed the direction of her attention. Her eyes were riveted on the photographs on the table. "One of them," she said. She stood so fast I fell back. The cup dropped off the afghan. Unlike the sphere, it hit bare floor to the side of the carpet and shattered.

"Who? That's Tom and Lu. One of who?" I stood, being careful to avoid the bits and pieces of broken cup, but Lorelei had already backed away from my outstretched hands.

"Them," she said, all calm lost. Tears were streaming down the face I'd washed clean.

"No one will hurt you here, Lorelei. I won't let them," I said. Some of the bruises I'd seen made me reluctant to restrain her. By the time I thought I'd better grab her, she had already rushed to the back door and opened it. "Wait. Rest here at least until morning. Don't go back into the woods at night."

Her arm slipped through my fingers and she ran surprisingly light-footed and quick. The pale blue of her dress was ghostly in the moonlight and soon disappeared in the thick growth of trees. I didn't think. I didn't even pause to shut the door. I ran after her. Without a flashlight. I ran into the mysterious, sentient wildwood even Granny said no one would ever understand.

The daytime forest can be shadowed and deep. When you're used to city streets, the tangle of tree and vine and the thick obfuscation of leaves can seem impossibly strange to navigate. Even in daylight, wilderness is changeable. A path can become a quagmire after a sudden rain or a dead end after a wind-felled tree—even worse is the off-path snarl of undergrowth and untamed branches.

But the nighttime forest is another world entirely. My worn path was surrounded by a cool velvet mystery, hazy and indistinct in the darkness. I jogged after the pregnant woman, my way illuminated only by starlight and a half-eaten moon winking between clouds, until the soft blackness my eyes could barely penetrate was ripped by the intrusion of sharp branches.

Lorelei had left the path. I followed. I could hear her for a while, crashing through the same growth that had me in its grip. My legs and arms were caught by briar and bramble with every step. My face was wet. It was either frustration or blood, I couldn't tell. There was definitely the sting of scratches on my cheeks and hands.

"Stop. Just stop. You're hurting yourself. Don't move," Jacob ordered. I froze because he'd startled me and then because he was right. He came out of nowhere like he always did. But of course it was more of an entrance in the middle of the blackest night. I barely saw a flash of eye and teeth. The rest of him was shadow, moving shadow, graceful shadow, but only shadow all the same.

"There was a Sect girl. I was trying to help her, but she ran away," I explained.

"So you followed her because two people lost in the wildwood at midnight are better than one," Jacob said.

"I'm not lost. I'm stuck. Two different things," I said. Jacob was shadowing around my legs and ankles now, pulling vines away from my skin, and I was acutely aware of my ridiculous nightgown and bare feet.

"I didn't have time to stop for shoes," I said. It might have been stupid, but even now if I could have seen well enough to pursue Lorelei I would have continued after her, bare feet and all. She was in trouble.

The kind of trouble I could feel in the shiver of empathetic horror down my spine.

"I think I've gotten you free from the briars. I'm going to pick you up. Because I'm wearing boots. And you could seriously damage your feet in the dark out here. Best-case scenario, a rock slices your sole. Worst case, you step on a copperhead. It hasn't gotten cold enough to discount that possibility yet." Jacob had already scooped me up. So easily. Too easily. I didn't have time to come up with a sane argument as to why I should walk back under my own power even with no shoes and scratched all to pieces. Because being cradled in his arms felt too safe, too sane, and I couldn't process those two feelings at the same time. Maybe because I'd never felt that way before.

"You must be hurt or tired or both," Jacob said. "I was braced for a fist or a fuck-you." There was laughter in his voice. In the pitch black, against my wild hair, I could feel the vibration of a chuckle he didn't quite allow to escape.

As soon as his boots hit the grass of the backyard, I wrenched myself down. I used too much force considering he easily let me go. I ended up stumbling forward like an awkward, half-naked zombie girl. I slowed my galumph on the porch and opened the door. I didn't slam it in his face, although I was tempted. The light of the living room lamps illuminated him in the open door. He wasn't exactly smiling, but his mouth was quirked.

The light also revealed that Jacob was scratched too. All along one side of his face.

Had the graceful man who seemed perfectly a part of the wildwood and at ease among all its vegetation been scratched when he'd helped me escape from the briar patch? I hadn't seen or felt it happen. He'd seemed perfectly calm and in control of every vine as he'd peeled it away from my skin. Even harder to believe that he'd run into a branch when he was coming to help me. I'd seen how he moved among the trees in daylight. Would he really be that awkward at night?

Jacob came through the door and shut it behind him. He slid the bolt into place with a firm snick.

"A Sect woman woke me up banging on the door. I let her in. She's very pregnant; it looked like she could go into labor at any time," I explained. "But something frightened her and she ran before I could do anything for her."

"That explains the nightgown and your bare feet," Jacob said.

I looked down at myself and wished I hadn't. Besides the scratches, my feet were filthy. Streaks of dirt, moistened from the night's damp, painted my legs and stained the edges of my gown. My thin gown.

More than my teeth clicking together indicated I was cold.

"You're freezing. Let me help you," Jacob said.

He didn't wait for me to reject his offer. He grabbed me by the hand and pulled me down the hall to the bathroom. He pressed my shoulder to urge me to sit on the toilet and I watched, shivering, while he turned on the hot water tap in the tub.

I was completely out of my comfort zone. One of the reasons I liked being Granny's apprentice was because, as the helper, I didn't have to accept anyone tending me. I didn't like feeling weak or needy. Never had. But I turned to place my legs over into the nearby tub when Jacob pointed.

He took the washcloth he'd found under the bathroom sink and wet it in the now steaming water. I watched, mesmerized, as he took the lavender soap from its dish and worked it into a lather with the wet cloth.

This was not even slightly okay.

Jacob didn't intend to be sensual. If anything, the expression on his face was exasperated concern—thin lips, furrowed forehead. But, as he washed and rinsed my feet and legs, everything changed. His lips softened. His brow eased. His eyebrows arched as if he found himself in the middle of a moment he hadn't expected or planned.

Like my pricked finger in his mouth.

I reached for the washcloth exactly as he released it. He straightened and stepped back and his damp hand went to his hair to push it back from his face. In the bathroom light, the scratches looked angry and painful, but he had been worried about me. And somehow the flash of tattooed tree at his wrist said I should understand.

"I'll finish up," I said, releasing him from the suddenly awkward ministrations. He nodded and left the bathroom and I finished with much rougher and efficient scrubbing. I rejected the urge to continue the gentle swipes my body had interpreted as caresses. Something about Jacob's scratches was bothering me. If I ruled out the idea that he'd been as clumsy as I had been in the dark forest, then I had to accept they might have been caused by... fingernails?

Jacob was standing near the woodstove when I came out of the bathroom. I ignored him as I went over to pick up the pieces of broken china on the floor. Or I tried to. I was still shaky and awkward. As I tossed the shattered cup in the trash, I managed to slice a finger. I bit my lip to keep from hissing and went to the sink to wash off my hand, quietly wrapping a paper towel to catch the blood. When I turned back around, Jacob was in the middle of the rug with the glass sphere in his hand.

Suddenly, I remembered holding the sphere before the Sect woman came to the door. Trying to connect to whatever it was that Sadie had felt when she'd touched the glass. My cheeks heated and the rush of blood made the scratches tingle and sting again. I hid my embarrassment by shuffling through several drawers to find an old cookie tin full of first aid supplies I'd seen when I'd first moved in.

"Why did she run away from you after you let her inside?" Jacob asked.

I opened the first aid kit awkwardly with one hand and the crook of my opposite elbow. Jacob took pity on my one-handed operation when I tried to open the adhesive bandage I'd chosen. He walked over, placed the orb on the counter and reached to take the bandage from my good hand. With two hands, he easily ripped it open. I held my breath while he wound the bandage around my cut finger. We were practically holding hands while the poor Sect woman was out there, somewhere, frightened and alone.

When he was finished, he stepped away, waiting expectantly for me to answer his question.

"She was upset. I thought I'd calmed her down, but she freaked out again when she saw the photographs on the coffee table. I couldn't stop her, so I followed her. She ran off the path. I got lost, and then tangled. That's where you came in," I said. "You must have seen or heard her too…"

"No. I didn't. You must have been much louder than she was. I only heard you," Jacob said.

"Those briars were painful," I said to excuse what must have been excessive shouting. "Then again, your face looks worse than mine feels," I said.

Jacob raised his hand to the injury on his right cheek as if he hadn't noticed the four wide scratches that welled with thickening blood. His eyes met mine, fast, and their usual mossy secrets had gone hard. There was no way his scratches had been made by briars. He knew that I knew it. I could see the scratches on my arms and legs. They were fine and thin and already drying.

"Must have been a branch when I was rushing over to help you in the dark." He slowly lowered his hand. I was alone in an isolated cabin with a man who had just lied to me. The knowledge made my chest tighten and a cool wash of adrenaline flow down my spine.

"What were you doing in the forest at night?"

It was a stupid question. Not because I didn't need to know the answer, but because I needed to pretend I hadn't noticed anything unusual about him being in the woods behind my cabin at midnight.

"Ginseng poachers work at night sometimes. They're easier to spot when headlamps give them away," Jacob explained. His eyes had gone soft again. Scientist at work. Nothing to see here.

I reached for the glass sphere and turned to hang it back above the kitchen window, using the move to cover my concern. Unfortunately, this time when I touched the sphere I felt a strange electric jolt run up my arm and then spread as an arc of barely perceptible energy throughout my entire body. I paused, but for only a second. It took every bit of subterfuge I'd learned as a kid to cover my reaction.

Sadie couldn't have felt such a strong shock every time she touched the sphere. What if Jacob had transferred even more of his emotion and energy to the glass just now because he was feeling more tension than he should be if he was telling the truth?

I turned from the sink to discover he had followed me into the kitchen area. He reached above my head to steady the globe that was spinning from the quickness of my move to hang it and get it out of my tingling hands.

This close I could get an even better look at the scratches on his face. *And I could very clearly imagine them being caused by a woman's defensive hand.*

"You shouldn't have opened your door to a stranger in the middle of the night." Jacob's face had softened. His eyes tracked over my face. Stupid to think I could completely hide my reaction to the globe from him.

It was automatic to look up at him. As it must have been automatic for him to lean over me to speak. I could see the vivid scratches on his face. Could easily imagine how they got there. But as always there was a voice deep down inside whispering that I trusted him even if he had secrets he couldn't share with me.

"I'm not here to hide behind bolted doors. We're supposed to help people. It's what we do," I said. My jaw was clenched. But I wasn't angry. There was a tension in me I couldn't identify. One that was uniquely tied to this man *who was currently standing between me and the woman I needed to help.*

There were whispers telling me to stay near him. Or to get even nearer. But I'd listened to less trusting instincts too often in the past. And those instincts were more like a shout. I stepped forward and for a second experienced full-body contact with Jacob before he allowed himself to be pushed out of the way by my forward momentum.

"Someone murdered Melody Ross. She'll never be able to help anyone, ever again," Jacob said to my back as I headed to the front door.

A harsh truth that didn't exactly capture the reality of her legacy kept forever in the Ross Remedy Book, with Granny and the trio and other wisewomen I barely knew. She continued to help long after she was gone, but only because there were women following in her footsteps. If I quit now, who would carry on Melody's legacy? *Sarah's* legacy?

"She still helps as long as any of us are helping." I paused and leaned against the door. The wood felt cool on my forehead and my fingers, but for only a second before I drew back and pushed the bolt open.

"Listen to yourself. 'Us.' 'We.' When did you decide to become a part of this?" He stalked forward, completely focused on me, as if he hadn't noticed I'd opened the door wide for him to leave. I didn't even know if his Jeep was outside. I hadn't heard a vehicle. I only knew I needed the energy I'd somehow absorbed from him to dissipate. And that could happen only if he went away and took whatever secrets he was hiding with him.

Jacob stopped a foot away from me. "She might come back. If she does, call me," he said. "I'll go back into the woods at dawn to see if I can pick up her trail." He waited for me to reply until it was obvious I wouldn't agree to call him. He pushed his hair back from his forehead with one hand in frustration. "Or call anyone—Granny, Lu. Just don't try to help her alone. Reverend Moon doesn't let people go easily. Trust me," Jacob continued. "We'll have to try to help her discreetly."

My eyes must have widened. My nostrils must have flared. Because Jacob noticed my silent rejection of his plan to keep me out of danger. His eyes narrowed. His hands settled at his sides and he stepped closer, barely glancing at the photographs on the table that had seemed to frighten Lorelei away.

He stopped beside me in the open doorway. A cool breeze from the night outside flowed over us. We stood shoulder to shoulder, him facing out, me facing in, and I refused to look up at him. I simply waited for him to leave. I could wait all night. He must have felt my determination. But he didn't walk away.

"I grew up in these mountains. Played in the wildwood from the time I could crawl. My mother was a minister's wife, but when he died, she was left a widow with a small child to feed. Folks helped. They sure did. But my mother wasn't from around here. Not originally. She never understood my desire for the woods. She found Granny and the women like her strange. Different. And, unlike my father, she could never reconcile their beliefs with her own. So we had to go. I followed her and my father's Bible off the mountain. All the way to Charlottesville. But I never left. Not really. The wildwood already had me. And it will never let me go." When his story had trailed off, I lifted my chin to meet his eyes. The halo from the nearest lamp didn't illuminate his expression. He'd stood in the open doorway as if it was a shadowed confessional.

"I don't know what that means," I said.

"Yes you do. You already know. You feel it yourself. Might have felt it before you put the first foot in Morgan's Gap," Jacob said.

"Granny says she brewed me here," I said softly. The breeze died, having left a heavy lock of hair on Jacob's forehead.

"Maybe she did. Or maybe you were called in ways even Granny wouldn't understand," Jacob said. His last "maybe" sounded pained. And somehow I understood because an echo of a similar pain was in my own chest. If the wildwood was causing us to be drawn together, his secrets and my reservations were keeping us apart.

"Sarah's mother said that some people hear the wildwood," I replied. I needed him to go. I wanted him to stay. Most of all, I wanted to hear more about his past, about his plans and dreams and the reasons why he always seemed to show up, wherever I was, especially when I needed support.

"Lots of people hear. A select few *listen*," Jacob clarified. He paused. I saw his chest go still. His lids lowered. I could barely see the shadow of his lashes against the lighter color of his cheek. "My father was a minister, but he was born on this mountain. He listened."

"Are you one of the select few?" I asked. I had always considered myself a loner. Even after Sarah came into my life. In my mind, we were outcasts, together. Taking on the world by ourselves. In Morgan's Gap, I was either beginning to believe in community or my circle of outcasts was growing. I had fewer reservations about Jacob than I'd had only a few moments before. All I needed to accept the connection growing between us was for him to be open to it as well. And open up with me about where he stood, what he believed and who had caused those scratches on his face.

Then, we could work together to find Lorelei, to help her.

I cursed the lack of light when Jacob stepped out on the porch. Had he nodded or had his sudden movement simply caused a noncommittal shifting of shadows? I didn't know. I couldn't be sure. Trust was for suckers. Something I'd always believed. But when I closed the door and locked it behind him the heat in my belly had changed to a cold hollow. Granny had said we were all here for love, but she'd been wrong. Jacob was in Morgan's Gap for something else. And ultimately, whatever it was kept us apart.

Her mother was proud.

Sarah did all the usual things she did when her mother was presiding over a birth, but she couldn't help noticing the warmth of her mother's smile when she handed her towels. Or the shine in her eyes when she asked for some tea.

If the Sect woman hadn't gone into labor, Sarah would have gone to the wildwood garden this very afternoon to complete the ritual. She was to become a wisewoman like her mother and her grandmother and her great-grandmother. And all the mothers all the way back to the Old Country... and beyond.

The first Ross was said to have been born from woman, but fathered by the Tuatha Dé Danann, an ancient Irish race with supernatural abilities. Hill folk. Fair folk. Fairies. It was only a story, but her mother always said there was a grain of truth in every fairy tale.

Beneath her breath, Sarah practiced the words she had learned from the Ross Remedy Book. The revelation of the ritual had happened that morning after breakfast. Sudden. But not so sudden. She'd been waiting and checking the book every day for a long time. Tomorrow was her twelfth birthday.

Her mother had completed the ritual when she'd been a year younger than her.

"You'll be shown when it's time," her mother had said. Always patient. Always certain.

Sarah had been afraid her time would never come. She'd studied. She'd helped. Little by little, she learned as much as she could by her mother's side.

They helped the Sect woman deliver her baby, but there was an undercurrent of celebration in addition to the happiness of birth. Tomorrow was her birthday. And it was time for her to join the ranks of Ross wisewomen who had ministered to the Morgan's Gap community since long before she was born.

Twenty-Six

I *rushed to the garden* at first light after my strange dream about Sarah. It had been brief and hazy. In all my other dreams, I had been Sarah, looking through her eyes, feeling her emotions. This one had been vague and distant. A strange flash of an intense moment in her life and then it had been gone. I'd tossed and turned the rest of the night. Worrying about Lorelei. Hoping Jacob would find her or that she would somehow make her way to Granny in town.

There was no sign of her in the woods.

Only the usual tangle of vines.

I pushed all thought from my mind of what it had been like to be carried back home out of the dark woods by Jacob Walker.

After a quick shower, cool enough so my skin wouldn't recall the hot washcloth in Jacob's hand, I pulled on jeans hardened by the wind and fresh from being baked in the sun on the outdoor line. I used the blow-dryer only long enough to keep my hair from dripping on my clothes. It was a bright, sunny day so even though we were headed toward winter, I needed only a flannel shirt as a jacket over my T-shirt. I'd been outdoors enough that my skin was slightly tanned and sprinkled with freckles. To that, I added a smudge of gloss, a smear of mascara and some powder.

I'd rarely worn makeup this summer, but I was trying to hide my sleepless night and the bags under my eyes from Granny.

When I came out of the bathroom, more than ready to go, I stopped in the hallway outside of the kitchen. Charm was on the counter, but what startled me was what was beside him.

The Ross Remedy Book was open on the counter.

Charm sniffed around its edges, but there was no way the tiny mouse could have retrieved the book from my fox bag, carried it up to the counter and then opened it. The book weighed several pounds, at least. Charm's weight would have measured in ounces.

As quickly as I had frozen, I burst into action. I rushed first to the back door and then to the front. Both doors were shut tight and locked by a dead bolt and by the sliding bolts I'd installed myself. After checking the doors, I went through the house to make sure no one had managed to get inside while I had been to the garden in the early morning hours.

The cabin was peaceful and quiet. Charm and I were the only living souls inside the house.

"The book was in my bag before I hit the shower," I said to Charm as I came back downstairs. He was still sniffing around the book as if he was also trying to figure out how it had gotten in its current position with no help from me.

I turned around in a circle in the middle of the living room. Nothing else was out of place and the embroidered fox bag was exactly as I'd left it, hanging on the back of a chair.

One thing immediately caught my attention: The remedy book was open to a page I didn't recognize.

I'd studied all the way through the book a thousand times. I thought I knew it from cover to cover. But from where I stood in the living room I could suddenly tell the book was open to a page that was thicker than the rest. I moved toward the kitchen counter to get a closer look and as I did Charm placed his front two paws on the page and sniffed as if he too was clued in to the page's oddity by my reaction.

I could see the page was different because it was larger than the rest of the pages in the book. It had been folded into the size and shape of the other pages, but the creased paper had increased its thickness.

Charm looked up at me expectantly as if to say he couldn't unfold the page, but I should. He stepped back as I reached to do exactly that, carefully and gently, because it was obvious the unusual insertion was older than the rest of the book.

The paper was yellow, stained and slightly brittle. Its creases were permanent and greatly defined. They'd obviously been first folded ages ago and rarely unfolded in the life of the page.

It was a part of the book. Down the center of the opened folds, a stitching held the page in place almost in the dead center of the remedy book. I couldn't tell what the thread was made of—cotton or something thicker like sinew. I could only tell that the stains on the paper were a combination of age, and soil, and possibly something darker—like blood.

There was tight and tiny scripted writing on the page. But what caught my attention, besides the stains, were the sketches of black-berry bushes, finely wrought in indelible ink, although they must have been rendered many, many years ago.

On the yellowed paper, the ink looked greenish-brown, but its color didn't negate the drops of blood that trailed from the forefingers that had also been sketched on the page.

An old wives' tale? Or a ritual the Ross women had practiced for generations?

I'd had to resort several times to a silver magnifying glass I'd found in a kitchen drawer when I'd been studying the older recipes and remedies in the book. I rummaged for it now so I could read the words my unfolding had revealed. My hands shook. I was clumsy as I skimmed the glass over the page.

In my dream, Sarah had been excited and nervous because she was preparing for a rite of passage. It must have been very close to the time her mother was killed because she'd been the same Sarah I had first met except for the lack of shadows under her eyes. I hadn't seen the remedy book in my dream, but Sarah had been happy because she'd finally earned her place among the wisewomen on the mountain. How had Melody and Sarah known the time was right? Did this page reveal itself only when it was time to follow in the footsteps of all the Ross women who had come before?

Sarah had murmured words I couldn't understand. The words I tried to read under the magnifying glass were written in what seemed to be an archaic form of English. I could make them out, but I resisted the urge to whisper them out loud. If this was some kind of a spell, I didn't want to set something in motion I couldn't control or, worse, something that hadn't been meant for me.

It was one thing to learn to make blackberry preserves, bread and pickles. It was another to perform a ritual that involved thorns, blood and the Ross family's legacy.

Sarah had wanted me to come to the mountain. Granny had given me the book. And, now, this page had suddenly appeared. Had I merely missed it before? Had it been there, folded, all this time?

My mind tried to rationalize what it couldn't explain, but my heart knew the page hadn't been there the night before. It had appeared after I'd dreamed about it appearing to Sarah. It wasn't the first time I'd noticed a page that hadn't seemed to be there before. The bee balm ritual had been illuminated by lightning when I needed it. Now this.

Did that mean it was meant for me or did it simply mean I'd awakened something through my connection to my dead adopted sister?

Jacob had already pricked my thumb on a blackberry thorn, but that moment had been dark whimsy that had morphed into something more. Maybe he had set something in motion. But there was a clear process of steps listed on this page I had yet to follow.

Both forefingers pricked, deeply enough to drip blood on the ground.

Promises made to cultivate and cherish the land.

Life and growth celebrated and accepted from sacred earth.

It was a recipe like all the other pages of the book, but one that didn't involve baking, canning or preparing a poultice or tisane. I folded the page, returning the instructive sketches and text to its slumber. Charm watched me with curious, blinking eyes. Granny was expecting me. I'd called her that morning using an ancient wall phone with an echoing connection. I wasn't sure the page had been meant for me. It would be presumptuous to rush into the wildwood and complete a ritual that was meant for Ross women.

Besides, I felt a stirring deep inside my bones. The decision to establish such an intimate connection with the wildwood garden was a momentous one. Such a connection would entail me giving up the walls I'd always depended on to keep me safe and independent from others.

I closed the book. And, not entirely sure I would mind if the folded page disappeared, I shoved it back in my fox bag as I left the house.

With curls still slightly damp, I jumped into the old Chevy and pumped the clutch. Every time it started was an adventure in figuring out what magic combination of lever, pedal and prayers would cause it to fire up and chug its special blend of blue-tinged smoke to the sky.

Charm stayed at home. It wasn't an abandonment. It felt more like he was holding down the fort and although I couldn't imagine the little rodent being able to do much to defend our home I appreciated the intention inherent in the sparkle of his eye and the twitch of his nose.

All the movement made me feel less helpless, until I hit the outer limits of town only to encounter a roadblock. Two county squad cars were parked by the side of the road and two sheriff's deputies were stopping cars entering or leaving town.

"You're the one living out at the Ross cabin. I heard Joseph got this old fella up and running again," the deputy said when I stopped and rolled down my window with a crank that sounded like the hounds of hell. "Seen or heard anything unusual out that way? We got ourselves a missing person alert. A runaway. Girl by the name of Lorelei Moon."

I held the crank with one hand and the ancient loose steering wheel with the other as dizziness slammed into me. Moon. Wife? Daughter? Sister? Some version of all three? Nausea rose at the back of my throat and I had to swallow its bitterness down before I could speak.

"No. I'm sorry, officer. It's quiet out that way." The deputy didn't seem to have half of Jacob Walker's observational skills. He didn't notice my shaking hand on the wheel or the squeak in my voice while I lied through my teeth.

"All right, then. Drive safely and let us know if you see or hear anything," he said. He hit the side of the truck a couple of times as a goodbye or to urge me along; I couldn't be sure. The hollow metallic thumps made me jump and let off on the clutch too quickly. I had to grab for the wheel to keep the truck on the road as I depressed the gas to keep the chugging engine from stalling. The deputy laughed. No doubt amused by my lack of skill and not alerted at all to my guilty mental state. So, really, who lacked skill in this situation?

What if I lied for the girl when what she really needed was professional medical help? What if the authorities only wanted to help Lorelei Moon?

I'd run away from bad situations too many times to fall for those nagging doubts. I'd seen the way the townspeople treated Reverend Moon. I'd seen the way they made way for him and treated him as someone to respect. I'd seen Lorelei's fear.

Maybe she'd made her way undetected all the way to town. Maybe she was hiding with Granny or one of the other wisewomen right now.

There was no one hiding at Granny's house. CC met me at the door and I told Granny everything that had happened while she helped to pack my new willow basket full of deliveries. We both thought that a stroll through town meeting our regular customers would be the best way to find out if anyone had seen Lorelei. When I got to the part about the strange shock I'd received from the glass orb and the story Jacob had told me at the door, Granny stopped packing the basket and closed her eyes as if she was in pain.

"She never should have taken him away. He belonged on the mountain. Anyone could see that," Granny fretted.

"Well, he's here now," I said. The basket was full, but I lingered. I hadn't told Granny about feeling rejected because I hadn't yet shared with her the pull I felt toward Lu and Jacob. It was such a deep and pervasive thing. Why talk about heartbeats and blood circulation. It just *was*, indefinably *there*.

"Maybe. He's here and he's not here. I can't explain it. I don't understand," Granny said. She opened her eyes and shuffled items in the basket as if she was embarrassed by her moment of weakness.

"He's holding something back," I said. "And it might be my fault." The basket still sat on the counter. I gripped its handle tightly without picking it up because I'd taken myself by surprise. I'd been ready to trust the wildwood about Jacob last night. I'd been ready to accept the connection. He had walked away from that readiness. I'd felt rejected, but what had I really done to deserve his trust? I was still an outsider by most mountain standards. I was definitely still guarded and defensive most of the time.

Granny put her hands on her hips and looked at me, hard. She didn't say a word. She didn't have to. I knew she was waiting for me to go on.

"There's… something… happening. Between us. And Lu. Between all three of us. A growing connection. And maybe I'm the last person in the world anyone with any sense would want to be connected to."

I finished in a rush that made Granny soften, smile and step forward to place her hands on either side of my head as if she needed to hold me in place before I decided to fly away.

"Whatever is going on with Jacob Walker was going on with him before you even arrived. Stop blaming yourself for the difficulties and darkness in this world, Mel. You cannot take that on. It's just another way of adding layers of insulation between yourself and others. Another kind of armor that keeps you apart."

I let the warmth of her palms and the truth in her wisdom soak into me.

"But a trio…" I tried to begin again, only emotion weighted my tongue and tightened my throat.

"Do you think Sadie, Kara and Joyce were always so easy together? The kind of ease they've developed takes time. And none of them, not a one, has as much power as you do. Sparks are flying." Granny teasingly tugged my hair as she lowered her hands. "In more ways than one. It's completely natural. Let them fly. Just be prepared to accept the connection when it happens. Because it will. The wildwood doesn't play." Granny pointed to the basket and I picked it up. I had deliveries to make and townspeople counting on us no matter what else was going on. "Oh, not to say nature can't be mischievous, and Jacob Walker can be too. Don't let his strong, silent act fool you. He's quick to tease once he knows you. And his watchful eyes don't miss a thing! But, Mel, the wildwood knows what it's doing. If it's urging you, Jacob and Lu to come together it's because you're needed. As a trio. More powerful together than apart."

I paused on my way to the door and looked at the woman who had taught me so much in such a short time. When we'd made the rye bread together, I'd felt a camaraderie I hadn't felt before. But now, with all my fears and weaknesses out on the table, I felt more than friendship. Granny was family. My family.

"I'll do my best," I promised.

"I know," Granny said. She put her hands in her pockets, rummaging around for space. "We all will. We'll all do our best."

As I walked out the door I heard her whisper "I just hope it will be enough."

As I walked from back door to back door around town, I bumped into more deputies on foot, handing out fliers and going from house to house. Several ladies' auxiliaries from local churches had also been mobilized. They had their own almost-uniform of cardigan sweaters and sensible loafers as well as hard hairstyles that didn't move no matter the breeze.

The women bothered me more than the deputies. They were like the Sect women in too many ways. Flocking without thought in whichever way they were directed. Had they never seen the mad look in Moon's eyes or the youth of some of the pregnant girls he herded through town? Did they really value choice and individuality so little?

And what of the babies forced to be born and grow up in an oppressive community ruled by fear? Lorelei had run away for a good reason. I only wished I could find her so I could help her get away.

Violet Morgan was in the salon when I pushed my way through the front door. No one else was there. Including Becky, who must have stepped out. Violet had a head full of the foil folds that indicated she was having her hair colored. The acrid scent of peroxide burned my eyes and nose. She dropped a magazine onto the table in front of her when I walked in.

"I'm not going to judge you for reading an article about an actor," I said. The sexy Swedish actor who smiled from the cover of the entertainment magazine had won multiple awards. His acting ability paired with his natural charisma was deadly. I didn't blame Violet at all.

"I wasn't." She leaned over and pushed the magazine away.

"Did you like the preserves?" I asked. I shared my best smile, but it must have been scary because Violet blanched like I had snarled.

"Tom helped me gather them," I continued.

"Please. Stop. You can't…" Violet began. Her eyes darted from me to the door. I wondered if Hartwell Morgan ever checked up on her mid-appointment. To be sure she wasn't chatting or looking at sexy magazines.

"…be your friend?" I supplied the impossible finish for her. Hoping that by saying it aloud she would hear how ridiculous it sounded.

"Yes. That. We can't. Hartwell doesn't like…" Violet stalled again. I took pity on her and lost all trace of flippancy. She really was miserable. And I already suspected her husband was nothing to laugh about.

"…women like me," I said.

"I don't think he likes anything, really," Violet said. She sagged against the back of her chair, still having the presence of mind to protect the foil on her head by tilting her chin forward.

"I heard he wants to be governor," I said. I hadn't only heard it. I'd spent some time at the tiny library in town to confirm the rumors. Mildred Pierce was a widow who kept several rooms' worth of books and historical materials in the bottom story of a large Southern colonial near the courthouse. Much of it devoted to the town's founding family. The Morgan family was a popular topic in newspapers and websites that leaned toward extremism—tax cuts for multibillionaires, corporate interests, doing away with environmental regulations. I walked over and took several bottles from the basket and placed them on the stylist's station. I could get payment later.

"It's all about the natural gas pipeline," Violet explained. "He needs more political clout to enable the energy companies to extend through Morgan's Gap. He's heavily invested in fracking." Real talk. Not the breathless niceties she was allowed to say.

"Fracking destroys everything," I said. I'd seen photographs of mountains in Tennessee and Kentucky completely denuded of life. I'd taken the opportunity to research more than the killing on my laptop when I was visiting Granny's. I knew more about the process now than I had and I felt even more confident in my placement of the "No Pipeline" bumper sticker on my truck.

Most of the mountaintops got washed away by high-powered water cannons to get to the shale layers that held pockets of oil and natural gas deep beneath the ground. Cheaper and safer than mining. So much worse for the environment. Especially when you considered the construction of the pipelines and the inevitable leaks of methane and oil during transport.

"I know," Violet said. She leaned over and opened the magazine I thought she'd been reading to reveal a smaller magazine hidden inside the larger one. She hadn't been reading about the Swedish actor. She'd been reading about the environmental impact of fracking and pipeline construction. The article was paired with horrible photographs. Streams full of dead fish. Children who had to have clean water shipped in on container trucks because their local ground water was contaminated.

"The wildwood would be devastated," I said.

"No more chanterelles or blackberries," Violet said.

"No more rye bread or pickles," I added.

"Hello, ladies." The bell above the shop door jangled and a deputy stepped into the salon. Violet flipped the magazine closed and sat back on her chair. I lost my equilibrium because the natural, open expression she'd shared with me changed so quickly to one of polite blankness. "Just gonna leave a stack of fliers here."

The deputy tossed a handful of fliers on the table. There was no photograph of Lorelei. Only a crude drawing and a physical description. But Violet gasped and her face shone as white as the peroxide on her hair.

"Hartwell knows. He's called in help from the next county. And the state police. Don't worry. We'll find her," the deputy said.

He left as quickly as he'd arrived. I held tight to my basket and met Violet's frightened eyes.

"If they find her, it won't be good. It's never good for the ones who run if they're caught," she whispered. "Not that it's good for those of us that don't run. We're all caught, sooner or later."

Like dot matrix art that finally reveals itself to you when you focus your eyes right, Violet Morgan became clear to me. She was a Sect woman. She might no longer wear the homespun dress or the kerchief in her hair, but she had the look in her eyes.

"Moon gave me to Hartwell when I was sixteen," she said. There was shame in her voice. As if she thought she should have run like Lorelei. Anger bubbled up from the place in my gut where fury for men like Moon and Hartwell always lived.

"He had no right. He didn't own you. Or your future. And Hartwell doesn't own you now. You aren't a possession," I said.

"I know that. I've always known it, really. But they don't let you go. They will never let me go," Violet said. Tears welled up in her eyes until they were thick pools I couldn't believe she didn't spill. But crying would smear her perfectly applied makeup.

She'd always had to be so careful. I could see it in the way she held herself even now as we spoke about unspeakable things that everyone in Morgan's Gap knew but didn't mention. The whole town was culpable. Including me. Because I had seen that flock of frightened women and I hadn't known what to do. How do you save a person who has been caged in a culture of nonentity since birth?

Granny had been trying. Maybe her whole life. Melody Ross had tried too. She'd saved the ones she could, but how many had died in the woods or been given away, chattel to men like Hartwell Morgan? Violet's cage was gilded, but that didn't make her life sentence any less harsh.

I remembered Jacob telling me the Sect had broken off from the Mennonite church fifty years ago. No wonder Reverend Moon was part of a rogue group. Even the most backward religion wouldn't turn a blind eye to what basically amounted to trafficking. Would it? I shuddered.

"Moon signed over almost all the land he owned to Hartwell. That land provides a strip straight through the county along the National Forest. In exchange, Moon lives undisturbed in the way he sees fit. Hartwell and his supporters and the supporters of the pipeline protect the Sect. I have nowhere to go," Violet said.

I left my basket on the table and wrapped my arms around her stiff shoulders. I ignored the sting of peroxide in my eyes. "You could come to the wildwood with me. We'll figure something out."

"I would never bring my troubles to anyone else's door. If I ran to the wildwood, Hartwell would follow me. Tom…*People* depend on the wildwood being a peaceful place. A sanctuary. I wouldn't destroy that," Violet said. There was a thread of steely resolve in her soft voice I hadn't heard before.

"But Hartwell wants to. It isn't only about money, is it? He hates the wildwood because of Tom," I guessed. "And he knows you care about Tom."

"Tom is Hartwell's brother," Violet said. "He ran away a long time ago, but after my marriage he checked on me. Always in secret, but he came to see if I was okay. No one else did. No one but Granny. She helped me with the birth control pills."

The scarred man everyone called Mad Tom was a Morgan.

He'd run away from home, but he had found a new one. In the wildwood. With Melody Ross? I couldn't be sure based on only an expression in an old photograph.

"One of them," the pregnant Sect woman had said before she'd run away.

She must have been talking about Tom Morgan. But why would she be afraid of the Morgans? Hartwell had his docile wife. Why would his family seem a threat to Lorelei? I knew his support of the Sect ran deep. Moon had purchased it with the land he'd signed over to Hartwell. And with Violet. But what other arrangements with the Sect did Hartwell enjoy? My blood turned cold in my veins.

"We'd better get you rinsed, Vee!" Becky gleefully shouted in a singsong voice that drowned out the bell above the door as she pushed it open. "Oh, hi, Mel. I didn't expect you today."

"I needed to help Granny with a few things so I decided to make my rounds while I was in town," I replied. "You can pay me for that moisturizer later. Go ahead and take care of Violet's hair."

I made sure to keep my goodbye to Violet casual even though my mind was racing. Had Tom's family had anything to do with Melody's death? And what about the car crash that had killed Sarah? The Ross women had no political clout and the wisewomen were a tiny ragtag group of people. Would Hartwell have really thought they could stand in his pipeline's way? Had he seen them as enough of a threat to justify murder?

I reached for the reassuring warmth of Charm before I remembered he had stayed at the cabin today. I kept seeing the fracking photographs superimposed over the wildwood garden every time I closed my eyes. But, worse, I heard the cree-cree of the weighted rope in the black locust tree.

He never slept. There was a spot where he curled on the back of a chair, but when his eyes were closed and his respiration slow and steady he was still ever alert. He had been made to be alert, watchful, ever ready.

Charm had watched his mistress leave from a hidden corner at the top of the kitchen cabinets where cabinet met interior wall. The outer walls were log. They provided no place for him to travel without being seen. He preferred the walls that had been constructed with several porous layers of material. Ones pervious to his sharp teeth and digging feet. He'd established a route from the kitchen to the upstairs to the attic in the wall that held the cabinetry.

But he waited for the sound of the truck to fade away before he entered the small hole he'd gnawed in the wall. Because his instincts warred inside of his fuzzy chest. She was going alone to wherever she went. Empty pocket. Cold shoulder. His head grew dizzy with the sense she was driving toward danger without him. Not good. Bad. The same way snakes were bad. Lurking. Coiled in wait to strike. Someone, something lurked around his mistress. The one he'd been sent to aid. It was wrong to let her go without him. Wrong to leave her alone. Yet, it was also right. There was another instinct driving him. A Thing That Needed to Be Accomplished.

Once the sound of the truck had diminished to nothing in the distance, Charm entered the wall. He followed the route he'd made up, under and around wiring, through several more holes he had diligently chewed until he came to the place in the attic where a loosened corner of ventilation screen allowed him to reach the outside.

He paused, as a real mouse vulnerable to predators should. Rising up on his hind legs and lifting his nose to the air. He sniffed, but smelled no predatory death close enough to endanger him. Wings, claws, fangs were all busy flapping, scratching and chewing elsewhere.

The logs the cabin had been constructed with long ago were rough-hewn and easy enough to grab with his handlike feet. He ran down log by log, zigzagging to find the purchases he'd marked with his scent by using them time after time.

Then he paused at the ground sheltered by the shadow of the house.

He sniffed again and this time he caught whiffs of animals very unlike the birds, cats and snakes he needed to fear. Just as he still held hints of lavender, mint and chamomile forever in his gray-and-white fur, he smelled fur and feathers and scales that contained wildwood fragrances deep within their atoms.

The garden called them as it called him. And they must go as he must go. To the source. To their reason for being. To the other half of their mistresses and masters. To the wild.

Charm ran from the cabin to the wood line. His small mouse legs were only slowed by the quick mouse instincts that kept him from being eaten until he finally reached the garden clearing. Others had already assembled, still others came from the trees, the undergrowth and the sky at the same time as him or shortly thereafter.

A deer-who-was-not-a-deer foraged beneath the sunflowers. Charm joined him there, picking up the fallen seeds, not to satisfy a mousey hunger, but to answer the call that had brought him here in the first place. He was the living connection between human and the wild. As were all the creatures merging into a crowd around him. A bright red bird that still held the scent of the wax paper from which it had been made with precise folds and whispered wisewoman's words fluttered down. It perched on a bowing sunflower's head and plucked a seed that hadn't yet fallen to the ground, cracking it open with its sharp once paper beak. A mink, sable brown and slinky, slithered from out of the briars. Its fur smelled of mothballs and its eyes were a solid beady black, but too wide and too open because they had once been buttons sewn into a velveteen toy for a child.

After a while, the trees were filled with as many birds as leaves, and a thick assorted pack of dissimilar creatures formed a strange menagerie snaking around the garden and by the stream.

Last of all came the handsome russet fox they'd been waiting for. He stood at the mouth of the path that led from the cabin, arriving from the same direction Charm had arrived from. Sometimes, recently, Charm had ridden on the fox's back, clinging to the bristly ruff around the fox's neck. Unlike many of the other creatures, the fox's scent was very nearly the scent of an actual fox. He'd been quickened many years ago, fashioned by a woodsman's hands out of fragrant cedar and rubbed to a fine polish with linseed oil. He smelled strongly of those things, but also of the moss he slept on and his forest home. The fox rarely went to town. He never curled into a pocket or on the back of a chair. His connection to the wildwood was greater than all the other wisewoman-made creatures because his master had left him for a long time.

So long that the connection through him between the wild and the human had almost been lost.

Charm took the fox a few of the sunflower seeds and dropped them in front of his nose. The fox licked them up, then sat in the midst of all the creatures. The garden clearing grew silent, save for the slight sound of creaking from the black locust trees as they swayed in the wind.

Twenty-Seven

*G*ranny *was packed and* ready to go by the time I returned from deliveries. She sat primly on an antique sofa in the formal front parlor. The velvet upholstery was tufted, the wood frame was scrolled and the proper name for the sofa was probably something like "settee." I hadn't been in the room before. The door to it had always been closed.

"I'm going back to the cabin with you," Granny proclaimed.

Like the room and the sofa, Granny was more formal than I was used to. The dress she wore still had numerous pockets, but it was made from a shiny black jacquard fabric with a raised design that reminded me of patterns I'd seen before. In Sadie's bean arrangement and in the basket she'd woven for me before she'd even met me.

"I don't need a babysitter. I can handle Jacob Walker or anyone else who shows up," I said. But Lorelei's genuine fear and Violet's as well made my bravado fall flatter than usual. My pulse was quick and my chest was tight and I wasn't as opposed to company as I might have been a few days before.

"I didn't like the look of the dregs this morning and there was a raven on the back fence. Pretty as you please. An egg-born raven not wisewoman made. No good can come from a portent like that before I've even had my second cup," Granny warned. She rose from her perch in a flash of black skirts that echoed the dark portents she claimed to have seen that morning.

I glanced around the room, trying not to stare. The walls were covered in framed photographs. Every inch of wallpaper was covered and standing frames covered the tables and shelves. Much like the ones in the box in the cabin, the photographs depicted people, many of them women and children, but unlike the cabin photographs, some of the photographs in Granny's private parlor ranged back in time to vintage black and white.

The small old woman surrounded by a room packed full of photographs made my breath catch, then rush out in a startled sigh. I knew what I was seeing: all the people Granny had helped on the mountain. There were hundreds of them. Too many to catalog or count. There were even loose photographs tucked into the edges of frames.

I picked one of these frames up from the nearest shelf and examined the faces more closely. The family resemblance was obvious. I flicked through the loose photographs. They represented generations. Had Granny known and helped them all?

"If you'll grab my basket from the kitchen, we can be on our way," Granny said. She picked up a carpetbag that didn't seem too heavy so I let her carry it out while I placed the frame back on the table. Emotion swelled inside my chest as I took one last look around the room. I was reluctant to close the door on it again. I wanted to leave it wide. To celebrate what one woman's work had done for this community. Hippy. Kitchen witch. Granny. Some used those terms in a derogatory, dismissive way. Others called her Granny with respect. *Wisewoman.* I was only beginning to understand what that calling entailed. I closed the door and turned the key in the lock of the ancient door. She kept her memories close. I needed to respect her wishes in spite of my urge to shout her contributions to the world.

I went to fetch her basket.

She'd shared those photographs with me. For inspiration? For revelation and greater understanding? I couldn't be sure. But I was fairly certain she wanted me to feel the simple gravitas of her life's work. So much effort. So little recognition. And that was somehow part of the job.

I'd left my own emptied basket in the bed of the truck when I'd returned. Granny's basket was packed full of unusual supplies—bandages, poultices and ointments, unlabeled bottles with cork toppers filled with viscous dark liquid.

"What is she prepping for?" I asked the empty room before I realized that CC was nowhere to be seen. His usual place on the counter was vacant beside a plate of crumbs.

I looked around for the fat cat as I headed for the door. He was gone. Just as Charm had been that morning.

Granny had put her bag in the back of the truck. I tucked the basket in beside the bag and tied everything, including my empty basket, down with a bungee cord lashed to a rusty chain that had been left over from some kind of cargo decades before.

"I didn't see CC," I mentioned as I climbed up behind the wheel.

Granny tsked her tongue against her teeth. Her fingers worried with the seat belt after I fastened it around her, twisting it in her wrinkled hands.

"It was only a bird, don't fret," I said.

"If you continue your studies, you'll learn that noticing is part of our lives. We make a habit of seeing what other people can't or won't."

The only other person I'd met who seemed as observant as Granny was Jacob.

"Did you pack your basket before or after you'd seen the raven?" I asked. The truck started with its usual roar and I popped the clutch in a way that didn't shame me in front of the neighbors. I didn't stall out and the truck didn't leap forward with a jerk.

"After," Granny said. From the corner of my eye, I saw her lips thin into a tight worried line. I was halfway out of town before I noticed the taste of blood. I'd worried my own lips with the edge of my teeth until I'd made myself bleed.

The sheriff's office still had both lanes blocked with a checkpoint on the road that led in and out of town. Granny was more subdued than usual, but she spoke to the deputy who stopped us and he barely made us pause because she had helped him with a bum knee he'd gotten from high school football.

"Go Eagles!" Granny said as we pulled away. The deputy laughed, but Granny had only smiled a grim smile that made my chest constrict tighter around my heart.

The sun was setting. The driveway to the cabin was shadowed. When a raven the size of a toddler rose up with a sudden stretch of wing from a fence post near the old barn, I almost ran the Chevy off the driveway. I jerked the wheel and slammed on the brake, but this time I forgot to press the clutch at the same time. The vehicle jerked and its engine stalled. Granny cursed and we both watched as the raven lifted up into a sky that would soon be as black as its feathers.

"Let me guess. Not egg born," I said.

"I...I don't know. Can't be sure from this distance," Granny said.

To be honest, I wasn't sure it mattered. A wisewoman-made familiar of that size wouldn't be a welcome sight right now either. Not when I was still uncertain about my place in all of this. Granny was so spooked it had rubbed off on me. The weight of a wisewoman's work was greater than I had imagined. We lived precariously between humankind and our wild surroundings, trying to establish peace between the two.

How easy was it to upset the symbiotic relationship that kept us all safe and sound?

Right now, it seemed the balance had been disrupted a step too far. Whether or not it was my imagination or a sixth sense, the world around us seemed tense, expectant, ready and waiting for…

There were no vehicles in the driveway when I parked the truck near the house. I went around to help Granny get out. Sometimes her joints stiffened when she sat too long. The place was silent. Too silent. Not so much as a cricket hummed. The sun had sunk below the mountain and the forest was completely dark against a blue-black sky.

"If she's out there, she's hurting. All alone," I said, trying to penetrate the shadows to see what I could see. A wink of eyes startled me, reflecting starlight and the lamplight that beckoned from inside the house. I'd left the light on in the living room, but it wasn't strong enough to illuminate the creature that looked at us for only a moment before it was gone.

"Maybe hurting less alone than where she came from, though," Granny said.

She made it out of the truck and stretched before following me toward the porch. I paused only to grab the baskets and the carpetbag from the back.

"I tried to get Violet to come with me today. I invited her out to the cabin. To the wildwood. To stay," I said.

Granny slowly climbed onto the stoop and waited for me to unlock the front door. Even with the lamplight shining from the window, the porch was gloomy. The reflection of eyes in the woods had unsettled me. Between my shoulder blades, a spot like a target tingled. I didn't whirl around to peer into the darkness. I didn't want Granny to see me shaken and nervous.

"Of course you did, but Hartwell would never stand for it. He'd burn this place down before he allowed you to take what he considers his," Granny said.

"Violet is a human being. Not a possession," I replied.

CC meowed from the kitchen counter as we came in the door. I wasn't surprised to see him. It was a long way from town, but CC was Granny's familiar and much more than he seemed.

"That is not your counter, Cat," Granny chuckled. "You won't find any cookies there."

"Sometimes, but not today," I corrected. Not that I had made Granny's sunwort cookies. After that first night in Morgan's Gap, I'd decided I needed to dream. It had seemed as if only Sarah's memories were revealing anything to me. Now, I felt the blend of knowledge from her memories and my lived experiences since I'd come to Morgan's Gap. I needed her memories less as I accepted my place on the mountain more.

Before I closed the door, a coyote laughed. Sound carried strangely in the mountains. The animal could have been on the opposite side of the hollow or it could have been around the corner of the house. I'd heard coyotes before, but I still closed the door and slid the bolt home so quickly my fingers fumbled over the usual task.

"They're restless," Granny said. Her lips had thinned again. "You might have more company tonight. You should turn the porch lights on, just in case."

"Lorelei?" I asked. I flicked the switch closest to me and the amber bulb on the porch flickered on. As Granny sat down to take off her shoes, I crossed to the back door. I turned that light on as well. The amber bulb on the back porch barely illuminated the backyard. But even in its meager light I saw a fox sitting at the edge of the yard where the wildwood path began. I'd seen the fox before. Or Sarah had. Sitting exactly in the same way. But before I could call to Granny the fox stood and stretched and trotted up the path that led to the garden.

As if it had been waiting for us to get home.

"They're restless tonight," Granny repeated without answering my question. I turned back around to face her. Her mouth was tight with concern and her eyes were dark. I didn't press her for more information. She was sharing only feelings and hunches. She didn't know anything for sure.

Charm had appeared on the front window ledge. His little body was backlit by the front porch light. CC meowed again as if to confirm what Granny had said.

"Nothing to do now but wait," Granny continued. And suddenly the tight feeling in my chest was identified. *Anticipation.* But not the good kind. Granny's worry over dregs and portents hadn't caused the feeling. I'd been feeling it all day. Constricting more and more, minute by minute. It was tangible. Physical. The atmosphere around us had thickened and my clumsy manipulation of the bolt frightened me because I felt like I couldn't move as fast as I should.

"I'll put the kettle on," I offered.

What I really wanted was an excuse to go to the remedy book. I suddenly knew what I had to do. The ritual had appeared for a reason. For me. Jacob had inadvertently begun it with the thorn prick. Had he known what he was setting in motion? He'd said it was an old wives' tale. But I'd felt the gravity of the moment when he had taken it a step further than he'd intended.

The wildwood gave us the garden. And from the garden we accepted our connection by baking and breaking the bread and consuming the blackberries, herbs and other things that grew.

But, for the connection to be completed in a perfect cycle, we had to give something back to the wildwood as well. I'd willingly allowed Jacob to give the wildwood a drop of my blood, but that drop had been only the beginning. If I was to truly embrace the life of a wisewoman and follow in Granny's footsteps, I needed to complete the ritual and fully accept the cycle of connection between the garden and my heart.

Granny hadn't tried to stop me or come with me. She'd taken one look at the Ross Remedy Book I clutched to my chest and she nodded as if she knew what I was about to do. I left her on the sofa with CC warming her lap and I went out into the gloaming.

It took all my nerve to slide back the bolt on the back door. Only moments before, I'd locked out the world. Now, I ventured out into it, armed with only an old book, some ancient scribbles and a few words. I murmured the words I'd heard Sarah mumble in my dream. Or the closest approximation to them I could manage. For her, I thought the page had probably revealed itself in Gaelic or some long-dead language very like it. For me, the tight cursive scrawl was in English. I would use those words in the garden. But on the way up the path I needed Sarah with me.

She had been sent away before she could complete the ritual and become a full-fledged wisewoman. She'd wanted nothing more than to live and work beside the mother she loved and admired. The killer had taken that future away from her when he'd killed Melody. Then, if our car had been intentionally run off the road, he'd taken any future away from her.

Reverend Moon? Hartwell Morgan? Or their acolytes? Hired hands who would even kill for the men that directed them.

I couldn't resurrect Sarah and give her back the life that had belonged to her. I could only complete the ritual the remedy book had offered to me. In her place? Maybe. Or maybe I'd earned a place of my own.

I was thankful the path was smooth and well traveled. I'd brought along a flashlight, but it was that strange time in between sunset and moonrise when the world was in shadow, but not shadowed enough for a light to do more than create dizziness and glare. The expectant hush we'd experienced in the cabin was even more pronounced here. No more coyotes called. The birds were asleep for the night. Even a distant whip-poor-will cut off in mid-song as if it had broken the silence by mistake.

We were all waiting for something. The whole mountain world. But the wildwood garden was only waiting for me. I sensed its welcome when I came off the path and into the clearing. The gurgle of the stream was louder at night. The quiet amplified the rush and tumble of water over rocks no matter how small. There was no breeze. Nothing stirred. I hadn't seen any more eyes reflect the glare of my light. At the edges of the garden, the black locust trees had been some of the first to drop all their leaves and on this clear night their silhouettes were dark against the sky.

I wasn't afraid.

All my worries about Lorelei, Jacob, the Sect and Moon and Hartwell Morgan receded. The remedy book was solid in my hands. The ground was even more solid beneath my feet.

And Charm was in my pocket.

Promises made to cultivate and cherish the land.

Life and growth celebrated and accepted from sacred earth.

I made my way to the blackberry bushes. I traveled the same route Jacob had traveled that day when he'd found me trimming. I didn't leap over or step around. I took no short cuts. I followed the winding rows and recognized in them the patterns I'd seen. In the beans. In the basket. In the sphere. In Granny's dress. A spiral. The garden's rows represented life itself. Forever growing and expanding outward to encompass all. Not only the Ross women. Or people with happy families. *All*. I had been rootless my whole life without realizing that putting down roots was up to me.

Even without leaves, the blackberry was a massive tangle of twining, twirling vines. My trimming hadn't made them any less dense. In the deepening darkness, the bush was impenetrable by sight. I suddenly thought about fairy bushes, portals the fairy Sidhe had enchanted to travel from our world to other realms. Sarah had loved to tell stories about the fae. I'd clipped these vines during daylight. I knew they were only blackberry bushes. But, at night, it was easy to imagine them as otherworldly. Influenced by the fae that had been enticed to join with the first Ross woman centuries before.

My hands were cold. By the light of the flashlight, I could see my breath. It fogged from my chilled lips and I tried not to think about poor Lorelei. I needed to focus. By strengthening my connection to the garden, I would be better prepared to help her.

I dropped to my knees in front of the blackberry bushes. I placed the flashlight on the ground so its beam shone on the book I'd placed beside me and, with one flick of my wrist, I opened it to the folded page. Even the folds of the page opened with a touch or two. As if the ritual was already in motion before I knelt down.

I had been carefully following the steps set out in the Ross Remedy Book since I came to Morgan's Gap. Page by page. I had never been a cook so the recipes had seemed magical to me, a particular kind of kitchen alchemy you had to practice to understand. But with greater understanding came the realization that magic exists in the simplest things.

Root. Vine. Thorn. Blossom. Magic you could see, taste and touch.

This ritual was as simple on the surface as all of that. But its implications ran as deep and complex as the root systems hidden beneath my knees.

With an emissary quickened by garden's growth.

I reached into my pocket and cupped my hand around Charm. He grasped my fingers with his paws and I lifted him out. I raised him to my nose and breathed in his stored-up, closety scent of lavender and yarn. Simple. And not. But the *not* didn't intimidate me anymore. I remembered my fear of growing the yeast. Of ruining the blackberries. I was no longer afraid. I could follow a recipe. I could stand where others had stood before. I placed Charm in the middle of the opened page in a place of honor. He assumed his usual pose on his back haunches.

Both forefingers pricked, deeply enough to drip blood on the ground.

I had gone down a list of instructions in the book many times. This was no different. And yet, it was. When Jacob had pricked my thumb, he'd barely drawn blood. The "injury" had been quick and slight. The pain fleeting. It had been the feel of his hot mouth and lips that had sensitized the sting. Causing it to throb for hours if not days afterward.

I knew from the sketches I needed to make the blackberry thorns penetrate my skin seriously this time. Just as sketches had helped me test the seal on the blackberry preserves and spoon off the blackened foam on the yeast. What was a recipe, really, if it wasn't a perfected ritual written down for others to follow? A treasured remembrance to help others learn the way to go.

This pricking was to be my promise to the wildwood.

In *blood on the ground.*

I reached for the nearest vine or it reached for me. Night had fallen. Pitch black surrounded the halo of light created by the flashlight's beam. All I knew for sure was that the vine was closer than I expected. And a larger thorn than I'd seen before came easily to my searching fingers. Before I could pause or feel trepidation, I pressed my forefingers into the thorn, each in turn. Pressed hard until the thorn penetrated deep into my skin. The pain was sharper than I expected. I cried out softly and Charm hummed, a strange sort of trill that sounded like encouragement.

I released the vine and held my hands high. My fingers throbbed and I watched as droplets, driven by my thudding heartbeat, seeped from the pricks to trail down and fall. Beat by beat, the drops splashed into the loose soil of the earth I'd cultivated all summer.

There was a sigh as the silent night woke up in a soft, cool breeze against my face.

Did the wind cause the forest to stir or did the stirring forest cause the wind? I didn't know. But I suspected the latter as I spoke words in an ancient tongue I didn't know myself. I recognized their meaning even though the language was strange. As the garden absorbed the blood I'd given to the ground, the wildwood returned my promise, using my own lips to utter a reciprocal pledge to me.

"*Buanaich.*"

Abide, continue, and persevere.

"*Maille ri.*"

Together.

Only then did I feel the tears on my cheeks. Not from pain. There was hardly any pain at all. I cried because I'd accepted the connection. I'd felt an echo of this relationship in the way I'd loved Sarah. That echo had called me here, to this place, to this life.

I would live in the wildwood and the wildwood would live in me. And together we would help Lorelei.

Twenty-Eight

*M*y *cell phone buzzed* at 11:00 p.m. Granny was dozing on the couch after being watchful for hours. The veggie soup I'd taken from the fridge and reheated had amounted to two cups' worth and I'd urged Granny to drink most of one of them while I sipped the other. At the sound of my phone, she sat up and narrowed her eyes as I answered. If she had been at the top of her game, she probably could have intuited what the call was about before I could relay the message.

"Get the downstairs bedroom ready," Sadie said with no preamble. "Company's coming."

Granny had already given me some spare furniture from the attic of her house in town. *Just in case.* At the time, I'd been happy to fill the empty room. Now, I knew why it might be needed. I'd set up the lower bedroom with an old single sleigh bed and a waterfall dresser with a wavy mirror that had seen better days. With pillows and bedclothes borrowed from Joyce, the bedroom was as ready as I could have made it for Granny or for anyone else.

"Sadie says company's coming. To have the bedroom ready," I said after I'd thanked Sadie and disconnected the call.

"Well, she could have told us something we didn't know," Granny grumbled, but all the watchful energy I'd seen in her the last few hours had gone. The near nap had rejuvenated her. She sat calmly as if she had settled into the idea of whatever was going to happen.

Neither of us jumped when a thud came at the back door. I stood from the armchair and went to answer it, glad the wait was over. Granny did jump up from the couch when a baby's cry sounded at the exact moment I slid back the lock and opened the door.

"Lorelei," I gasped, but I couldn't say much more because the tattered figure had been leaning against the closed door. When it swung open, she fell forward, kept from hitting the floor only by me. I caught her with my whole body, grabbing her upper arms and cushioning the tiny bundle in her arms with my breasts. There was blood. So much fresh blood. It transferred from her and her bundle to me, smearing across my shirt.

"Let's get her inside," Granny ordered. "Lorelei, we're going to lay you down on a nice, warm bed. Don't worry. We're going to help you."

"Everything's going to be all right," I added. But my voice shook and I was trying to convince myself as much as the new mother. Beneath the blood, Lorelei's face was paper white and her hair a damp tangle. Her clothes weren't only stained with blood. They were also dirty and torn.

"Good girl. You used your skirt to wrap the baby. The crying is good, honey. Strong lungs. Clear airway. You've done real good," Granny crooned. She wrapped her arm around both the mother and the child on the opposite side and together we walked Lorelei into the bedroom. She couldn't walk quickly and I could feel shivers wracking her frame. The part of her skirt she'd ripped to make a blanket for the newborn had left her legs bare all the way to her hips.

I rushed forward and swept back the quilts, but I left the top sheet spread. Between the two layer of sheets and the mattress cover, the mattress would be protected.

"Go and bring back a stack of clean towels and my basket of supplies. And turn the hot water on in the sink when you pass," Granny ordered. The bathroom was directly across from the bedroom. Close enough that I would be able to clean Lorelei and the baby up comfortably while Granny assessed their conditions.

By the time I came back to the bedroom with the towels, Granny had rolled up her sleeves and washed her hands and forearms. I followed her example after I set the towels within her reach.

"Lorelei, I'm going to take a look below and make sure you've passed everything that needs to be passed. Then, we're going to wash you up and I'll pad you. Okay? I've done this many a time for women on this mountain and it looks like you handled most everything on your own," Granny explained.

"I bit the cord," Lorelei said. I had wet a towel while Granny examined and washed Lorelei "down below." I used my towel to gently wash her face. I'd never been present at a birth or closely after a birth before. My hands were shaking and my own face was wet. I'd always considered myself badass, but I'd never known anyone as badass as Lorelei.

"You did right. You did right," Granny said. She'd finished washing up Lorelei's thighs and legs. She urged her to lift her hips and she placed a double layer of towels under her bottom before placing a padding made of rolled bandages between her legs. "There now. Clean and dry."

I took all the soiled towels into the bathroom and washed and rinsed them before putting them in the hamper for a later laundering. Granny followed me to wash her hands again. We both would need to change our clothes when we finished.

"I'm going to check the baby now. Do you have a shirt or a night-gown that buttons in the front so Lorelei can attempt to feed the baby? She's had a shock. The warmer we can keep her, the better," Granny said.

I ran upstairs to my bedroom to fetch a flannel pajama top that had been Sarah's. I'd kept it even though it was too small for me. With its long sleeves and soft material, it would be perfect. I also brought back a soft fleece throw, which would be better for the baby than a ripped piece of bloody cotton.

"A girl, and a perfect one at that," Granny said. "Ten fingers. Ten toes. Healthy lungs. You did well, mother. You did well."

Granny had washed the baby off and disinfected and clipped the cord that Lorelei had desperately bitten. The newborn kicked and cried on a towel at the foot of the bed while her mother looked down at her from her propped cushion of pillows.

"I knew she was a girl. I dreamed about her. She told me to run away," Lorelei said. I came to her with the pajama top and helped her shrug into it. Her shivers had stopped, but the flannel would help her even more.

"It's time to feed her," Granny said. "She needs to be skin to skin with her mother."

Granny nodded to me and my throat closed tight and hot around a bubbling up of emotions I'd never experienced before. My arms refused to respond. I was stuck in place.

"Pick her up and place her on her mother's chest," Granny instructed. "Nothing to it."

Of course, there was everything to it. I'd never touched a newborn baby. I'd definitely never placed one on its mother's breast. Such a simple thing. Such a simply awesome thing. I couldn't move.

"You know, there's nothing more qualifying than two willing hands.

Lots to learn in this life. For sure. Lots to learn. But all you need to start is willing hands and a loving heart. Don't scoff. I'm getting to know you. All piss and vinegar. Skin three feet thick. But you've got the hands and heart. You just haven't learned to trust yourself with them yet," Granny said.

The wildwood was in me and I was in the wildwood. Rooted, strengthened, a part of the cycle.

She leaned over and picked up the softly crying infant herself and all the air I didn't know I was holding whooshed out of me. But before I could feel deflated, Granny placed the squirming baby in my hands. Instinctively, I brought her close to my chest. She snuggled in looking for nourishment and her need sent me hurrying to the bedside even as tears burned behind my eyes.

"My baby girl," Lorelei said. "My baby girl."

I awkwardly leaned and transferred the baby from my hands to her mother's chest. Granny had followed me so it was her wrinkled, experienced hands that helped Lorelei position the baby's mouth to suckle. Crying made way for eager snuffling sounds as the baby began to drink.

"You did the right thing, Lorelei. That baby did not steer you wrong," Granny said. "Never ignore your dreams." She reached and pulled the pajama top closed around the back of the baby to keep out drafts from the room. We both pulled the quilts over Lorelei's legs.

Only then did I remember that Lorelei was a young runaway hiding from a man with very powerful friends in town.

Granny brewed an herbal tisane for Lorelei to help her uterus contract and to help her milk come in. Right now, she said, the baby would be getting the rich yellow colostrum a mother's body produced in the weeks prior to childbirth. But the steaming hot cup of steeped herbs would help in the production of nutrient-rich breast milk.

"What if there's a problem? Doesn't she need medical attention?" I whispered in the kitchen.

"Women used to always do this at home. Especially on this mountain. I doubt Lorelei would have been taken to a hospital if she'd gone into labor at the settlement," Granny said. "But I'd prefer to have her checked out. Just to be sure. It isn't safe to have her on the road tonight. Especially not when they're looking for her. We'll have to talk to the others. See what favors we can call in to get her down to Charlottesville or even Richmond."

"You've done this before," I guessed. "You've helped Sect women escape."

Granny settled into the armchair. She looked tired and about fifty years older than she'd looked at the beginning of the evening. "It's harder to get the women out. The babies are easier. They can blame miscarriage. Or even hide their pregnancy altogether. You'd be surprised how many of the Sect women know nothing about how their own bodies work. There aren't very many older Sect women. They have a life expectancy closer to women who lived in earlier times. Poor health care. Multiple pregnancies. Bad nutrition and abusive living conditions. Lorelei was very smart to escape."

We'd washed up and changed our clothes, but I was suddenly reminded of Melody Ross's bloody nightgown. The one she'd been wearing when Sarah had found her hanging in the black locust tree.

The blood hadn't been hers.

And it had been very like the blood that had stained Granny's dress and my shirt and jeans tonight.

"Melody helped a Sect woman deliver a baby the night she was killed," I said softly.

"Never ignore your dreams."

"Melody stood against Reverend Moon and unlike the rest of us she made no secret of it," Granny said. "We had no proof that he killed her. How could we? The sheriff is in Hartwell's pocket and Hartwell stands with Moon."

The remedy book was on the counter. Granny hadn't needed to refer to it. She'd had the tisane already made up in one of her pockets, but I had flipped to the page so I could read through the recipe. One day I might need to make it myself. Hands. Heart. I had those things. And, more importantly, I was finding myself more and more drawn to using them. To help. It was a simple drive. One I'd always had. With Granny, in Morgan's Gap, with the help of the wildwood garden, I'd recognized that drive.

When I'd held the newborn girl my small contributions to her warmth and safety had felt significant. Small *mattered*. I still grieved, but putting myself to work had softened my loss. The dreams had brought me closer to understanding Sarah and Melody. But they had also brought me closer to understanding myself.

"Maybe Melody revealed her killer to us in other ways," I said. I paged through the remedy book pointing to all the drawings of hearts and moons. "Mixed in with the other doodles and notes, the hearts and moons don't stand out. But, if you look at all the hearts and moons throughout the book at the same time, you can tell they've all been drawn in charcoal pencil by the same hand," I said. "Melody knew she'd been too bold against Moon. She was in trouble. And this was her way of passing on a silent warning to her daughter."

"But whoever killed her that night ripped the book to pieces," Granny said. "It took me years to repair it. Sarah never saw it again after that morning."

"You sent her away. To keep her safe. But they found her. They didn't give up looking and they found her," I said. I moved around the counter to perch on the arm of the sofa across from the woman who had tried to save my friend.

"They found *you*," Granny said. "And I had sent Sarah to you. I didn't want her to be alone after she'd lost her mother. I didn't know what else to do."

I was glad I had already lowered myself to sit. Granny suddenly looked ancient, as if keeping all the secrets she'd kept for so long had sucked the living right out of her. She was more of a mummy than a wisewoman in that moment and I wasn't prepared to hear what she was about to utter from her dry, parched lips.

"You were born here. On this mountain. In this house. Melody delivered you. She was pregnant at the time herself. And the first breaths you took, you took against her belly, separated from Sarah by only her mother's body," Granny said. "I was here. I often came to help in those days when I was spry. And I'm the one who carried you down the mountain a week later, through the woods in a sling on my back. Your mother went back to the settlement. She claimed she'd miscarried. But, of course, your remains were never found."

"But Sarah was older than me. By a year," I argued.

"I changed your birth date. It was easy enough to do in those days when a hospital wasn't involved in your birth," Granny explained. "There are plenty of people who have left the mountain for work in the city. Folks who sign off on the papers we need when we need them. You were the older, more experienced sister Sarah needed when I had to send her away."

"How did you find me when you decided Sarah had to be sent away?" I asked. "You couldn't have kept track of all the Sect women and babies you helped."

"We wrote nothing down in any way that someone else would

understand. I keep my own recipes and remedies. I added a note or a doodle here and there to help me remember. Every single birth. Every baby. As we all did. All the wisewomen on the mountain who refused to look the other way," Granny said. "But I wasn't as careful as I should have been before Melody's murder. There were hospital visits. Too many people involved who might have been open to bribes. It wasn't until Melody's murder that I imagined the Sect babies might still be in danger even after we helped them leave the mountain. I hadn't realized how far Moon would go to keep control and keep his world hidden from outsiders. He has eyes everywhere. Fanatic believers willing to do anything for a man they think is the mouth of God." She had clasped her hands in her lap and she worried her fingers together as if her fingers were rosary beads and she was saying an unspoken prayer she'd said many times before.

I had a mother. One who loved me enough to want to save me. From Reverend Moon and the horrible life a girl would have growing up shadowed by his perverse beliefs. She'd risked her life in the same way Lorelei had risked hers. Had she been as young? As vulnerable? As abused? What kind of life had she returned to after she'd sent me away? I'd never allowed myself the luxury of thinking about my birth parents. To survive, I'd had to focus on the present not the past. Even more so when Sarah had come into my life.

I'd been born on the mountain. In the wildwood. My blood knew it. My heart knew it. And now my brain struggled to accept the truth— Sarah hadn't bequeathed special abilities to me. There was every possibility that I had Ross ancestors of my own.

"We'll need to call Sadie. Tell her what's happened here tonight. She and Joyce and Kara will tell the others. Together, we can decide what to do to help Lorelei. I don't think it would be safe for her to go back. The way she talks, she was openly rebellious. And she's been away too long. Moon involved the whole town and he'll want to make an example of her," Granny said.

"Why do you think they found me instead of Sarah?" I asked. I wasn't ready to change the subject, not even for an urgent matter at hand.

"Because Jacob Walker's mother told Hartwell Morgan's father what I had done. Tess was never really one of us. But I trusted her and she betrayed that trust. Her husband had died. She was an attractive young widow. I never saw a Morgan yet who could resist a vulnerable woman. He seduced her and she told him everything. It didn't much matter back then. The old Morgan didn't have the same ties to Reverend Moon that Hartwell has developed. Oh, he enjoyed deviling me and the others about it. Threatening to expose us. But it was only a game to him," Granny said. "He must have passed on what he knew to Hartwell before he died. Long before then, Tess had learned better than to trust the Morgan family. She had taken Jacob and left Morgan's Gap. But she couldn't take back the secrets she'd revealed."

"So Hartwell must have told Moon what his father had known. About the babies you and the other wisewomen had 'stolen.' Then, Melody openly stood up to Moon. More than anyone else had dared. And Hartwell was willing to help Moon silence Melody because he'd gotten in with the Sect too deeply. He owed Moon for the land. For Violet," I said.

"For more than Violet, probably," Granny said, with a grim set to her mouth. "When Melody had the audacity to fight Moon, he must have killed her. But it might not have ended there. He would have been furious that Sect children were being raised by 'heathens' elsewhere," Granny said.

"And if Hartwell decided Sarah knew too much and was a danger to his political aspirations, he wouldn't rest," I added. "She didn't know as much as he thought she did. Melody had sheltered her from the worst of it. But he couldn't have known that. His paranoia and misogynistic personality would have assumed a free wisewoman was trouble. Especially the daughter of a wisewoman like Melody Ross."

"He might have decided if he tracked down all the Sect babies we'd saved he would eventually find Melody's daughter," Granny said.

"We moved around a lot. Our caseworker despaired of finding us placements. Because I wouldn't stand for…" I began.

"I know it wasn't perfect. I haven't had a good night's sleep in thirty years. But I still believe what I did was better for you and the other babies we were able to smuggle away than the Sect settlement would have been."

Granny's shoulders were rounded and her chin quivered low. I jumped up and wrapped my arm around her, leaning my cheek against her mop of curly hair. My curls meant something more now. Something I would explore later when the shock wore off. But I was glad I'd accepted the garden's call before I knew my heritage. My connection was more than tradition. It had been completely a matter of choice.

"You saved me and you gave Sarah years she wouldn't have had," I said.

"I didn't understand until that morning Sarah found Melody's body that we were really dealing with life and death. Abuse. Neglect. Certainly, danger and freedom. But I never realized the Sect would go that far," Granny said. "I think Melody knew. And she still didn't back down. The night she was murdered I was busy in town. A breech birth. But she must have tried to protect the Sect woman who had come to her for help. Moon had had enough. Sarah wouldn't have been an impediment. He would have assumed he could silence her at any time."

"And Hartwell Morgan. How far did he go to help Moon?" I

wondered. Hartwell had blood on his hands if he'd helped the Sect at all. It was hard to imagine the shiny politician actually involved with hands-on violence.

"He comes to the settlement. He hurts the girls he visits. Reverend Moon doesn't care," Lorelei said from the hall.

Lorelei stood at the bedroom door with the swaddled baby in her arms. My gut convulsed and I had to swallow hard against a sudden rush of bile that burned the back of my throat. Hartwell Morgan was as much of a monster as Moon. Granny had lived a long time. She'd heard it all. But Lorelei's confirmation of what she'd probably suspected made her face go white as parchment. Neither of us spoke. I, for one, couldn't. We went to help Lorelei use the bathroom and settle the baby in a drawer we'd taken from the dresser and lined with a quilt. We placed the makeshift cradle beside her when she came back to bed.

Sick rage gnawed at my insides and Granny was no longer pale. Her anger had livened her cheeks with red spots of color and she looked less like a dry and dusty mummy ready to give up. She was the first to break the silence.

"I will try to get you and this baby off the mountain, Lorelei. Down to Richmond where we can help you disappear. But it won't be easy," Granny said. "And it might be dangerous."

"I been living dangerous for a while now. The Sect men are raised to be mean. They say it's their right. And we don't have say in nothin' that goes on. When Hartwell started visiting, some of the older women tried to stop it, but they quieted down after a couple disappeared. That's when I knew I had to run away before my baby was born," Lorelei said.

"Have they gotten so used to killing women that get in their way?" I asked.

Granny didn't reply. She tucked the blankets around Lorelei and then pulled me out of the room. I took one last look at the baby, sleeping peacefully beside her mother. What kind of life would she have? The ache of wanting it to be better than her mother's or mine ate me up inside.

Granny asked for the phone when we got back to the living room. I looked out the back door at the wildwood while she called Sadie. The amber glow of the porch light didn't illuminate very far into the woods, but I watched as a fox came and sat on the path. It could probably see my silhouette in the window of the back door. There were probably hundreds of foxes on the mountain, but I felt like I was looking at *my* fox. The one I'd seen earlier that night and hunting on a frosty morning. The one I'd seen in my dreams. He watched the house for a long while and then turned and disappeared into the shadows where the amber porch light didn't reach. In the background, Granny murmured directions to Sadie, telling her that we might be in greater trouble than we'd realized.

"They're going to come for her, aren't they?" I asked. I'd thought the anxiousness of the day had been explained by Lorelei's arrival. But now I realized it hadn't diminished. I could feel something else was coming. The knowledge prickled my skin and made my blood feel thick in my veins. Granny was a formidable woman and I was no slouch. I'd fought with everything I had my whole life, including my fists. But we had no weapons and we couldn't even call the sheriff because he was on Reverend Moon's side.

"They'll come for her. But we've got friends too," Granny said. CC stood up and yawned with a mighty stretch on the sofa. I hadn't seen Charm since before the mother and baby arrived. I pressed my thumbs into my forefingers where the fresh pricks still tingled. Reminding myself that I wasn't alone.

Granny saw the movement. She couldn't possibly see the two tiny red dots on my scarred hands, but she nodded. At one time, long ago, she must have decided to complete the ritual herself.

"Welcome, child," Granny said softly. Her eyes were bright with unshed tears. My decision had been one she'd invested in body and soul. She'd sacrificed flagging energy reserves to teach me and guide me along the way without pushing because she'd known I had to decide for myself.

I went to her and she raised her gnarled and wrinkled hands, palms facing me, in front of her chest. I reached out and she showed me how to press our fingertips together, not clasped, but touching. Palm to palm, prick to prick. I'd never noticed the slight indention in each forefinger. They'd been lost in the calluses and stains caused by her life's work.

"Wildwood born," Granny whispered, honoring the new life we embraced when we'd embraced our connection to the garden, the forest and the land.

"Wildwood born," I replied.

The air was suddenly filled with the faint fragrance of blackberry jam, dill, peppermint, dandelion wine and rye bread. Each scent came and went like a memory, but richer, fuller, more. And with each scent I remembered the people I had shared them with. This was our mountain. It had claimed us as we had claimed it. And now it was time to defend it.

Twenty-Nine

B eams of light shot through the windows of the house from in front and behind at the same time, then a skittering knock sounded at the back door. It took me a second to understand that powerful flashlights in the hands of multiple people were being trained on the cabin.

"We need to stop them from taking her or the baby for as long as we can," Granny said.

"They'll have to kill me to take that baby," I replied. I knew then with a cold, certain exhilaration that I'd never needed a baseball bat for home defense. All I'd ever needed was a lifetime of struggle to hone my own sharp heart.

The quiet, almost scratching tap came again at the door. There was a teasing quality to the sound. As if the person knocking was being purposefully playful with his knuckles against the wood. It made me shudder. I had no hope of sending them away. I knew there would be a fight, but I went to answer the door as if crazed misogynistic freaks often came calling at the cabin in the middle of the night.

"How can I help you?" I opened the door because keeping it closed would have immediately escalated the situation. Moon stood there. His curled fist raised to tap, scratch again. The flashlight beams glinted off and around him like strobe lights. This was only me asking a visitor what I could do for them. No more. No less. Reverend Moon's black suit and starched white shirt wasn't stained with Melody Ross's blood. But it was easy to imagine him bloodied. The thirst for blood was in his playful knocks and the curve of his ugly smile. I tried not to imagine his hands crushing Melody's windpipe and driving her to her knees. What had become of the baby she'd delivered that morning? Had it died along with its mother for daring to want a different life than fate had given them?

There were at least ten men behind Reverend Moon. They all had flashlights pointed at the cabin and me. My vision was dazzled and I raised my hand to shield my eyes.

"We are looking for one of our own. A runaway. She's had issues with hysteria before. A danger to herself and others," Reverend Moon said.

Now I could see a few women with the men, off to the side and without lights of their own. Moon motioned for one of them to come forward and she did so meekly as if pulled on a string I couldn't see.

"Give us Lorelei and the baby. Let us take them back home where they belong," the woman said. The other two women whispered "where they belong" like eerie echoes. The hair raised on the back of my neck. They must have known how near her time was. And still they had chased her through the woods and hounded her to exhaustion. I well knew how they could wait and watch. They'd wanted her to come to me. This was never going to end with simply finding a runaway. Like Melody, I was not going to get out of the way. The sick rage in the pit of my stomach had long turned to ice. I fought the rise of despair. I'd been here before. In one house or another. A foster father friendlier than he had any right to be. A foster mother too quick with a pinch or a kick. A doctor who took the exam a few caresses too far while his nurse looked the other way. No one to protect me. No family. No friends. Alone in the world.

Lorelei and the baby weren't alone. They had me.

"You've come through the wildwood tonight. To my back door. This isn't your settlement. This is the Ross cabin. And you're not welcome here," I said. To Reverend Moon and his men. To the women who would enable him. I stood in the doorway and a breeze from the forest ruffled my curly chestnut hair.

Reverend Moon seemed fascinated by the play of hair on my cheek. He narrowed his eyes and looked at me. Hard. Was my mother still living under his control or had he killed her years ago?

"I've seen you before. In town. Yes. But…she's one of yours, isn't she?" he asked Granny over my shoulder. I could feel the presence of the older woman behind me, but I didn't turn around to check on her. I faced Moon and focused every bit of energy I possessed toward keeping him outside.

"Oh, it's more complicated than that, as you well know. No one belongs to me. Or to you. It's the wildwood that we all belong to," Granny said. "There are many who live in your settlement who aren't Sect any more than I am. The wildwood has them and they have the wildwood, deep in their hearts where you can't corrupt it."

"No!" Reverend Moon shouted. The other Sect men and women followed his lead, shouting their protests and cursing Granny's blasphemy.

Reverend Moon slammed into me with surprising force considering his age. I'm no lightweight, but against the whole crowd that followed him, I didn't have a chance to shut the door. Moon grabbed fistfuls of my hair and jerked me down to my knees. I cried out for Granny, Lorelei and the newborn baby. But two of Moon's men took my arms as I struggled to my feet in spite of the pain in my scalp that brought tears to my eyes. Moon didn't let me go. He liked the tears. He liked to hurt. Worse, there were more Sect people at the front door. The bolt I'd installed had held, but it did no good at all when one of Moon's women slid it back and opened the door.

"Take them all," Moon commanded.

No one argued even though one of "them" was a tiny, mewling baby who shouldn't be taken out in the cold, damp night.

Granny must have known she'd be no match for the burly Sect man who took her cruelly by the upper arm. She raised her chin and went where he pulled her as if he was leading her onto a dance floor.

But the look on her face. Even through the tears in my eyes, I would have thought twice about jerking her around. The Sect man didn't seem to care.

"Be careful. Don't hurt her," I said. Lorelei had locked herself in the bedroom with the baby, but it took only a few determined kicks to the interior door for the lock to bust. They dragged Lorelei into the hall. She clutched the baby to her chest, but when the women who had unbolted the front door jerked the bundle of blankets from her only a pillow fell to the ground.

I stopped mid-shout when I realized the bundle had been a decoy. Muffled cries came from the bedroom and it didn't take the Sect people long to find the baby Lorelei had carefully hidden in the drawer we'd padded with blankets as a makeshift cradle.

"Stop fighting," Moon said, pressing his face close to mine. His hands had tightened and I could feel the clumps of hair he gripped loosening from my scalp. I hadn't realized I'd still been writhing and kicking to try to get to the baby. I would have continued until Moon was left with nothing but bloody hair in his hands if Charm hadn't appeared on my shoulder.

I froze as if I'd obeyed Moon, but it couldn't be helped. My jerking might hurt the tiny mouse no one but me had noticed so far. Plus, there was nothing I could do against the crowd of Sect men and women who had us now except watch, wait, hope for a window of opportunity... For what, I didn't know.

My stomach roiled and a trickle of warm liquid trailed down my forehead into my left eye. Moon had made my scalp bleed. I blinked it away. I didn't care about my injuries. Only my friends mattered.

"Bring them," Moon ordered. He pulled and I followed. The men on either side of me were ready if I didn't and Charm was cuddled against the side of my neck beneath the hair Moon didn't have in his hands. I could feel him holding on, hiding, waiting breathlessly in the same way I waited.

For what, I wasn't sure.

My sick stomach plummeted when Moon led the way through the backyard and onto the wildwood path. Even though I cooperated, he pulled me in fits and starts because he enjoyed my distress. I couldn't help crying out at the first few surprising jerks, but then I sank my teeth into my lower lip to keep quiet no matter how much he hurt me. I was hunched over, but because of Moon's height I still managed to see some of what was happening.

Helplessness burned in my chest. It hurt more than my scalp.

Lorelei was begging for her baby. The woman who had opened the front door had her wrapped in only the cloth diaper Granny had fashioned from a towel. And she wasn't cradling the baby. She held her carelessly, ignoring her weak cries of distress.

"Please. Let me take her. She's cold and afraid," Lorelei said.

"You have done this. You have brought this on yourself with your shameless turn to heathenism," Moon said. He stomped without pausing up the path.

And then I knew.

He hadn't come to take Lorelei and the baby home. Even if we had given him the baby, he would have dragged us from the cabin.

Just as he must have dragged Melody ten years ago.

"Where are you taking us?" I already knew. The beams of light from the flashlights many of the Sect people held already illuminated the wildwood garden in the distance...and the black locust trees' branches that scratched at the night sky. I fought Moon's grip to turn my head enough so that I could see Sarah's sapling as he pulled me into the clearing.

"Your people will learn to stay away from our women with your filthy concoctions and your demonic brews," Moon said. "Or I'll send you all to the Maker to face His judgment."

"Doesn't your Maker frown on murder?" Granny asked. I could finally see her. Still straight, with her shoulders back even though, from the looks of the man's grip on her arm, she'd been pulled up the path almost as roughly as I had been.

Moon suddenly dragged me into the garden over the dormant flower beds and toward the black locust tree with the crooked limb just right for a rope. I stumbled and cried out as my lower lip came free of my teeth.

"I am my Maker's hands and feet and voice in this world. And I go about His business. Abomination must be stopped. We don't kill. We *cleanse*." If Moon shouted it would have been less sickening, but he chose to utter "cleanse" close to my face again so that his hot spittle burned my cold cheeks.

A subtle shifting of the night breeze rustled the dried foliage, vines and branches all around us. I focused on Sarah's sapling. I wouldn't be dying in the garden. It wasn't time to join my sister yet. My heart swelled with the knowledge as if the wind had whispered that certainty to me.

"You must have thought you'd gotten away with it. The killing. The desecration of the garden. Subjecting those poor girls to abuse for the power and pleasure it gave you. But the wildwood bides its time, old man. It buries its roots deep," Granny said. "It reaches its branches to the sky. It scatters its seeds and bears its fruit, and then, one day, it calls an army home."

Charm growled and several of the Sect people nearby exclaimed. A beam from someone's flashlight fell on my shoulder like a spotlight, but they didn't stare at Charm for long because animals started pouring from the wildwood path and the trees—all the animals I'd seen before—ravens, coyotes, crows and squirrels, rabbits and deer, including a giant buck with sixteen points and a scar along the right side of his face.

Then, up the path, one by one, other surprise guests began to appear. Sadie, Joyce and Kara. Charles in a dapper walking suit as if he was out for a stroll and May with her arm linked in his. The glassblower. The carver. Joshua, the mechanic. The waitress from the diner. Becky the hairdresser. The woman who sold the fungi Tom collected. The potter. I'd served many of them bread at Gathering. And others still I recognized from my delivery rounds. Townsfolk who weren't fooled by Hartwell Morgan. Artists and artisans and craftsmen. People who lived their lives more connected to the wildwood than most people did these days.

People like me.

"You thought you'd come here and find a vulnerable woman you could hurt and harass or even kill. Again," I said. "You were wrong."

Lu had come up the path too. Blood crusted the lashes of my left eye, but I could see clearly with my right. My tears were gone. I didn't know who had called all the people here. Sadie wouldn't have had time to make the calls and even if she had they wouldn't have arrived way out here so soon.

I'd asked for the wildwood's help. Maybe this was its reply.

Several of the Sect men made a break for the trees. The giant buck leapt forward and lowered his rack. He managed to block all but two from getting away. And from out of the wildwood, Tom Morgan came. He ignored the two men who had made it into the wildwood. I heard their shouts of distress as the brambles and briars caught them. By the sounds of their thrashing, the thorns were biting deeper than they had bitten me the night I had chased after Lorelei.

Charm gurgled near my ear and a laugh bubbled from my lips in response. Moon's hands loosened in my hair as if the sudden crowd of townsfolk and his men's desertion had weakened his resolve.

Or maybe it had been my laughter.

Tom laid his hand on the side of the buck and the deer raised his head high. Side by side, they blocked the other Sect men on one side of the garden while the people from town blocked the path back to the cabin. The big mechanic, Joshua, was over six feet tall and as broad as a weight lifter.

I watched as the other animals gravitated toward people. I had been right. Me and Charm. Granny and her cat. The trio had their creatures. It seemed there were many other wisewomen and woodsmen in Morgan's Gap. The wildwood had used the animals to summon them together when we needed them the most.

"You have no jurisdiction here. I'll call Hartwell and the sheriff's deputies will bring the girl and her baby home," Reverend Moon said.

I lashed out. It wasn't wise. I'd long ago learned that violence only got me in worse trouble, but the scrappy orphan girl who wasn't actually an orphan reared her head against an oppressive system she couldn't stomach for one more second. The wildwood helped us. But we still had to help ourselves.

Unfortunately, Moon let go of my hair and found my neck as I lunged toward him. He had long arms and I barely landed a glancing blow against the side of his face with my fist before both hands closed around my throat. He pushed me back and drove me to my knees in front of him, his superior height and weight behind his grip. His freakishly skeletal fingers wrapped, tight, against my windpipe. I couldn't scream. I couldn't breathe. I clutched at his hands and beat at his arms, trying to break them free.

I heard shouts. My friends would try to help me. But some of the Sect people hadn't given up yet. There was scuffling and fighting all around us. I had no way of knowing if anyone would get to me in time before Moon did to me what he had done to Melody. My head was tilted back. I could see only the contorted horror of Moon's hate-filled grimace and the crooked black locust branch looming above us.

And I couldn't budge his cruel fingers pressing into my windpipe.

The vision in my one good eye swam with black spots, but the spots didn't prevent me from seeing Moon's shock when Charm scurried from my shoulder to one of his hands. Or his pain and rage when my small familiar sank his teeth into Moon's flesh. I croaked in horror as Moon shoved me away. Because I saw him shake his savaged hand and fling Charm into the blackberry bushes.

The blackberry bushes.

Even after all I'd seen and learned, I wasn't sure I believed in the fae. But I had seen enough to trust in the magic of the wildwood garden. I was on the ground when Moon tried to grab me again. I used my whole body wrapped around his legs to tumble him into the briars where he had thrown Charm with no compunction.

In that moment, as Moon fell, I allowed the magic that lived in me to reach out to Lu. I'd seen her. She was here. But more than that I *felt* her. I felt her energy, her light, her music, her magic. She was always here. In me. Our connection zinged through me in an instant.

But there was another connection to be made.

A trickier one.

Jacob.

I hadn't seen him tonight. But I felt him. He was here. His energy came to my call, melding with mine even more fully than Lu's. And I released every inhibition that had prohibited me from fully accepting our trio's strength. Three. Three. Three. Barely perceptible, I felt another trio add their silent pleas for the wildwood's help to ours. Sadie, Joyce and Kara. I didn't know if it would work. I could only merge with my trio and ask the wildwood to answer our call. But combined with the other trio and drawing strength from all the friends and familiars around us, it was enough.

The wildwood answered.

I was stunned by the speed in which the thorns cut into the screeching reverend. Vines twisted and tangled and bit, deeper than deep into Morgan's hands and arms and legs and face to hold him and keep him from doing any more harm. He was left with a blackberry vine crown piercing his forehead and more blood trickling into his eyes than I had in mine.

Buanaich Maille ri.

Abide together.

Moon's gruesome predicament had caused all the fighting around us to come to a standstill and into the lull a dozen people in military-style black apparel appeared out of the trees. Some of them wore night-vision goggles. And several had guns.

"Ladies and gentlemen, if you would all direct your attention toward these badges, thank you."

Jacob was the one who had spoken. I wasn't surprised to see him. I never had been really. I had always felt his presence; I just hadn't allowed myself to accept that heightened perception. Until now. He was dressed in the same uniform as the others. That was a shock. The secret he'd kept from Lu and me finally revealed. Dozens of flashlights had fallen on the ground. They lit up the wildwood clearing well enough for me to see the scratches on Jacob's face had begun to heal. They no longer looked angry and red. Silly for me to notice, sitting by the blackberry bushes with blood drying on my face and a savaged neck. It was dark. I couldn't be sure. But Jacob's attention seemed to linger on me. Not long. But long enough that I was certain he'd cataloged every scrape.

He held one of the badges he referenced flipped open in the palm of his hand.

"Federal agents, Reverend Moon. And you'll find us much harder to influence than Hartwell and his deputies," another agent added.

A Sect man stepped threateningly toward one of Jacob's people and the man drew a gun that gleamed in the eerie half-light. He didn't have to speak. The Sect man stopped in his tracks. Lorelei rushed forward at the opportunity to take her baby from the Sect kidnapper. She immediately wrapped the pajama top she wore around the infant as she soothed her against her breast. None of the agents protested. Every decent person in the clearing breathed a sigh of relief to see the baby back where she belonged. Safe in her mother's arms.

"All of Reverend Moon's people need to turn and drop to their knees with their hands behind their heads," Jacob said. Several of the townspeople had raised their hands in the air when the federal agents had appeared. They tentatively lowered them as Jacob identified his targets.

My breathing was ragged, but oxygen tasted sweet. Especially when Charm crept out from under the bushes and climbed into my outstretched hand.

One of the Sect women began to weep and pray, but the others were silent as the agents came up behind them to cuff their hands and pull them to their feet. Even Reverend Moon didn't speak. At least not until Violet Morgan appeared from the path. In this light, the blood on her face and hands looked almost black. Her hair was damp and matted. Her dress was torn. She limped, but I couldn't tell if it was because of an injury or because she wore only one shoe.

"I came as soon as I could," Violet said. She looked at Tom Morgan when she said it and I knew she was checking him from head to toe to make sure he was okay. Hadn't I felt Jacob's eyes on me when he appeared, doing the same thing?

"Worthless whore," Reverend Moon cursed. Then he screamed. As one, my trio had reached out to the wildwood. It was too dark for most to see, but we could tell the vines had twisted their thorns deeper into his forehead, and he was silent after that.

"He tried to stop me," Violet said. "I . . . I'm not sure if he's a . . . alive."

Jacob lifted a communications device from his belt and spoke into it. I assumed he was sending other agents to check on Hartwell Morgan. Conflicting emotions warred in my tight chest. I was thrilled that Violet had fought back against his violent abuse, but I was afraid she would be in big trouble if she had killed him. I was glad that some of the blood on Violet's face and hands and hair might be Hartwell's and not hers. It was a ferocious gladness I refused to reject. Any pain Hartwell had suffered he had deserved.

Lu pulled me up from the ground. I hadn't even seen her approach. She held me tight with a supportive arm across my back. We stood hip to hip and I reached to wrap my arm around her back too. When I did, I encountered warmth and feathers. A bird startled from her shoulder, and in this light I couldn't see exactly which creature the wildwood had sent to my best friend, but a sudden, fierce recognition rushed through me.

A small doe approached Violet, but the former Sect woman didn't act surprised or afraid. In fact, she reached for the animal and leaned against its sturdy back. She allowed it to help her to walk. She didn't have to go far. Tom and the large buck came to meet her. And Violet let go of the doe to step into Tom's embrace.

"Hartwell supported Moon. He looked the other way and even participated…" I began. My voice startled me. It was little more than a scratchy whisper and every word caused me pain.

"We know, Mel. I came back to the mountain to investigate Hartwell Morgan and the Sect settlement. And not only for dirty politics. The land grabs skirt the edge of what's legal, but the human trafficking, the disappearances and abuse. The killings. We've been gathering evidence for years," Jacob said.

"Tess took you away from Morgan's Gap," Granny said. "But she must have told you what she knew. She must have told you about us trying to help the Sect women and about Morgan's corruption."

The federal agents walked their prisoners around the townsfolk. Their vehicles must have been left down the driveway where they couldn't be seen or heard from the house. They had watched all evening, waiting for events to play out.

"Lots of Sect folk wanted to run away. They aren't bad. Just didn't know what to do," Lorelei said. "I'm sorry I scratched you. I thought you were one of them trying to catch me and take me back."

"You were afraid. Fighting for your baby's life. I understand," Jacob said. "There'll be further investigation. Interviews. We'll take witness accounts. There'll be counseling and medical care as well as legal aid."

Lorelei *had* scratched Jacob's face. She hadn't realized he was trying to help her that night. Instinctively, I had known I could trust him even though I'd been able to tell the scratches hadn't been caused by vines. She'd been desperate and it had made her fast and strong. She'd slipped away from both of us. Once he'd lost her, he'd come to help me. I would always wonder if the wildwood had tangled around me to keep me from chasing after her in the dark. Far-fetched to some. Maybe. But I knew, now, that the wildwood was alive around us.

Two of Jacob's agents were trying to pull Moon from the blackberry bush. The wildwood garden wasn't cooperating very well… until Jacob approached. My tension loosened as he came nearer and the vines loosened at the same time.

Jacob had risked blowing his cover that night. If the wildwood had held me, he had been the one to help me back home. At that point, he'd known Lorelei didn't want to be found. I might have chased her right into a less benevolent hunter's arms. I shuddered at the thought of what I would have done, alone, against Moon and his followers. Or that I might have disrupted the government's investigation by making them come forward too soon.

I'd known all along there were secrets in Jacob's eyes. I'd been right. But the night's events had left me disoriented. I couldn't reconcile the man who had pricked my finger with the blackberry thorn with this no-nonsense government agent. He'd helped his agents free Moon. They were none too gentle as they pulled the reverend to his feet.

"I hope we can talk sometime soon," Jacob said as he left Moon to his people and stepped toward me. He also scanned my face intently and, I thought, halfway lifted his hand toward my neck. Lu reflexively squeezed me closer and he lowered it before I could be sure. He nodded as if acknowledging Lu's concern. For now. "Right. I have work to do," Jacob said. "The rescue squad is on the way. We'll leave Violet with you while we evaluate the situation with Hartwell." I didn't know how to reply. The wildwood had brought us together, but he'd been undercover all this time. Just as I was going to turn away, a four-legged creature rushed from the wildwood path. I recognized the fox, with its handsome white ruff and russet fur and the brush of its flowing tail. It came to twine around Jacob's legs and then sat beside him, straight and tall and watchful as ever.

The fox looked directly at me.

I met Jacob's intense stare with a startled stare of my own. Suddenly, more puzzle pieces fell into place—the hiking stick, the orb full of electric emotion, the blackberry thorn, Gathering, the fox watching over... me?

"His father was one of us," Granny said. As if Jacob wasn't right there listening to us. "I thought he was too. Then he went away with his mother and I wasn't sure exactly where he stood when he returned."

In spite of what we'd accomplished as a trio tonight, I still wasn't sure. He'd always seemed like he was more a part of the wildwood than anyone else, but he'd kept so many secrets from me. From us. I squeezed Lu back and I could feel support radiating from her in empathetic waves.

Jacob's colleagues had Reverend Moon in handcuffs now. He glared toward me, but the blood on his forehead and around his eyes made his threatening expression more clown-like than monstrous. The fox stayed where the wildwood path ended when Jacob stepped into the backyard. In the chaotic aftermath of the confrontation, Jacob paused near me and we stood quietly face-to-face.

"I see him. All the time," I said, referring to the fox that suddenly leapt away from the path in a reddish flash that was quickly gone.

"My father carved me a toy fox from the branch of a cedar tree when I was a toddler. Granny was the one who spoke the spell. It's one of my first memories," Jacob said. He kept his voice low, but Granny missed nothing in spite of her age.

"I said a few words, but even as a baby that boy was connected to the wildwood. It was his heart that created his fox familiar," Granny said. "It's always the heart."

"A kestrel showed up at the shop," Lu said. "I thought he must be injured. But my grandmother knew he'd come for me." She gave me a parting hug before she went to help Granny with Violet.

Charm had reclaimed his perch on my shoulder. Now, he touched my flushed cheek with his pink nose as if confirming what Granny had said. He had been meant for Sarah, but he had chosen me. Tiny, determined, ferocious. A kestrel for Lu. Of course. Beautiful. Fierce. Protective. I'd seen the tiniest falcons swoop and soar over the tree-tops. Just like Lu's voice.

"Now you know why I couldn't resist the hiking stick," Jacob said. His lips tilted into a halfway smile that I'd seen before, but it was somehow different. More open, more real. Not as much left to hide.

"I need to help Granny with Violet," I said. Unsure of how to proceed. Would he be leaving the mountain now that his work here was done? What about the wildwood and Lu? And me? We'd exchanged gifts. Even though I was new to all this, I understood his acceptance of the carved stick meant more because he shared Granny's... *our* beliefs.

Before I could turn away (or run away), Jacob had lifted his hand to take a stray curl from the side of my face into his fingers. He gently twirled it as if the chestnut lock was the most fascinating thing he'd ever seen.

"There's someone in the Sect settlement I think you're going to want to meet," he said softly. This time there was no one around us to overhear. Granny and Lu had taken Violet back to the cabin. Tom had followed. The townsfolk had disappeared back that way as well. Deep down, I'd known. The wildwood had been whispering this truth to me for a long time. Had Sarah known my biological mother was in Morgan's Gap? I thought maybe she had. That sending me here had been as much for my mother as for hers.

"Granny said dark curls indicate Ross blood," I said. I looked up at the thick waves on top of Jacob Walker's head. They looked even darker in the amber light.

"Old wives' tales," Jacob said. "Diluted by half a dozen generations."

"But the wildwood knows," I said. The wildwood had stood against Reverend Moon and Hartwell Morgan tonight. With our help. Jacob's and mine. We'd come back to the mountain. To work. To grieve. To reconnect with something we'd lost. Lu had been here all along. Supporting her community with her musical gifts. More responsible than anyone but Granny for bringing all the artists and artisans together. The people who were most open to hearing the whispers from the world they drew inspiration from.

"A trio," Jacob said.

"We'll see," I replied. Our connection couldn't be denied anymore. It was there to tap into or not as I pleased. I wasn't irrevocably tied to anyone or anything. Wildwood magic, once you recognized it, was a choice. We could take it or leave it, day by day. Right now, I had a lot to process about this man who could very easily be a part of me, body and soul, if I allowed him to be. I finally turned, pulling my curl from his fingers. And he let it slip easily from his hand.

Thirty

*H*artwell Morgan *wasn't dead.* Although Violet had been covered in his blood, the head injury she'd given him with one of his high school football trophies hadn't killed him. She'd managed only to save herself from his fists and leave him unconscious on the floor of their ugly home.

I thought of his life being spared as I packed my suitcase, knowing that some of his victims hadn't been so lucky.

Violet hadn't wanted to return to her gilded cage even with Hartwell in jail, so she'd moved in with Granny for the time being. Every bedroom in Granny's Queen Anne Victorian was full, including one made up as a nursery for Lorelei's baby. The brave Sect girl was a huge help with Violet's recovery. The mayor's wife had suffered a sprained ankle and a broken nose as well as a chipped tooth, but even bruised she looked more beautiful than ever with her hair soft, wearing jeans, and singing Appalachian lullabies for the baby.

With suitcase in hand, I paused in the doorway of the nursery and waved. Violet smiled. We'd already said our goodbyes.

Fallout from the Sect settlement raid and ongoing criminal investigations had rocked the town. Morgan's Gap was subdued as it headed into its usual Christmas festivities. There was no mayor to oversee the parade or the lighting of the tree. And all the local churches experienced a sudden diminished interest in their ladies' auxiliaries. More than one household on the mountain resumed the vintage tradition of carrying in a Yule log from the wildwood to fill their hearth and home with warmth...and connection...around a blazing fire.

I had been at Granny's for over two months to help out with Violet, Lorelei and the baby. And to recover from my own injuries. But, also, because I was shaken. By what we had done. By what the wildwood had done. By the ugly confrontation in the woods and the not-so-ugly conversation with Jacob afterward.

I wasn't ashamed to admit I seriously considered bugging out. Old habits die hard and I'd run from relationships much less intimate than the ones I'd found in Morgan's Gap. It was a quiet evening in front of the fire with Lu and Jane that had made me realize I was changed. The harmonica player's reluctance to marry and move to the mountain had completely disappeared after the Sect attack. Lu had carried her over the threshold of the shop only a week after. No officiant necessary beyond the music they made together.

But Granny had helped me bake them an elderflower wedding cake. They'd eaten slices by firelight while I had basked in the wonder of suddenly having two sisters, three mothers, a grandmother and a town full of aunts and uncles.

My suitcase was packed only for a return to the cabin and the winter work that waited for me there. I loved Granny's house and Morgan's Gap, but I missed the black locust trees and the wildwood path. I missed the forest stillness...and a certain quick fox I hadn't seen in a while. No one tried to stop me when I decided to go home. I loaded my basket with supplies and drove the old Chevy with practiced ease out of town.

Smoke curled from the chimney when I rounded the last corner of the driveway. The weather forecast was calling for snow. The heavy, moist atmosphere caused the smoke to fall and linger around the metal roof rather than dissipate in the air. I parked the truck and carried several bags of groceries, my basket and my overnight bag into the cabin.

I wasn't afraid. The fire wasn't an intrusion. It was a welcome. I saw Tom's buck cross the backyard and I knew Violet must have told Tom I was returning. The fire was just beginning to heat the house and I was grateful for his help. Tom had been the one who had pulled the photograph box from the closet. He'd wanted me to know that Sarah was his daughter and that he was a friend. He hadn't understood I would be frightened by the arrangement of frames while I was gone. Violet had explained his reasoning to me. Tom could communicate better with her than with anyone else. He and Melody Ross had been in love, but his father wouldn't allow him to marry her. The morning she'd been killed, Tom had been badly injured by a Sect man who'd been ordered to keep Hartwell's brother away.

Hartwell had confessed to helping Moon murder Melody Ross. But he had drawn the line at murdering his own niece. It was Reverend Moon who had hunted Sarah and me down. And Sect men who had run us off the road.

I hadn't met the Sect woman who had run away to give me a better life. Not yet. She was embroiled in the investigation process and I wasn't sure how to introduce myself. It was enough, for now, to know she was alive and well and free. There would be time enough for a meeting.

And to decide where we went from there.

I was becoming used to motherly women in my life. Sadie, Kara and even Joyce mothered the entire town, but they seemed to especially relish that role with me. Maybe because I'd never known a mother's love. Once I had allowed it, they had swept into the vacuum with honey, harmony and dandelion wine.

I put the kettle on and prepared my mug for peppermint tea. I'd dried numerous bundles of fragrant leaves from the bank of the creek near the wildwood garden. So there would be plenty of my favorite brew to last through the winter. I still had a tin of valerian too. Occasionally, I allowed myself to soothe nightmares away. But I was more rooted in the present now. More often than not my dreams didn't disturb my rest.

I retrieved the Ross Remedy Book from the fox bag Sarah had given me. It was time. While I'd been in town, I'd ordered a fountain pen from a stationery shop in Charlottesville. I took it out now, along with the small bottle of greenish-brown ink and the refillable converter. The pen had been crafted out of cherrywood. I inserted the converter. Then, I opened the bottle of ink. I carefully went through the motions of filling, wiping the nib and putting the pen back together. Process was important. I'd learned that now. Mindful attention to details I would have skipped or rushed through back in my former life. To fully connect to wildwood magic, you had to breathe, take your time and appreciate.

The weight of the pen was pleasant in my hand. A promise of the contributions I would make to the book that had helped to save my life. I placed the prepared pen beside the remedy book. Then I screwed the cap back on the bottle of ink and set it aside.

I'd already chosen the place where I would add Charm's likeness to the book. There was a glaringly bare spot on the back of the blackberry preserves recipe. The first major task I'd accomplished and my first taste of the wildwood. I could still vividly recall the slightly sharp, woody and rich taste of the plump berries.

I'd practiced many sketches of Charm in pencil on scrap paper. I'd also practiced with the fountain pen since it had been delivered. But the first line I scratched on the remedy book's page sounded loud and momentous. It also stood out from the other faded marks, in color and in freshness. I'd wanted that. The contributors to this book had mattered. Their individual efforts needed to be defined. Recognizing Melody Ross's drawings had helped me determine that Moon and Hartwell were more dangerous than we had realized.

Since then, I'd asked Granny to help me identify some of the other Ross authors. I planned to add a descriptive key in the back of the book identifying as many contributors as we could determine. I'd also spoken to Mildred Pierce about adding to the library. I wanted to add books on Appalachian arts and crafts. The history of natural medicines. Granny doctors. She'd been clearing out some of the Morgan paraphernalia as we talked and seemed very interested in what I had to say.

Charm came to life beneath the gentle scratches of my nib. I drew him as I'd first seen him, on the windowsill in the moonlight, when the owl had hooted and I thought he was only a dream. The sketch was small. It nestled in the bottom right corner of the page, but it was the perfect size and shape for the outline of the window around him.

There was also a fox on the page. Granny agreed that Sarah must have doodled the foxes. They were in the same style as her other drawings. She'd probably grown up seeing Jacob's fox in the wildwood. It seemed to like to hang out near the wildwood garden. Much like Jacob Walker. I suspected Sarah must have known the fox was important. The same way she had always known where to find lost dogs in Richmond.

When Charm was finished, I watched the ink lighten slightly as it dried.

I was a part of the Ross Remedy Book, now. Forever.

I already had some ideas to try in the spring when the flowers started to bloom again. I would practice and perfect. I would "trial out" any recipe I came up with, as Granny would say, on the trio and Granny herself. It might be many seasons before I added my own concoction to the book, but I would. It was a goal I'd set for myself now that I was carrying on in the Ross tradition.

My most important goal was a big one and it would take a long campaign of building enthusiasm in the Morgan's Gap community. I wanted to bring back the tradition of apple butter day by next autumn. I'd been inspired by Lu's market. And Sarah's memories. There were a lot of churches to contact and the old cannery to revitalize, but I wasn't intimidated. I'd faced worse obstacles in my life and overcome. And for this project I had my newfound wisewoman family to back me up.

I left the book open so the ink wouldn't smudge before it was fully dried. The kettle had been softly whistling for a while. I prepared my drink, then, using the afghan as a shawl, I carried my steaming mug to the front porch. I wondered if Jacob's fox was too wild to seek shelter from the looming storm. Puffs of white from between my lips joined the peppermint-scented steam as I shamelessly watched for the fox.

To no avail.

Directly following the night we'd stood up to Reverend Moon, I had watched for Jacob every day. I expected him less frequently now. I couldn't help recalling the feel of his hot mouth on my finger, but that was a private weakness for no one else to see.

I'd read too much into everything.

I could blame only lack of practice and rusty social skills. Those were improving. From only Sarah, my family had grown by so many. Almost every person who had shown up that night to help us was part of my circle as I was a part of theirs.

I finished my tea and went back into the cabin. The fire Tom had built in the woodstove had created a cozy haven from the temperature dropping outdoors. I rinsed my cup and went to the living room to warm my fingers. They still ached sometimes when I allowed them to get too cold. I'd watched for the fox for too long.

Charm appeared on the front windowsill. He had ridden in the basket from town, but since we'd arrived he'd been scarce. Probably exploring the whole house to make sure not a dust mote was out of place. He watched through the window as if waiting for the snow-flakes to begin to fall.

The Jeep didn't take him by surprise. My fingers hadn't stopped hurting. They were still stiff when they reflexively clenched and I hissed at the pain. I tossed the afghan on the chair and forced them to loosen by shaking them at my sides while Jacob parked. He climbed out, but he didn't look toward the cabin. His eyes were directed at the wildwood when he reached in the backseat and retrieved the cherry hiking stick. It was the first time I'd seen him use the gift. My chest tightened around my lungs, constricting my breath. Snow had begun to fall. But, Jacob didn't come to the front door. I watched him slowly stroll around the side of the house—all strong, controlled grace—his eyes still on the trees.

I went to the back door and through the glass I saw him appear in the backyard at the same time the fox jogged from the wildwood path. The snow had already lightly dusted the ground. It swirled around the fox's feet, disturbed by the swish of his tail.

Jacob leaned to scratch the ruff of the fox's neck and the quick crea-ture paused long enough to allow it before he skipped away. Jacob straightened and met my eyes through the glass. He paused, much like the fox, and I looked my fill. He'd trimmed the messy waves of his hair. Not short, but definitely shorter. His bangs no longer threatened to obscure his vision with every move of his head. His clothes were different too. He wasn't in uniform, but he wore straight-legged jeans instead of hiking pants and his shirt was more stylish too. A button-up oxford under a peacoat, both black, with the coat's lapel left open to the elements.

Only his old boots were the same. Trusty hikers that I'd been right to assume had been used to log a lot of miles on mountain trails.

His pause ended as suddenly as the fox's had. He came toward the cabin and I opened the door. Snow flurried in around me, melting kisses against my cheeks.

"The first snow," he said. Flakes clung to his curls and to his collar. I invited him inside, resisting the urge to dust his shoulders. He stomped his boots and knocked the tip of his hiking stick on the stoop before he accepted my invitation.

"Your fox is welcome to come inside too," I said. Charm made a noise from the windowsill that was either affirmation or argument. I couldn't be sure. But it didn't matter because Jacob leaned his hiking stick against the wall and shrugged out of his coat while shaking his head. "He won't come. Too wild. He'll curl up in a pine thicket with a friend, then come out and hunt in the drifts tomorrow morning."

I went to the kitchen to reheat some water. Jacob moved to stand beside the woodstove.

"I haven't seen you around." I prepared two mugs of peppermint tea this time, glad I'd purchased a set. My pulse was too quick. My words even quicker. The heat in my face wasn't caused by steam, but I hoped he wouldn't notice when I delivered his tea.

"It's been a crazy time for us. Wrapping up this case. Tying down all the loose strings," he said. He took the tea from me and I stepped back quickly because I'd accidentally leaned too close.

"Am I a loose string?" I asked. I cradled my mug in my hands, appreciating the warmth on my fingers. Then I sipped, appreciating the distraction of having something to do even more.

Jacob paused again. I saw his gaze drop to my neck. The bruises had faded. I was fine. Steam rose, but I wasn't even sure if he was breathing while he watched me trying to figure out why he was here.

"In a way, but not because of the case. My work has complicated things between us. I wanted to give you time to decide how you felt once you knew who I was and what I was about," he said.

"Do I know? I'm not sure. I think at times you were more yourself with me than you were supposed to be. At other times, you were obviously working. Digging for information. Trying to keep your distance," I said.

"And failing," Jacob reminded me wryly. Would I ever forget the shocked look on his face when he'd taken my fingertip between his lips and licked the thorn prick? That hadn't been Federal Agent Walker. That had been wildwood Jacob. Through and through.

"Once you said, 'the wildwood knows.' Do you really believe that?" Jacob asked. He had followed my retreat by one step. I had to tilt my chin to meet his eyes. I probably should have backed away. But I didn't.

"Beliefs are built over a lifetime, aren't they? I believed it when I said it. These last couple of months I've been living at Granny's. Away from the wildwood. I missed it. Felt like I needed to get back. Needed not wanted. And then when I got here I still wasn't satisfied. Like something was missing," I said. Beliefs were built over a lifetime. Trios were as well. Sadie, Kara and Joyce had taken years to form the alliance of power they used to help the rest of us. Something told me my alliance with Jacob and Lu could become even more powerful if we allowed it.

"Or like someone was missing," Jacob said. Steam no longer rose from his cup. He leaned to set the cooled liquid aside on the coffee table. As he moved, he brushed me with his arm and the scent of forest shadows and woodsy air teased my nose.

I still clutched my cup to give me something to do. It took several tugs from Jacob before I realized he wanted me to release it. He set my cup beside his and then straightened to face me again.

Somehow we were closer together still. I hadn't moved. My feet might as well have had roots anchoring me to the ground. Not because I didn't want to be closer. But because I didn't know how. In spite of having more loved ones in my life, I was still too used to standing alone.

"I've known there was more to this world than most people understand before I could walk and talk, but I strongly believe in conscious decision. That day when I found you pruning the blackberry bushes, something came over me. Attraction. Fascination. A connection I couldn't ignore. But I didn't mean to set something in motion that hadn't been mutually agreed upon," Jacob said. He took another step and I still didn't back away. He'd given me plenty of time to move. He wasn't touching me in any way. "I wanted the wildwood to know you, to accept you. I won't lie about that. But..."

"You think the wildwood influenced my attraction to you?" I asked.

"I tasted you that day. It wasn't planned, but that moment started something," Jacob said.

"I choose my path. I always have. I always will," I said. He leaned forward. Maybe I whispered and he couldn't hear. Or maybe he wanted to be closer. "I was open to the experience, and it shook me, I won't deny it. But it didn't start anything between us that hadn't already started."

"When I accepted the hiking stick, I knew it meant something more than you intended," Jacob said. I could feel the soft air of his words teasing across my lips.

"You're wrong. Deep down, I knew," I said. "And if the wildwood is a matchmaker, I don't mind."

The confession was the last bit of encouragement he needed. He had given me more time than necessary to allow me to run away. And I had proven I had no intention of going anywhere. He pressed his mouth against mine and our lips opened, to merge, to taste, to remember the thrill of magic between us that had started even before the thorn prick and the first flick of his tongue. He tasted of peppermint. Or we both did. I pressed into the solid warm strength of him, and he wrapped his arms around me. Finally. As close as I'd always wanted to be. Or almost. Heat rose as mint mingled and our hands found their way under clothes. His bare skin was a revelation—all smooth and masculine and vulnerable somehow in spite of his strength. From his murmurs of appreciation against my lips and then my neck, and then more intimate places, he discovered revelations of his own.

Much later, Jacob fished a photograph from the jeans he'd retrieved from the floor.

"She wants to meet you," he said. "I don't think there's any doubt from her past and her appearance, but she's agreed to any testing you might require if you want to be sure first."

I'd seen the woman in the photograph before. In my mirror every day and in the photograph of the Sect woman with the baby Tom had placed on the counter for me to find. I wrapped myself in the afghan to go to the closet and retrieve the old photograph to compare the two.

And to get a closer look at what I knew now to be a baby picture of myself.

There wasn't much to see. The photograph was yellowed and I was wrapped in a blanket. But even with her face turned away from the camera, the young woman looked so like me I wondered if the only way I'd missed the resemblance was to refuse to see it.

"I don't want to put her through anything else. This is enough for me. I'd be happy to meet her," I said. But then I had to lean against Jacob when another horror occurred to me. "Does she have any idea who my father is?"

"Not Moon, Mel. She told me that. She was given to one of his closest acolytes. A Sect man who died after being bitten by a copperhead about five years later," Jacob explained.

"Thank God it wasn't Moon or Hartwell," I said. My whole body had collapsed from relief.

Jacob held me and I allowed myself to be held.

There was a scratch at the back door.

I was the one who stood to answer it. When I opened the door, the fox looked up at me. We stood like that until Jacob came to pull me back inside. I had started to shiver from the cold. The fox shook itself free of snow and followed us.

Sarah had known. The fox had been in her life long before mine. But she'd shared her premonition when she'd given me the embroidered bag. She'd somehow known that the fox and I should be together.

I dropped down and placed my hand on the fox's damp head. He didn't shy away from my touch.

And Jacob closed the door.

Acknowledgments

Lucienne Diver patiently read numerous early versions of this book. Her support was invaluable. The wildwood never would have existed without her. Thank you for finding a home for the wisewomen and the book of my speculative heart, Lucienne!

My sons are scientists. Deciding if they were born scientists or I somehow raised them to become scientists is impossible. I couldn't have written *Wildwood Whispers* without watching three growing children discover the world and commit their lives to a deeper exploration of the universe. This is simply who they are and I suspect nature and nurture both played a part.

And what can I say about Nivia Evans? I've only known a few special creatives in my life who inspire worlds with mere conversation. After speaking with Nivia, I hang up the phone and my head is so full I have to immediately put pen to paper. It's been such a joyous privilege to work with her and the entire Orbit team.

My mother, Elaine Meador Craighead, is the Appalachian woman behind the character of Granny. Canning, remedies, porch swings and pie—all magic of a sort. Not to mention tales of eccentric ancestresses and mountain lore. I grew up hunting for fairies in blackberry bushes and trying to catch robins with salt. For haints and hollers. For tonics and tall tales. For books. So many books. Thank you, Mom.

This book is dedicated to Todd because he's the one who brought me to a cabin in the wildwood. The perfect sunny spot for a family, all my rescued pets, and a writing chair in the trees. Love always.